"Mr. Carter, Robert, listen, I don't pretend to understand what you've been through, but I do know that you're not going anywhere," she spouted sternly.

"Am I under guard then?"

"Under guard?" She tilted her head. "Yes, I suppose you are, under my guard, and you're not going anywhere until I say you can."

Robert lay back quietly to take stock of the situation and his surroundings. After a careful scan of the room, he finally noticed his present attire. He moved his hand over the soft shirt of some finely spun cotton upon his chest. Then he touched his face. His beard was missing. He lifted the sheet and saw his bare legs and strange underdrawers, also of finely spun, tightly woven cotton. He tried to shake his head to clear it, but then he gasped for breath as pain made him wince. His eyes closed tightly. The muscles in his neck ached and strained. *What's happening here?*

Wings

Waltz In Time

by

Diana Lee Johnson

A Wings ePress, Inc.

Paranormal Time Travel Romance

Wings ePress, Inc.

Edited by: Pat Casey
Copy Edited by: Sara V. Olds
Senior Editor: Pat Casey
Managing Editor: Elizabeth Struble
Executive Editor: Lorraine Stephens
Cover Artist: Chrissie Poe

Wings ePress Books
http://www.wings-press.com

Copyright © 2002 by Diana Lee Johnson
ISBN 1-59088-946-0

Published In the United States Of America

February 2002

Wings ePress Inc.
403 Wallace Court
Richmond, KY 40475

Dedication

In memory of
Sarah Warren Prince Osborn
(my direct ancestor)
who died May 10, 1692,
as a direct result of the Salem Witch Trials.

To my daughters,
Renée and Melissa,

my grandsons,
Stefen and Alex.

and my new granddaughter
Madelyn Marie

Prologue

Union Encampment Near Fredericksburg, Virginia
December, 1862

"Hello, Father." The young Union officer, Lt. Harry Carter, glared at the Confederate Colonel he held prisoner. The Lieutenant squared his shoulders and stood erect in his crisply tailored uniform. "I've been waiting for you." Throwing his head back far enough to look down his nose at the taller man in gray, he gave a haughty tilt to his chin. His hands remained tightly clasped behind his back.

"They told me you were ill." The Confederate looked confused and spoke warily. "Are you better?" Then his eyes widened with realization. "Or was this some ruse to get me into enemy camp?"

"I knew you wouldn't be bright enough to see through the messenger. I'm quite well, no thanks to you." His left eyebrow arched as his upper lip curled in a sneer. "We thought you could be useful to us. I'm sure you have a great deal of information." Menacingly he circled the Confederate, his gaze fixed on his rebel father.

"My men will know that I have been captured when I fail to return in twenty-four hours as I promised." Robert Carter did not show concern for himself.

"Your *men*!" Harry spit the words out with contempt. "Those cut-throat, ignorant rebels you call your men couldn't find their way to the necessary without a leader. You aren't much of a leader, but you're better than nothing." His voice carried the harsh Philadelphia accent of his grandparents, instead of the warm southern drawl of his father.

"Harry, why are you doin' this?"

"Captain Perry and I are looking to be promoted." He smugly mused, still circling. "If we serve up some good intelligence about Jackson's forces, well, it's only a matter of time." He cocked his head.

"Joshua Perry?"

"The same." A tenor voice came from behind Robert. "I won't say 'at your service' for you are obviously at mine, Colonel."

"I should have known someone else was behind this. Still can't live with the fact that Beth preferred me to you, can you?" No fear sounded in the tall Confederate's voice, only contempt and a little satisfaction knowing his comment would make his enemy's blood boil.

"It was *not* a matter of preference. You kidnapped her and forced her into marriage. It was your fault she died, dragging her out there to Kansas, where she couldn't get competent medical attention."

"I neither dragged her, nor did she lack for medical attention. You forget it was your Philadelphia doctors who couldn't save her. I sent her home as soon as I knew she was expectin' a child. As far as force is concerned, I'm not the one who tried to rape her to make her marry me. That's the kind of low-down trick only someone like you would attempt. Just like lurin' me here, tellin' me Harry was dyin'. You bastard!"

Perry took out his saber and held it to Robert's throat. "I could kill you right here and now and say you were caught spying on us." His calculatingly cold voice seeped through clenched teeth.

Robert noted some apprehension on his son's face.

Perry raised the saber higher and stuck the tip into Robert's forehead until it bled.

"Captain, you said he wouldn't be hurt. We'd just get the information we needed and leave him tied up somewhere." Harry urgently whispered in Perry's ear.

"Losing your nerve, boy? This piece of filth should never have been your father. I should have. You owe him nothing. He never cared about you. Who was always there for your birthdays?"

"You were, Uncle Josh."

"And who taught you how to ride a horse, and shoot a gun?"

Harry didn't reply. He simply cast his vacant eyes to the campfire.

"There, now, let's get down to the business at hand." Perry stuck a cigar in his mouth. "Tell us how many men are with Jackson, and their exact location."

"Go to hell, Perry!"

"I never thought this would be easy. In fact, I never intended it to be. I *will* have my sport with you, Carter. Maybe you'll talk, maybe you won't. Maybe you'll survive." Perry cast a wicked glance in the Confederate's direction. "Maybe you won't. No matter." He shrugged. "I will extract a certain pleasure from watching you squirm."

"I never agreed to--" Harry broke in, putting a tentative hand on Captain Perry's arm, but without a moment's hesitation, Perry hoisted his revolver by the barrel ' and clubbed the young man, knocking him cold.

"Your boy is soft! He hasn't the stomach for war, or much else. He was easy to manipulate." Perry looked toward another soldier, jutting his chin toward young Carter to direct the man's attention. "Get him out of here and see he doesn't interfere."

The man saluted and enlisted the aid of another to drag Harry from the camp.

One

Fredericksburg, Virginia
February, 1993

Virginia Berkeley rode past the old house as slowly as the light traffic would allow. She smiled to see the face of the house being shored up. She didn't dare pull into the private drive now that the house was sold. She just went down the road a little farther and turned around to take a second look as she resumed her path toward town.

Some time ago, when her friends first showed her the house, her remark at seeing the "For Sale" sign was, "Darn, I didn't get 'rich and famous' soon enough! I'd buy that house and fix it up."

If Ginny had been well off, she'd have probably done just that.

Quite by accident, her friends had found the house--with the "For Sale" sign in front of it--near their home. An old, falling down mansion, with the porch supported by two-by-fours nailed lengthwise together to hold the high roof, so it wouldn't collapse. Knowing her fascination for history, they took Ginny there when she'd visited them a few months ago.

The moment she spotted it, Ginny felt overjoyed. "It's at least early-to mid-nineteenth century, though it looks as if the current structure could be a re-build on the original foundation. I guarantee it was used as somebody's headquarters in the Civil War." She mumbled her observations more to herself than to them for her friends weren't quite as enthusiastic as she. They snickered at her assumption of its use. As they turned to leave the grounds, Ginny spied it. A marker!

"I knew it! I knew it!" she shouted excitedly as she cleared a vine away to read the inscription. "'Burnside's headquarters, December 11-13, 1862.' That's when the battle of Fredericksburg was fought!"

When she got home from that trip, Ginny wasted no time looking up everything she could find about the area. In one of her many Civil War volumes, she found a reference to the Phillips house, the home Burnside had used as his headquarters, and later burned as he retreated. She found a drawing done from a photograph taken when the house was burning. Indeed, the house was similar in shape and size to the one her friends found, but slightly different in façade. Of course, it would be. It had been burned. There was no mention of the name of the home on the marker. Perhaps she could find out more.

Someone had lived there well into modern times, as evidenced by the remnant of a swimming pool in the back yard. The last her friends told her, the house had sold and someone was fixing it up, and putting in a new septic field. Ginny felt glad someone would preserve the house, since there was no chance she would become rich and famous before it collapsed.

~ * ~

Ginny continued the final couple of miles to the inn where she booked the last room. "Relax!" she ordered herself out loud, as if ordering could make it so.

"I wonder if Mary remembered to mail those plans… Did I leave that note for Ken? Damn it! Forget about work! Think about… Think about horses, carriages, Rebel yells, hooped skirts, Robert E. Lee...his sad eyes...that's it. Make a mental note. Go back to Stratford Hall while I'm down here." She smiled. "If I keep talking to myself while I'm down here, I won't need a vacation, I'll be in a *padded cell*."

She would just have to keep her thoughts in her head and out of her mouth as much as possible. Sometimes she found it difficult, though. Looking at something interesting for the first time, she just naturally wanted to share her enthusiasm. She wondered if her first husband, Harry's ghost were in the car, coming along for the ride. He'd listen to her ramblings. Heck, she wouldn't be surprised if he donned a Confederate uniform, or a Union one, just to torment her. No, he'd never wear a Union uniform. He was a Virginia native, too, a Shenandoah Valley native. He'd wear gray and butternut.

As she chuckled at her own thoughts, Ginny had to admit she would now probably look sideways at any Confederate with dark hair, slightly over six feet--just in case. She looked in her rear-view mirror as she pulled away from the house. She glimpsed a scene which she then replayed in her mind to capture. A couple of men in dark clothes, uniforms perhaps... dragging another man in lighter clothes...toward a small stone building. She turned her head quickly to glance back, but there was no one stirring. No, her mind played a trick on her. She was just imagining. She shook her head, then looked in the mirror again--nothing.

A horn sounded and she realized she was sitting still. The doctors were right. She needed a rest!

"Harry, don't do this to me," she whispered aloud.

She thought about her first husband, dead now, killed in an accident several years after their divorce. He wasn't a bad man. Raised without family, he had no idea there were times when family should come first. He cultivated his friends, being at their disposal at any hour of the day or night. His biggest failing was a violent streak that, when aroused, flared without any warning.

It was no longer painful to remember him. As a matter of fact, she didn't really remember that much about their ten years together. Mercifully, only a few funny memories remained. The rest was a clinical memory, like a book she once read or a story she'd been told.

There were times when strange little things happened around Ginny. Like her office door closing for no reason, or articles disappearing from one place and reappearing in another. Ginny would laugh and say Harry had come back to pester her. For the door, she had no explanation, for the articles, well, Ginny wasn't the most organized person, and she didn't have time to be. Her mind and her body were always going in ten different directions. That was how she functioned best.

~ * ~

For a few moments, Ginny stood outside the inn and just surveyed Sophia Street, which ran parallel to the river. This was an old place, indeed. The neatly restored buildings showed their age to some degree--windows were odd sizes, and clapboard siding sagged in places. Doors were shorter and sometimes narrower than modern doors, and granite and brick stoops curved in the middle, the result of long years of wear from many feet clad in many styles.

Some of the buildings seemed to have always been stores of one kind or another. After all, Fredericksburg's Rappahannock River made it a main port in the eighteenth century, though it was hard to imagine it being so deep at one time. Other shops were former houses or perhaps inns, like this one at which she was stopping. They all displayed distinct additions made over the centuries reflecting different styles of architecture. Sidewalks were tilted at various angles, slanted, and uneven, some concrete, some brick, some stone, all demanding particular care in walking.

Ginny felt welcomed the moment she entered the little eighteenth century inn on Sophia Street. She surveyed the lobby and let her mind wander to picture what all the walls must have witnessed. It wouldn't be difficult to picture George Washington stopping here. *He stopped everywhere else.* In times past, townsfolk scurried around with bustles and hoops, top hats and forage caps.

Turning the register toward herself and reading Ginny's name, the clerk spoke, interrupting her reverie. "Ah, Ms. Berkeley, you have our last room. It's furnished in about mid-nineteenth century. I hope that will be satisfactory."

"Quite," Ginny said quietly, trying not to break her own spell but reveling in her good fortune.

The clerk left the desk to show Ginny to her room. "This way. Do you need help with your luggage?"

Ginny had a firm grip on the small suitcase, her tote, her laptop computer case and her shoulder bag. She rarely gave in to any frailty. "No, I can manage, if it isn't too far."

"Not far at all, just down here." The young woman pointed.

Good, I'm on the first floor, not a bunch of stairs to climb.

At the end of a short and narrow hall were two or three steps, and another couple of rooms. That was where Ginny's room was nestled, in an addition to the original inn, probably itself about mid-nineteenth century.

"Perfect," Ginny whispered, as the clerk opened the door to reveal a huge four-poster bed. Ginny never slept in one. No canopy. *I'd probably feel too closed in.*

Each post of the bed was topped with the traditional carved pineapple indicating Southern hospitality. The windows appeared to contain original glass, clear enough to see out, but creating wavy images as your eyes moved about.

She was shown the bath, given a few little housekeeping hints--where to find ice, drinks, restaurant hours, etc.--and the clerk disappeared leaving Ginny standing in the center of antique and history heaven. She dropped her bags exactly where she stood and spun around, taking in the whole of the room at one time. Four poster bed, roll-top writing desk, wardrobe, dresser with antique mirror. On it sat a washbowl and pitcher, though she knew she had a full bathroom. There were electrified, antique-looking, perhaps authentic antique lamps.

She looked around the room a second time. Her features softened as the muscles in her face relaxed and day-dreams began to filter through her mind. Her brow furrowed as she contemplated the area. Something seemed strange. Something was missing. Oh, yes, television, telephone, clock. She cautiously pushed at the top of the desk. When rolled back, it revealed a modern telephone and digital alarm clock.

She opened one side of the wardrobe to find a normal cedar closet, but there was a partition in the center. Opening the other door she found a hidden shelf with a small color television. Under that was another shelf with an empty ice bucket and glasses.

It's perfect! Caught up in her imaginings, she stayed herself from shouting aloud. *I can close the bathroom door--not when I'm in it, though, I'm too claustrophobic-- pull down the desk top, close the wardrobe, and voilà! Eighteen hundreds, here I am.* She flopped happily on the big bed. It would be no trouble at all to transport herself backwards in time, mentally, of course.

On her way into town, Ginny had seen a few signs of the sights to come. In a couple of places, men were beginning to set up camp. Two or three women, wearing long skirts, walked down the street. Nothing overwhelming yet. The actual two-day re-enactment wouldn't start until the day after tomorrow and she was in no real hurry to don the hoops. She put on a simple long wool skirt and knee-high boots to ward off the February cold of Fredericksburg. She wanted to wander about town, get the "lay of the land" so to speak, before deciding whether to participate or just be an observer.

~ * ~

Down the street Ginny trooped, looking in all the shop windows. Studying her own reflection in one window, she tilted her head and wondered why she wasn't born a hundred and fifty years before. She would have fit in.

She stopped at a used bookstore and spied a book about the Reconstruction Era in Louisiana. She didn't have that one in her steadily growing collection, so she bought it. Then she slipped into an art gallery. It dealt in prints from famous modern-day artists who specialized in the booming business of recreating the images of the Civil War.

One print after another struck her fancy. She was beginning to get caught up in the times. An original oil caught her eye, the *Monitor* and the *Virginia*, commonly called the *Merrimack*. Ginny was chock-full of these bits and pieces of information, like an encyclopedia with no index. Oh, but she would love to buy it, or a dozen other prints, each well over two hundred dollars, unframed. Framed, they were totally out of the question.

When I'm rich and famous, I'll cover my walls with these treasures. She released a slow sigh. She dared not indulge herself too long here, or she might throw caution to the wind and her bank account to oblivion and buy a print. With a longing backward look, she left the gallery which had to be showing as sadness in her eyes, because she was destined to have none of the expensive pictures.

Only a few doors farther down the street stood another such shop. Ginny stood outside for several moments and tried to decide whether to go in and enjoy a few minutes of make-believe, or stay outside, and resist temptation and disappointment. She inhaled deeply, let her breath out in a quick rush, and decided to tackle the temptation.

Again, all the pricey prints fired her spirit, but then she gazed upon one that tore at her heart more than any other. It was titled "Generals at Prayer." On a church pew sat Robert E. Lee and Thomas J. "Stonewall" Jackson, heads bowed in prayer.

Ginny moved her hand toward the print--her fingers passing lightly over Robert E. Lee's aristocratic, yet humble, face. His sad eyes were probably much like her own as she denied herself the frivolous purchase for which she longed.

Every time she saw his likeness, she felt the anguish of Lee's position. He loved the Union. Though he held no slaves himself, there were those inherited from his wife's family of which he was custodian. But he couldn't fight against his beloved Virginia.

Ginny could never decide who she admired most, Robert E. Lee or Abraham Lincoln. Both were men of great sorrows, great vision, heavy responsibilities, fierce loyalties, towering strength, brilliance beyond their times. Both were misunderstood, maligned, torn by empathy; both stood for beliefs in which she could share. She felt a strange kinship with them.

Friends often teased that she must have known them in some past life. Had she been alive those hundred and thirty years ago, Virginia Berkeley didn't know which side she would have found herself on. Her head was with the Union, but her heart was with the South.

Vaguely aware of men's voices, Ginny stood in the gallery and looked at the somber print. There was no one in the shop when she entered except the shopkeeper. She had paid no attention to any comings or goings, never noticed the faint tinkle of the bell which hung suspended above the door. She sighed. She had to quit thinking about the past. She turned to leave.

Looking up to find her way, Ginny had her breath stolen from her. She stood squarely facing three men in complete and, what looked to her to be, authentic Confederate garb. Not the perfectly tailored gray uniforms of romantic movies about the war--real, butternut and many-shaded grays with little uniformity about them at all. Bedrolls over their shoulders, mess equipment, canteens, each different hanging from a variety of belts--and guns, real antique guns--well, maybe replicas. Ginny was no expert.

She could only snatch her breath in short, shallow gasps. It just wouldn't come. She came face to face with reality, hundred-year-old-plus reality. Her eyes watered. She bit her lip to keep an involuntary screech from escaping as her hand clutched at her chest and willed her lungs to fill. Still her breath would not come. It felt as if the color had drained from her face. Her gaze fixed, she stared at the three men laughing and talking with the shopkeeper.

Her mouth refused to close. Her eyes opened so wide they ached as she swallowed down one lump in her throat after another. Why did this hit her so starkly? She should have expected it. But suddenly here it was, unannounced, so real.

At last her breath came easier. From the glance he gave her, one man noticed her out of the corner of his eye. He seemed to sense her awe and gave her an understanding, lazy smile, then he tipped his hat. "Ma'am," he said quietly and smiled broader, his eyes fixed on hers.

Ginny smiled back, but she couldn't speak. She just floated out the door of the shop.

~ * ~

Ginny wandered toward the inn. "So this is how it feels," she whispered to herself. "I like it. I want to be part of it. I'll wear my hoops and, and I'll talk to visitors, if I'm spoken to, that is. I won't make a spectacle of myself by approaching people. I'll just mingle." Her heart lightened as if her entire body was smiling on the inside, and her green eyes must be dancing with the mischief she was feeling.

She walked less than half a block when someone was calling after her.

"Ma'am!"

She couldn't imagine the call was meant for her until she realized the voice could be the same as the man who had spoken in the shop. Ginny turned, gave him a questioning look, but said nothing as she stared up into his face.

"I just wanted to apologize. I think we caught you a little off-guard, didn't we?"

"Well," Ginny began slowly, "I guess you did. I wasn't paying any attention to other customers."

"I know. You were kinda lost in the pictures, weren't you?"

Ginny felt the warmth of a blush creep upon her and looked down.

"I guess you could say that."

"Jonathan Blackburn's the name." He swept his hat from his head and offered his hand to her.

She reached out. "Virginia Berkeley."

"I noticed you 'cause o' your hair. My sister's got red hair, but it's not all kinda gold and red at the same time like yours. Hers is more like Raggedy Anne. Used to tease and call her that sometimes." He chuckled. "My ma's hair was the color o' yours, best I can recollect m' gram sayin'." He cleared his throat. "You live hereabouts, ma'am?"

Ginny couldn't decide if his drawl was natural or put on for the occasion.

"Just visiting. I live closer to Washington."

"Will I be seein' ya in costume later on?"

"Could be, Mr. Blackburn." Ginny turned and began to stroll toward the inn.

"Mind if I walk with y' aways?"

Ginny chuckled and glanced around. "I suppose not. If you promise to be a real Southern gentleman."

"Yes ma'am. I promise." He nodded cordially as he straightening to his full height and pulled himself to her side. "Have ya met anybody interestin' down here?"

"Only you. I just got here a little while ago. Where are you from, Mr. Blackburn…? uh…" Trying to determine his rank to keep up the pretext, Ginny eyed his uniform, but she had no earthly idea of the insignias.

"Oh, Sergeant, ma'am."

"Sergeant Blackburn."

"I'm from North Carolina, a little hole-in-the-wall near Murfreesboro. You wouldn't have heard of it. I come to every one of these re-enactments I can. I'm real interested in the Civil War, kinfolk back then, ya know. I c'n see you're interested, too."

"Yes, I am."

"Got kinfolk from then, too, have ya?"

Ginny grinned. *That drawl of his is real.*

She shrugged. "I suppose we all do, somewhere."

"Mine was here at Fredericksburg. My great-great, uh, well, ya know, grandfather was a colonel in General Lee's army. Story has it we had relatives on the other side, too." He lowered his voice to a whisper.

"Really, that's very interesting, Sergeant." Ginny lowered her voice. "I won't breathe a word to your friends." She wanted to hear more about Jonathan Blackburn, but she needed to let him return to his friends. He was just a young man and she didn't want to appear forward.

Probably in his mid- to-late-twenties, Jonathan stood about five-feet-ten or eleven, sandy brown hair, with a sparse attempt at a beard. The scant whiskers were darker than his hair, and through them Ginny could see the straight cut of his jaw. When he smiled his eyes, an unremarkable brown, sparkled with flecks of green making them a hazel color. He was handsome. He was also genuinely pleasant and she enjoyed talking with him. There was an immediate connection between them.

Making small talk, mostly, about his relatives who were in the war, they walked along all the way to the inn. When Ginny stopped, indicating it was the end of the walk for her, the young man became a little flustered.

"Well, guess I'd best be gettin' on back to m' buddies." He took his hat off again and fingered it. "We'll be a-campin' just down there." He nodded toward the river. "If ya need anythin' or want t' visit a real camp site, you'd be more'n welcome."

Ginny gave him a warm smile. "Thank you, Mr. Blackburn. I might just take you up on that."

"Jonathan, please ma'am."

"Jonathan," she obliged in amusement. She saw no harm in calling him by his first name. He wasn't much older than her daughters.

"Yes'm." He nodded shyly and turned to leave. "I'll be lookin' for ya, Miz Berkeley."

"Good night, Sergeant Jonathan Blackburn."

Ginny opened the front door of the inn and cast a backward look toward Blackburn. A crooked little smile escaped her lips as she berated herself.

You've done it again, Virginia. You've made friends with a young man. It's either young men or old ones. Never manage to find your own age, or if you do, they're taken. But he is sweet, and he did seem to enjoy your company.

As she shook her head, a breathy chuckle slipped out, then her face slackened a little. Loneliness threatened to tinge her mood.

At least the young man appeared to share her interest in history. He could prove an amusing diversion this weekend. Ginny gave a deep sigh as she lamented his youth. But for the difference in their ages, he could prove *more* than amusing.

Two

Ginny tossed and turned all night. When she slept, she dreamt about the Battle of Fredericksburg. Something about men being captured. She supposed she could attribute the dream to her talk with Jonathan. Giving up, she rose early. She must find a way to unwind.

She wished her best friend, Terry was with her to enjoy this adventure, but if Terry were there, Jonathan would probably lavish his attentions on her instead of Ginny.

Terry was very important to Ginny, more than Terry probably ever knew. Though they were total opposites, they understood each other. They could share anything and never feel condemned or judged or preached to. There was almost nothing similar about the two.

Looks were the first clue. Terry was slight--*slight!* She was just downright tiny. Ninety pounds, soaking wet, five-foot one, blonde, blue-eyed. Ginny was always heavier than she should be. Taller than Terry, though only a couple of inches, her size otherwise made her look much larger. "Mutt and Jeff," Ginny used to call them.

Terry was an immaculate housekeeper. Housekeeping was *not her bag*, as Ginny would put it. She loved to cook, but hated cleaning up after herself. Terry had nice things, antiques.

Antiques meant nothing to Ginny, except family heirlooms. Terry was artistic with her hands and could paint. Ginny's art was of mind, and voice; she could sing well. Terry worked outside, kept horses, gardened. Ginny hated the outdoors if it meant bugs, or dirty hands, though she loved animals.

"You can go outside, muck out stalls, feed the horses, rub them down and come back looking fresh as a daisy and smelling like nothing worse than fine leather. I can just walk out to the barn with you, and I come back looking, *and smelling,* like I've been in the saddle for days without a bath," Ginny teased Terry when last she was on the farm.

When her doctor ordered Ginny to get away from her stressful job for a few days, she'd wanted to go to Terry's. Her husband, Jim was retired and Ginny wouldn't be disrupting their routine. It seemed the perfect solution. She enjoyed being around Jim almost as much as Terry. He gave great hugs, something Ginny never got enough of, and he seemed to genuinely like her company, and her cooking. She didn't get to cook for an appreciative man often.

But when she called, Terry and Jim were having company, first one family then the other. They were tied up for the next two months.

"We can work something out, Ginny," Terry had insisted, but Ginny wouldn't impose.

"No, that's all right, really. It's not important. I'll call again soon. We'll make it another time." Ginny tried to hide the catch in her voice. She was disappointed, but what's new? Sometimes she thought "disappointment" was her middle name. Maybe it was branded on her forehead.

Then it had been back to square one. Depressed, Ginny had hung up the phone. That was when she grabbed the AAA book and the newspaper and found this Civil War weekend getaway. "Costumes are encouraged for all visitors during the long weekend celebration. There will be many available for rental by various establishments. Antique photography will also be available." The article went on to say that an area of several blocks in the old part of the city would be cordoned off to cars for two days, and during certain hours each day, only persons in period costume would be allowed to walk those streets or ride in carriages. The rest of the time, everyone, costumed or not, would be mingling. "Costumes need not be authentically detailed, but must outwardly reflect the Civil War era."

Now Ginny was here alone, except for meeting Jonathan Blackburn, that is.

~ * ~

Ginny having risen early, wanted to get a complete feel for the part of Fredericksburg that would be cordoned off tomorrow. She also needed to find parking for her car outside of the restricted area. Just as she thought, the early morning made it easier and she moved her car to the safe parking area, only blocks from her inn.

Now Ginny strolled back to the inn to get breakfast. The late winter sun barely peeked through the naked trees. Ah, she caught a whiff of bacon on the chilly breeze. The men hearty enough to camp out during the night were about making their breakfast over open fires. She wandered just close enough to watch for a few moments, but not close enough to be noticed.

A smile of amusement crossed her lips. The men in their trousers and long underwear emerged from the tents. She looked away in embarrassment as one man was scratching in a rather delicate area. It reminded her that she never succeeded in breaking her first husband of that habit. As she turned to go, her face collided with a man's chest. It was Jonathan Blackburn.

Ginny chuckled as she rubbed the end of her nose. "My nose just got too familiar with your chest, Sergeant!"

"Sorry, ma'am." He looked down at her apologetically. "Come t' look in on us?"

"Well, er, uh," Ginny wasn't sure how to answer that. She wasn't spying on them. "I smelled the bacon, and..."

"I'm glad ya came. Would ya like to have some breakfast with us? I'm sure the Captain wouldn't mind a little feminine company. It ain't so very cold in camp."

"Oh, no, that's quite all right. I'll just be getting back to the inn. By the way, where are you off to so early yourself?" She regained her wits.

"Uhh," he looked down sheepishly, "well, ya see, we cain't do ever'thing just like in the ol' days. They make us use the portable, uh, 'little boy's room.'" His face blazed.

Ginny stifled her smile. "Oh, well, that does make more sense."

"Yeah, a fella could freeze his bu--buns off." Seeming a little more relaxed, Jonathan chuckled.

Ginny began to snicker, and Jonathan joined in. In a moment, they were engulfed in side-splitting laughter, and Ginny took his arm as they headed for the camp.

"Lady about!" Jonathan called as they strolled.

Men scurried hither, thither and yon as they approached. It intensified the air of amusement. By the same fire as the bacon sizzled, men were drying or warming their socks.

"Coffee?" one middle-aged private offered.

"Thank you, no. I never acquired the taste. But I appreciate the offer, really."

He nodded and went on about his business, passing out coffee to the others in camp as they held out their cups. One of the men offered Ginny a camp chair, which she accepted graciously. She was now very interested in talking with these men and finding out what drove them to these re-enactments.

"Well, actually, this isn't a re-enactment. That is, we aren't going to re-fight the battle of Fredericksburg, or anything like that. This is just to add a little atmosphere to the celebration the city is putting on. This is like a picnic compared to some of the re-enactments." A man in a captain's uniform spoke. Ginny learned he was an engineer from Richmond who'd been caught up in this pastime since his college days.

"Yeah," Blackburn chimed in, "I'd rather be camped out in the cold than the re-enactments of Manassas and Gettysburg in July. These wool uniforms are comfortin' in the cold, but in July--they ain't just hot and scratchy, we, well, we cain't always stand how the other fella smells."

"Or ourselves," another observed.

They all laughed and Ginny smiled.

~ * ~

After an hour of listening to their stories, and being shown their garments, equipment and other paraphernalia, Ginny realized these were dedicated men.

Ginny shook her head. "I'd never imagined re-enactors gave such attention to detail. The level to which you're all involved is simply amazing. And some of you go all over the country to do this?"

"Yeah," a man in a sergeant's uniform spoke up. "Me and the captain even went to England as American representatives in an international re-enactment."

"Wait, now let me get this straight," Ginny puzzled. "A re-enactment of the American Civil War--in England, with people from around the world?"

They all nodded.

"Now that I'd like to see."

"You can't imagine the striking impression it makes on an American to see all these men in blue, or gray and butternut shouting orders with English, Scottish, and Irish accents, not to mention the Danes, Germans, Belgians and I don't know how many others."

The winsome expression on the captain's face let Ginny know he had pleasant memories of it as he pictured it in his mind.

"You know," the captain continued, "we don't too often think about how many of the soldiers probably had foreign accents. After all, America was full of immigrants in the middle of the nineteenth century, especially on the side of the Union.

"In the South there were Cajuns and Creoles from Louisiana and Mississippi, the Acadians who fled Nova Scotia, and lots of Irish who fled the potato famine…" His voice trailed off.

"Okay, guys, I'm hooked. When you see me again, I'll be in costume, too."

~ * ~

As Ginny strolled back to the inn, more and more people milled about in costume and many more soldiers, even some in Union blue. They would be relegated to the camps on the other side of the Rappahannock River tomorrow. From the vantage point of her new friends' Confederate camp, she could see the campsites being set up.

When the actual Civil War Days celebration got under way, the two sides would be able to see each other across the river, but today, everyone, blue and gray alike, was welcomed in Fredericksburg. It brought an eerie feeling to have these men mingling here. They should be separated, not ambling around together as it if they weren't at war. It confused her sense of time-transport. Maybe she could pretend today was just before, or just after the war.

No more cars, not until this festival is over, she told herself. But she wouldn't do without the plumbing. After all, if she were affluent enough, she could have a water closet, and even piped-in water, cold though it may have been in the eighteen hundreds. She could just imagine the rest.

When the celebration started, she'd do her best to refrain from electricity. She vowed not to use her computer, unless she got a spectacular idea.

At last, I can indulge my desire to write, but I'll try to stay in period as much as possible to make my impressions seem real. But if an idea is just too tantalizing, I'll have to use my computer to capture it, but only as long as the battery lasts. With the backup battery, I'll have about six hours.

I'll write with a pen. She pulled a roller-ball pen from her purse. Well, not a quill, maybe a pencil! No, not a pencil. Ginny was never able to stand the grit of graphite on paper. She'd just have to imagine she was using a penholder and nib. *I do have my limits.* She smiled. She wasn't one of these re-enactment devotees anyway.

Ginny would use a little of this morning to make some notes in her computer. It wasn't the beginning of the festival yet.

~ * ~

After about an hour alone in her room with her computer, someone knocked at her door. She didn't respond quickly, thinking someone must have the wrong room.

A voice then called out, "Miz Berkeley, you in there?" It was Jonathan Blackburn.

"Jonathan?" Ginny queried as she opened her door.

"I got a real treat for ya, Miz Virginia. Would ya step out here and take a look?"

She followed Jonathan down the narrow hallway to the little lobby. He nodded toward the window. "How'd ya like to take a spin in that?" He pointed to an authentic-looking buggy. "Borrowed it to take ya out, if ya want to."

"Want to? Oh, I'd love to. It's a…a…runabout, isn't it?"

"Yes." A male voice came from behind them. A distinguished-looking man in a Union colonel's uniform joined them. "My grandmother in Pennsylvania used to drive one just like it." He tipped his hat and continued through the lobby doorway to the outside.

"Let me get my coat!"

Jonathan winked as he grinned, his thumb pushing up his Confederate cap. "Yes'm."

~ * ~

Ginny ran to her room, took her coat out of the closet, then feeling a twinkle in her eyes, snapped her fingers. She should make the most of this opportunity. Throwing down the coat, she grabbed her high-necked Victorian blouse and skirt. She threw open the drawer where her rolled up hoops were tucked and quickly maneuvered them into their sleeves inside the skirt. Her boots would be fine under the skirt.

She pulled her hair back in the ivory bow with the snood attached and tucked in all the ends. Tossing her "Scarlet O'Hara" cape over her shoulders, she grabbed her rabbit muff, and scurried into the lobby.

~ * ~

In the lobby, Jonathan stood fingering his hat as he waited.

"Hope I didn't keep you waitin' too long, Sergeant."

He wheeled around and rocked back on his heels. "Wooee!" he screeched in a voice that would win a hog-calling contest. "Now that was worth waitin' for, it surely was." His tone softened to a pleased murmur. "You sure do look like a real Southern belle, ma'am."

She nodded with an appreciative smile.

"Hope ya won't mind if we just sorta meander past the camp, so's I can show ya off. I know the Captain would like to see you all decked out like this."

"I don't mind at all, Sergeant. I'm so grateful to you for this opportunity. You don't know how much I've always wanted to take a carriage ride with a gentleman. The closest I've ever gotten were the crowded paid rides in Williamsburg and Charleston. This is going to be a real adventure."

"Maybe more of an adventure than you think. I've never driven one of these things."

She gave him a wary glance, then laughed. "There's a first time for everything, so they say."

He clucked and flicked the reins. "I did get a quick lesson from the owner of the rig. I think I can manage. I do know somethin' about horses."

"I'm sure we'll be just fine."

Ginny really enjoyed the company of this young man, though she couldn't imagine why he wanted to spend time with her. She was old enough to be his mother, almost--well, older sister, anyway. She shrugged. For once, she wasn't going to question, she was just going to enjoy.

Shortly after they began their ride, the carriage jerked a little, and to steady herself, Ginny reached for Jonathan's arm. His mouth tilted into a smile, so she threaded her left arm through his right then put her hand back in the muff with her other hand.

Jonathan's smile broadened, and he sat taller in the seat.

~ * ~

Jonathan stopped at the camp and the men came out to meet them. The Captain reached up, put his hands on Ginny's waist and easily hoisted her down to the ground. It was her imagination, she knew, but for the first time in her life, she felt light as a feather. Of course, the Captain was a large man with his feet firmly planted on the ground.

The afternoon sun beamed down, warming the air. When they finished their duty visit at the camp, the Captain again helped Ginny up to the carriage seat via the little fold-down step.

"Where to, ma'am?" Jonathan's voice was chipper and full of fun. "I'm at your service."

"Don't you need to get this carriage back to its owner?"

"No ma'am. I got it for the whole afternoon. The owner's originally from Murfreesboro, we struck up a conversation, and he offered it to me. After today, he'll be hauling payin' customers, but today, he wasn't doin' anything particular. I told him there was a special lady I wanted to impress, so he offered. Don't have to have it back 'til sundown."

"Impress? Why would you want to impress me, Jonathan? I'm already impressed, by your uniform, your knowledge, your interest in the period I love most." *Your interest in me.*

"I just, hell, I don't know. I'm not very good with words."

"Try, Jonathan," Ginny whispered.

"I, well, I saw this kind 'o longin' look in your eyes, like you wanted to be part of this. Like you wanted to join in, but just didn't know how." He hung his head as if he was afraid of saying something wrong. "Guess that sounds silly. I don't know you, but I feel like I do. Like we're old friends, or we should be. Stupid, huh?"

Ginny looked him squarely in his big, brown eyes. "It doesn't sound stupid at all. You're right. I'm not much of a joiner. I'm always afraid I won't be accepted. I've never felt as comfortable as you make me feel, and I appreciate it, Jonathan." She leaned close to him and, like a feather, kissed his cheek lightly.

Jonathan flushed wildly and swallowed hard.

"I didn't mean to fluster you, Jonathan." She held out her right hand. "Friends?"

"Yes ma'am!" Jonathan took her hand in his and gave it a mighty jerk of a handshake. "Now, where would you like to go?"

Ginny shrugged. "I truly don't know." She thought another moment. "Wait! I *do* know. Do you think we could manage a couple or three miles?"

"Sure! We can do anything you want." On the last words his voice lowered, and gentled. "This is your afternoon, and I'm yours to command."

Ginny stared at him for a moment, unsure what to think of this young man. She wasn't going to let herself think about him as anything but a friend. He was too young.

"How old are you, Jonathan?"

"Now, ma'am, I don't think that's exactly polite, is it?"

"I don't have to be polite. I'm the *old lady* here." Ginny tried to sound as if she was joking, but she was quite serious.

"Why is it important?"

"What?"

"Age."

"It isn't, not until you pass forty. Then for some reason it seems very important, especially if you're alone." Ginny's voice became hollow, distant.

"Can we leave it at I'm over thirty?" He put his hand over hers, without being suggestive or threatening, but just friendly.

Ginny gazed deeply into his eyes, seeing the softness of the brown for the first time. They were warm and sincere. She swallowed the lump in her throat, then, composing herself, wiggled a bit on the seat.

"Humph." Ginny smiled. "Touché, Sergeant!" *Thirty and one day, maybe.*

She told him about the house being restored outside of Fredericksburg. "It would really be a kick to drive up in this buggy, just for a look."

"Point me in the *right* direction." Jonathan's voice returned to its more companionable tone.

Ginny looked around for a moment to get her bearings, then pointed toward the bridge over the Rappahannock.

"Tell me, Jonathan, what do you do for a living down in North Carolina?"

"Oh, no, I'm in costume, you're in costume. You're not trickin' this country boy into comin' back into the twentieth century 'til I'm *good* and *ready*. We're here in Fredericksburg. The year is eighteen sixty-two," his voice became soft and pensive, "and for just today, you're my lady."

Jonathan's words touched Ginny's heart. A peacefulness overtook her, bringing with it a smile as she clung to his strong arm.

Three

Ginny succeeded in finding the huge old house. Workmen were all about, busily laying the pipes and backfilling for the huge new septic field on the right. Others were busy with carpentry work, securing the facade of the lovely frame dwelling. Jonathan skillfully maneuvered the buggy into the gravel drive.

Ginny chewed her lip apprehensively. "I don't know if we should be here."

"Well, I'll just have to find out." He jumped from the buggy and approached a man in a hard-hat who seemed to be directing the bulk of the workmen. "'Scuse me, sir." He tapped the man on the shoulder.

"What the hell--?"

Jonathan cut the man off. "My friend and I just drove over from Fredericksburg. Do you think the owner would mind if we just took a little look-see? We won't bother nothin'."

Without removing the hard-hat or his mirrored sunglasses, the man glanced to the buggy. Ginny flashed him her most dazzling smile.

"Uh, sure, no harm, I guess. Just watch out for the construction. Don't get too close to the house or the septic field.

Better take the carriage around back, though. We got trucks coming in and out here. We'll be knockin' off for lunch soon, so be careful. The new owner won't be standing for any liability."

"Thank you, sir. We'll be careful. I'll watch out for the lady." Jonathan tipped his Confederate cap and dashed back to drive the buggy to the rear of the house.

Ginny continued to smile, but the man was intent upon his work and didn't give her a second look.

Jonathan hardly stopped the runabout when Ginny stood to get down by herself.

"Ah-ah-ah," Jonathan shook his head vehemently. "You wait to be assisted like a proper lady of good breedin'."

Ginny snickered then folded her hands back into her muff to await his assistance. She reached out her hand toward Jonathan as he rounded the carriage, but Jonathan ignored it and put his hands about her waist. In one smooth motion, he lifted her and set her gently upon the ground.

Ginny was taken by surprise. She hadn't thought him so strong. She flushed and lowered her eyes in embarrassment. Then she raised her chin and tried to make light of the situation.

"That's a good way to hurt your back, Jonny!"

Jonathan smiled. "I like my women with a little meat on their bones. The preference runs in our family."

Ginny's breath left her suddenly, as if someone punched her in the stomach. She had no ready reply for him. She was flustered, but a little flattered, too.

"Jonathan, really, you must remember *my age.*"

"Why? You remember it enough for *both* of us. And I liked it when you called me Jonny."

31

Ginny's face warmed as a furious blush crept up it like a thermometer plunged into boiling water. She didn't recover her composure for several moments that seemed to her like an eternity.

"I'm sorry, Miz Virginia. I didn't mean to confound you so. I'll try to be more mindful of my words, but I have a habit of saying exactly what I'm thinkin'."

"I suppose that runs in the family, too? Jonathan, I'm flattered, but it does make me a little uncomfortable just now. I enjoy your company, but..." The tone of her voice faded.

"I understand." His whisper resounded with disappointment. "I want us to be friends. I've never been comfortable around women. They always scare me spitless."

Ginny laughed, a contagious, high pitched, melodic laugh, like singing a scale. She enjoyed his colorful expressions.

This time Jonathan blushed and rubbed his chin hard to recover his composure.

Ginny pushed the muff up her left arm, far enough to expose her hand. Then she used both hands to lift her skirt so she could explore the property.

"I promised the man we'd be extra careful," Jonathan remarked as he followed her into the back yard.

Suddenly, all the noise of the carpenters, and the clatter of the gravel being scooped into the drainage system ceased. Ginny noted the quiet with a questioning look on her face.

"He said they was about t' stop for lunch."

"Oh, perfect. Now I won't have to tune the noise out to imagine."

~ * ~

About ten yards from the back of the house, Jonathan hesitated as Ginny stopped and turned around to look at the house. Her gaze moved slowly from one end to the other, then to the second floor and again scanned from one end to the other. Then she just stood staring, at nothing in particular…no, staring into oblivion, past the house. She froze in place like in a trance. Even her breathing seemed to stop.

"Miz Virginia," Jonathan said softly to get he attention.

She made no response.

"Miz Virginia!" he said more loudly, for he noticed the dead stillness of her entire body, and the distant look in her green eyes.

Ginny put her finger to her lips. "Shhh, I'm just getting impressions, Jonathan. Don't be alarmed. I like to picture appropriate settings in my mind and meld them into the scenery. I'm not crazy, I promise."

Jonathan gave a slow little nod, as if he understood, but he didn't. He stood staring at her, and watching for any change in expression.

"Can't you picture it, Jonny? Once this house was the hub of a huge farm, the center of family life. I don't see the two-by-fours holding up the porches. I see fresh white paint on a proud home, built to hold a huge family. I see lots of trees close to the house for shade, rocking chairs on the veranda, fields full of workers, content because they're treated like family…"

Jonathan rolled his eyes. "I see a '7-11' store, a gas station, and a parcel o' houses."

"Oh, Jonathan, stop looking with your eyes. Look and listen with your heart, with your *imagination*."

"What else do you see, Miz Virginia? Can you see anyone special?"

Ginny didn't answer. Her gaze darted to one side and her head swiftly followed. A brief impression of the vision she imagined the day before, when she looked in her rear-view mirror as she left the house behind, crossed her mind.

Jonathan turned to look in the direction that had Ginny so enthralled. He didn't see anything.

Just the slightest hint of a smile found its way to Ginny's lips. Then her head tilted and her eyes narrowed, as if she was listening intently to some distant sound. Her right hand found its way to her face, her fingers touching her lips lightly as she turned, heedless of the long skirt swishing about. She ambled toward a small stone building.

"Smokehouse, most likely," Jonathan offered as he followed.

The wooden door was old, but intact, and latched from the outside by a piece of wood which swiveled on a center nail into a rusty metal latch on the door frame. Jonathan reached in front of her, turned the wood, then opened the door. The hinges were very rusty, so he moved gingerly trying not to cause any damage to the ancient door.

"Yup, smokehouse all right. Still smells a little like bacon or ham." Jonathan's chest swelled as he demonstrated his knowledge.

As he opened the door, it wasn't a smokehouse Ginny smelled. It was a vile, stale, insufferably pungent odor which turned her stomach. She peered into the darkness of the little building, but hesitated to enter but Jonathan crowded behind her, inadvertently forcing her inside.

In an instant, Ginny's heart began to pound, and her breath left her completely. The hair on her neck stood up, and her arms and legs were relegated to goose flesh. She backed against Jonathan in such a panic that the force of his body landing against the door wrenched it from its rusty hinges and it crashed to the ground.

Jonathan'd never seen such complete terror in anyone's eyes as he glimpsed in Virginia's at that moment. She ran wildly out into the yard, clutched at her chest, then fell to her knees in the frozen brown grass, her body shaking violently. When Jonathan reached her, he saw tears drowning her eyes, but not yet falling.

She couldn't speak. She could only shake and sob. Jonathan fell on his knees in front of her and held her to his chest, shushing, lulling, rocking her as he held her ever tighter. She allowed the closeness and eventually clung to him. She had terror in her eyes, her chin quivering, as she tried to tear herself from his embrace. He held her tighter until her body stilled.

Ginny wanted to blame her reaction on her claustrophobia, but she knew in her heart, if that was part of it, it was only a small part. Something evil lurked in that smokehouse. Something she didn't want to feel, or think about.

"I…I'm…" She tried to speak, but she wasn't yet ready.

Jonathan just kept holding her, burying her head in his shoulder, smoothing her hair, making soothing noises to calm her.

"I'm so sorry, Jonny," she began with a weak voice. "I…I should have told you how claustrophobic I am. I just can't stand small places. They frighten me to death." Ginny's voice was tiny, muted, child-like. She could not make it sound normal.

"Shhh," he stroked her cheek. "It was clumsy of me to follow so closely that it forced you inside. I'm an oaf!"

Oaf? That wasn't a word Ginny expected to hear from him. It broke the spell of horror. She let go of a nervous little giggle, but even that embarrassed her.

"There, that's better." Jonathan sighed. "Think you can get up, now?"

Ginny nodded.

He held her shoulders solidly to assist her, but as she got to her feet, her knees just wouldn't support her and they buckled, like a wobbly colt. Without the slightest struggle, Jonathan swept her into his arms and carried her the few yards to the buggy. Ginny hadn't imagined anyone could whisk her up so effortlessly. There was quite a strong young man inside that Confederate uniform.

He placed her on the seat of the buggy and rushed to climb in himself. He took the reins into his left hand and put his right arm around Virginia, forcing her head down on his shoulder. Then he split the reins, one to each hand with her still inside the circle of his right arm. He steered the horse with both hands and kept her head captive on his shoulder.

Fleetingly, Ginny worried about the workmen seeing them like this as they left, but no one was about. They'd all left the premises for lunch.

~ * ~

Ginny and Jonathan made their way back to town. By the time they came to the bridge over the Rappahannock, Ginny was composed enough to straighten in her seat which forced Jonathan to remove his arm from her shoulders. He let his right hand join his left on the reins but Ginny kept her left arm firmly curled through Jonathan's the rest of the way to the inn.

Not a word was spoken the entire return trip, until Jonathan lowered Ginny to the ground.

"I'll see you to your room."

"No, that's not necessary. I feel so foolish."

"You've nothing to feel foolish about. Everyone is afraid of something. Me, I *hate* snakes. I mean I fairly panic at the sight."

Ginny smiled. "Thank you, Jonathan, really, but I'm all right. I did so appreciate the ride and the good company. Like I said before, I always wanted a ride in a private carriage. I'm just sorry I spoiled it." She hung her head.

"Spoiled it? You've gotta be kiddin'! I just got to play 'knight in shining armor'. You didn't *spoil* anything." He kissed her forehead.

"Perhaps I should call you 'Sir Galahad.'"

"No, 'Jonny' is just fine. Look, I'll return the rig to my friend and come back to make sure you're okay."

"That isn't necessary."

"Would Sir Galahad just go off and leave a lady like that?"

Ginny smiled and shook her head.

"Darn tootin' he wouldn't. Now, you get on in and get warm and comfy. I'll be back in two shakes of a lamb's tail, and we'll have dinner together. Then I'll see for myself that you're okay, so I can go back to my camp cot with a clear head."

Ginny took a deep breath to protest, but Jonathan put a finger to her lips to stop her.

"*No,* I won't listen to *any* arguments. Now, go on inside." He shooed her with both hands.

Ginny did as she was bid, all the time wondering how she came to be so close to this *young* man. When he came back, when she completely recovered, when they finished dinner, she would know how to respond to this gallant boy. Perhaps he *was* over thirty, he certainly acted like it, but he looked about twenty-four, and regardless, "I'm forty-two."

~ * ~

When Jonathan returned, Ginny was ready to go to dinner. She'd changed into slacks and a high-necked sweater. She'd put her costume away until tomorrow, when it was really needed.

The little dining room at the inn was picturesque with a big fireplace. Two embroidered antique fire screens sat on their claw-footed stands in front of it. The fire crackled and popped as its light danced in Virginia's emerald eyes and flickered extra gold highlights into her coppery hair.

She looked at Jonathan and thought what a warm brown his eyes were, like the color of a deer, and as soft. They were large and expressive making her feel cozy and safe.

~ * ~

As Jonathan escorted Ginny back to her room, Ginny found herself wishing with all her heart Jonathan was a few years older, or she a few years younger. She rose to her tiptoes to give Jonathan a kiss on the cheek at her door.

"I'm not goin' yet." He shrugged matter-of-factly.

"Jonathan, you must." Her voice was soft and cajoling.

"Nope."

She began to protest, but hardly drew a deep breath.

"Now, just hear me out. You were pretty darn shaken back there at that house. I'm afraid you'll have trouble sleepin' with all the wind whistlin'. 'Sides, I'm not in any hurry to freeze my b--buns off in a tent just yet. My intentions are entirely honorable. I know how you feel about me. Just say you'll let me sit on the bed and hold you until you get sleepy."

"Jonathan!"

"Okay, just one arm." He held up one arm, smiling. "I'll just put one arm around you. I won't even take my boots off."

"Jonathan, you're embarrassing me."

38

He stepped back from her and took both her hands in his. "They're like ice, Ginny. I know your mind isn't settled yet. Please. I'd do the same for m' sis."

She closed her eyes and breathed out. It was against her better judgment.

"I'll be a perfect gentleman, I promise. I'll just think of you as Raggedy Anne. Don't you trust me, Virginia?" The hurtful honesty in his voice touched her.

"I trust you, Jonny. I just feel like such a fool. I'm a big girl. I've lived alone for years."

"Do you prefer to face everythin' alone, Ginny?"

His words moved her. No, she didn't like facing everything alone. She didn't like facing much of anything alone. His accent was thinner now; he seemed older, worldlier. But what kind of signal would she be giving him if she let him come in?

Her gaze darted from side to side, her breath quickened. He ran the back of his fingers along her cheek and she was lost. Her eyes closed and she realized she felt safe, cared for, and understood for the first time in years.

"You'll go when I feel drowsy?"

"Promise." He raised his right hand.

~ * ~

"Go on into the bathroom and change," Jonathan said, once inside. "I'll just put my overcoat at the foot of the bed so my boots won't soil the covers."

Ginny took her nightgown and robe into the bathroom, changed, and took out her contact lenses. Her glasses lay in the bedroom. She didn't tell Jonathan she couldn't see anything but blurs when she returned in moments to find him sitting on the left side of the bed, uniform, boots and all, with the right side of the covers turned down for her. He patted the bed next to him.

With a tentative smile on her lips, she climbed into the high bed and he pulled the covers up over her, gently, lovingly. Then he stretched out his right arm for her to lay her head against his chest.

She did so, but bolted up as soon as her cheek hit his wool jacket.

"I'm not just scared of small places. I'm allergic to wool." She rubbed her cheek, looking at him sheepishly.

"No problem." He began to unbutton the jacket as Ginny looked on fearfully. Under it was a modern white T-shirt.

"You cheater! That's not Confederate issue!"

He flung the jacket toward a chair and welcomed her head again to his chest. Until her cheek felt the softness of the shirt over the warm, hard chest, Ginny hadn't realized how exhausted she was. As Jonathan ran his hand softly up and down on her upper arm, she began to drift off. Safe. She felt really safe. How she welcomed that forgotten feeling.

She snuggled cozily to his chest and threw her right arm over him in her slumber.

If he tried to get up to leave, she would wake. He simply slid down a little on the bed, boots and all, and dozed off himself. After a few of the re-enactments he'd been in, he could sleep anywhere, in any position.

Four

Jonathan awoke first. He would have loved to make a trip to the bathroom, but he wouldn't disturb Virginia's peacefulness. He watched her for a few moments. There was no strain or care about her face. She looked years younger than she claimed to be, an almost a child-like innocence about her slumber.

His right shoulder and arm were almost numb. Ginny's head hadn't moved from that side of his chest all night. It seemed to fit snugly into the curve of his shoulder, as if he had been molded just to hold her head. He touched the slender fingers of her right hand, there next to her cheek upon his chest. She didn't stir. Then he touched her cheek, softly as the kiss of butterfly wings.

He hoped he wasn't imagining the slight smile that crossed her lips as she took a deep breath and unconsciously snuggled to him. Then her eyelids fluttered. With a startled jerk, she gasped and scurried to her knees on the bed. She said nothing, but looked frantically about the room as daylight streamed in through the windows.

Ginny swallowed hard, then her mouth fell open. Jonathan chuckled at her deep chagrin. Still without a word, she scrutinized him. "You…you're still dressed. You haven't even taken off your boots. Her face flushed bright red.

"Jonathan, you spent the entire night in such discomfort. Why?"

"Because I couldn't bear to disturb your sleep. Somehow I felt like you needed that deep, peaceful slumber, Ginny. I'm sorry if I overstepped myself. You were so tired and, well, I can sleep just anywhere at all. Honestly, I didn't mind. I slept very well."

She smiled, but her smile faded quickly, "Oh, Lord! What will your camp friends think?"

"They'll think exactly what I told them last night. I went by before I returned the buggy. Told 'em my friend invited me to hoist a few beers, and if I had one too many, they needn't look for me 'til mornin'." He reached his hand to hers. "Don't fret, please."

Ginny sighed heavily.

Jonathan stood up, stiffly. "Miz Virginia, your reputation is entirely safe with me. I am a Southern gentleman, you know."

She smiled. "Thank you Jonathan. I must admit that was the soundest sleep I have enjoyed in years." She thought about telling him it was the first time she'd felt "safe" in a long time, but he probably wouldn't understand her meaning. "I feel so refreshed."

"Then, ma'am, since my duty is finished, I should return to my post." He snapped to attention and saluted.

"Won't you let me buy you breakfast, Jonathan?"

"Thank you, no, ma'am. They'll be cooking over the fire back at camp. I kinda like that. I'll just be goin', after I put my jacket back on, and, if it's not too bold, could I use the facilities one time, before I get back to the 'porta-potty'?"

Ginny laughed and signaled her approval by waving toward the bathroom.

She had brushed her hair and straightened her appearance by the time Jonathan emerged.

"I'll be takin' my leave, ma'am." He put on his hat after he nodded politely.

"Thank you for everything, Jonathan."

"Will I see you about town later, in your costume?"

"Probably." She paused. "Tell me something, Jonathan…"

"Only if you take t' callin' me Jonny again."

She nodded. "Jonny. Tell me why it is your North Carolina accent fades in and out?"

He rolled his eyes a little and grinned.

"You noticed that, did ya?"

Ginny nodded again.

"Well, it's like this. I grew up mostly in Ohio with my grandmother. My mother died right after I was born, and my father took my older brother, but left me and my older sister with Gram until I was through sixth grade. Then I went to North Carolina to live with him and my brother. My sister stayed with Gram. I get a little confused at times."

Ginny laughed. "I just wondered because my accent seems to get thicker at some times than others. It depends on who I'm talking to, what I've just been reading or writing… I get teased about it a lot."

"See that's one more thing we have in common." He turned toward the door. "I'll make myself as inconspicuous as possible as I leave. I hope you have a pleasant day." He opened the door.

"I already have, Jonny. I already have." Her voice was a mere whisper. She stood on tiptoe and gently kissed his cheek.

He said not another word, but walked quietly down the hall and left by a side exit.

~ * ~

In the dinning room, Ginny seated herself at a table by the front window so she could watch the foot traffic. She wanted to see just how many and what kind of costumes she could expect.

43

An occasional Confederate uniform went by, then a couple of women in full costume, then an older man in a great coat, riding boots and bowler hat. By the time she finished breakfast, the waitress was dressed in a modest period skirt, blouse and pinafore.

This was an adventure. A real getaway. It would be fun, if she let herself dissolve into the masquerade.

She left the check and appropriate money on the table and the waitress came toward her. "I hope you don't require Confederate money."

"No ma'am, greenbacks are just fine."

They both smiled at each other.

~ * ~

Even the desk clerk was now dressed in a little more elaborate fashion, befitting her station, than the waitress. In her room, Ginny dragged out all her paraphernalia and dressed in costume. She didn't own any appropriate slippers or high-topped shoes, so her boots would have to suffice. The skirt was dark green, like her cape, with a lighter green flounce around the bottom. It was very heavy material, so with her knee-high boots and panty hose her legs should be warm enough. The cape would warmly cover the rest of her.

She put on her ivory satin blouse with the large collar of delicate ivory lace, and pulled her hair back in an appropriately matronly manner, clipping it in the ivory satin bow with snood attached. She pushed the curls of her shoulder length hair into the snood. Then once she put in her lenses so she could see, she put on only a moderate amount of make up to look natural.

She remembered to bring the small green leather bag that closed with a leather drawstring. She purchased it years ago at a Renaissance festival, to go with her cape, but had never yet used it. Too small to hold much, she placed in it her room key, some money and a handkerchief, one of her grandmother's.

"There! Guess that's as good as it gets." She looked into the full-length mirror on the inside of the open bathroom door. She put on her green velvet "Scarlet O'Hara" cape and headed toward the lobby. She didn't want to put the hood up, not until she saw how cold it was outside.

~ * ~

The sun beamed brightly, and, though there was a nip in the morning air, there was no wind to make her shiver, so Ginny left the hood of her cape down so the sun could warm her hair.

She walked down the street toward the bridge that separated the City of Fredericksburg and its Confederate troops from the Union troops on the other side. She nodded and smiled to passersby as she strolled. Her costume was a sham compared to the other ladies she met who wore chemises, corsets, crinolines, heavy stockings and garters, and sturdy, high-topped shoes, but she could blend in quite well. Who'd know what was underneath but herself?

She crossed the street toward the Chatham bridge and stopped at the warehouse which had survived since the eighteenth century. This was the boundary of the festival area. Automobiles would be allowed to cross the bridge, but only to continue on William St. in a straight direction for the three blocks of the festival area which ended at Princess Anne Street. From the railroad station on Lafayette Blvd. to William St., for the length of Sophia, Caroline, and Princess Anne, no cars could be seen. Outside of that area, automobiles were allowed, but parking spaces were almost non-existent.

A couple of surreys would ferry people from farther parking areas, while smaller carriages, like the runabout Jonathan used, would sell rides.

The first Union camp sat some three or four hundred yards downstream on the other side of the Rappahannock. Men in blue milled about, cooking over carefully contained campfires, and heading up the hill to the partially camouflaged portable toilets.

Through the brush on the up-river side, a single figure approached the bridge. She watched from her vantage point at the old warehouse. The man was dressed in Confederate gray, but his clothes looked dirty and disheveled. He wore no hat, but some kind of dirty bandanna about his head and a brown cape thrown haphazardly over one shoulder.

He staggered toward the bridge. As she watched him for a moment, she wondered if he had simply imbibed too much the night before and just awakened from sleeping it off, or was some kind of pervert. She didn't want him to spoil her illusions, so peeking toward the bridge, she hid behind the warehouse.

For a moment the man stood, scanning the bridge and the river, then he crouched down on the walkway of the bridge and looked toward the Union camp. Ginny decided to leave before this disgusting character made it across the bridge to harass or molest her.

"Either drunk, or crazy," she whispered to herself and turned to stroll down the river side of Sophia street toward Jonathan's Confederate camp.

~ * ~

"Good mornin', madam." The Captain swept his plumed hat from his head and bowed.

"Good morning, Captain."

"Won't you join our humble group for a while?" He offered her a camp stool and reached for her hand to assist her.

"Thank you, Captain…uh…"

"Childress, ma'am, at your service. I apologize for not properly introducin' myself yesterday."

"Virginia Berkeley, Captain Childress." She offered him her hand, which he kissed gallantly.

"A fine family name, Berkeley, and an even finer Christian name. Would you care for some coffee?" Obviously he had forgotten that she refused it the day before.

"Thank you, no, Captain, I have become accustomed to doing without in these desperate days of the war. I fear I should abstain lest I desire something which I can have nowhere else, and become a wretched camp follower." She tossed her head and batted her lashes coyly.

The Captain nodded with an amused look on his face. She fell right into the part of a Southern lady. He would continue to portray the noble Confederate Captain.

"Alas, my dear lady, I do understand. I myself have been forced to take alternate brews from time to time. Tomorrow, when our supplies have abated, we shall have a truce to exchange good Virginia tobacco for Yankee coffee beans."

"Do take care, Captain. I hear those Yankees can be a devilishly clever bunch."

He nodded again. "I thank you for your concern."

"I got some chocolate, ma'am," a young corporal offered as he pushed his cup toward her. "M' ma sends it t' me, and I got some milk from a...local farmer." The young man hesitated as he concocted his story.

"I'd be delighted, Corporal..."

The young man jumped to attention. "Hilliard, ma'am."

"I'd be delighted, Corporal Hilliard. I'm pleased to make your acquaintance. Give your mother my regards and tell her what a perfect gentleman her son is, when next you write."

The boy snickered, but regained his composure and continued the guise. "That I will, ma'am."

This was fun. This was really fun! Virginia Berkeley was having the time of her life and this was only the first day.

By now several of the men gathered around, but Ginny didn't see Jonathan.

"Captain, is Sergeant Blackburn about this morning?"

"Present and accounted for!" His voice rang from one of the white tents as he came out.

"Good morning, Sergeant."

"Good mornin', Miz Berkeley. I trust you slept well?"

She felt a slight warmth about her face, but took a breath and continued the play. "I did, Sergeant, thank you. I passed a most restful night."

"It was rather a good thing you decided not to accept my invitation to join my friend and I in a drink. We got carried away and slept if off in a tavern."

As they spoke, Ginny felt someone's eyes on her. She glanced about the camp as unobtrusively as she could.

"Somethin' wrong, ma'am?" Jonathan asked.

Ginny took a deep breath and shook her head. "No, Jonathan, just an overactive imagination. I keep feeling as though someone is watching me."

"Only about ten of us is all," the young corporal joked.

"Why Corporal Hilliard, I declare. You are a *scoundrel*. But you needn't tell your mother that."

A few feet from where Ginny and the Captain sat, a young man brought out his guitar and began to strum it. Ginny recognized the tune of "Lorena" and hummed it softly for she didn't know the words.

Suddenly, the Captain began to sing it in a glorious baritone voice. When he finished, Ginny slapped her hands together to applaud.

"Ooo!" She flung her hands in the air. "I didn't realize they were so cold. I shouldn't have forgotten my muff." She blew on her stinging hands. "I should go back for it." She began to rise, but Jonathan put his hand on her shoulder to stop her.

"Give me your key and I'll fetch it, Miz Virginia."

"No, Jonathan, that's not necessary. I've intruded quite long enough."

"Intruded! My dear, you are no intrusion."

"You're very kind Captain, but I'm sure you men have other things to do besides entertaining me."

"But you are entertaining us, at least you will be when we find a song you know the words to and you sing it for us."

"Oh, no, Captain, thank you, really."

The men applauded and whistled, which went over none too well with the few camp wives nearby. They kept their distance when she was about. But Ginny shrugged and decided not to care. This was her vacation, her day-dream, her getaway. She would love to sing with them...for them. She'd been letting her singing speak for her heart for years. It kept her wits about her in times of deep distress. She'd had many such times. It brought her closer to God as it touched others. One day, she hoped writing would do the same.

"Surely you sing, madam. Your humming is so melodic. Your voice is clear and carries well, though only a hum."

"Well, yes, I sing, in church and at weddings...and in the shower." She chuckled.

"See, Miz Virginia. Let me get your muff," Jonathan insisted.

Ginny reached into the tiny green pouch, brought out her key and handed it to him.

"I won't be long. It's just down the street. Don't sing nothin' 'til I get back." He scurried away.

"Well, my dear, tell us what songs you know, from our time, that is."

Ginny drew an absolute blank for a moment, but calling all her wits about her she remembered some songs. "Well, I guess I know just about all of Mr. Stephen Foster's songs... and 'Shenandoah'... 'Barbara Allen,' 'Battle Hymn--' no, uh," she stammered as she cut off the Union song "Battle Hymn of the Republic." "Dixie!"

The men whistled and shouted.

"Benson, can you play 'Dixie'?"

"Does a cat have whiskers?" Benson asked.

"Play it slowly." She inclined her head toward him.

"Lieutenant, ma'am."

"Thank you, Lieutenant, I'm sorry to be so bad with rank insignias."

"What key, ma'am?"

"Good question. I don't know what key is most comfortable for 'Dixie.' I'm a soprano, Lieutenant, does that help?"

"Try this one on fer size, ma'am." He played the last phrase and just as Jonathan returned with her muff, she nodded that the key would do.

"I wish I was in the land of cotton... Old times there are not forgotten, look away...look away...look away...Dixie Land." She began slowly, melodically, capturing the attention of everyone in camp, and everyone passing on the street as well.

By the time that she finished her heartfelt rendition, there were tears in nearly every eye and a dead stillness about them all. Then the Captain rose from his camp chair and bowed to her, whispering, "Lovely, just lovely, my dear." He applauded almost reverently. Then the crowd joined in. She had captured their hearts.

"It is a beautiful song, isn't it," she said quietly.

"It was just a song to me until now," the old man who passed the inn that morning in the bowler hat spoke up.

Ginny's face heated, it must have been beet red by the time the crowd quieted. Everyone asked her to sing more, and she did. Shenandoah, Barbara Allen.

"Captain, there's a special favorite of mine, I wish you would sing. I'm sure you know it."

He looked at her questioningly.

"Aura Lea."

The men cheered and the guitar began. The Captain's voice rose beautifully and the resulting applause was thunderous.

"What say we end this with something everyone can sing?" Ginny shouted above the pleas for them to continue to entertain. "How about 'When Johnny Comes Marchin' Home'!"

All the uniformed men stood and the visitors even danced about as they all sang. It seemed great fun for everyone, but particularly for Ginny. She became one of them, one of these historic re-enactors. She wasn't on the outside looking in as usual. She was participating.

~ * ~

The morning flew by. Ginny should leave and give these men the opportunity to go among the crowd and socialize. The camaraderie had brought them to this place. As she bid them farewell for a while to return to the inn for lunch, she looked past the log building in front of which they were camped.

The man from the bridge peered at them, at her, actually. He looked disreputable. Even from this distance of many yards, his face seemed distorted, his eyes looked wild, his costume not only dirty, but tattered in many places.

"Captain, you really should see about that man over by the house."

"Man?"

"Yes, at the rear of the log house. He has on what might pass for a poor Confederate uniform at the end of the war, but he looks quite mad."

"Well, my dear, we do attract a few strange ones." He looked toward the building but the man was gone.

"Oh, he was there a moment ago. It's probably just as well you didn't see him. I'm not sure you'd want to invite him to join you. Whoever he is, I hope he gets some help if he needs it." She shook her head, but could not shake the look of the man she assumed was a bum of some kind.

"I hope we will see you again soon." The Captain bowed and kissed Ginny's hand.

"I'll walk you back to your inn," Jonathan offered, and she took his arm.

Five

The walk back to the inn was pleasant enough, though Ginny was uneasy, feeling again someone's eyes upon her. At one point she turned suddenly to try to catch a glimpse of the figure that seemed to be stalking her, but she wasn't quick enough to get a clear look, or, at least, he was quicker. *If he were there at all.* She shrugged to herself.

"Jonathan, please have lunch with me. They did have restaurants in the nineteenth century."

"I should be sharing the hard tack and fat-back in camp." He chuckled, indicating by his sour expression that he was none too fond of it.

"I'm sure someone can eat your share." Ginny tugged at his arm playfully.

"Well, ya talked me into it, Ma'am, but I insist on payin'."

"You're not supposed to have modern money, Jonathan. Keep your hands in your pockets. I owe you for yesterday's adventure, and last night's good company."

Jonathan wanted to tell her he would have gladly been more than company, but he knew Virginia wasn't interested in a brief liaison with a younger man, and he would settle for her friendship.

~ * ~

After lunch Jonathan and Ginny walked around the town a bit more. As a couple, they provoked much interest with the tourists, and, never letting on that she was a tourist, too, Ginny enjoyed stopping to chat with them. She called on every bit and piece of historical information from the imaginary files in her brain, and quite entertained those who dared to stop them to talk.

"Jonathan!" Ginny exclaimed as she looked across Caroline Street. "A photographer! Oh, Jonathan, I hate having my picture taken, but I've always wanted one in costume like this. Would you?"

"A picture with you?" Sweeping his cap from his head, he bowed deeply from the waist. "Why, Miz Virginia, I would be honored."

The antique camera, backdrops, props and costumes had been moved into a vacant store for the festival. The photographer picked out an appropriate hat to go with Ginny's outfit, removing her cape and placing it on a peg in the back of the photograph. Her bow and snood would not show in this stately posed photograph. The hat was red, a ghastly color against her golden red hair, but it mattered little for a sepia colored antique photo.

The photographer posed them as they would likely have been for a period picture, and for effect, draped a Confederate flag over Jonathan's arm.

"Come back in an hour, children," the old photographer said. "They'll be ready then."

Ginny stifled a giggle as they raced from the store. "Children! Did he really say, 'children'?" Then she burst into bubbles of laughter.

"He did! I told you, you looked no older than I when your eyes sparkle and your cheeks color with delight, especially when you're happy." He took her face in his hands.

"Jonathan, stop!" She recovered slowly from her laughter as her face heated.

He dragged her to the next store front. There was a dark curtain behind the glass of the window and they could see their reflections clearly. "There! You look, and tell me, honestly, that you think I look younger than you." He squared her shoulders pointing her toward the glass.

"But you *are* younger…much younger. I look like an old-maid aunt you're indulging.

"I didn't ask for chronological analysis. I asked what you see."

Ginny would never admit it aloud, or even clearly in her own thoughts, but it was true. They looked relatively the same age. This charade made her look as young as it made her feel. Would that she could stay like this, but, in a week, she'd return to the old grind at work, at home. Resolving to think of nothing but this time, and her new, handsome, and very good friend, she raised her chin in the air.

~ * ~

Ginny had told the photographer to make two eight by tens and two wallet-size copies, if the picture turned out, then Jonathan and she had wandered about for the hour the photographs would take then returned.

They did turn out. They turned out beautifully! "Oh, Jonathan, I shall treasure this always. I'll put it right above my computer to help me imagine when I write, and I'll always remember my gallant sergeant in gray." She touched his cheek and met his fawn brown eyes as tears of happiness gathered in her own.

Neither spoke for some moments as they turned and strolled arm in arm down Caroline Street to William Street then back on Sophia to return to the rebel encampment. With the festival now in full swing, each time they approached an officer in

Confederate uniform, Jonathan stopped and saluted and Ginny nodded pleasantly.

A caped figure lurked in a narrow alley-like walkway between two buildings. As they walked past Ginny caught a chill that made her shake all over. An unpleasant, stale odor, like last night's garbage assailed her. As they passed, Jonathan turned to look over his shoulder and made her sure he had smelled it, too. He shrugged and kept moving.

~ * ~

Jonathan walked Ginny all the way to the door of her room. "Sure you're up to stayin' alone tonight?" He grinned slyly as he took her key and unlocked her door.

Ginny smiled at his boldness. "Yes, Jonathan, I think I can manage tonight. Thank you for your concern."

"Ma'am," he tipped his hat, nodded politely to her, then turned to leave.

"Jonathan…" She called him back. "Thank you for the lovely time yesterday, and for staying last night. I don't know what got into me, but I did appreciate your kindness." She kissed him in a sisterly fashion on the cheek, but he did not turn again to leave.

He leaned his face down toward hers and gently kissed her lips, not wantonly or demandingly, but beguilingly, honestly, softly.

"I been wantin' t' do that for two days. I wanted to know how you tasted." His voice was a whisper to which Ginny made no reply.

She stood staring after him as he turned and strolled down the hallway. He didn't look back, but she couldn't move. She swallowed the lump in her throat as she leaned against the door. Then she absently reached behind her to the knob and opened it, stumbling backward as it gave way.

~ * ~

Inside her room the awesome feeling of the gentle kiss did not leave her as she removed her cape, unzipped her boots and dropped her skirt to the floor. She unbuttoned the tiny pearl buttons on her blouse as she walked toward the bathroom. Her face was still blank but glowing as she gazed into the mirror. With her first two fingers, she traced the tender feeling of his lips on hers, wondering why he kissed her, and why she let him?

Such a handsome *young* man--the operative here word being "young." She ran both of her hands down the length of her face and inhaled deeply, chasing any thoughts of interest from her mind and her body. "You've been alone too long, Virginia!" she told herself. "Get a grip!"

She pulled the bow and snood from her hair and started the shower running. Her shower took much longer than usual as she found herself unwillingly daydreaming about the handsome young Jonathan. She finally scoffed at herself. "Wonder if he has an older brother?"

Wrapping her freshly washed hair in a towel, she dried her body and put on her nightshirt. Though it was winter, she hated long gowns like the one she wore last night for modesty's sake. She always slept restlessly and got tangled up in the length of the gown or managed to have it bundled up to her waist in short order. Nightshirts were better. She really only needed something about her shoulders which she always kept above the covers.

She combed out her wet hair, fastened a clip to keep it from her face and let it dry partially in the air as she sat in the lady's chair by the fire. Its high back comforted her fatigued shoulders; its winged sides offered their restful corners to cradle her head. She stared into the gas fire, which danced about on the artificial logs looking almost like a real wood fire. It was much safer to have these old fireplaces converted like this, and cleaner. No ashes to dump or sparks to fly out. No fire screen was even needed.

Well, she'd have to keep her mind on something besides Jonathan. Maybe it'd help to think about something like converting her own fireplace when she returned home.

The wind seemed to be picking up outside tonight. Wonder how the men were faring in their tents? Wonder how Jonathan was faring anyway? At the window, she drew back the curtain to peer into the darkness for some sign of the weather. As she put her face close to the window and shaded her eyes from the inside light, she gasped and let out a startled screech. A man stood looking straight at her through the windowpane.

She threw the curtain back down, grabbed her robe and headed for the hidden telephone. The desk clerk answered.

"A man…" she said breathlessly. "There's a man looking in my window!"

"A man, Miz Berkeley?" the clerk asked.

"Yes."

"Hold on a minute. A sheriff's deputy is eatin' dinner here," he said.

Silence fell on the other end of the phone. It seemed forever before the clerk picked up again.

"Ma'am, the deputy is on his way outside to look around. I'm on the way to your room."

The phone clicked on the clerk's end. Ginny stared at the phone for several seconds . Then someone knocked at her door.

"He's here." Ginny slammed the phone down and rushed to the door.

~ * ~

Ginny opened the door a crack, peering cautiously around the edge. When she assured herself it was indeed the desk clerk, she opened the door wider.

"Sheriff's outside checkin', Ma'am. Just what did you see?"

"A pair of eyes...wild, fierce eyes. A beard...scraggly hair..."

The desk clerk squinted. "'Scraggly?'"

"Scraggly! Dirty, stringy, long."

"Oh, yes, I see."

Flashlight in hand, the deputy came down the hall. He nodded toward Ginny, who stood there with her wet hair hanging and clutching the front of her robe to keep it closed.

"Didn't find anyone ma'am. Maybe it was just a shadow of a tree in the wind. Strong wind a-blowin' tonight."

Ginny straightened indignantly. "I know a pair of eyes when I see them, and they were looking directly at *me*."

"Yes ma'am," the deputy said quietly. "Well, there's no one out there now. We'll ride by ever'-so-of'en tonight, ma'am. You needn't worry."

She cocked her jaw in disgust. Not wanting to make a scene, she gave the deputy a glaring look and retreated behind her door.

"Maybe I should have let Jonathan stay again," she whispered to herself. Then she thought about it a little more. "Bad idea, Ginny, you might have been tempted to act stupidly." She chastised herself again. Then her resolve melted as she thought about his fawn-brown eyes.

She'd never cared for brown eyes. Harry had brown eyes, just a sort of muddy water brown, but Jonathan's eyes were warm and soft. *If I were ten years younger.* The thought gave her a smile. "If I were ten years younger, I'd still be married to that womanizing son-of-a--" She caught herself speaking aloud. Her second husband, who kept two women on the side, worked mostly nights so he had excuses to come and go at strange hours.

Ginny had to give him some credit, though; he was great in bed. She had no idea just how much practice he was getting. It was no wonder he was always exhausted, spreading himself so *thin.*

She'd hardly settled back into her chair by the fire when a gentle knock came to her door. Well, she could answer it, but then again maybe not. It might be the deputy. Maybe he took a second look around and found something, or someone.

"Yes?" She called from where she sat.

"Miz Virginia?" The voice was just a heavy whisper, but Ginny recognized it as Jonathan's. "Miz Virginia, you all right?"

She darted to the door and opened it part way. "Jonathan! What on earth are you doing out in this cold? You should be under a dozen blankets in your tent."

"I saw someone snoopin' about with a flashlight. We can see this place from the camp, ya know. I wanted to make sure you were okay." He shuddered suddenly as if a chill gripped him.

"I'm fine. Come in here where it's warm." Ginny was covered well enough in her burgundy fleece man's robe. Her hair was still damp, and she wore no make-up.

"*Well*, now you see me at my *worst*." She chuckled. "Just try to tell me I look younger, then I'll know you're a pathological liar."

He just stood, looking at her.

"Sit down, for cryin' out loud, *Jonathan*."

"Yes'm." He took the low-backed arm chair opposite hers.

"Might as well take off your coat and stay a while."

"I don't want to intrude, Miz Ginny. I just wanted to make sure--"

"I know, I know, I'm okay. Well, I am, but I could use the company. I was just thinking about you, actually."

"Really?" He stood to shed his greatcoat. She hadn't seen him in it before. But this night was colder than it had been in the last two days.

"I wish I had something to offer you to drink." She wagged her head regretfully.

"No need, ma'am. I just downed a few with the fellahs."

"Oh," was all she said. Hopefully, that didn't mean he was a little drunk. He didn't seem drunk. He just seemed relaxed. Maybe that wasn't so good either.

"What happened tonight?"

"Nothing, I guess, Jonny. I thought I saw--NO! I *saw* a man looking in my window. I think he was the grungy-looking man I saw near your camp. The one I told you I saw acting like a lunatic on the bridge. They didn't find anyone."

"Want me t' stay with ya tonight?"

"Uh, thanks, Jonathan, I'm fine, really! But you don't need to run off."

Jonathan seemed to be studying her face.

"I wish you wouldn't scrutinize me so. No make-up, wet hair, I guess I am a sight."

"No, it isn't that. I just was noticing your hair, how different it looks all dark and wet, and it took me a moment t--" He stopped abruptly.

"Took you a moment to what?"

He smiled, "Pardon me, ma'am. I just had to focus in to find your eyebrows. I thought they were missin'."

Ginny laughed. It was true. If she had no pencil on them, her eyebrows were such a light strawberry-blond that they didn't show up at all. With her tongue she moistened the index finger on each hand and stroked them along her eyebrows. When they were wet, they showed up a little. "Better? See there are some advantages to modern make-up."

They laughed.

~ * ~

After talking for about an hour with Ginny, Jonathan said a polite goodnight and left her with a kiss on the cheek.

As she closed the door behind him, Ginny traced the place his lips had touched so warmly and smiled wistfully. She wasn't sure if she was glad he left without making any advances, or sorry.

Six

Jonathan showed up bright and early Sunday morning, the second day of the festival. Ginny answered the knock at her door. Dressed in the long peasant skirt, no hoops, she still looked like she stepped out of the nineteenth century…or so he said.

"Jonathan?"

"Mornin' Miz Virginia. I wasn't takin' any chances this mornin' that your mystery man might keep you from joining us in camp. 'Sides thought you might be more comfortable with an escort."

"Thank you, Jonathan, but I'm all right. I thought I might wander across the bridge today and visit the Union camp."

Jonathan rubbed his bearded chin. Then he chuckled. "Not afraid they'll hold ya hostage?"

Ginny laughed. "Oh, I doubt it. I have no particular worth to the Union."

She was glad to lighten the mood. If the truth be told, she hadn't sleep very well last night. She saw the face in the window every time she closed her eyes.

~ * ~

"Had yer breakfast, yet?" Jonathan asked Ginny in the hallway of the inn.

"No, I'm not really hungry this morning, Jonathan. I thought I'd just get out into the fresh air and maybe work up an appetite."

"Didn't sleep last night, did ya?"

Ginny didn't answer.

"Your eyes look tired, Ginny."

Wonder if he meant "tired" or "old?" Two bad marriages left her feeling like an old used car with too much mileage and bald tires--not a valuable vintage automobile. Jonathan should be dating someone her daughters' age. Why did she keep reading her own meanings into his words?

"Would ya like to go to church, Miz Virginia? Well, not church exactly. We're havin' our own little service with a chaplain and everything in camp. I was hopin' I could fetch ya."

Ginny looked up into his eyes. "I think I'd like that, Jonathan. I think I'd like that a lot."

~ * ~

The morning was sunny but very cold. Ginny clung to Jonathan's arm, and though she had the hood of her cape up and her hands in her muff, she just couldn't shake a deep chill.

The clearing where the men were camped was full of people. Many more Confederate uniforms than Ginny had seen in one place before, and many civilians. Everyone was dressed in period, or near period costume. As Jonathan escorted her to a waiting empty camp chair in the front row, the Captain reached out for her arm. It was like being an honored guest. Ginny never felt special or important like this. She relished the feeling.

She was used to attention when she sang, but that was different then: she was someone else--a personality she put on like a cloak--confident in her voice and delivery of a song. This was just Ginny being Virginia, or was it? She was acting. That was almost like singing. But she didn't feel like she was acting. It was just *fun*. She felt at home, comfortable, cared about with these re-enactors, but particularly with Jonathan.

They used no hymnals, nor Bibles for the service, except those the chaplain held. In order to be heard in the large crowd, there were some unorthodox microphones and speakers camouflaged rather ingeniously. Lieutenant Benson played his guitar and a man Ginny had not yet met, played his harmonica into hidden microphones for the hymns. At the close of the service, the Captain seemed to signal the chaplain, who then reached for Ginny's hand to lead the last hymn, "Amazing Grace". After they sang the three most well known verses, the chaplain handed her the microphone and asked her to begin the first verse again. She hid the mike behind her muff.

The crowd was silent; even Lt. Benson's guitar was still and she sang a cappella. She hadn't realized everyone else was going to stop singing, but she didn't falter as her lone voice rang out, clear in the crisp air. She scanned the faces to include them, as she always did when she sang in front of an audience. As she searched, she saw the men in the Union camp across the river standing in silence. She could hear her own voice carried on the breeze from some unseen speaker.

The Confederate congregation stood in silence for a moment, even after the benediction, while from the Union camp arose a cheer from men with hats waving in their hands.

The captain escorted Ginny from the front of the group. Jonathan stood tall, a proud look on his face as she reached for his arm. He said nothing as his brown eyes, moist with waiting tears, caused a lump to form in Ginny's throat.

"Today, my dear," the captain began, "you can watch while we exchange our tobacco for Yankee coffee. The cease-fire was called until one o'clock to give us a chance for our church service and tradin'. In a few minutes I'll be sendin' a detail of men to the middle of the bridge to meet with a delegation of the Union forces. Would you like to accompany them?"

"Oh, yes, Captain. I was just telling Jonathan this morning I thought I might walk over to the Union camp."

"Well, I hope this doesn't mean you plan on tradin' any secrets, my dear," the captain said in a joking manner.

As Ginny lifted her head to laugh, she spotted someone in the crowd of people. It was him! She was sure it was the man from the bridge, the man she saw through her window last night. Trying not to lose sight of the man, she tugged at Jonathan's coat sleeve to get his attention but when Jonathan leaned down to listen to her, his head blocked her view. By the time she told him what she wanted, the elusive figure had vanished again. Had he been there through the entire service? It was possible. There were so many people.

~ * ~

Jonathan was one of the delegates to go to the bridge, and Lieutenant Benson was in command. Ginny was the only civilian invited to go, though the bridge was crowded with on-lookers. Lieutenant Benson dutifully asked the Union captain if Miz Virginia Berkeley could accompany them back to camp. The captain bowed and extended his arm to Virginia.

"I won't be gone long, Jonathan," she called as she left with the Union escort and the tobacco.

"Sir!" Jonathan shouted and saluted. "Permission to accompany Miz Berkeley, Sir!"

The Lieutenant nodded. Jonathan took off his side arms and approached the Union Captain. "Sir!" He snapped to attention again. "Request permission to accompany the lady, Sir! I am unarmed!" He saluted.

Ginny's eyes sparkled with amusement, and the public cheered Jonathan on. She didn't care if all this was just make-believe, she was enjoying every moment. The Union captain granted Jonathan's request and the Union escort encircled him and Ginny.

"Jonathan," Ginny whispered. "What was that all about?"

He leaned close to her ear to reply softly. "You don't think I was going to let my best girl go off with some damn Yankees, do ya?"

"Jonathan!" She giggled like a schoolgirl.

"I don't have much longer, Miz Virginia. I got to be startin' back for home before supper. I just wanted to be with you as long as I could."

"Oh, Jonathan!" She turned to look into his buckskin colored eyes. "I don't want this to end." Pain knotted in her stomach and she felt tears gathering in her eyes. She wished she hadn't let that last sentence slip, but nobody had ever wanted to be with her so urgently. Must it end so soon?

"Mustn't show any weakness around the enemy, Ma'am." Jonathan tried to lighten the mood and Ginny forced a slight smile.

~ * ~

With the exception of more luxuries, things in the Union camp weren't much different from the Confederate camp. There were fewer tourists visiting this side of the river, but the men were very much like her grays on the other side.

A Colonel commanded the Union camp. Having no idea, Ginny had to be told his rank. The only ranks she could recognize were generals, and now sergeants.

"It is a pleasure to have you with us, Miss Berkeley." The colonel held out his hand for hers as she was introduced. He kissed her hand then cast a wary glance with his hazel eyes. "I trust you have not come to count our troops or seek out secret papers."

"Why, Colonel, I wouldn't dream of it. I am your guest, after all, and if you so choose, I could well be your prisoner. I would not spy on you."

The colonel's and Ginny's mouths curved in cunning smiles as he escorted her to a comfortable chair with arms.

"You travel in luxury, Colonel, compared to our poor boys." She snickered a little trying not to break the spell again. "I was curious to see your encampment and uniforms. I am most drawn to this period in history."

"Ah, but you persist in keeping company with the wrong side, my dear."

"Wrong, Colonel? I hardly think so, though I admit my entire family is full of Yankees. In my heart, I am like General Lee, first, last, and always a Virginian!"

"Well said, my dear." The colonel acknowledged with a nod. "You have a very devoted escort in this sergeant, to walk into an enemy camp, unarmed."

"Yes, Jonathan is my champion, my Galahad." She smiled up at Jonathan who flushed with embarrassment, but seemed an inch taller with pride.

"Well, Colonel, this has been pleasant, but we must be getting back."

"Ah, but surely not before you sing for us. I was told it was your voice we heard over the speakers. How about singing the Battle Hymn of the Republic?"

"Colonel, surely your jest!"

"Forgive me. Whatever you would favor us with would be appreciated."

"Well, it is Sunday, perhaps another hymn. Do you have a favorite, Colonel?"

"Of course, but I'm afraid music of this period is not my forté. Perhaps 'Rock of Ages'?"

Several men with instruments gathered. A concertina, harmonica, guitar, and violin, or "fiddle" as they would probably have referred to it.

"You start, and we'll follow," the elderly man with the fiddle offered.

Ginny began slowly, "Rock of Ages cleft for me…" and the camp was still.

When she was finished, men shouted out other hymns and songs.

"I'm afraid I'm not sure of the dates of these songs either, Colonel. Would it compromise your camp if we just made sure we sang some 'oldies'?"

"Not at all."

They sang "In the Garden," "The Old Rugged Cross," and one or two others. Then, as she had in the Confederate camp that first night, Ginny wanted to leave them with a rousing tune. "Dixie" wouldn't have been a very good idea, and Jonathan would certainly not approve of her singing the "Battle Hymn of the Republic." She thought for a moment then began.

"Do not wait until some deed of greatness you may do. Do not wait to spread your light afar…" "Brighten the Corner Where You Are" was a cheerful melody to which everyone could clap in time, once Ginny got them started.

~ * ~

When it was over, Ginny stood and, taking her leave, gave a slight curtsey to the men. Jonathan would be leaving all too soon, and she wanted to have a little more time with her new friend. They waved as they were escorted back to the bridge. The escort left them at the middle, and they walked the rest of the bridge alone.

"I've had such a good time, Jonathan. I wish it didn't have to end."

"Do you have to go back to work tomorrow?"

"Oh, no. I took the whole coming week off. I needed to get away for a good while, but anything I do after this will be so anti-climactic."

"I'm gonna miss you, Virginia Berkeley." Jonathan took her hands in his. "But you have things to do and people to meet."

"I'm going to miss you, too, Jonathan. Could we write? Maybe we could see each other again sometime--" She cut her words short, fearing she was presuming too much.

"I'm not much for writin', but I'll make the effort. Don't promise how good, or how long my letters'll be."

"That doesn't matter. I like to write. Any reply will be fine." She took a business card from her tiny green bag.

"I do have reason to come back this way. Perhaps..." He stopped. "You're very special, Virginia, do you know that?" There was a sincerity in his voice Ginny hadn't heard before.

She blushed, her face on fire. She wasn't special, not to anyone and it made her sad to think about it. She made no reply as she dropped her eyes from his.

"Virginia!" He took her chin in his right hand and tilted her face toward his. "You are special, and don't you ever think otherwise. And that's an order!"

"Yes, Sergeant." Her voice was soft and trembling, as she tried to swallow the lump in her throat. For just this one instant, she wanted to forget the twelve years she had on this dear man. She no longer thought of him as a boy, but he was too young for her to think intimately about--not in good conscience. If she couldn't keep the interest of a man her own age, why should she risk trying to keep the interest of a younger one, and have people talking about her as well?

The silence was becoming uncomfortable. She wanted to break the mood. "Don't suppose you have an older brother, do you?"

Jonathan laughed. "As a matter of fact, I do. He's forty-one, single, too!"

"You'll have to introduce me sometime."

"Maybe. But you're much too good for the likes of him."

She wanted to cry out that she wasn't "too good" for someone like him, that she was lonely, and wanted to love and be loved, but she dared not say a word.

"I'm sorry I gotta be packin' up and leavin'. I really did enjoy myself." Jonathan's eyes were sad and pensive. Ginny knew he wanted to kiss her, but she dared not kiss him. She would be lost, and she wouldn't let herself care that way about someone with whom a relationship was impossible. She touched his cheek, then threw her arms about him tightly, burying her head deep in his hard chest, and totally forgetting the wool about him.

When she moved away from him, her cheeks were damp from tears and raw from the wool. "I…I have to go, Jonathan." She turned to leave him there at the edge of the camp. She hoisted her skirt and darted for the inn. Like all her other dreams, this was short-lived and she must be the one to end it.

~ * ~

Ginny couldn't walk through the lobby with her splotchy red cheeks and puffy eyes, so she passed the building to enter by the side exit Jonathan discreetly used the morning before. As she rounded the corner of the building, she came face to face with the shabbily dressed Confederate who'd been stalking her.

She gasped, but did not scream. It was daylight, there were people within screaming distance, and there were no vehicles into which he could spirit her off. She had to keep a cool head.

"What do you want?" Her voice was sharp and agitated.

"Who are you?" came his raspy response.

"Who am I?" She choked. "Who the hell are you?"

"Are you a spy?" He had a strangle hold on her arm now and she was becoming frightened.

"A spy?" she shouted in disbelief.

"Yes, a spy! I saw you go to the Union camp. You and that, that, turn-coat!"

She had a lunatic on her hands, but what should she do? Should she humor him, scream for help and chance provoking him? She didn't know, but she had to stay calm. He must be really caught up in this play-acting of the festival.

"Of course I'm not a spy." Hoping to distract him and escape, she spoke in a calmer tone. "I was invited to visit the Union camp to entertain. We were in a brief period of truce, to exchange coffee for tobacco. I went over to the Union camp with the permission of Captain Childress."

"Captain Childress?" He ran his fingers through his dirty hair, blinking and sighing as he did. "I don't know him."

"He's the commander of the encampment here." It was not easy to keep her voice even with her arm in the vice his hand made.

"The boy. Who was he?"

"The young sergeant?"

He nodded.

"He was Sergeant Blackburn."

"I don't know him either." He hung his head and closed his sunken eyes.

It was only now that Ginny's senses began to function. She became acutely aware of a pungent odor coming from the man and his dirty uniform, or semblance of a uniform. He ran his fingers through his dirty hair again and she could see what looked like dried blood on his head. That must have been why he had what looked like a bandage on his head the first time she saw him on the bridge.

She reached out tentatively toward the wound. It was filthy, infected. "You need to get to a hospital," she urged.

"No hospital. Not 'til I figure out what's goin' on here." He pushed her hand away, which didn't upset her. His hair and the wound could be teeming with varmints.

She almost gagged. "You can't go around like that. Let me call someone, please." She spoke softly.

"*NO!*" he shouted and turned as if to run, but instead he sank onto a stone garden bench near the side door of the inn. Putting his head in his hands, he wept.

"Please, don't." She kept her voice calm and reassuring as she reached for his hand with no thought to the smell or filth.

"Nothing is right. Everything is so confused. People look the same for a moment, then they look different. Lights, lights are not from candles and gas, carriages approach the bridge with no horses…" He grabbed great hunks of his hair in both hands and, cowering and rocking as he sobbed, sank from the bench to his knees on the cold ground.

"Are you by any chance trying to tell me that you think it's eighteen sixty-three?"

He looked up at her. "Is it sixty-three already? I didn't think Christmas was here yet." His words were beginning to slur, his eyes becoming glazed.

"Look, I don't know who you are, or where you came from, but let's get one thing straight right now. We're just playing at the nineteenth century here. It's just a Civil War festival, that's all. You and I both know it's nineteen ninety-three."

He jerked to his feet. "You lie!" He tightly grabbed both her wrists. "You stand there in those clothes and make sport of me. I have been shot, beaten and imprisoned, but I know who I am, and what the century is, even if I am not sure of the exact date."

She struggled to free her hands, but he was strong; though he looked as if he could not whip a squirrel.

"Let go of me!" She tugged harder. "I'm telling you, you've had too much to drink, or the blow to your head has scattered your brains. It is *nineteen ninety-three*."

"Do not mock me." He whispered through tightly clenched teeth.

"Look, I'll try one more time. We are all in costume for a festival." She pulled her skirt high enough to show her bare knees, covered only by panty hose, over her boots. "Does this look like the underwear of anyone from the Civil War?"

His eyes were wide, then his face reddened.

"Put your skirt down, woman. Have you no dignity? Are you some camp-following harlot, that you should be so brazen? This is mad."

"You won't get an argument from me on that." She flopped her skirt back down. Then her voice softened. "Look, why don't you go home and sleep it off."

"Home? I don't live around here. I'm from Petersburg."

"Then head for Petersburg. It's only a couple of hours away. It's early, you can make it, if you're in any shape to drive."

"Two hours? Drive? Drive what?"

"Here we go with the second hundred years bit again," she grumbled under her breath.

He began to shake uncontrollably, and as Ginny got her first good look at him, she noticed the raggedness of his uniform, or whatever it was. Against her better judgment, Ginny must try to help in some way. "Look, step inside with me. I'll get you some coffee and something to eat."

"I could use somethin' t' eat, but I'd rather have whiskey than coffee."

"Don't you think you've had enough booze?"

He gave no reply, but stared at her.

"Okay, okay, whiskey. Just come inside out of the cold." Glancing around to make sure they weren't seen, she led him in the side door. She couldn't take this derelict into the dining room; the smell alone would send everyone fleeing. She didn't want anyone to see her taking him to her own room. "Do you know your name? I can't just say 'hey you.'"

"Of course I know my name, madam. It's Robert William Carter! *Colonel* Robert William Carter."

"Pleased to meet you, Bob."

"Robert!" he corrected sharply.

She rolled her eyes and inhaled disgustedly, biting her tongue to keep from lashing back at him.

She opened her door and pushed him inside. "Just stand here a moment. I'll be right back with something to eat, some coffee and a whiskey. Don't even sit down until I've covered a chair. And that's an order, Colonel. Just think of me as--as a general."

She whirled about leaving him standing there his mouth frozen in a gape, his eyes wide.

Seven

Ginny was gone far longer than she intended. She balanced the tray precariously with one hand while she fumbled for the key and finally unlocked the door. Without looking up, she began talking the moment the door was open.

"The kitchen was closed, but I talked the bartender into making you a turkey sandwich. I hope you like t--" Her words were cut off in horror as she found his body sprawled upon the bed, *her* bed, "What the hell do you think you're doing?" She screeched in anger, her jaw set so tightly it ached as she slammed the tray down on the dresser and stormed to the bed.

"Hey! Get up! You can't just flop down on *my* bed in those dreadful clothes!" Even in desperation, Ginny couldn't help thinking about the way she passed up an opportunity with wonderful Jonathan, there in her bed. Now, look what she had in his place!

Not a muscle on the body moved, not even an eyelash. "Robert! I said…" She tugged at his arm… "Get up!" Still nothing. She leaned closer. "Maybe he died," she whispered, staring, praying for some sign of life. "God, don't let him be dead. I'd have to try CPR and I'd never be able to get that close without throwing up… And I'd have to explain how he got in my…" Just then she saw his chest rise. She closed her eyes and drew in a deep thankful breath, but leaning over him, she got too much of his scent and began to choke.

"You really have to get up. Y...you can take a *shower*." She looked back at him in exasperation and threw up her hands in defeat. "You're out cold, aren't you?" She heaved a disgusted sigh and went over to her chair. Her elbow on the arm of it, she rested her head on her hand, thumped her finger against her cheek and tried to decide what course of action to take.

"It could only happen to me. I finally get a man my own age in my bed, and he's crazy, smelly, and stone drunk." But of all the distasteful smells, she hadn't noticed alcohol among them. Maybe he wasn't drunk; maybe he was sick, besides in his mind. Maybe he had some dreaded disease. She looked back toward the bed.

"Maybe I could clean him up a little so he didn't smell so god-awful. Maybe if I got those dirty clothes, I could send them to the cleaners..." She stopped talking to herself and studied his face--from the odor-free safety of the other side of the room.

I should get something for that head wound, she pondered. *Or maybe I should get practical and just call the sheriff and let him worry about it. But how would I explain how he came to be in my bed? Nope. Not a good idea, Ginny. Think again.*

I could take his clothes while he's passed out, drop them off at the cleaners, dash to a drug store and get some things...peroxide, gauze for a clean bandage, rubber gloves for me... She cocked her head and looked at him again. Holding her grandmother's handkerchief to her face, she tried again to rouse him, but it was hopeless.

She decided to start with his boots. Not a good idea. She got hold of the right one and tugged. It finally came off, but the odor gagged her until she ran to the toilet and vomited. She pinned a hand towel about her face and recovered her attack mode. When she managed to get the other boot off, she grabbed the small can of disinfectant spray she kept in her tote bag and sprayed--first his feet, then the inside of the boots. She dared not look inside them. Anything could slither out. His feet had, what appeared to be, hand-knitted socks on them, two pair, complete with wear holes.

The cape was on the floor. She grabbed it and stuffed it into the plastic laundry bag provided by the inn. The socks were beyond help. She had sprayed them with disinfectant for now. They could stay where they were. She unbuttoned his wool jacket. It was hand-sewn, too. The gold braid on the sleeves meant nothing to her except it was supposed to look like an officer's uniform of some kind.

Trying to get away from the smell, she moved as quickly as she could. She slipped his left arm out, then his right. Then she yanked hard on it. It would either come out from under him, or it would tear to shreds. Either way, it would be off. His shredded cotton shirt remained. Like the socks, it was beyond caring about. She may as well leave it until she could wake him up to shower.

His trousers actually buttoned all the way down the front. Someone had paid attention to detail. She unbuttoned them and tugged them off from the bottoms of the legs. She expected him to have underwear on. He didn't. She ran for a towel and threw it over his middle. Coughing and sputtering, she wasn't even tempted to look. This was no object of her or anyone else's affections. This was a dirty, stinking, disgusting, putrefaction of flesh.

She quickly emptied the pockets and threw the contents on the dresser without even looking at them. She stuffed the jacket and trousers in the plastic bag and twisted it tight. Then she saturated the air with disinfectant, until she couldn't breathe.

Ginny grabbed her jeans and a flannel shirt which had belonged to one of her husbands. She couldn't even remember which one any more. She changed in the bathroom. Tearing off the towel mask, she wrote a message in lipstick on the mirror. "Don't try to leave! I will be back."

She darted for the door with the plastic bag and her purse. As she left, she hung the "Do Not Disturb" sign on the door.

~ * ~

Walking up to the front desk, she took in a great breath of air and tried to act nonchalant. "Is there a cleaners anywhere that's open on Sunday...and a drug store?"

There were. She politely refused the clerk's offer to send the bag out, so the clerk gave her directions. The cleaners were just a block outside the festival area, and a modern drugstore only two more blocks. Ginny asked for a piece of paper and sat in the lobby for a moment. She made a list of everything she could conceivably need to turn this body into a person.

I didn't know I was volunteering as a nurse. Just call me 'Mother Bickerdyke'! Oops, wrong side, she thought as she jotted. She mouthed as she wrote, "Rubber gloves, disposable towels, peroxide, Neosporin, aspirin, dry shampoo," *if there is still such a thing. He isn't going to wake for hours.*

"Plastic drop cloth, gauze, adhesive tape, cotton, alcohol, socks, jockey shorts--no, boxer shorts might be easier to get on...but briefs may be easier to find--T-shirt, scissors, shaving cream... I've got my safety razor... No, better get a disposable one. More disinfectant!" She punctuated the paper exaggeratedly with her pen.

"Guess that's about it. Toothbrush! May as well really let him clean up." She rose with the determination of Stonewall Jackson.

Ginny scurried along the street, then paused to gather her composure and strolled into the cleaners. "Yes ma'am, may I help you?" A young woman asked.

Ginny swallowed. How should she word this? "Yes, well, in this bag is an old Confederate uniform and a cape. Uhh, seems the men in my friend's camp decided to play a trick on him and hid it in a garbage bag...with the garbage. It isn't in great shape, but it means a great deal to my friend. If you can clean it somehow without it falling apart, I'd be willing to pay extra."

"I'm sure we can take care of it." The girl reached confidently for the bag, but Ginny didn't let go right away.

"Uhh, don't open it out here, it might sort of keep other customers away. Could you just open a machine and dump it right in...by itself? You wouldn't want anything else near it, trust me."

The girl gave her a patronizing smile and opened the bag. Immediately her cheeks puffed out as bile rose in her throat. "I...I see what you mean." She walked back to the back with the bag and, the color still drained from her face, came back in a moment. "We'll have it for you this time tomorrow, I hope." She filled out the ticket.

"Look, I know it won't look like new, but at least, if you can just get the smell out?"

The girl smiled, nodded, then rolled her eyes before turning to another customer. Ginny left.

On to the drugstore. She pushed the cart through, throwing the items in as fast as she could. She needed to get back before he awoke and tried to leave. There were still a couple of things left on her list she couldn't find. She spied heavy-duty odor-eater insoles, perfect for his boots. They weren't on her list, but they would be welcome, and a cheap hair brush and nail brush.

"May I help you find something?" A young man drawled as he put stock out on the shelf.

"Yes, please, I'd really appreciate it. I have to get back to a sick friend."

"Sure, whatcha lookin' for?"

"Well, I need a plastic drop cloth..." Her voice trailed off as she continued to glance around her.

"'Fraid we ain't got that."

"Uhh, how about a plastic table cloth?"

"Oh, sure. Over here." He motioned for her to follow him. "Round, square, oval, rectangular?"

"Rectangular." She nodded.

"How big's yer table, Ma'am?"

Unwittingly, Ginny raised her hand above her head to judge. "About six-foot-two." Realizing what she was doing, she shook out her fingers and grinned. "It's standing on end, I just bought it."

He nodded and smiled warily. "This one's eighty-four inches."

She snatched it from his hand and threw it in the cart.

"Don't ya want to pick a certain color?"

"Oh, no, I'm not particular."

The boy scratched his head.

"What's wrong? Don't I look like the kind of woman who would enjoy a Mickey Mouse tablecloth?" she asked.

He gave an unconcerned look and a lethargic shrug of his shoulders. "Anythin' else?"

"Surgical mask."

"Ma'am?"

"I mean, you know, those masks you can wear to cut the grass?"

"Oh, yes ma'am." He pulled one off a nearby shelf. "Anythin' else?"

"Yes, I really need some kind of dry shampoo."

"For a carpet?"

"Uhh, no, no, for hair. Do they still make that stuff you just pour on and towel off?"

"Oh, for your pet?"

"Uhh, well… "

"That's the only kind we got. Over there in the pet section." He pointed and followed her as she walked tentatively toward the pet supplies. "This one's great! I use it on my dog in the winter. Ain't good to let 'em get too cold, but, boy, can he stink if he doesn't get a bath!"

"Is it harmful to humans?"

He smiled. "Uhh, no, if you're a might sensitive, you can use those rubber gloves ya got in the cart."

"Un-huh, well, that's about it, oh, except, do you carry any men's underwear, socks, ya know?"

"Sure do, right over on aisle three."

"Thank you, you've been most helpful."

Thirty-two inch waist would probably fit, but when she saw a package marked "32-34", that was a safer bet. Obviously, he shouldn't be as thin as he appeared. A package of Large T-shirts, and a couple pair of heavy socks, and, throwing in a couple of candy bars at the check out, she was off. He might need soothing, or she might need the energy.

~ * ~

The two full plastic bags were getting heavy about the time she got back to the inn.

She opened the door quietly, if he wasn't yet awake, she didn't want him waking up now. He hadn't moved. She grimaced at the odor and quickly set up everything in the bathroom. She now had a use for the pitcher and washbowl, and grabbed the deodorant soap and disposable towels. It wouldn't be a good idea to leave the kind of grime he sported on the white towels of the inn.

She put on the pollen mask, and, though she didn't like the closeness of it, it did bring relief from the smell. If she could just get him clean, throw the shredded shirt in the trash bag with the socks, the odor would have to subside. She put on the rubber gloves and placed the odor-control insoles in his boots but jerked her hand out as quickly as possible.

Then she set about tending to him. "No point in trying to dress the wound on your head until I get you clean," she whispered absently to him.

She took the plastic tablecloth out of the package. On it was Mickey, Donald and Goofy. She chuckled to herself. Those characters were more real than this one on her bed. The tablecloth was backed with flannel. That wouldn't slip well on the bedspread, but, it would feel better to his skin. The plastic would slide easily, and protect the bed from dampness and dirt. It was large enough to cover the entire top of the bed.

"Now." Trying to figure out how to accomplish getting the tablecloth under the length of him, she bit her bottom lip. She remembered helping to change beds in the hospital without moving the patient off the bed. She'd been a candy-striper in her youth. That had taken two people. She only had herself. She would have to adapt her tactics.

She accordion folded the tablecloth, raised his legs as high as she could and ignored the towel falling away. Placing the tablecloth under his thighs, she pulled half of it down the bed, under his legs and feet. Then tugging at it, after replacing the towel, she managed to get the other end up past his buttocks, but she had no leverage to get it any further.

Ginny set her jaw determinedly and climbed up on the bed. Only by straddling him could she manage to pull the plastic up under his torso.

"There!" She proudly tossed her head, paused for a breath, then set about her task. Robert's slightly open mouth accommodated his ragged breathing. She pulled the breath spray she carried from her purse and spritzed it inside.

If that didn't wake him, nothing would. It didn't. She pulled the shreds of shirt off from the front and heard only the slightest sounds of rending cloth. Turning her head away, she wadded it up and put it in the bag with the socks. She tied the bag securely and tossed it across the room.

She threw two disposable towels into the basin of warm water. Working up a good lather on the first one with the deodorant soap, Ginny wiped his face, and into his hair about the wound. She couldn't imagine what made the deep gouge.

She soaped his face and scrubby beard. What she thought was dirt around his eyes were simply dark circles, probably from lack of sleep. The face began to take a human form as she removed the grit. She gently worked on his neck and shoulders. On his left shoulder she noted a heavy round scar, about the size of a quarter. She continued to wash his broad chest, the patch of dark curly hair in the center of it. Then his mid-section, so symmetrically parted by a narrow trace of dark hair. His navel… She stopped there and took the other towel to rinse off the soap.

Taking his left hand in hers, she lathered it with the soap, scrubbing lightly with the nail brush. She brought the washbowl to the bed and dipped the soapy hand in it to rinse. That alone was enough to make the water unusable. She went to change it.

She washed down his left arm, thoroughly. It was strongly muscled, though a little thin, like his entire body. His shoulders were broad and hard with muscles, but his ribs showed through his chest.

By kneeling in the middle of the big bed, she repeated her routine on his right arm. On the inside of his right arm, just above the elbow, another scar, a long straight line, like a knife slash. *Some surgery, perhaps.*

She swallowed, trying to decide whether to tackle the middle of him, or his legs. She elected to do his legs and feet first. Maybe then he would awaken and finish the rest himself. He had not awakened when she finished.

"Oh, what the heck. I've been married twice, for cryin' out loud! What's another male appendage?" She flipped off the hand towel and tried not to look as she gently soaped and rinsed. She didn't need to look; feeling was quite sufficient to make her shudder, with memories, and desires, with thoughts of Jonathan, and what she might have enjoyed. Though flaccid, he was not what she would call small, and the two appurtenances suspended were quite sufficient to invoke some sweet remembrances of passion.

"Shoot! It's just a job, Virginia Berkeley. Get on with it. Half the smell's gone. Get rid of the rest." As she worked, she wondered how she could have ever thought about becoming a nurse when she was a child.

Before she could turn him over, she should attack the hair. She got out the dog shampoo and read the label carefully. "It does say it's not harmful to pets or humans. It can't make that grimy hair any worse, can it?" Talking to herself was really becoming a habit.

She sprayed on the foam, and rubbed it with another disposable towel. It did work, the towel turned grungy brown. And it said it killed lice, ticks and fleas. At least there wouldn't be anything crawling about. She lifted his head and got as much of the back as she could. It did make a difference. It smelled sweet. It smelled... She took off her mask and sniffed the air. It smelled like tutti-fruity gum. "He'll probably kill me for this."

Leaving the wounded left-side exposed, she carefully turned his head to the right and mustered all her strength to turn him over. She only needed to roll him. The plastic was sufficiently large and she could move to the other side of the bed to finish the back side of him. She got both hands under him, beneath the tablecloth, one in the middle of his back and one on his buttocks and pushed quickly, thrusting him to the other side of the bed.

Proud of her accomplishment, Ginny peeled back the plastic cloth. She failed to stifle a horrified scream. Not a loud one, for what she saw stole her breath.

Open, bleeding, inflamed streaks, like whip marks covered his back. The white flannel back of the cloth on which he had lain was covered with blood and pus. She must have started them bleeding when she wrenched the shirts from him. She couldn't turn away, she couldn't breathe, and as she stared at the horror, a flood of tears streaming down her face.

"Oh, Lord! Who did this?" she whispered. Her face contorted as she gently blotted the shredded skin and tissue with a clean, soapy cloth. She had to clean it, but lord, how it must hurt. He didn't move. If he wasn't just asleep, he must be unconscious. She must get this done quickly before he came to. She couldn't stop the tears as she continued to bathe and rinse. She opened the bottle of peroxide and dribbled it over his back to bubble out the infection as she bathed the balance of him.

Each stroke of the cloth was now tender and sorrowful, and her chin quivered as she bit her bottom lip. How could anyone have done such a thing to another human being? Why?

She blotted away the peroxide and continued bathing and rinsing until she ended with his dirty feet. He was clean now. The odors were leaving the room with the exchange of air. She opened the window slightly and turned up the gas fire to help the circulation. She laid a large white towel across his buttocks, and struggled to put clean socks on his feet to keep him warm.

She returned her attention to his back, and dribbled the peroxide again and again. It took many, many dousings before the bubbles subsided. Then it took the entire tube of the anti-biotic cream to cover the open stripes. Her heart still somewhere in her throat, she hadn't nearly enough gauze to cover his back. But she had the T-shirts, a package of three. She took one out of the package and cut it off just below the neck and sleeves. She taped the double thickness of clean, white cloth to his back.

Gently now, she managed to remove the plastic beneath him, and climbed upon the bed next to him.

Just staring down at him, she sat on her knees for a long time. His back was covered with the soft, white cloth bandage, his rear, by the draped towel. Gently, she moved to turn him over again to his back, but this time she sat there, cradling his head on her own lap, looking down with compassion upon his dark features. She stroked his hair, his cheek above the beard, his eyebrows and her heart bled as surely as his body.

At last, she climbed down from the bed. Time to finish her task. She pulled a pair of the briefs from the package and struggled to get them up over his legs and into place. She noticed more about his male appendage as she did so. He wasn't circumcised, a rarity at his age. It wouldn't have even occurred to her, except her first husband was not, and until she married the second time, she hadn't known the difference.

Now she must turn her attention to his head wound. She cleaned his left temple. Gently, reverently, she dabbed on peroxide, until the bubbling stopped Then she coaxed a last bit of antibiotic cream from the tube and placed a clean bandage over the wound.

She draped a towel over his neck and shoulders and tried to comb at his hair and beard. The beard didn't look like it belonged. First she started to just trim it, but trimming was not exactly her forté She wound up cutting it closely, then shaving his face. She uncovered a strong, square-cut jaw, with a little scar on his chin. It was a handsome face--tired, a little gaunt, very pale--but handsome, beyond question.

He appeared to be forty-five to fifty, though only the slightest bit of gray shown in his dark hair. She would have liked to trim the tutti-frutti hair, but that would have to wait until he could take a proper shower. For now, she would just brush it and smooth it out. Besides, she was no better at trimming hair than beards, and she didn't think she'd like how he might look bald.

Ginny slipped the neck opening of another T-shirt over his head, then carefully pulled one arm and shoulder through a sleeve, then the other. Gently lifting his upper body, she managed to struggle it down over the bandaged back and handsome chest. She went over to the wardrobe and pulled out the burgundy fleece robe she wore the night before. It had belonged to her father, and she never traveled without it, like taking part of him with her since his death.

She held the robe to her cheek and walked over to the strange man on her bed. No one ever had that robe on but her father, and, after his death, herself. She laid it lovingly over this injured body that she allowed to fall into her life. Then she sat in the big chair, put her feet up on an ottoman, and drifted off to an emotionally exhausted sleep.

Eight

Sometime during the night, Ginny awakened to a thrashing sound. It took a moment to get her bearings and determine how she came to be sitting and sleeping in the chair. Her eyes, suddenly raw with grit, she realized she hadn't removed her contact lenses before she fell asleep. She dashed for her purse, then into the bathroom where she removed and cleaned them quickly. Contacts safely in their case, glasses in place, she stumbled out into the dim light of early winter morning.

When she focused through her smarting eyes and regained her perspective, she realized the noise was coming from Robert. Tossing and shuddering violently, he emitted small gurgling sounds as if he were drowning. His breathing was severely hampered.

Ginny dragged herself to the bed. "Robert?" She whispered and nudged him lightly. "Robert?" She called more loudly as he did not rouse to her first inquiry. Still he made no attempt to open his eyes. She could see little clearly as the obscure light cast shadows upon the room and her eyes, tendered by leaving her lenses in, refused to focus.

She walked to the bathroom and closing the door but for the width to admit her fingers, flicked on the light. She could then see something of the restless form on the bed. Walking closer, she adjusted her eyes to the near darkness again. The sliver of light cast by the opening, illuminated Robert's face, drenched in perspiration.

Ginny took a damp cloth from the washbowl where she left it after the cleansing job she subjected them both to. She ran it gently over his face. Then, as she smoothed the hair from his eyes, she snatched it back, as from a hot stove. His forehead scorched and unnerved her.

His body was shaking and shivering as if extremely cold, yet his temperature was obviously very high.

"You're burning up, she whispered. "What do I do now? I can't get any aspirin down you if you won't *wake up*." Aspirin would probably do little to help. No doubt he needed the strongest antibiotic known to man.

She studied him, trying to figure out how to get something into him to help break the fever. "I could dissolve some aspirin in water, if I could get you to drink it." Then she shook her head remembering an admonition from a first aid class many years before. "Never give liquids to an unconscious or semi-conscious person," she whispered to herself in the darkness.

"Well, I'll be damned if I'm going to get aspirin suppositories for you. I'll just have to try to cool you down until you wake up."

Removing the soda she had chilling there as her emergency stash, Ginny dipped the cloth into the melted water in her ice bucket. She popped the soda can top, took a hearty swig and returned with the cold cloth.

She wiped at his face, then his arms, and finally raised the T-shirt to run the coolness over his chest. The warmth radiating through her as she touched him came from much more than fever. She must ignore the tingling sensation as she bathed the muscled form.

Robert's eyelids fluttered momentarily. Then they opened, looking questioningly into her eyes.

"Hi. Remember me?" Ginny said cheerfully. But he didn't answer. He simply gawked at her. "I'm Virginia."

Still no recognition from him. His eyes were glazed, and beads of perspiration formed on his forehead as fast as she could mop them away.

"Robert!" Ginny tried to rouse him further, but he came no closer to full consciousness so she quickly grabbed a glass of water and the bottle of aspirin. "Just stay awake long enough to get these down." Her teeth clenched as she spoke.

"Robert, take these!" She commanded as she held out the aspirin and propped his heavy shoulders up. He was too heavy for her to keep upright and manage the glass and aspirin. She pushed herself in behind his shoulders and reached around him on either side, one hand holding the aspirin, one the glass of water.

She would never have gotten them into his mouth had he been fully cognizant of his surroundings. No doubt he would have accused her of trying to poison him. But in his daze, he allowed her to place them inside his mouth and she forced the water glass to his lips. He took only a couple of swallows before his fevered head fell, limp and heavy against her breasts.

Ginny sighed and closed her eyes. "Thank God!" She absently leaned her cheek against his head and touched his cheek with the back of her fingers. Smelling the horrible tutti-fruity smell of the cleaner made her smile. She sat there for several moments with the dead, warm weight of him against her body. *Have I done the right things? Am I helping him? He's in such bad shape. I don't want to make him worse. I'm not a nurse. He's not a squirrel with a broken leg. He's a man; a man someone hurt badly.*

She lifted him back to his place on the damp pillow. Then, as she looked down upon his face, a sweet sadness overtook her. His features were drawn, not just by the fever, but by some deep, inner pain she could not fathom. She reached down and softly pushed the cool cloth about his face. She prayed the aspirin would help break the fever. He needed the rest, but tossing about with fever was not going to bring refreshing, healing sleep.

She put the cloth back in the washbowl and pulled a straight chair up to the bed. She studied his countenance and wondered from whence he really came and how he landed in her lap. At the same time, she was remotely glad he did. Something about him touched her heart. It would have been a shame if he was a drunk or junkie, or perhaps crazy as a loon. But here, in her bed, clean, shaven, it seemed such a waste. "So many women, so few men…straight ones anyway."

She stifled a snicker at her own words as she smoothed back a wild strand of semi-clean, strangely scented, black hair. Ginny ran her thumb softly under his troubled eyes, dark and puffy with circles of unrest and sickness. She traced his eyebrows, one at a time, smoothing the unruliness into broad, well-formed lines, as she wished he would open his eyes. But, if he did, the illusion being created in her mind would be shattered. Perhaps the mystery was better than the reality. With her fertile imagination, she could dream about her version of his story, and be convinced it would be more interesting than the truth, whatever *that* was.

~ * ~

The time Ginny spent next to him, occasionally mopping his brow, thoughtfully tracing the lines about his mouth and eyes went unmeasured. The morning crept in, and still she sat, imagining the lines in his face were gradually disappearing as she tenderly cooled them, sponging him off now with alcohol for its cooling evaporation as she remembered from some distant illness of her second husband.

His breathing seemed a little less ragged now. Perhaps it was her imagination; perhaps it was the aspirin allowing him a little more restful sleep. Whatever, she was being drawn into his world, under his spell. Ginny learned long ago to keep her romantic perspective in check when it came to flesh and blood; and whatever else this enigma might be, his fevered presence attested to the fact that he was flesh and blood

~ * ~

A good time to catch a shower, Ginny pulled herself from his side. It would clear her head and distance her from her dreaming. It would also get her out of the clothes she unwittingly slept in. With his slumber more peaceful, she should be able to maneuver in and out of the shower easily. She would have to make it as quick as possible, however, for she didn't like the closeness of the small room, and she could hardly leave the door wide open, her practice when alone, with this stranger in her boudoir.

Ginny took the quickest shower on record and washed her hair so fast, she wasn't sure she even used shampoo. She used her hair dryer to remove all traces of moisture from her towel-dried body in order to be able to wiggle into her clean clothes in the little space of the bathroom. Having reached her saturation point for the confined space, she burst through the door into the bedroom with little thought of what, or who, was on the other side.

Breathless and quivering, her eyes closed, she tried to recoup her composure.

"Have you been out in the rain?" Robert sat on the bed, his eyes open, though blank. He inquired, in a coarse and feeble voice.

A startled squeak escaped her lips as she heard him speak. Her composure now further eluded her. This person of questionable character was awake, and here in her room. Her gaze darted wildly for something, anything that would give her some direction, or even some protection. Suddenly frightened, she wondered how and why she befriended this, this…her mind could not put a word to him.

"I mean you no harm, Madam. Please rest assured of that. Even if I meant you harm for some reason unknown to me, I have not the strength to lift my own self from this bed."

Her heart softened as she looked squarely at him and relaxed. He was shaking, and, indeed, looked as if a slight puff of air would push him back down. Ashamed of her wariness, Ginny dropped the towel with which she was drying her hair, then rushed to the bed.

"Please, don't try to get up. Just lay back down." She kept her voice soft and reassuring as she lifted his legs back up on the bed.

"Madam, I have no wish to cause you any further discomfort. If you will give me my uniform, I shall be on my way."

"On your way, indeed. You haven't the strength of a kitten, but you think you'll be on your way." She chastised him as she pressed him back down upon the bed. "Just lie there a moment, and collect your thoughts. I'm going to order us something to eat. You'll feel better if you eat something."

"I've no doubt I would, Madam, but, I need to be on my way. I have been away from my men too long. They will have given me up for dead, or worse, think I have deserted." He looked at her with intense sincerity.

"Mr. Carter, Robert, listen, I don't pretend to understand what you've been through, but I do know that you're not going anywhere," she spouted sternly.

"Am I under guard then?"

"Under guard?" She tilted her head. "Yes, I suppose you are, under my guard, and you're not going anywhere until I say you can."

Robert lay back quietly to take stock of the situation and his surroundings. After a careful scan of the room, he finally noticed his present attire. He moved his hand over the soft shirt of some finely spun cotton upon his chest. Then he touched his face. His beard was missing. He lifted the sheet and saw his bare legs and strange underdrawers, also of finely spun, tightly woven cotton. He tried to shake his head to clear it, but then he gasped for breath,as pain made him wince. His eyes closed tightly. The muscles in his neck ached and strained. *What's happening here?*

His head filled with a million questions, but it throbbed so he could not form any of them into words. A single anguished tear trickled down one cheek as he sighed heavily.

"I don't understand," he rasped, both hands to his temples.

"I don't understand, either, Robert," Ginny whispered as she approached him cautiously. "I can't explain. It's something we'll have to find the answers to together, but to do that you have to be rested and get some strength back. To get strength back, you have to eat something. This time I'm going to call. I'm not taking a chance on leaving you."

Ginny approached the desk and rolled the top back. She picked up the telephone and called the desk to ask that sandwiches, coffee, and such be brought to the room.

Robert watched the charade with interest and suspicion, but asked no more questions of the strange woman who spoke into an even stranger toy, unlike any speaking tube he'd ever seen. She must be quite mad, and the sooner he could gather enough strength to leave, the better.

His gaze was fixed on her as Virginia took a comb to her wet hair, and fastened it with a clip to keep it out of her face. Then she approached the bed. He had thought himself a brave enough soldier, yet he shrank from her touch as she reached to feel his forehead.

"Since you're awake, I'd like to take a look at that back and make sure it's clean."

"Are you a nurse, then?"

"Well, I'm you're nurse." She gave him her most reassuring smile. "Now, roll over, and let me have a look. I wasn't sure just how clean I got you last night."

He reluctantly obeyed, turning on the bed. His stifled moans and involuntary shudders clearly evidenced his pain from the assorted wounds and strained muscles.

"I'd sure like to know who did this." Ginny made conversation as she carefully lifted the T-shirt to his shoulders. "Now be as still as you can. I can't promise this won't hurt, and I can't promise some of the bandage I made won't be sticking to you, so hold tight." Slowly she began to peel the T-shirt material bandage from his broad back. It must have hurt tremendously, but Robert didn't flinch. Not a single muscle moved as she exposed the tender skin. No part of the material had stuck to the wounds.

That was lucky. Ginny carefully inspected the long, infected streaks of torn flesh.

"Well," she said with a sigh, "I must have done something right. They're clean and not so red. The peroxide and antibiotic cream have allowed them to close some. I didn't realize I knew what I was doing. I'm sure you could use a tetanus shot, though. Maybe we can see to that later. For now, I'm just going to put some more antibiotic cream on and leave off the bandage. The clean white T-shirt you're wearing should suffice since nothing appears to be weeping too much."

Ginny grabbed a second tube of cream. Tenderly, she applied it, all the while biting her bottom lip as she imagined the severe pain these whip-marks caused, this time using one with a mild anesthetic added.

"You don't have to be such a he-man, you know. I wouldn't think any less of you if you screamed a little."

"There's no need. You are not hurtin' me. Your hands are so gentle that it feels like a soft feather is touching my back. I'm grateful for your kindness." His voice had softened, no longer so dry and raspy.

Ginny rolled the shirt back down over his back, and Robert turned to face her.

"Are you a spy?" He asked softly, in an almost apologetic tone.

"You asked me that yesterday. I'm not a spy, okay?"

"Then you are a Southerner?"

"I'm a Virginian!" she said indignantly. "How do ya think I got my first name, anyway?"

He leaned his head far back and took a deep, cleansing breath.

"I think I shall take your word."

"Well, I'm glad that's settled."

"I'll have to trust you for now."

"Oh, that's kind of you. How about me having to trust you enough to let you into my room? To clean the stench from your body. To dress your wounds? Now that, my friend, is trust." Her hands were perched indignantly upon her hips.

"I apologize. You are right. You have shown nothing but kindness. I stand sufficiently rebuked, Madam."

"My name is Virginia, Ginny for short. I don't like being called 'madam'."

"My apologies again, M…Miss Virginia."

Ginny smiled. It reminded her of the way Jonathan addressed her. She missed him already.

A knock came to the door making Robert flinch with alarm.

"Take it easy," Ginny commanded, waving her hand at him to stay put. "It's just the food. Once you've eaten, you'll improve more rapidly." She approached the door, her hand still waving to Robert to calm down and stay in the bed. She opened the door, took a tray and signed a paper. Then she closed the door again and turned toward Robert.

"You missed the meal last night. I got enough to make up for it today, though. Choose your poison," she chortled.

He looked quizzically toward her.

"That means, oh, never mind. We have turkey, ham, and roast beef sandwiches. Which do you prefer?"

"Uhh, anything is fine, really."

She handed him a sandwich, opened a carton of milk and placed a straw in it. "Here."

Robert suspiciously eyed the paper in which the sandwich was wrapped as he opened it. He smelled the sandwich, shrugged, and began to devour it. He inspected the container of milk as well, but as the word 'milk' was boldly printed upon it, he appeared satisfied of its contents. He removed the straw and put the point of the carton to his lips

Hardly stopping for a breath, he finished two sandwiches and three cartons of milk.

"My, you were hungry!" Ginny smiled as she collected the trash.

Yes, Ma'am. I can't remember the last time I ate, or even tasted milk, though that seemed a little watery… No cream on the top, but it was good anyway." Then Robert's stomach growled loudly. He placed his hand against it. "Guess I shouldn't have eaten so fast."

You just relax, and it'll settle down." Ginny gently pushed against his shoulder to get him to lean back against the pillows she had propped up.

"I can't remember the last time I slept in a bed either. I'd forgotten anything but the ground or an army cot, in better days."

"Robert, can you tell me where you've been? Lately, I mean."

"No, I'm afraid that wouldn't be advisable, madam, er, Miss Virginia. It's not that I don't trust you, ya see. It's just, well, I'm not sure exactly what's happening here and I don't want to give away any military secrets."

Not wanting to alarm Robert, but neither wanting to go along with his pretending game, Ginny rolled her eyes and sucked in her lips. She cleared her throat purposely. "Well, I guess you'd best get some more rest, uh, Mr. Carter."

"Colonel Carter." He corrected her.

She swallowed and acquiesced. "Colonel Carter. We'll talk more after you rest. I'll go see about your uniform, if you promise not to try to leave this room."

He nodded.

"Don't expect they managed to save much of it, but I'll see."

~ * ~

Ginny blow-dried her hair and re-fastened the clip at her neck before she grabbed her coat and headed for the pharmacy. There on her credit card, she placed a call to her doctor and asked him to give the pharmacist an order for her antibiotic, telling him she left it at home. It certainly couldn't hurt Robert to have some penicillin in his system.

Then she took the dreaded trip to the dry cleaner's. They had done their best, but there was little to be done for the wool uniform. The cape fared well.

"The material was in really poor condition, but we did the best we could." The girl handed the plastic covered garment to her.

Ginny smiled in acknowledgment as she paid, then left with a sigh. She knew she would have to find something for Robert to wear. She had seen a small men's shop a few blocks away, so she headed in that direction.

She estimated Robert's size in relation to her two ex-husbands. Tall as the taller of them, she thought, but thinner, much thinner, hopefully not as a rule, just as a current condition. She bought a pair of jeans with a thirty-four-inch waist, estimated him more at thirty-two inches at the present, and a belt to draw up the excess. A solid gray flannel shirt, might make him feel at home with his uniform in near shreds.

~ * ~

Robert was sleeping soundly when Ginny returned to the room. She left him that way and decided to catch a few winks herself after the hectic night. Sitting in the chair to sleep, however, proved uncomfortable. Ginny put a sweater on over her clothes for added warmth, and took out her contact lenses, which were irritating her tender eyes after only a few hours. She walked over to the chair and ottoman where she passed the last night.

"I need to lie down," she thought to herself. "Perhaps, on my side, on top of the covers, hugging the edge of the bed."

As she gently lowered herself to the bed, she thought warmly of the night Jonathan held her in his arms. One long sigh escaped her as she closed her eyes. She could no longer worry whether her position would give Robert any ideas, should he wake before her. She was too tired to care.

Nine

It had been after dinnertime when Ginny lay down on the bed. She slept soundly, though clinging tenuously to the edge of the bed. When she awakened, a faint glow shone at the window as just before sunrise. She felt rested and must get up while Robert appeared to still sleep.

She fumbled for her glasses in the near darkness and tiptoed to the window to close the drapes she had left open the evening before, expecting to only take a brief nap.

She could not see Robert's face as she maneuvered carefully about the room. She slipped into the bathroom to splash water on her face and brush her hair. She brushed her hair, but her mouth had a pasty taste and feel, so she grabbed her toothbrush. She could hardly wait until Robert was cognizant enough to brush his own.

She eyed herself in the mirror for a time wondering what to think about this character she allowed into her life. He must be totally deranged, but he hadn't yet been conscious long enough to really talk to him. He was certainly ill, of that there was no doubt. He was handsome, now that his face was clean-shaven. She could almost picture him with clean, neatly trimmed hair.

Ginny inhaled deeply, letting her breath out slowly fortifying herself as she opened the door. She crept into the dark room, trying to adjust her eyes, but was suddenly grabbed from behind. Two large hands closed about her arms and held her motionless. She froze for only a moment, then, after the initial shock wore off, she tried to break free, but the hands were strong.

"Robert!" Her tone was sharp. "What-the-hell do you think you're doing?"

"I'm trying to figure out why you speak like a man, who you are and what you want of me!"

"What *I* want with *you*? Let's try what *you* want with *me*. Or better yet, what do I *do* with *you*?"

He still did not release her, though she struggled to turn to face him. His strength surprised her, for he seemed weak as a kitten.

"If you don't let go of me--" She spoke softly through clenched teeth. "You can just take care of yourself!"

Robert released her, not really knowing why he felt the urge to take her captive in the first place. Virginia pulled away defiantly as though she had shaken him loose of her own power.

"Humph!" She snorted. "That's better." She rubbed at her arms. "That hurt, you big goon. Just who do you think you are anyway? I don't see anybody else willing to help you. You sure have your nerve." She continued to rub the places on her arms which he had held so tightly.

Robert hung his head as he placed both hands to it in total confusion. "I…I'm sorry. Please forgive me. I am indebted for your kindness. I…I just don't understand any of this. One moment I'm being held prisoner, and the next I'm free to wander about in a world I don't recognize."

As he finished, Ginny could see tears slowly making their way down his wan cheeks. Totally unaware, he stood there in only the underwear Ginny provided. Emotion and physical weakness overtook him and he sank to his knees on the floor, his face in his hands, sobbing uncontrollably.

Ginny joined him on the floor. Kneeling in front of him, she would have liked to ask some of the thousand questions swimming about in her mind, but it didn't seem the time.

"Robert," she reached to take his hand, removing it from his face. "Robert, shush now, we'll figure this all out. I promise we will."

Like a lost child, or a stray puppy, he looked up with disbelieving, despondent eyes. Ginny could no longer resist the urge to hold him and, turning her head slightly to avoid the pungent smell of his breath, and his tutti-fruity hair, she pulled his head to her shoulder.

Robert clutched her tightly as his entire body trembled with emotional release. It felt good to hold him. Ginny felt complete for the first time in years. She closed her eyes and imagined lifting some great burden from him. She rocked back and forth on her knees making soothing, shushing noises as he clutched her.

~ * ~

Nearly an hour later, Robert's sobbing ceased. Ginny's legs were numb from supporting his weight as well as her own on her knees.

"Robert?" She questioned softly, but received no reply. "Robert?" she whispered again, seemingly unheard.

She couldn't tell if he was unconscious or simply cried himself back to sleep. She leaned forward, easing him to the floor. Indeed his eyes were closed and he made no move at all as she lowered him.

"Okay, what now, sleeping beauty? I can't carry you to the bed, Robert!"

Heaving a great sigh, Ginny struggled to her feet, shaking out her legs to relieve the prickling, sleepy sensation. She grabbed a pillow and blanket from the bed and returned to the body on the floor, then struggling to lift his head placed it on the pillow. She covered him with the blanket. Well, she could just proceed with her normal routine. Robert didn't seem to be going anywhere any time soon.

Ginny collected clean clothes, and her makeup bag and headed for a long, steamy shower. She stepped over Robert as if he were a sleeping Labrador, took a deep breath and closed the bathroom door. The little room didn't seem as confining as it had before. Somehow, with Robert right outside the door, after holding him so closely, she felt calm, unthreatened by being confined.

Her face in the mirror brought a smile. Her eyes were warmer, softer, less exhaustion showing in the fine lines around them. What could it possibly be about this displaced, possibly deranged, yet quite handsome stranger that could make her glow inside?

She shook her head. Well, whatever. She turned on the shower. While it warmed up she disrobed, she thought of the man in the next room. She stepped into the steaming water letting it beat gently upon her face and soak her hair. Every muscle in her body seemed to relax as she contemplated her feelings toward the man on the other side of the door.

Odd as it was, Ginny didn't have the urge to hurry and escape the smallness of the bath. She shampooed her hair, applied her crème rinse, and let it soak in as she lathered up her body with sweet-smelling soap. She rinsed her body and turned her back to the shower to rinse her hair. A peacefulness took over with the rush of warm water.

She froze as a large hand settled upon her shoulder. She hadn't heard the door open, or the shower curtain behind her move, but following the hand, the unmistakable presence of a tall form obstructed the water from her naked back. The tutti-fruity smell of hair became hot and wet. She felt a soft, wet T-shirt stretched over a muscular, if somewhat thin, chest.

Why didn't she jump out? Why didn't she scream? Why wasn't she surprised? She had no answer. She just let herself lean into the form--feeling safe, feeling warm. Just feeling! Anything was better than the desensitized existence her personal life was lately.

As his arms gently encircled her just below her breasts, it was pleasant. Robert made no threatening move. His hands did not roam or stroke. They slid up his own arms as he drew her closer.

As the shock of his intrusion wore off, Ginny suddenly remembered his tortured back and that it was being exposed to the hot water and the clinging wet T-shirt. She spun around in his arms and looked into his face, the stubble showing on it from her shaving it over a day ago. Their eyes met, and he fixed his gaze onto hers. He did not look further, did not even gaze downward.

"Your back," she whispered, hoarsely. "The water, it must hurt."

He neither answered, nor blinked. He seemed oblivious. Couldn't he feel pain?

"Robert?"

"You smell good," he whispered as he gently put his cheek to hers.

"Robert, you have to get that shirt off. It…" She swallowed. "It's as good a time as any to wash your hair and give those lashes on your back a thorough cleaning." She tried to sound stern and demanding, but it was useless. Robert so disarmed her that her commands sounded more like bashful suggestions.

He didn't move to release her when she began tugging at the soaked cloth of the shirt. Begrudgingly, he disengaged his arms from about her waist and raised them just enough to allow her to peel the shirt from him. Virginia moved one hand across him and shuddered.

Robert smiled, secretly, as her body quivered, but he straightened his crooked smile as she lifted her face toward his.

"Turn around!" Virginia ordered, her voice cracking as she tried to sound authoritative.

"Yes, ma'am," Robert whispered and did as he was told.

Ginny closed her eyes and sighed with relief. Even if *he* was gentleman enough to keep his eyes from moving downward, *she* would soon let her eyes wander, and it would be better if they wandered over his wet derrière, than…

The sight of his torn back brought reality crashing in on her. She reached for the bar of soap, and decided perhaps her hand would feel less abrasive than a washcloth. She tenderly ran the soap over the healing flesh. She fought back tears. How could anyone have tortured another human being like this? Her hands moved slowly, reverently over his skin. The cleaning could only help the healing, but she was so afraid of causing him unnecessary pain.

Robert was gratefully aware of her tenderness. He couldn't remember the last time he felt a woman's touch, much less such a compassionate one. It just now occurred to him that he had absolutely no idea where this water was coming from, already warm and so clear. This was not the time to ask. He needed to just revel in the feel of the water, in the feel of her.

"Here." She handed the soap through beneath his right arm. Feeling her there with him made the origin of the water totally unimportant.

"The front is up to you! I'm going to shampoo that mess on your head."

The secret smile returned as Robert ran the soap about on his chest, his underarms, his arms, his waist, as he contemplated removing the wet underdrawers. "I can't manage to get any lower until you stop working on my head." He chuckled.

"Then just stand there!" She reached around and took the patch from the gash on his forehead.

Two complete soapings of his hair left it only somewhat improved, but the third seemed to do the trick. It was dark and straight, while the hair on his chest was lighter and very curly.

Oh, but it was good to get rid of that *pet* shampoo smell. After being married twice, it had seemed natural, but it suddenly occurred to Ginny that she was standing, stark naked, in the shower with her bare breasts touching a perfect stranger.

Well, not perfect, but certainly interesting.

She was too surprised to be embarrassed at first, then cared only to get him clean. She jerked suddenly, threw a handful of crème rinse on his head and pulled the back of the shower curtain aside enough to retreat as he was pulling off his wet briefs.

"You can bend over and wash the rest of you now. Throw your wet underwear in the sink. I'll, uh, I'll be in the other room." She grabbed her robe, two towels and swung the door open in one fell-swoop. "Rinse your hair once more," she shouted through the door. "Towels are on the rack. Take your time." Her voice dropped to a whisper. "Please, take your time."

~ * ~

Ginny needed all the time she could get to recover from the shower episode, get dry and dressed, *fully* dressed. Her face had to be crimson. It was warm enough to heat the room. Should she dress and go out for a while? No, it would be even harder to return. She must stay and face him down. He was the one who invaded her shower. Her stern look faded to a distant smile. It was a rather nice invasion.

"Virginia, get a grip!" she said sharply to herself. "It's not like you've never seen a naked man. You were married--twice! And you've had a couple of flings." She hesitated. "Yeah, but not lately." Her voice had changed, even though he wouldn't be able to hear her. "Ya gotta admit, girl, that was one nice specimen...a little too lean just now, but those muscles..." Ginny's alter-ego nearly chastised her for not enjoying the view while she had the chance--all the view.

She rolled her eyes with disgust at her own thoughts, then dashed about combing her wet hair, and wiggling into clothes with her still-damp body. She must be completely calm, and *completely* dressed.

Just as she thought she'd gotten a good hold, the handle of the bathroom door turned and her heart was in her throat.

As the door opened, Ginny sighed with a little relief. At least Robert had the good sense to wrap a bath towel securely about his waist. His hair was wild and dripping wet. She grabbed one of her own damp towels and reached up toward his head.

"Sit down, for cryin' out loud, and let me dry this mess before it gets tangled up again."

Without a word, Robert did as he was told, sitting on the foot of the bed. Ginny moved to face him and began towel-drying his long hair. He didn't say a word as she retrieved a comb from her bag and tugged at the snarls. With his hair wet and combed back, she could imagine it neatly trimmed. Clean, he was startlingly handsome.

She threw another pair of briefs in his direction. "Put these on. Then let me put some more medicine on that back."

Robert stood and began to open the towel. Though she would secretly have liked to watch, Virginia spun around as if she were embarrassed.

"These strange drawers are rather fitting."

Ginny turned back around to find Robert admiring them in the mirror.

"Just *sit down* and let me look at that back." Ginny tried to be stern, but he was certainly appealing, standing there in just a pair of briefs, with little left to her imagination. She could never understand how men seldom seemed embarrassed by their own nakedness, even though many are quite odd-looking.

She gently covered the lash marks with antibiotic cream. Now she would introduce Robert to deodorant. "Lift up your arms."

He did as he was told. Ginny ran the ball of her roll-on deodorant under his left arm.

"That's cold!" he protested as she repeated under his right. Then she helped Robert put the last T-shirt on, and handed him her father's robe.

Ten

Robert put on the soft robe and ran his fingers over the sleeves. "I've never felt such a fabric, at least not meant for a man, and this certainly doesn't look like a woman's wrapper..." He paused momentarily, eyeing Virginia purposefully. "But then you seem to be wearing boy's clothing, and spectacles you don't always need."

Indeed, Ginny stood there in her bare feet, jeans and sweater. She looked down at herself as Robert moved toward her.

"I must say, however, that never have I seen a boy fill a sweater in such an intriguin' manner." Inches from her, towering over her, he looked straight down at her two plump breasts. "I am feelin' greatly refreshed. What a shame you fled the..." He faltered for a word. "The shower? I have seen a gentleman's free-standing shower before, with a hand pump to circulate the water, but never have I known one to be connected to a hot spring as that seems to be. What carries the water away from the large tub, clay pipes like in Boston?"

For a split second, Virginia seemed to process his words. She just stood looking upward into his eyes.

"Hot spring?" she asked as she realized what he had said. "Gimme a break! Don't let's start that garbage again. I'm sure you know all about indoor plumbing, showers, bathtubs, toilets..."

"I have seen some cold water piped indoors in cities or in very wealthy homes. Never have I seen such a wonder as this. The tank must be very high, indeed, to obtain such a forceful stream and why doesn't the elevation cool the water? It did not take me long to discern the use of the water-filled commode. The hole in it lent recognition. It is very different from the water closet I saw once in Philadelphia."

Ginny rolled her eyes and turned away in disgust, but Robert caught her by the shoulders and faced her squarely. "I don't wish to argue. Could you not just humor me for a moment? What harm could it do?"

Indeed, what harm could it do? Didn't she just finish a few glorious days with Jonathan, pretending to be from another time? She sighed. "All right. I'll try, but--"

Robert put his index finger to her lips to halt her conditions. She sputtered once, then fell silent as he ran the calloused tip of his finger along her bottom lip. Then he followed his finger with his own lips and she offered no resistance. The stale mouth odor was gone.

She leaned into the kiss and let herself feel the warmth. Perhaps he found the toothpaste and extra brush she bought. Maybe he used hers. Oh, what difference did it make? She was enjoying this kiss, though it made her think about Jonathan and feel sad she hadn't given in to temptation with him, instead of standing here feeling something for this obviously disturbed...possibly insane...definitely exasperating...perfectly beautiful man.

When Robert leaned back from her, she could not open her eyes. Ginny didn't want to come back from the far away place he had taken her.

"You're lovelier with those big green eyes open, you know," he whispered close to her ear.

Her eyelids flew wide and she glared at him--unable to respond in words, wanting to respond physically, but thinking better of it. Unable to face him, she cast her gaze to the floor and lowered her chin.

Robert gently took her chin in the palm of his large hand, and raised her head toward him.

"Please excuse my forwardness, but don't ever be ashamed of your feelings. I have known many women who were incapable of enjoyin' such a simple thing as a kiss."

She smiled at him with her eyes and he understood, moving his hand to her cheek. Ginny closed her eyes and turned her face in his hand and kissed the inside of his fingers. Then watching his eyes, she backed away slowly. She couldn't remember seeing such warmth radiating for her, at least, not for a very long time, except from Jonathan. It was comforting. It put her at ease, and she was ready to play along with his time-game.

~ * ~

After minutes of staring at each other, Ginny realized her feet were freezing. The thermostat was hidden in the bathroom. She darted in and punched it up a notch, then returned to the room and grabbed a pair of socks for herself from her bag, and a pair for Robert from the drugstore bag.

"Here, put these on before you catch pneumonia, if you don't have it already." She thrust the socks at him. "And get back in bed!"

Robert gave her a devilish smile and sat on the bed to put the socks on. "I've always wanted to be ordered into a beautiful woman's bed." He chuckled.

Ginny screwed her mouth to one side and shook her head. "Don't let it go to your head. I just want to make sure you're in good physical condition when the men in white coats come to collect you."

Robert didn't respond.

"It will be warmer in here soon," she remarked as a shiver ran down her spine.

"Should I build you a fire?"

She watched Robert as he glanced at the fireplace in one corner of the room, where logs were already be in place.

"It's a gas fire. Wood is too much of a fire hazard. The clerk already said they closed off the chimneys."

"Then if the room is to get warmer without the fire, where is the stove?"

"The stove is in the kitchen. The furnace is, well, I don't know where the furnace is--but it doesn't matter. Trust me, it will get warmer. But I'll turn on the gas fire anyway."

"Oh, I do trust you." Robert smiled, and as he was ordered, he climbed back into bed. "Are you coming, too?"

Ginny heaved an exasperated sigh. "Don't push you're luck, Bobby. You might wind up out in the cold on your--" *magnificent*, "--buns."

"Yes ma'am. I shall obey your orders to the letter. The last time I failed to obey orders, I was captured."

Ginny let it pass with just a roll of her eyes as she reached for her glasses.

"You know your soap smells wonderful, but it tastes absolutely terrible."

"Soap?"

"Yes, I gathered the toothbrush in the box was meant for me, so I used it with the soap. My mouth felt cleaner, but I couldn't seem to get rid of the taste. And what is that glass-like material in which the box was wrapped? It's wondrous, indeed, for lettin' one see the contents."

"You're good at this, aren't you, Robert?" Ginny sighed, wondering how long he had practiced this time-travel routine. He must be the most experienced re-enactor of all.

"Madam?" Robert questioned.

Ginny sighed. "Oh, never mind. Next time use the tube of toothpaste. It won't taste so bad."

She pulled a chair closer to the bed, and, vowing to herself to be as open-minded as possible, sat down to talk. She reached for the bottle of pills sitting on the night table, removed one, and handed it to Robert with a glass of water. "Take this."

"What is it?" Suspicion still shown in his eyes.

"It's *mold*!" Defiance edged her voice. Then she collected her calm. "It's an antibiotic."

Robert just gave her a puzzled look.

"Look, you trust me and take this to help you get better, and I'll trust you and listen to your story, or your questions, whatever. Deal?"

"Deal?" He nodded. "Deal."

"Will you tell me first why you wear boys' clothes, when you were so beautiful in ladies'? And why you wear no proper, uh, no proper ladies' under things when you do wear a skirt?" He remembered her demonstration, raising her skirt to prove she was not from his time, before he collapsed.

"Mind, I'm not complainin'. As a matter of fact, I think it very wise for women to avoid some pieces such as corsets. They must restrict breathin'. I also noticed that you wore none, yet you seem to have some sort of harness about your--bosom." His voice dropped at the word "bosom." "I felt it when I grabbed you."

Ginny lifted her eyes to the ceiling, inhaled deeply and let her breath out slowly. "I'll tell you what." She began as placidly as she could manage. "You take my word that I'm not from your time, and I'll take your word you're not from mine. We'll start on even ground. You tell me about your time, and I'll tell you about mine. And leave my underwear out of the discussion."

"That sounds agreeable." He observed her. "Interesting spectacles."

With that settled, there was first a long silence, then they both spoke at once. Ginny sighed. Obviously each raged with questions, and knew that they would probably not believe the other's answers.

"Sorry, ma'am. Ladies first."

Ginny smiled. "Oh, no, I'm liberated. You start. I think your story will be much more interesting than mine." Robert looked so natural in her father's robe. No one ever seemed man enough to wear it before, but Robert did, at that moment.

"I don't know where to begin. I have so many questions about my surroundings, but I'm sure you want to know where I've come from, and I want to know how I got here."

"Well, why don't you start with the last thing you remember before you started skulking about town the other day."

"I remember seeing you from the bridge. Then later I saw you and…" He hesitated, not knowing how much to reveal. "You and a young man in uniform go into enemy camp and return to our troops as if it were a planned meeting."

"Jonathan and I were invited to the Union encampment." Perhaps she should humor him more to get him to talk. "During a brief truce."

"Jonathan?" he whispered.

"Yes, the young man, his name was Jonathan Blackburn, Sergeant Jonathan Blackburn from North Carolina."

He nodded. "You mentioned him before, didn't you?"

"But what do you remember before the bridge, before I spotted you?" Ginny prodded.

"I was a prisoner… There was smoke, a fire outside… I…I was in a small place… I was dying… They left me for dead. I…I awoke to find the door knocked off its hinges, and the sun was shining in, and they were gone."

"Who was gone?"

"The Union soldiers. The ones who captured me. The ones who tricked me."

"Did they put the whip marks on your back?" Ginny's curiosity was aroused. Just how far would this man go to concoct his story? Or were there some re-enactors among the Union men who were still fighting the war in some bizarre manner?

"Yes, but I don't think they were ordered to… I think they were acting on their own. I think they wanted somethin'."

"What?"

"Information. I don't know. My head is full of brief images. Feels like it's stuffed with cotton. One of them kept calling me 'Robin'. It was strange; nobody ever called me that but…"

"Who?"

Robert didn't answer. He stared ahead for a moment and swallowed back a lump in his throat. Moisture gathered in his deep blue eyes.

"Who, Robert? Who called you, 'Robin'?"

"It was a joke. Beth used to pretend she was Queen Elizabeth and I was the Earl of Leicester, Robert Dudley, whom it was reported Elizabeth called 'Bonnie Robin'. It was just a pet name, that's all." He became agitated.

"Who is Beth, Robert?" Ginny's voice was soft, full of compassion.

"She was my wife. She died in thirty-nine."

"Thirty-nine? Robert, unless you're terribly well preserved, you weren't any more alive in nineteen thirty-nine than I was."

He stared at Ginny with blank eyes, then closed his lids slowly, and shook his head. "No more. It's time to stop this play-acting. Where's my uniform? I must return to my men!" Robert jumped from the bed. He was angry, confused, his breathing became rapid and irregular. His gaze darted from one wall to another, to Ginny, to the robe he was wearing and he began to shake uncontrollably.

"Robert!" Ginny shouted trying to get his attention. "Robert. Stop this. Sit down!"

"No, you want me to betray my men. You want information, too. You can kill me, but I won't tell you how many troops we have or lead you to…"

There was a fury about him Ginny couldn't control, couldn't understand. Ordering him did no good. She must regain his confidence. "Robert, darlin'." She spoke softly, letting every bit of Southern drawl she could manage melt into her own, normally slight accent. "Whatever are you thinkin'? I'm just as much a Virginian as you. My last name is Berkeley. Remember? Doesn't that mean anythin' t' ya? My family goes back to Jamestown. How could I possibly do anythin' to bring harm to Virginia?"

Robert looked at her out of the corner of his eye. His shaking, probably a direct result of his high fever, lessened. He sank back onto the bed, drew his knees to his chest and buried his face against them as he hugged himself with both arms.

Making shushing noises as she sat next to him, Ginny ran her fingertips through his damp hair. "Robert, you've got to rest. You need to regain your strength. We'll talk more later. You won't have to tell me anything except what you want me to know. And I'll answer any questions you have for me. I promise. Later."

Slowly he uncurled his body, and Ginny managed to get him to lie down. She drew the covers over him, but he shivered. Ginny sprawled, fully clothed, on the bed beside him, ran her hand across his forehead, stroked his neck, his arm, anything to calm him down to sleep.

Sometime as she caressed and soothed, his shivering stopped, and the ordeal caught up with her as well. She had her head upon his chest, her cheek snuggled to her father's robe. It was the most peaceful time she'd had in years. She was trying to make Robert feel safe, but his body next to hers made her feel safe enough to really sleep. And she did

~ * ~

Virginia was sleeping soundly when the warmth of the room, and the warmth of her on his chest awakened Robert. He wasn't used to such heat, and his body still felt warmer than normal.

He opened his eyes just as he was about the give in to the urge to throw off the covers. When he realized Virginia was snuggled to his chest, Robert didn't want to disturb her, but he was so warm. Gently, he moved his left foot, which was closest to the edge of the mattress, until it broke free of the covers. He managed to get one of his legs out from under the warm quilt. That provided the relief he needed, for the moment.

He turned his gaze back to the amber-haired woman, whose face looked more peaceful than he thought anyone had a right to look in these troubled times. She was a stranger, she was forward, demanding, exasperating; yet she'd shown him nothing but kindness.

Was she really from a different world? Was everything outside this room another time? Perhaps all this was but fevered dreaming. And if it were all a dream, what would he finally awake to find?

If this was a dream, he wished it would never end. He wished he would never have to return to being a Yankee prisoner, to knowing that Harry arranged his capture. He squeezed his eyes tightly closed. Perhaps he would open them, and this would all be gone. But when he opened them again, he still lay in this strange room with this strange woman sleeping soundly upon his chest.

He looked down at Virginia's face. Her hair ornament came undone, and her hair lay in disarray. Robert took his left hand and smoothed the hair from across her face. It was a pleasing face. He ran his finger across her pale eyebrow, down her jaw to her chin and across her lips. She stirred a little, but just snuggled harder against his chest. His right arm had been stretched out across the bed, partially beneath her. He drew it around her shoulder and held her tightly to himself.

It felt good. He wanted something to hold on to in this chaos. He kissed the top of her head and she moved her face upward toward him, almost mechanically, without opening her eyes. Then his lips found hers, and they were soft and warm and responsive, but still she did not open her eyes.

Robert gently raised up and Virginia slipped over on her back next to him. She seemed to be almost smiling. She was so inviting. He'd been alone so long. He had been at war so long with no comfort. He kissed her again, and this time suspected the stubble on his face pricked and seemed to wake her.

Robert moved to suspend his chest over her. Looking deeply into her sleepy eyes, he smiled and she smiled in return, then, trying to keep his whiskers from her soft skin, he gently planted his lips against her cheek. Virginia turned her face and grasped his lips firmly with her own.

He relished her boldness as she returned hungry kisses.

He let his hand rove beneath her sweater, and cupped one breast, bra and all. He was frustrated by her "harness," and he groaned to let her know it. Virginia reached behind and loosened it. Then Robert managed to free the plump object of his attention from the harness and contented himself for a moment just holding one large breast in his fingers, massaging, maneuvering, caressing.

Ginny pushed her father's robe from his shoulders and ran her hands over the hardness of his chest and his shoulders. She would have pulled off the T-shirt, but thought of his wounded back. The soft, subtle shirt left little to her imagination anyway, though she would have loved to run her fingers through the fluff of curly hair on his chest. She reached up beneath the shirt and gently grasped handfuls of the softness as Robert pulled off her sweater, and then the "harness."

Now both his hands reveled in the large, malleable breasts as Ginny felt them come alive to his touch. Her crests became hard, demanding, inviting his lips to follow his hands.

Ginny slid her hands inside his briefs and seized handfuls of his buttocks--grabbing, massaging, stroking; then pushing the briefs down, freeing the massive hardness that she longed to find her. Robert fumbled at the button and zipper on her jeans until she slipped from them herself. Then he seemed intrigued by her panties, playing at the waist, and leg openings, until Ginny could wait no more.

She grabbed at her panties, slipped from them then threw them across the room. At the same time, Robert cast off his briefs and the robe. When he began to pull at the T-shirt, Ginny used her hands to stop. She merely slid the front up enough to feel his skin next to hers.

Neither of them uttered a single word, but they communicated every thought, every desire so expertly, as though they had been lovers forever.

Robert gently raised Ginny's right leg and kissed the back of her knee, then lifted her left leg and kissed the back of its knee. Her legs were now raised and parted, inviting him to enter. He looked into her eyes again, as if asking permission.

"Yes" she whispered, and guided his member to the moist warmth it sought.

Robert suspended himself there, only the tip of him entering her for seconds, as if he were trying to decide if he should continue, or perhaps just basking in the sensation. Ginny knew she must have him, all of him and she stretched her arms until her hands reached his buttocks and pulled him into her forcefully.

Robert inhaled deeply, his jaw tight as he threw his head back in wild celebration of the sensation. Ginny's breathing almost halted after a gasp with his first thrust, then she breathed deeply and sighed as if all the tension had been released from her. She moaned long and low and Robert's excitement soared.

It seemed like only a few strokes before Robert found release, and she squealed softly as his warmth drained into her. But he would not leave Virginia unsatisfied. After only a moment he began to move again, slowly, deliberately. His release had not affected his hardness or size and he stroked and kissed her as he continued to move inside her.

He pushed all the right buttons, sensing her climb steadily toward her summit. He could tell what touches and kisses made her climb higher, and he continued until he knew she was about to come, then he thrust one last, deep, thrust and she moaned in a low, earthy tone, as she clutched him tightly, then fell limp beneath him.

Yet he did not leave her, but remained suspended above her, and deeply inside her, as he kissed and fondled and stroked her into placidness. Then he planted his lips upon hers as he slowly withdrew his body.

He sank to the pillow and drew her to his chest. They were warm, sticky and satiated. Only one word passed between them in this hour of lovemaking--Virginia's whispered "yes". For the first time in many years Robert felt as if he had been lost and now found.

Eleven

It was noon when Ginny rose lazily from the bed. She felt renewed, and knew she must help this man who made such beautiful love to her. She must help him, but how? She put her robe on instead of getting back into her jeans and sweater. She floated about the room gathering her make-up, hot rollers, and clothing from the wardrobe.

Perhaps she should be upset about the morning's happenings, but she couldn't bring herself to spoil the warm feeling she had inside. Of course, she shouldn't have made love with a stranger, but at first she thought it was just a pleasant dream. By the time she was sure it was real, there was no turning back. She didn't want to turn back. She was tired of being lonely.

As she closed the bathroom door to curl her hair and get dressed, she didn't even mind the smallness of the room. There was someone wonderful on the other side of the door, and she would put her best foot forward. While the curlers heated, she refreshed herself with a quick shower and took care not to get her hair wet again.

While the hot rollers sat in her hair, she put on her make up, and donned panty hose, low heels (but not flats)--Robert was very tall--a Victorian blouse and a long skirt. She put her contact lenses in and brushed her hair out. When she opened the door, Robert was sitting up in the bed and wore an expectant look on his face.

"Now, that's more acceptable." He smiled at her, his deep blue eyes shining.

"I just thought I would do what I could to make you feel more at ease." Ginny turned slowly for his approval.

"T'would be a shame to spoil such loveliness by coaxing you back into my bed…"

"*My* bed!"

"Yes, I stand corrected."

"We're going to leave this room, if you feel up to it, and get something to eat, and see a little of the outside world."

"After this morning, I feel 'up to' most anything." Robert gave her a rakish grin, rolling his eyes, as he emerged, stark naked from the waist down, from the bed covers, and advanced toward her.

She sidestepped him and slapped him with the robe he had cast to the floor earlier.

"Bathroom's all yours. You'll find a razor and shaving cream out on the sink. Just holler if you don't know how to use them." She smirked as she gave his bare bottom a playful smack, which obviously startled him, but pushed him toward the bathroom.

"Don't get that T-shirt wet," she called after him. "It's the last clean one until we buy some more."

Robert closed the door behind himself.

She rolled her eyes and chuckled. "I hope he puts the seat up."

The bathroom door opened. "I find neither shaving brush, nor razor. I can get along without a brush, but how do I shave without a razor?"

Ginny walked indignantly into the bathroom.

"Here is the razor." She picked up a disposable safety razor. "And here is the can of shaving cream." She snatched up the can. "You don't need a brush. The lather is already made when it comes out. Just shake the can like this, and push the button." She demonstrated.

She took a handful of the lather and slopped it over his face.

Robert was annoyed. "I still need a razor!"

She picked up the safety razor again, took one, rather careless, swipe at his cheek to demonstrate, then exited to the bedroom.

"And here's your underwear!" She tossed the briefs from the bed to him.

Robert's wide eyes and his speechlessness puzzled her. Could there really be something to this time warp? Could he really be convinced he was from another time? Of course he couldn't be, but he could think he was.

Robert began to get the hang of using already warmed water from the tap. He finished his shave, splashed off the remaining lather, and emerged from the bathroom.

"You've gotten your T-shirt wet. I told you to be *careful*."

"I'm sorry, the water comes so fast."

Ginny grabbed her blow dryer and pointed it in his direction as she turned it on. Fifteen hundred watts of heat were suddenly coming in his direction from something that resembled a large pistol. Robert blinked, then held his hand up in the hot stream.

"That's wonderful! Is that how this room is heated?"

"No. This is a hair dryer. It's for drying your *hair*." She pointed it toward his hair as she rumpled it with her other hand.

"But hair dries on its own. Why would you need it?"

"So you can shower, dry off, and go outside on a cold day like this without freezing or getting pneumonia, which you probably already have."

"My shirt is *dry*. Can you dry socks and gloves like this? It would certainly cut down on frost-bite if we didn't have to go around in wet socks in the winter."

Ginny put her fingertips to her temples and sighed. "Patience, I must have patience," she whispered to herself. She could tell him about a giant machine called a clothes dryer, but he wasn't ready for that yet. First she had to introduce him to cars, telephones--no, first they had to eat, then get him a haircut.

"Where have you hidden my uniform?"

"Your uniform is cleaned, but needs a great deal of mending. I have something else for you to wear today." Ginny reached into the bag and brought out the flannel shirt and jeans and held them out to him.

"I appreciate the gesture, but I can't be caught outside, out of uniform. I could be shot as a spy. They already tried that once."

"Robert, there is no war outside, at least not between the North and South. Look," she walked to the window and drew back the curtains.

The sun was bright, and felt good on his face, but Robert's eyes strained to adjust.

As he looked out, he saw mechanical conveyances passing by on the well-paved street. People passed in clothing much like Virginia had worn earlier. Feeling like a lost child, he swallowed and cleared his throat uncomfortably. "I shall wake up soon, I know it, or perhaps…perhaps I have died and this is heaven," he whispered.

Here," Ginny walked across the room and rolled back the desktop to reveal the telephone. She dialed the time and put it to Robert's ear. Then she turned on the television and he nearly jumped out of his skin.

"Robert, you know about the telegraph, right?"

He nodded, his face still frozen, his eyes wide.

"Well, from the telegraph transmitting a sound, they found voices could be transmitted, hence, the telephone." She pointed. "Then they found out how to transmit sound through the air without wire, that was radio, then voice and pictures through the air." She pointed to the television.

For the first time, Ginny could see his complete bewilderment was real. This wasn't just an act. Robert truly believed he lived in the nineteenth century. Of course, that was impossible, but *he* believed it. Perhaps the trauma of the beating coupled with the fact he was obviously a re-enactor. She didn't know, but she would go slowly, and try to be understanding from now on.

"Robert, put on the jeans, and the shirt. I guess you'll have to wear your own boots for now, but we'll get you some shoes later. Let's have lunch in the dining room, and you'll feel better. We'll both feel better."

Robert did not utter a sound, but took the shirt and let the robe fall to the floor. Then he pulled on the jeans and fingered the zipper until Ginny offered to help. The socks she had given him earlier were still in place. Slowly, he took his boots, which she had cleaned up considerably, and pulled each one on.

~ * ~

Robert followed Virginia silently to the dining room, and his gaze darted about at everything and everyone. He was out of place, out of step, out of time. How did he get here, and how could he get back? Did he want to get back? To what?

When they sat down, he stared at the menu Virginia handed him.

"What would you like?"

No answer.

"Robert, what would you like for lunch?"

Robert looked up from the menu and into Ginny's eyes with such anguish in his own that her heart broke. She wanted to hold him, to comfort him, but she must be strong. She must get through to him. He was now important to her. She wouldn't dismiss him as crazy.

Virginia ordered a hot lunch for them both. Roast turkey, mashed potatoes with gravy, steamed vegetables, and milk. Robert liked milk.

"Would you like a cup of coffee?"

Robert nodded.

The coffee was warm and real, no grounds in the bottom, and it was strong. Robert found a smile to give her after his first cup. When the food came, he was ready to eat.

"I don't know about you, but I worked up an appetite this morning." She gave him a wink, which he thought rather bold.

"I never seem to get enough lately--to eat, I mean." He smiled.

Virginia blushed.

After cleaning his plate and eating the entire basket of rolls, Robert relaxed.

"Dessert?" the waitress asked.

Robert nodded, his mouth still full of the last bite of bread. The waitress listed the desserts available that day, and Robert picked cherry pie and peach cobbler. Ginny smiled and ordered a piece of cherry pie to keep him from eating alone.

"I haven't seen this much food for months. Not since--" Robert stopped abruptly.

"Not since when?"

"Never mind. It isn't important. Besides I can't remember anyway."

"Robert," she reached across the table and took his hand "If we're going to help each other, if we're going to get to the bottom of how and why we've been thrown together, we have to trust each other, and answer each other's questions."

Robert nodded. "I'm sorry, it just seems like another life, another world. I can't make any sense of anything. The only thing that's real to me is you."

"Robert, I have a lot to tell you. You have to decide what to believe, but you can't do that unless I show you the outside. Are you strong enough?"

"I guess if I was strong enough, well…" He tossed his head toward their room. "I guess I'm strong enough for most anything, if you'll stay with me."

"You'd have trouble getting rid of me."

"Well," he stood and threw his napkin down on the table. "Where do we begin?"

"We begin by paying the check." Ginny giggled and took his hand as she grabbed the check and headed to the register. Not knowing how much cash she might need before this day's end, she took out a credit card and paid for lunch.

Obviously taking mental notes as they went, Robert watched in curious silence.

~ * ~

As they walked back to Ginny's room, it occurred to her she had a coat, but Robert had none, nothing but that cape, and that wouldn't exactly make him invisible. "Oh, uh, Robert. Wait a minute. I just remembered something I have to get. You wait here in the room for a moment." She turned the key and pushed the door open. "I have to run to my car. You need a coat. I'll be right back."

His expression showed great apprehension.

"Five minutes, that's all, I promise. Just five minutes."

He nodded. "I had a wool cape, didn't I? At least I did when I was captured. I gave my great coat to a young Lieutenant from Florida. He wasn't exactly prepared for our winter." He looked toward her. "I doubt you believe a word I've said, and what difference does it make? I'm beginning to doubt it all myself."

Ginny didn't stop to console him or even acknowledge his rambling. She held up five fingers and gently gestured for him to wait. She had a man's parka she kept in the trunk in case she had to change a flat tire or something and didn't want to get her clothes dirty. It once belonged to her first husband, and though he had been cruel at times, she couldn't bring herself to get rid of it after he was killed. He was about Robert's size, maybe an inch or so shorter, but that shouldn't matter.

Stupidly, Ginny didn't stop to put on her own coat before she dashed to the car. When she got back to the room, she was holding the brown parka, and shivering. The nylon of the coat was cold from being in the trunk so it would have done little good to slip it on. She flung it on the bed to let it warm up and stood shaking violently.

Robert immediately flew to take her in his arms. She buried her face in the flannel shirt and wrapped her arms around him. Oh, why had she gotten so attached, so quickly? She'd been holding her heart in check for years, feeling little or nothing, but he reached in and plucked it from her chest and held it in his hands. It was Jonathan's fault! He started her feelings again.

"You really are lovely, you know," Robert whispered, his mouth touching her hair. "You smell like this should be heaven. You feel like this should be heaven. I almost wish I could spend the rest of my life here in this room, with you, but I know I must find out what has become of my men, my life, my entire world." He kissed her forehead and she pried herself from him.

Ginny reached into the wardrobe for her velvet cape, and handed Robert the parka.

"Are you sure this is a man's coat? It is not wool, nor any other material with which I am familiar."

"It's called nylon, and it's a man-made fabric."

"All fabric must be made by man, except leather or fur."

"Yeah, right. I forgot. Well, I'll explain that later." A determined sigh for courage, Ginny grabbed Robert's hand and they were off.

~ * ~

Ginny stopped at the front desk and asked for the nearest barber. It would be senseless to try to get him inside a unisex haircutting establishment.

There was only one barbershop anywhere near the inn, and it was not in, what Ginny considered, walking distance.

"We'll have to take the car." She reached for his hand and led him to the front door of the inn.

"You keep saying that word. What is a car?"

"It's a 'horseless carriage'. An engine that's powered by gasoline runs it. That's a fuel made from oil. It's like a railroad engine that doesn't need tracks. Like *that*." Ginny pointed at a car about to pass in front of the inn as she dragged him through the door. Robert stared, following it with his gaze.

"I doubt I can handle it right off." His voice trailed away as he continued to watch the car.

"You don't have to. It's my car, I'll drive."

Robert raised his chin indignantly as she continued to pull him along.

"Robert, you're going to have to make concessions, too."

He nodded and followed her lead a couple of city blocks to a shiny blue "car." She used her key and opened the passenger door and gestured for him to sit. Then she reached down on the door panel and threw the door-lock to release the other side. Robert jumped with the noise of the locks being triggered.

She opened her own door and climbed in behind the wheel.

"I should have opened your door and assisted you," Robert muttered.

"I told you, I'm liberated. I open my own doors. I live alone. I fix my own plumbing, and do various other household repairs. Don't be so up-tight."

Robert shrugged dejectedly and sat in silence.

"Fasten your seat belt." She looked in his direction. "Here, like this." She demonstrated with her own. Robert pulled down the shoulder harness, but had no luck clicking the belt into place. Ginny reached for his hand and helped him.

She started the engine and let it warm up for a moment. Then as she pulled away from the curb, she could see Robert clutching at the armrests. He hung on so tightly that his knuckles were white.

"I'm a very good driver, Robert. Please relax. We only have a short ride to the barber. You'll feel better with a haircut. Then we'll buy you some more underwear and a jacket of your own. I don't think I like you in Harry's jacket."

"Harry?" Robert sounded alarmed.

"Yeah, that was my first husband's name, Harry."

"Oh. First husband? How many have you had?"

"Two."

"Where they killed in the war?"

"No, Harry was killed in a car. My second husband, well, I threw him out when I found out he had a girlfriend, and only married me to get his bills paid."

"Are you rich?"

"No, not hardly, especially after Harry and Joe got through with me. But I have a good enough job to keep body and soul together."

"Job? You are employed?"

"I should say so. That's why I took this little vacation, to get away from work."

"What kind of work, a dress shop or millinery?"

"Robert, women have all kinds of jobs now. What do you do?"

"In the army, I'm an engineer. I was in the Army Corps of Engineers before the war. I resigned my commission to join the Virginia troops under--" He halted abruptly.

"Oh, I get it, military secrets, well, that's okay. Women are engineers now, and doctors, and lawyers, and construction workers, and, well anything you can name, except fathers." She laughed at her joke, but it didn't seem to strike Robert as funny. He looked as if he was puzzling over it.

"Well, here we are, just a plain old barber shop," she remarked as she parked the car.

"You maneuver this machine expertly."

"Why, thank you Colonel. I consider that high praise coming from a chauvinist like you." She bounced out and around the front of the car as Robert fumbled looking for the door handle with no success.

Ginny opened his door, and they entered the barbershop.

"You tell him how you want it cut, just not too short. I'll be right next door getting a newspaper."

"Wait!" Robert shouted as he grabbed the straight razor from the barber's hand. "Now, *this* is a razor." He thrust it toward her.

The barber just looked at him with wide eyes.

Robert replaced the razor in the barber's hand.

"Excuse me, she's never seen one of these before."

The barber half-smiled and nodded.

Twelve

While Robert was safely busy, Ginny went down the block to grab a newspaper and a couple of current magazines. Perhaps that would convince Robert of the date. She wondered how to tell him the Confederacy was no more, that they lost the war. Perhaps she wouldn't have to be the one to break the news. Maybe she should take him to the battlefield, or better yet, the cemetery; no, maybe that was too morbid just now.

~ * ~

Armed with what she thought would convince him, Ginny returned to the barbershop just as Robert was getting his shoulders brushed off. He looked like a new man, not that the old one was hard on the eyes, but his haircut suited him, and he could pass for any era he wanted now. And he was even more handsome.

"Your eyes show approval, perhaps?" he asked.

"Yes, oh, yes. You look splendid."

He chuckled. "Splendid is not a word I would have associated with my looks."

Ginny stared. "Oh, *I* would. I *definitely* would." She spoke in a breathy voice.

"Come!" Robert grabbed her arm. "Show me more."

Anything you want immediately came to her, but she had the good sense not to say it as she looked behind him to the close fit of the jeans on his muscular thighs and curved derrière.

~ * ~

In the car Ginny started the engine, but she didn't pull away from the curb. She had to take one more, long look, and glanced over at the passenger seat. Robert was gorgeous.

Maybe I should have left you the way you were. Now every woman we meet will notice you. I don't have a chance. Though she did not vocalize these thoughts, she couldn't keep the sadness from her face.

"What's wrong? Don't you like the haircut?"

What difference did it make if everyone noticed him? He didn't belong to her, he never would, and she should resign herself to that right here and now.

She forced a smile. "Nothing, nothing's wrong. The haircut looks fine."

"Good. I feel better, I really do. I'm ready to face more of what your world has in store. I still have no idea how I got here, but I'm beginning to be glad I came."

"Yeah, well..." Her voice was small and lost. A deep breath, and she was ready for school to begin again. This was silly; she was fine when she had control, in the room, in the car, when *he* was unsure. Now he began to get some confidence. She didn't like weak men. So what was the problem? The problem was she already felt as though she was losing him, and it hurt.

Without a word she shoved the newspaper in front of him. He looked at the headlines, the date, the pictures. He showed little emotion now, taking it more in stride.

~ * ~

"Aren't you comin' in?" Robert asked Ginny.

Ginny had driven in silence to the Fredericksburg battlefield. Out of the corner of her eye, she watched Robert watching everything...and everyone, especially the women. He had excitement in his eyes where there had been sadness, eagerness where she had seen uncertainty. She would distance herself. She wouldn't let herself be hurt. That was a joke! It already hurt. At the visitor's center at the battlefield, she pushed him into the slide show presentation.

"I'll be out here," she muttered with a sigh. "I've seen it all, several times."

"Virginia," he took her hand. "I can't do this without you. You're my anchor."

"That's a good analogy." she scoffed. She couldn't resist his pleading eyes and finally sighed and shrugged as she accompanied him into the little theater.

Even in the darkness, she could see Robert's expressions, from remembrance to disbelief. His face was pale and showed such a broad range of emotions. Ginny rarely took her eyes from him. She had seen all the slides several times before, but she was seeing them through Robert's eyes this time. She had heard all the commentary, but now she heard it through Robert's ears.

He wasn't some re-enactor caught up in his own fantasy. He had *been* there. She knew that now. But that made her position even more ambiguous. What should she do with him, for him? This puzzle would not be solved easily. There had to be some reason he was transported to this time, perhaps even a reason he was dumped in her lap. She must try to help.

Robert didn't move a muscle when the slides were over, he didn't even appear to breathe. It was obvious to Ginny he was trying to let all he had seen and heard sink in. She let him remain as long as she dared, but another presentation was about to start.

"Robert," she whispered. "Robert, we have to go." She took his arm and stood, trying to pull him up beside her. When he stood, he was not erect, he slumped, he was beaten, and he was disillusioned. "Robert, we'll figure this out. I promise." She led him from the theater like a broken old man. His eyes were dull and blank.

"Robert, you're a Colonel, right? Then there must be some record of you." She pulled him toward the little bookstore of the center. "Look, Robert, here are books about various Virginia regiments. Do you see yours?"

He didn't even look where she pointed.

"Robert, please. I want to help, but I can't do this alone. You're the only one who knows the facts."

He still did not respond.

"Damn it, Robert! I refuse to feel sorry for someone who won't help himself. Some soldier you must have been." She dropped his arm and walked away. She was outside and down the front steps when he came running after her. He grabbed her arm and spun her around to face him, then he wrapped both arms around her tightly and clung to her.

"Please, don't leave me, Virginia," he whispered. "I need a little time to understand this. We...we lost the war...but it took over two more years of fighting... General Jackson was killed only a few months after...after I left and came here." His voice was cracking. Then he looked toward the gray winter sky and shouted, "God in heaven, why am I here?"

Ginny quickly led him to her car. Leaning the seats back a little, she held his head on her shoulder. "I pray God will answer your question, Robert, for I certainly can't."

"Virginia, I know now that the war is over, that I have somehow traveled over a hundred years, but I have to know about myself. There could be no harm now in telling you I was in Jackson's brigade. I was in the 5th Virginia. Will you go in and see if they have a book... I can't go back in there right now. I don't think my legs would carry me a step."

Ginny reached to wipe an escaping tear from his cheek and found his face very warm. "Robert, you're not well. I have to get some more of that antibiotic in you. I'll go in and look for a book, if you promise to sit here quietly."

Robert gave a slight, defeated snicker. "Where would I go?"

~ * ~

"You get in bed. I'll get the antibiotic and some aspirin." She rushed to the bathroom for water. Her face shown with worry as she handed him the three pills and the glass of water.

"Robert, maybe I should take you to a hospital or at least to a doctor. They couldn't possibly tell you were from another time. People haven't changed."

"No!" He grabbed her hand tightly, his eyes pleading. "No one but you must know. I have to tell you everything I remember. You have to help me figure this out. My brain is so muddled." He put a fist to his head. "Some memories are just pieces. I think I lost consciousness a couple of times when the Federals had me." He shook his head in exasperation. "Where are the books?"

"Whoa, now, hold on. What you need right now is some rest. We'll look at the books later."

"I can't rest! I can't think... I can't stop thinkin'... I'm so confused."

"I know, and rest, a little sleep, will make everything fall into place. I promise you." She smoothed his hair from his face and he grabbed her cool hand and held it to his cheek.

"You should just leave me to my troubles. This is not your problem."

"Shhh. I've made it my problem. I want to help. I... I care about you."

"I am tired."

"I know."

"Sit with me?"

Ginny smiled and climbed up next to him on the bed, kissed his cheek and laid beside him on top the covers.

"Now, you go to sleep."

"Virginia, you're wonderful."

"Yeah, that's what they all say 'til they get to know me better," she joked.

"I mean it. I haven't cared for anyone in a very long time."

"That's an understatement. Now, close those big blue eyes."

~ * ~

Ginny stayed with Robert on the bed until he was sound asleep. He went quickly from being ready to conquer the world to being ready to leave it. As ill as he had been, he could not have much endurance, but he didn't seem to realize it. She must make sure he did not overdo anything later. She wanted him well. She wanted him to stay in her time, but he could disappear as suddenly as he appeared.

Ginny had brought back three books from the battlefield store. One on Jackson's Division, one on the 5th Virginia and a small one on the Battle of Fredericksburg. Quietly she looked through the books, slowly finding pieces of the puzzle, but she didn't like what she was finding. She found an account of a Colonel Carter in a brief, glowing report to Lee made by Stonewall Jackson late in 1861. Another brief reference early in 1862, but what she found in a report by another Colonel from December of 1862 near Fredericksburg, made her blood run cold.

She found a report which speculated that Colonel Carter deserted upon finding his son's Union Division to be in opposition under General Burnside. This colonel went on to say Jackson thought it more likely Carter was captured, but no one on sentry duty saw or heard anything, and there were no signs of a struggle in Colonel Carter's tent. Jackson requested that Carter be put on the missing list instead of absent without leave, for the time being.

She could find no further reference to indicate what final status was given to Carter, whether he remained on a missing list or was reported as a deserter. Biting her lip, she closed the book. How could she let Robert see this? How could she let him know he may have been labeled a deserter?

She must make him tell her his story before she let him see anything she found. She would convince him she needed his entire story before she could look anything up. If she told him of her writing and research and all the Civil War books she had at home, perhaps he would take her word.

In the turmoil of the afternoon, Ginny forgot to get any more clothes for Robert, so she took a moment to wash out the T-shirt and briefs he'd already worn, which were still lying wet in the bathroom sink. It felt strange to be handling men's laundry after so many years alone.

~ * ~

Robert looked much better when he awoke from some three hours of sleep. It was past dinner time, but Ginny knew he must eat, so she ordered in, thinking she would wake him when the food arrived, but it hadn't come yet.

She sat on a chair next to the bed as he stretched and yawned.

"Hungry?"

"To look at those books."

"No, not yet. You promised to follow my orders, Colonel. And the first one is that we eat. Dinner should be here any moment." The words were hardly from her mouth when a knock sounded at the door.

As she opened it, a tray was wheeled in with two covered plates, milk, a rose and candle, and a bottle of champagne, compliments of the inn management.

Ginny had ordered two steaks, baked potatoes, salads, green beans, and dessert. Not having any idea how Robert liked his steak, she just ordered them both "medium."

She tipped the desk clerk, who served, when needed, as waiter in the little inn, and tossed Robert the robe he wore before.

"Smells heavenly."

Robert seemed cheerier, and she was glad. Perhaps he would be able to tell her enough to shed some light on the things she'd read. It was obvious to her that his reference to being captured was true. His back seemed proof enough of that, but she was curious to know just what happened, if he could remember.

"Robert! Slow down. You'll choke eating that fast."

"Sorry, I just want to get to the books."

"The books will be there; whenever we finish will be soon enough. Now drink a glass of the champagne and relax."

"I warn you, champagne makes me amorous," he whispered with a sly smile.

Ginny lowered her chin and looked up at him with wicked eyes. "Funny, it has the same effect on me, and this is my second glass."

"Then I'd best catch up." Robert downed the full glass and poured another.

Ginny wanted to keep him from the books, just for the evening, but selfishly, she also wanted another session like they spent that morning, before he might relapse into his moodiness upon learning of her discoveries. Besides the champagne might also loosen his tongue and he might not be suspicious of her many questions about his capture. If she could piece some of the puzzle together first, perhaps she could soften the blow.

Ginny began to unbutton the top of her blouse. Champagne, or any other wine, also made her very warm. She was gaining Robert's undivided attention, so she fluttered the lace of her blouse and fanned herself demonstratively.

"I shouldn't have had that champagne. It makes me so *hot*."

Of course the word "hot" did not have the same connotation to Robert it did to her, but he fingered his collar and stretched his neck uncomfortably.

"Robert…" Ginny got up from her seat. "You look flushed. Is your fever worse?" She put a cool hand to his forehead and ran her other hand gently down his cheek, pulling his head against her chest.

Robert swallowed and took a deep breath.

"You should go right back to bed after you finish your dessert."

"Are…aren't you going to have dessert?" he stammered.

"No, I don't think I have room. I don't like to…" She paused purposefully. "Go to bed on a full stomach. I really think we should find some way to relax tonight, and start on the research tomorrow. You could tell me something about yourself. We could get better acquainted."

Robert smiled slyly. "Perhaps I could interest you in another shower?"

That would be one way to keep him from getting at the books while she showered. She rolled her eyes. "Well, it wouldn't do any harm to clean that back again, and you certainly can't be expected to do it yourself without breaking something open." *Good thinking*, she congratulated herself.

She didn't have to ask him twice. Robert was up from his chair and untying the robe as he crossed the floor toward the bathroom.

"Coming?" He tossed a look over his shoulder.

"What am I doing?" Ginny whispered to herself, but she followed obediently.

~ * ~

Robert reached to close the bathroom door, but Ginny caught it quickly, "No, no reason to do that." Then she consciously dropped some of the excitement from her speech. "It's too crowded for both of us to undress in here." She stepped back into the safety of the bedroom, but Robert followed.

He took her hands from the buttons on her blouse, and began to unbutton them himself as he kissed her. She not only responded to his kisses, but began to tug at his shirt and pull the tail out of his jeans. Then she pushed the shirt off his shoulders and, trying not to hurt his tender back, gently rolled the T-shirt up.

Ginny ran her hands over the back of his jeans. Spreading her fingers wide on each cheek of his buttocks, she massaged the intriguing muscles.

Robert carefully removed her blouse, let it float to the floor, then gave a disgusted sigh. "The harness," he whispered.

Ginny started to reach behind herself to unfasten the hooks, but instead, Robert moved behind her.

"I should master this. It can't be any worse than bridling a horse." His voice was soft and amused.

He unfastened the hooks and slipped the straps from her shoulders. Then he pulled her back against his chest and caressed her head with his cheek as he let his hands wander around her waist and come to rest, one on each of her breasts.

Ginny gasped with the feel of his fingers, spider-webbing her breasts. It sent wondrous shock waves through her. How natural his hands felt to her--how strong, but gentle his touch. She unzipped her skirt and let it fall, standing there in only her black panty hose, he in his jeans. She leaned forcefully against his chest and reveled in the feel of his great hands.

"I love your brand of 'skin to skin' combat," she whispered. She turned and planted kisses against his chest. She kissed the deep scar on his left shoulder.

"Manassas," he whispered.

Then she kissed the inside of his right arm, running her lips over the length of the scar above his elbow.

"Sharpsburg," he whispered again.

"What? Nothing from the Shenandoah Valley?" Ginny whispered playfully.

"Not where it's likely to be seen." He gave a breathy snort.

She unsnapped and unzipped his jeans and pushed them down along with his briefs. Her hands lingered on his firm derrière. She imagined the muscles were so hard from hours in the saddle.

As his hands roved over her flesh to the thin panty hose, he became fascinated with them. "I've never seen anythin' so sheer, nor felt anythin' so smooth. How does one make such a fabric and where are they sewn together. I--"

She kissed him. "Robert?"

"Yes."

"Shut up." Trying to remember his back, she pushed him down on the bed but she was aroused. She wiggled out of her panty hose and climbed onto the bed, her torso on top of his. "Robert, do you feel up to this?"

"It matters not what I feel." He looked down. "My partner has a mind of his own."

Ginny's hand drifted down his side until it reached his thigh, then her fingers wandered toward his center, and she felt a lumpy scar she hadn't noticed when she bathed him. Her hand stopped there on his inner thigh.

"Shenandoah?" she asked and he nodded.

"Your skin is so soft and fragrant, your hands so, so soothin'," the tone of his voice lowered, "…so seductive."

"I love the feel of your body next to my skin. I can't remember anything feeling quite so good."

"Anything?"

"Well," she blushed, "maybe one thing." Then remembering how it felt inside her, she ran her fingers up the length of his "partner," and slowly moved to straddle him, finding him easily.

Robert was shocked, but not repulsed. It seemed very natural to him, though he'd never quite experienced this kind of behavior outside of a brothel and that comparison was poor. This was different. There was no hurry, no ulterior motives here except mutual satisfaction. Ginny gave no impression of promiscuity. She simply radiated tenderness, love, affection and passion, unbridled and most welcomed, passion.

"Do you mind?" she asked thoughtfully.

"Not at all," he whispered as she began to move rhythmically. Robert rather appreciated having both hands free to wander over her softness, caress her pendulous breasts so tempting above him. Enchanted by Virginia's directness and expertise, he held himself in check for many minutes until at last she squealed and shuddered with satisfaction.

Then, without leaving her, he gently maneuvered them on their sides, and then Ginny to her back as he rose above her. It was clear she was happily exhausted, but still she moved in concert with him until Robert too approached satisfaction.

Suddenly, Ginny moved with greater purpose, and as he found his release, she again moaned and gasped. Obviously, Robert found all her right places a second time. He felt strangely proud of his accomplishment. She looked strangely amazed.

Had Ginny taken the time to think rationally about what she was doing, as she usually did, she wouldn't have made any advances, or at the very least, she would have felt guilty about doing so. This was Never-Never Land. This entire trip turned into one fantasy after another, and she didn't care to dissect any of it. It was probably the first time in her entire life she just decided to enjoy and "go with the flow," as she had often been advised.

Thirteen

Robert and Ginny showered together after they made love. Ginny gently washed his back with an anti-bacterial soap. The more she could keep the infection down, the less scarring he would have. Touching him sent wondrous sensations through her.

It felt good to hold each other as the warm water pattered down. Ginny showered with neither of her husbands. Only once had she taken a shower with a boyfriend she dated for over a year between her marriages, or, as she most often referred to them, her two disasters.

It was a sensuous experience now as before, but with Robert, it was a bonding. Feeling his clean skin against hers made her feel complete. He was like a missing part of herself. It was almost frightening. It seemed the more determined she was to keep her feelings in check, the more she needed to be with him, to touch him, hold him, understand him, and most of all, to help him.

Perhaps it was her interest, bordering on obsession, for the past, particularly the Civil War, that gave Robert this power over Ginny. If his flesh pressed to hers had not been so real, Ginny would have easily convinced herself he was a figment of her own imagination. But her imagination was never this vivid.

It could not create the magnitude of passion she experienced with Robert, for, having never before experienced it, she could not have dreamed it existed.

~ * ~

After their shower, Robert and Ginny, both bodies naked and clinging to each other, retired to the bed for sleep. Once, during the night, Ginny got up and went to get a couple of aspirin. The champagne gave her a slight headache. The moment she withdrew her arm from Robert's chest, and her head from his shoulder, he jerked awake.

"It's all right, I'll be right back," she whispered in the darkness.

In seconds she returned.

"I missed you," he whispered and kissed her forehead. "Come back where you belong." He coaxed her head to the hollow of his shoulder and Ginny ran her hand over the skin covering his ribs. There wasn't much meat covering those ribs, what was there was muscle, but Robert was too thin. She could fix that, she thought as she stroked him back to sleep, if she only had the time.

"It's scary, how complete we feel together, Robert."

"Shhh, it scares me, too," he whispered.

A tear slipped silently from Ginny's eye. How ironic it was she finally found a soul-mate, the definitive piece of the puzzle of her existence, and he couldn't be hers. He didn't even come from her world, and he could be snatched away at any moment.

Ginny had loved before, she had been "in love" before, but never had she felt this completeness. It brought her a kind of personal peace. She would enjoy it as long as it lasted, and hope it would be implanted firmly enough in her memories to last a lifetime. This magnitude of feeling could certainly not hurt her writing, if she could find a way to put such depth into words.

But it wasn't her writing that was paramount in her mind now. It was trying to get to the bottom of Robert's story, without losing him in the process. If she let him know of the speculation of his possible desertion, she might make him disappear, or perhaps drive him back inside himself, broken and sullen. It would take all her wiles to manage him.

Even in the soundness of his still-fevered sleep, Robert was considerate of Ginny. Without opening his eyes or seeming to arouse in any way, he would tighten his arm around her or touch her cheek. It had been much too long since Ginny was held in a man's arms, and never had it seemed so natural as this. Never had she found reason to shed her normal self-consciousness so easily, nor felt such strong desire with no thought to the future or feeling of being used.

This time-traveling, battered and ill soldier showed her the kind of tenderness she could heretofore only dream about. Sometimes she wove those dreams into the stories she wrote, but never did she think she would really experience it first hand. She was jealous of it, wanted to protect it for as long as it would last, but how?

If she helped him exonerate himself, would he then be free to go back from whence he came? Should she let him believe he was thought to be a traitor, a deserter, and perhaps by so doing keep him in her time? What was she thinking? Of course not! She must help him. She owed him that much for just the last two days, which gave her more affection than she knew in a lifetime.

Besides, if indeed, he had traveled through time, what gave her any idea she could control his staying or leaving? She must do everything in her power to give him his life back, for hadn't he done just that for her?

Ginny turned her head slightly on his shoulder and placed her lips against his bare skin. Even that small gesture caused electricity to flow from him to her. Yes, she must help him, and by doing so help herself. She kissed the side of his chest and drifted back to sleep.

~ * ~

Ginny awoke first. She didn't scurry about the room getting dressed, for fear it would awaken Robert before he was well rested. Her father's robe drawn about her, she simply retired to the foot of the bed, sat studying him, thought about all the feelings he evoked within her, and tried to plan her strategy for helping him get to the bottom of the stories he didn't even know yet.

If only she had all her books from home. She had a collection of well over 200 books about the Civil War which she used for reference and for entertainment. Maybe she could take Robert home with her... Maybe not. What if he disappeared halfway up Route 95? What if his time-traveling visit was tied to Fredericksburg? If Fredericksburg, how far out might she be able to take him? He came from somewhere outside of town when she spied him on the Chatham Bridge.

"It's not bad enough I don't know where to start to help you," she whispered to herself. "I don't know any of the rules for this situation. How can I keep from breaking the rules, if I don't know what they are?"

Silent tears escaped down her cheeks. She might do more harm than good, or she might do something to cause him to flee or disappear as quickly as he appeared.

"All my life I've been more likely to do nothing at all than take the chance on doing the wrong thing. I'm not the one to help you. I don't know how to take chances..."

Now the crying came in earnest and she put her face in her hands and wept quietly.

Robert opened his eyes and moved to hold her. "What's this?" He put his arms around her inside the robe. "Have I done something which I shouldn't?"

His gentle arms around her made her cry even harder. She needed to get all her fears out, once and for all. Stroking, kissing her forehead, shushing her sobs, he pulled her down to lie with him.

"Are you sorry we made love?" he whispered, as if trying to guess what made her cry. She gave a negative shake of her head. "Are you *afraid* because we made love?" Ginny didn't move to reply in words or movement, unsure what he meant. "Are you afraid I would not respond honorably, if..." He continued, but faltered for words. "If I, if we, uh..."

Ginny smiled through her tears. "If you made me pregnant?"

The word assailed his ears. Robert swallowed hard at her frankness, his face flushed that he could not be as frank, considering the last twenty-four hours.

"Oh, darling Robert." She wiped her tears with the edge of the sheet. "Such *chivalry*. I wouldn't have such thoughts, even if it were possible. If I know nothing else, I know you are a man of honor."

"What do you mean, if it were possible? Do you doubt my virility?" He was indignant.

"Not hardly!" She laughed and kissed his neck. "Robert, I have battle scars, too. I can't have any more children. Trust me."

"I'm sorry."

"Please, don't be. I'm not."

"Was it...a cesarean birth?" His fingers crossed her abdomen, and he felt a long scar.

"No, but, I didn't know that was commonly known in your day."

"It was not too common a practice, not often successful, but that was how my son was delivered moments before my wife died."

"Oh, I'm sorry. But no, it wasn't a cesarean. My daughters were born in the normal manner." Ginny wasn't about to tell him it was the aftermath of a terrible beating she sustained from her first husband. Nor did she wish to explain what a hysterectomy entailed. "Let's just leave it that I can't have any more children."

Robert's face turned sad.

"Robert, I don't mind. I don't want any more children. My daughters are grown and I like it that way. Does that shock you?"

Robert's gaze darted. He seemed to be searching his mind for the right answer. "I don't think so, but, I thought most women lost interest in, uh, making love when they could no longer bear children."

Ginny chuckled. "Maybe in your day, but not in mine."

Robert smiled at her honesty. "I wasn't complaining, mind you." He wrapped his arms tightly about her, then leaned back from her and slipped down to plant a kiss on her shoulder, her neck, then her lips. "I'm definitely not complaining," he whispered hoarsely.

Ginny gasped as he held her. "Neither is your 'partner.'" She wiggled beneath the covers enticingly as his prowess became evident.

"Madam, are you tempting me?"

She smiled. "I don't know. Am I?"

"Definitely!" He ravaged her with kisses.

~ * ~

"Robert," Ginny began later as they lay in solemn satisfaction, "tell me about your life, before the war."

"It wasn't much of a life, except for the two years I had with Beth. I am a Carter, but I don't suppose that means much in this day."

"A Carter, as in Robert "King" Carter, Carter Burwell, Anne Hill Carter?"

"Why, yes, Annie was a distant cousin."

"Then you're related to *Robert E. Lee.*"

"Well, in a manner."

Ginny swooned. "Oh, how wonderful."

"You should meet him, you'd like--" He stopped short, realizing it would be impossible. "You would have liked him. I realize he must be dead. Did he die in the war?"

"No, he died in 1870."

"I'm surprised losin' the war itself did not kill him. He never wanted it in the first place."

"I know," Ginny whispered, understanding how difficult this was for Robert.

He took a deep breath and let it out quickly as if to move on in time.

"What about Beth, Robert, tell me about your wife."

"Bethy was small, lovely, rather delicate."

"Figures," Ginny huffed disgustedly under her breath.

"She was Elizabeth Franklin Harrell of Philadelphia. Her mother claimed some relation to Benjamin Franklin, though I never saw any proof. Her parents didn't approve of me. I have a good family name, but no family money."

"Sounds like that other Robert--the 'Lee' one."

Robert smiled. "I'm afraid he was in better stead than I, however. I was career military as was he. Elizabeth's parents frowned on that, unless we would be content to be apart for long periods as I was assigned about to various posts. They tried to force her to marry the man they handpicked for her, but she refused. She once spent a week locked in her room for refusin' to receive the man."

Robert's gaze reflected a drifting away of his thoughts. Ginny watched him for a moment, wondering what he was remembering, then she touched his hand and he snapped back.

"How did you manage to win her hand, then?"

"We married without their knowledge or blessin', upon my graduation from West Point in thirty-seven. When I was settled at my first post, she joined me. I was still twenty when we married, youngest man in my class, and she was only eighteen. Her father could have had the marriage dissolved, if he caught us, but, by the time he found us, nearly a year had passed, and Beth was expectin', so he let us be.

"Tried to offer me a job in his law firm, pay for my law studies, but I liked bein' an engineer, except for the lack of advancement.

"After Bethy died, that didn't matter either."

"What about your son?"

"I had little choice but to give him over to his grandparents to be raised. What was I to do with a baby? Besides, he looked like his mother. I would have resented him, I think. I tried to get to know him as he got older, but Harry wanted no part of me. His grandmother saw to that."

"Harry? Oh, that's why you looked so funny when I mentioned my first husband."

Robert nodded. "Robert Harrell Carter. His mother made her choice of names clear before…well, anyway, his grandmother refused to call him Robert, thus Harrell, or 'Harry' for short.

"He's as headstrong as both his parents. Graduated second in his class from West Point, this year, um, eighteen sixty-two. Had to go there to prove he was a better man than I. I was eighth in my class. He thinks and talks like his grandparents.

Yankee to the core. Not that I object to him bein' a Unionist. I believe in the Union myself."

Ginny could see the pain in Robert's eyes as he spoke of his wife, and the bitterness as he spoke of his son.

He puffed a sigh. "Well, enough about my past. It's your turn to share."

Ginny didn't want to talk about herself, but if it would keep him away from the books a while longer, she would acquiesce.

"Well, I was born Virginia Lee Berkeley. I like to pretend that my middle name came from your famous cousin, but, in truth, it was the middle name of a deceased relative. I took my maiden name, Berkeley, back after my second divorce. My first husband gave me a beautiful set of twins, and a lot of grief. He died in an accident some years after our divorce.

"My second husband gave me a different kind of grief with his running around with other women, and both husbands cost me a great deal of money."

"It's impossible a man should want for more than you." He kissed the top of her head.

"Tell that to my second husband."

"I would, if I met him, but only after I gave him a sound thrashin'."

She chuckled. "I'd pay to see that!"

"That doesn't sound like much of a life, Ginny."

Ginny laughed. "It hasn't been, until now."

"Your daughters?"

"Total opposites, twenty-two years old… What can I say?"

"Twenty-two? Surely you jest."

"No, why would I kid about a thing like that?"

"But, you must have been a child-bride."

"Blessings on you, Robert. Not exactly, I was twenty. I'll be forty-three this year."

"But--" he cut himself off.

"Thanks, but I have to admit it."

"You look to be in your prime."

"Well, I should hope I am."

"Excuse me, I didn't mean to offend." Robert's voice was sheepish.

"I'm not offended." She kissed the palm of his hand she was holding under the covers.

"You're so vibrant, so, so very alive."

"I am with you. I can't say I felt very alive until I came down here. First there was dear, sweet Jonathan, then you."

"Who was this Jonathan?"

"The young man in the Confederate uniform you saw me with. The one you thought was a traitor."

"And what was this Jonathan to you?"

"Why, Robert, you sound jealous! I love it."

"I'm not, well, I'm just curious. How did you meet this fellow?"

"I just sort of ran into him, literally. I came down here for a rest, to get away from my job and the rest of my life for a while. Jonathan kindly invited me to camp, and took me for a carriage ride. He was just a nice *young* man."

"Did he, did you--it's none of my affair."

"*You're right. It isn't.* But no, he didn't, we didn't."

"I saw him come from this inn one mornin'."

"Yes, you did." She offered no more explanation.

"I don't want to think of anyone else touchin' you," he whispered as he grabbed her to him.

"Robert, I'm not in the habit of getting intimate with boys like *Jonathan*."

"I apologize." He cast his eyes downward.

"Please don't. I kind of liked it. I don't think anyone's ever been jealous over me. I could get used to it."

"Am I forgiven?" Robert whispered as he tightened his grip on her.

Ginny stretched and planted a moist kiss on his lips, her tongue playing at their juncture. "Does that answer your question?"

Fourteen

Robert and Ginny dressed and went to the dining room for a late breakfast. Ginny temporarily succeeded in keeping him from the books. This was another opportunity to get him to talk--and to put some weight on him.

"See anything that looks good to you?"

Robert raised his eyes from the menu and looked intensely at Ginny. "I thought I had already shown you."

Ginny smiled. "I'm flattered, but I meant do you see anything you want to eat."

Robert just rolled his eyes and smiled.

"Robert! Chill out."

She ignored the puzzled look on his face, realizing he had no idea what "chill out" meant.

"I think--" He stopped short and slammed the menu shut. "I think I can't order anything. It's just occurred to me, I can't let you keep paying for my meals, my clothes…" He rose abruptly from the table. "I'm embarrassed. You must think me a cad."

"Robert, sit down. I think nothing of the kind. This is silly. Even if you had money, it wouldn't be worth anything now. Well, I mean, it would be to a collector, but it wouldn't be spendable. Come on, I'm not spending that much on you, really. Please." She reached for his hand. "Robert, please."

"But just this morning I listened to how much your husbands cost you. I can't accept anything else from you... Well, not anything that costs money, anyway." He sucked one cheek in, and tilted his head downward to gaze up at her with a wicked roll of his eyes.

"Robert, sit down, now I'm getting embarrassed, please."

Robert sat, but held himself erect and away from the table.

"Robert, forget what I said about my husbands. I have a good job, and I can afford this vacation. Please let me help you. I care about you."

"I had a little money still in the pocket of my uniform, I thought. I was sure they didn't take that from me."

Then Ginny remembered emptying his uniform pockets on the dresser, and not even looking at any of it. She threw her napkin down on the table. "Wait here. I'll be right back." Taking the room key from her pocket, she got up and dashed to her room. She returned with the contents of his pockets.

"Here, this is what was in your pockets." She put the few coins, a button, and a charm of some kind on the table where they looked at them.

Robert picked up the coins, then tossed them back on the table. "I've seen the prices on this menu. I couldn't buy a cup of coffee with this."

"Robert, these coins are worth a great deal of money now. Seriously. They're worth much more than I've spent on you. This one alone..." She picked up the only gold piece. "...is worth much more than I've spent."

"Then sell them."

"I'd rather keep them. They mean much more to me than the money."

"They're yours. But it still makes me uncomfortable."

Ginny must change the subject. She would not be able to sooth away his discomfort with words. If only her husbands had possessed even a modicum of Robert's ethics.

"The button is obviously from your uniform, but what's the charm?"

Robert fingered the gold locket. "It isn't a charm. It's a locket. It holds a lock of Beth's hair. It was my lucky piece." His voice dropped to a choked whisper as he put the locket in his shirt pocket.

"Well…" She turned her attention back to the menu. "I'm hungry, and I intend to have a good breakfast."

Robert didn't look back at the menu, but drank the coffee the waitress slipped in front of them as they talked. When the waitress returned with her pad in hand, Ginny ordered one scrambled egg, bacon and toast.

"Sir?" The waitress turned to him expectantly.

"Oh, just the coffee is fine."

Ginny caught the arm of the waitress as she turned to leave. "Bring him the 'planter's breakfast'." She turned to Robert. "How do you like your eggs?"

Robert wasn't going to argue in public. "It doesn't matter."

"Scramble his eggs, too."

She turned back to Robert. "We'll have the coins appraised and you'll see how valuable they are. Then I'll show you all the receipts for what I've spent so far. Will that make you feel better?"

He nodded.

"Subject closed." She demonstratively pounded her hand on the table. Ginny reached across the table to where Robert's right hand rested and, without saying a word, put hers on top of it.

Robert raised his eyes and looked into hers. "I'm sorry. Seems like everythin' is different in your world. It just makes me uncomfortable to know I have cost you money. I should be payin' for everythin'. I'll adjust, I suppose."

"Robert, you don't have to adjust. I love you just the way you are." Ginny realized after the words escaped her that she really did feel a kind of love for Robert. It almost frightened her. She had opened her heart to this strange man, and felt no regret except that she didn't know when he might be snatched from her.

"I have been afraid to speak in such terms of endearment, for I have no right. Yet, I have not had such feelin's as I have for you."

"Robert, tell me about Harry. Did he have something to do with your capture?"

"I believe he must have, though images are not clear. I was sent a note through the lines at night, under a white flag. The note said Harry was gravely ill in the camp hospital and I would be granted safe conduct to visit him as they expected him to die.

"I did not wish to awaken my commandin' officer. We had been gettin' very little sleep with the Federals so near. I gave my corporal a note telling him where I was goin' and that I would return within twenty-four hours.

"I left with the Union messenger. We rode a couple of miles closer to town, on the other side of the river. It was only a small camp they took me to. I knew the whole of Burnside's forces were close at hand, yet they said Harry was in this camp. There was some excuse about him bein' contagious..."

"Did you see Harry?"

Robert ran a hand across his forehead trying to remember, trying to improve the images in his mind. "Yes, I...I did see him, but he was not sick. He stood and greeted me." Robert's eyes flashed as he related the scene and allowed Virginia to see through his eyes.

~ * ~

Robert's thoughts were a million miles away, and he had stopped talking after telling Virginia about his capture. The waitress brought breakfast, and after a moment of staring, Robert smelled the food. Virginia had been sitting quietly all this time. He was hungry, and he didn't want to remember anymore right now.

On the plate before him were at least three eggs, scrambled, sausage links, bacon, fried potatoes, biscuits and grits.

"Please bring a large milk, too," Virginia bid the waitress.

"Virginia, I can't possibly eat all this."

"Find room. You can fill in the spaces between your ribs."

Robert smiled and began to eat slowly at first, but everything tasted so good, he was soon nearly gobbling, politely, of course. Virginia seemed delighted to watch him fill up on the breakfast. She finished her meager meal long before Robert and sat watching him as if she enjoyed the sight of him eating with such relish.

There was little more left on his plate than a single bit of biscuit when he pushed back from the table and loosened his belt.

Virginia chuckled. "I'm trying to fill those jeans out."

"Well, a few meals like that will certainly do the trick. I don't really have the room, but I'd love some more coffee."

Virginia poured him another cup from the carafe the waitress had left.

"I don't think I've seen a breakfast like that since I was a boy visitin' at Oatlands."

"*Oatlands.* I've been there."

"It stands?"

"Oh, yes. It remained in the Carter family for many years, even after the war. Another family bought it, oh, I don't know, about the turn of the century, I think. They restored it."

"Would that I could see it again."

"Maybe you can. We'll see." Ginny was apprehensive. It wasn't that it would be a long trip, it was near Leesburg, but, she hadn't decided whether or not to chance taking Robert away from Fredericksburg. She really wanted to take him home with her, though she realized her little house would seem very modest to a Carter.

"I spent many wonderful days at Oatlands. My cousins always treated me as though I had a right to be there. It was a much happier time." His expression turned sad.

She touched his hand. "Robert, you'll be happy again."

"I am strangely contented with you, yes, even happy. It's been a long time since I felt any kind of warmth of feelin'. I could fall in love with you, Virginia Berkeley."

Embarrassed, Ginny shifted her gaze.

"Have I said something to offend?"

"No." Her voice had a startled crackle. "No, not at all." Perhaps it was her due to fall in love and be loved by someone who was only visiting from another time, after all, she always thought the last century much more romantic.

As they got up to leave the dining room, Robert fell in behind Ginny.

"You know," he whispered behind her ear. "I'm beginnin' to get used to you in boy's clothes. Doesn't leave a great deal to the imagination, but it does stir the blood."

"If you don't think this leaves much to the imagination, wait until you see what young girls wear, or even more shapely women my age," she whispered back.

"More shapely? I find your 'shape' extremely pleasin'. Never did go in for that corseted twenty-inch waist."

"Blessings on you, again, colonel. You're a wonderful liar."

"I *do not* lie, Madam." His voice was still a whisper, though strained. "Shall I prove my interest?"

Ginny smiled wryly. "Oh, sir, I fear I was simply the handiest device you could find."

Robert grabbed her shoulder and wheeled her around. "I say, not, Madam!"

By now they gained some attention of the patrons in the lobby and Ginny bit back a blush. "Robert, we're drawing a crowd," she whispered, her jaw set.

"I do not care. Take back your insinuation." His voice was still too loud.

"Okay," she whispered. "I take it back. You're crazy about me."

"So now you would label me 'insane' to be in love with you?"

Giggles were coming from the women in the room.

"My mental faculties are entirely intact."

Virginia ran from the lobby as Robert glanced around at the approving faces and bowed to brief applause.

~ * ~

Robert threw open the door which he caught as she attempted to slam it. She threw herself on the bed and, in embarrassment, buried her face in a pillow.

"What have I done?" He reached to touch her shoulder. She did not respond.

"Please, my dear, tell me what I've done to displease you."

"You embarrassed the hell out of me. I can't face those people again."

"I thought they seemed appreciative and I don't care for your language."

"I don't give a *damn* what you care for.

"Virginia, really. You're not a sailor, you know."

"Who the hell do you think you are, John Wilkes Booth?"

"No, Junius or Edwin, perhaps, but I'm much too old to be John."

164

Ginny turned over and looked up at his apologetic face. She realized he didn't know what John Wilkes Booth did after the war, but he'd probably seen him in person, and his father Junius or his brother Edwin. It suddenly became funny and she began to laugh.

"Edwin Booth. Or, or Junius. I'd forgotten their father's name."

"Well, I am forty-six years old. And I fail to see the humor."

"Forty-six, perfect," Ginny whispered.

"Far from that. Unless I'm unusually fortunate, I can't expect too many more good years. Of course, I didn't expect any more time a few days ago. And, frankly, I didn't much care, except for the men entrusted to my command, but now, now I do care." He took Ginny in his arms and held her close.

She wanted to melt into him, to become part of him, to never let him go, but he was only on loan, from another time, and she must just enjoy what moments she was given. She closed her eyes and gathered every sense of him she could in her mind--the feel of his hands on her body, his voice, and his laughter.

She inhaled his clean, manly fragrance, she touched his freshly shaved cheek, and she tasted his lips and the tip of his tongue. She absorbed the feeling of his arms about her, and her head upon his shoulder. She must remember it all before it disappeared.

"I'm sorry for any embarrassment I may have caused you. I shan't do it again. Forgive me," he pleaded in a whisper.

"I could forgive you most anything." She kissed him, then, studying his features, leaned away from him.

"Why do you look through me that way?"

"I'm not looking through you. I just want to remember every detail. I don't want to forget you, whenever you go back." She stifled a sob.

"What makes you so sure I'll be able to return to my time? What makes you think I even want to?"

"It's simple. I've never gotten anything I really wanted in life and I can't think of anything I want more than to keep you with me. Not even selling my first book is as important, and I never thought I'd hear myself say that."

"Selling a book?"

"Yes, I fancy myself a writer of sorts, but I can't seem to find a publisher."

"I should like to read some of your writing...sometime...later...much later." His words drifted off as he laid down on top of her, kissing her, caressing her, making her want him again.

Fifteen

Ginny sat up, straightening her hair a little. "Robert, I really don't know what to make of this power you have over me."

"Perhaps I'm just makin' up for lost time. One hundred and thirty years is a long time, you know."

"Maybe we're both making up for lost time."

"Surely you have had suitors of late."

"Surely I have not." She burst out laughing. "Seems like every man my age is either married or gay."

"Excuse me for my ignorance, but what has a sense of humor to do with the subject?"

"Oh, well, uh, 'gay' is a modern term for a homo..." She fidgeted with her hair. "A man who prefers other men instead of women."

"Surely there are few of those."

"Don't I wish. Of course, there are women who prefer other women, too. I don't have a problem with either one, but I just don't understand it. I accept it. Actually, gay men make great friends to women sometimes. We can't all be alike. The world would be pretty dull if we were. Suppose all men were as awesome as you. We plain-Janes wouldn't have a chance."

"Awesome?" He puzzled.

"Drop-dead gorgeous."

"Gorgeous?"

"Handsome," she sputtered.

"That's silly. You're not a 'plain-Jane'. You're a lovely, vital woman."

"Uh-huh, notice you didn't say 'beautiful.'"

"If I had, you would have argued with me, like you did before. I *am* beginning to know you."

"Probably, but it's still nice to hear." She gave a crooked smile. "I'm the type woman who is extolled by such praise as 'she's got a wonderful sense of humor,' or 'she's got a great personality.'"

"And what's wrong with that?"

"Nothing, if you're describing a faithful dog, or if that's all the attributes you have... Oh, can we change the subject? I don't want to hear lies anyway. Being with you makes me feel pretty, and that's head and shoulders above what I've felt for the last ten, no, twenty years. I'm not complaining."

"Are we back to you feelin' like you were 'the handiest device,' I believe you said?"

"If the shoe fits."

Angrily he grabbed her shoulders. "Virginia, I've heard all the nonsense I intend to from you. You're beautiful, desirable, and I love being with you. I love the fact that it was you who rescued me." His voice dropped to a whisper, "I...I love you."

"You don't have to say that, in fact, I think I wish you hadn't."

He looked at her questioningly.

"I mean, how will I give you up when it's time for 'Scotty' to 'beam you up?' I mean, when you disappear, or find a way back to your men, or whatever?" Her voice became small and feeble, the words sticking in her throat.

"How do you know I will?"

"I've already told you. I never get what I want out of life. If I get to taste it, I don't get to keep it."

"Virginia, I know we haven't known each other long, but I know I do love you. It's different from the love I had for Beth. This is a kind of sharing love, not just a giving love. I think this is better. We seem more on equal footing."

"Shhh." She put her fingers to his lips. "Robert, I think it's better if you show me. Actions speak louder than words…" She gave him an aggressive kiss and ran her hand down his chest to the front of his jeans. "Seems I have your 'partner's' attention."

He ran one hand across her silk blouse. "Appears I have the interest of two friends of mine, as well." His voice was low and throaty as he played across her breasts and rubbed her erect nipples with his thumbs. He spread his large fingers wide to grasp the volume of each breast.

Ginny unbuttoned Robert's flannel shirt. "We have to get you some more clothes. At least another shirt and some more underwear, and a pair of shoes. Those boots take too long to get out of."

Robert was scrambling off the bed, pulling at one of his high boots with one hand and fumbling with the zipper of his jeans with the other. This time he threw off his T-shirt and felt no fabric sticking to his back as he did. It was healing quickly with all Ginny's attention.

Watching in amusement Ginny was just sitting on the bed. She loved Robert's anxious enthusiasm, but she made no move to disrobe. When at last he stood there totally naked in front of her, she realized she was still fully clothed.

"Have I been too presumptuous? Are you…? Don't you…?"

Ginny crawled to the foot of the bed and, her arms open for him to come to her, she raised herself up on her knees. "I am, and I do, but I want to enjoy every moment. I want nothing rushed." She put her head against his bare chest and dropped her arms to encircle his waist where she knew there were no whip marks.

Robert took her chin in his hand, lifted her face and, gently, but soundly, planted a warm kiss upon her lips. Ginny ran her tongue along his bottom lip, then his top lip. Then she grasped his bottom lip between her teeth. As she played there upon his lips, Robert began to unbutton her silk shirt. All the while his "partner" was poking at Ginny's abdomen and making her giggle.

As he removed her shirt, Robert kissed each shoulder just below her throat. Then he dropped each strap of her bra and kissed the lines they made on her shoulders. He reached around her to release the hooks of her "harness" as she pressed her lips to his chest, planted small kisses, let her tongue play in the thick, curly hair, and kissed the tiny, hard crests of his nipples, to which he gave a shiver of delight.

The "harness" released, Ginny let her breasts graze lightly across his middle as she continued to kiss him and moved her lips to the heavy scar on his shoulder--the bullet wound he had received at Manassas. Stealing herself from the urge to throw her arms about his back and chance causing injury where there was healing, she ran her hands up and down his muscled arms.

Robert fumbled with the snap of her jeans and the zipper. Then, as he peeled them from her, he laid her down on the bed and leaned over her. He ran his hands up her thighs from her knees, then to her waist where he grabbed the cotton panties and slipped them down easily. Then he climbed upon the bed and suspended himself over her--his "partner" landing its tip in her navel.

"He's not very bright, seems he lost his way," Robert whispered and Ginny smiled. Then she planted her hands firmly on his buttocks and pulled him down upon her. His full length sprawled over her body. "I'll crush you."

"No you won't. I want to feel every inch of my skin covered by yours." She kneaded the muscles in his buttocks as she gritted her teeth. "It's so hard to remember not to throw my arms around your back."

"It will be well enough soon, but I rather prefer where your hands are right now. It makes me feel lecherous and lusty. I love to feel your hands on my body. It sounds wicked to say such things, but you've been so open with me. It gives me courage to say what I feel."

"That's as it should be, Robert. Please say whatever you can put in words. It isn't wicked. It's healthy."

"I certainly won't argue, for you have improved my health immensely, Madam." He looked very roguish as he spoke with one eyebrow raised and a lop-sided smile.

"You are a handsome devil." Ginny took his face between her hands and pulled him down to kiss him. As he lingered there, she ran her hands gently down his sides and felt the tip of one lash mark as she went. Her hands came to rest on his hips, her fingers digging playfully into his bottom. "I think your 'partner' is looking for a little bayonet practice," she whispered and moved her hands to guide him between her thighs where he settled into her moist center.

Robert's eyes closed and he held his breath. "I should like to stay here, like this, forever."

"You wouldn't get an argument from me," Ginny whispered as she nibbled his earlobe.

"I've never known love-making to feel this good."

"Oh, it's just that you've been away from it for a hundred and thirty years."

"You may have a point."

"Not me. That's your *partner*."

~ * ~

"Come on, get up, lazy. Just because you're a hundred and seventy-six years old, doesn't mean you get to lounge around all morning."

"I wasn't aware I was loungin' and until moments ago, I wasn't exactly doin' whatever it is I'm doing, alone."

Ginny threw Robert's underwear to him. She was already dressed. "We have places to go and people to see."

"What about the books?"

"The books will be here when we get back. I don't want anymore of your bulling-around. We're going to find a numismatist, and get those coins appraised. Then, if I can afford them, I'll pay you the difference between them and these." She held a few receipts up.

"It isn't necessary that you pay me anything, but I seriously doubt the coins could be worth more than you've spent. I saw a price tag on my shirt. Who ever heard of a ready-made shirt costing *twenty-five* dollars? That's highway robbery."

"Hey, I got off easy for that. I expected to pay much more here in old town."

"More! Lord-in-heaven. I could outfit a soldier for that."

"Not today, you couldn't."

"Well, I expect you're right. I remember the prices from the menu this morning. When first I saw the prices yesterday, I thought it was due to the food shortage of the war. It's very difficult remembering it's not eighteen sixty-two. We were camped closer to the enemy, an advanced unit, but on this side of the river. The bulk of Jackson's command was at Guiney's Station. Burnside was mustering his forces on the other side, readying for an assault of Fredericksburg."

"What was the last day you remember, Robert?"

"I can't exactly say how many days I was in Federal custody. The night I got the note was December 9. It was a Tuesday. I know I was in Perry's hands for at least two or three days, but he left suddenly and I was there in that small stone room. I don't know how long. I was unconscious for some period of time, but suddenly the door was thrown open. The light nearly blinded me. I lay there for some time tryin' to get my wits about me, tryin' to muster the strength, and the courage to go outside. I had smelled so much smoke and heard so many horses and cannon fire--I didn't know what to expect.

"I certainly didn't find what I expected. I was sure all the buildings nearby had burned, yet here a huge old house was standin'. Though in somewhat ill-repair, it was, none-the-less standin' there, and it appeared someone had been workin' on it. It was very early mornin', no one seemed to be about the place. I began to walk, or more nearly stagger, down a road.

"The next thing I'm sure of was seein' the camp at the river. And the bridge, where I didn't expect it, and you on the other side."

"You looked so poor and dirty. I had no idea all this..." She eyed him as he dressed. "Could be under that filthy, ragged uniform."

"Virginia, about my uniform. You said it was here?"

"Yes." She opened the wardrobe door. "I had it cleaned as best they could. I'm afraid it's in really bad condition."

"I don't care about the uniform. My cape, is my cape there?" His voice was hushed.

"Yes, it actually fared better than the rest of the uniform."

Robert sighed with relief.

Ginny was curious. "What's so special about the cape?"

"Bethy made it for me, when I graduated West Point. It's Union blue on one side and brown on the other. She made it so I could wear it with my army uniform on the blue side, and with civilian clothes on the brown. I wear it on the brown side with my Confederate uniform. I had my orderly take the 'US' button off the blue side, so I'd never make the mistake of pullin' it on in the dark with the Federal color out."

Robert took the hanger from Ginny and gently removed the cleaner's plastic.

"It is my cape. It is in one piece." He held it tightly to his chest and, hunched over the cape, stroking it, he sat down on the bed.

"If she were not already dead, it would have killed Beth to know that this very cape could have been my undoin'. Perry was goin' to sew one of his buttons on the blue side. He plucked my 'CSA' button from the brown side and ground it into the dirt floor of the little buildin' he threw me into. Said, after he finished with me, he'd turn me in as a spy to be shot.

"I guess the troops moved out too fast for that. I tried the door. Though I was weak, I know it was locked from the outside. I hadn't the strength to break through. I thought if I rested, perhaps..."

"Did Joshua Perry have you whipped?"

"Have me whipped? No, he reserved that honor for himself alone. Asked me how I would like bein' treated like one of our slaves. It mattered not to him that I did not hold any slaves, nor had I ever done so. We were too poor. He had my tunic and shirt removed, tied me to a tree far from camp and gave me twenty lashes with his whip. He is, or was, an expert with a whip. It gave him more pleasure than I have seen on any man's face.

"I shiver to think what would have become of Beth if her parents had succeeded in coercing her into marrying him, or if he had succeeded in forcin' himself upon her to make her marry him.

"He had a terrible scar on his chin, which hurt his pride immeasurably because it disfigured a cleft of which he was proud. Beth gave him that scar with a letter opener when he ripped away her gown in her mother's own drawin' room. Since he was unable to charm her into submission, he thought he'd just take her. Then she'd have to marry him. He never forgave her for that night. He had always worn only a mustache and sported a bare chin. After that, he took to a full beard and combed it so as to cover up the scar.

"Strange what things I remember clearly, while others seem blurred."

Robert suddenly began to quiver as if very cold. He drew his arms about himself and shivered.

"Robert, I've forgotten your antibiotic this morning." She got one pill out hurriedly and grabbing a glass of water, thrust them toward him. Robert took them, downed the pill, but could not stop shivering as, caressing the cape, he sat there on the bed.

Ginny knelt on the floor in front of him and pulled his head down to her shoulder, both of her hands in this thick hair, she held him tightly. "We'll figure this out, Robert," she whispered. "You have my promise."

Sixteen

Well past lunchtime by the time they left the inn, Ginny decided it would be fun to introduce Robert to "fast food." After all, he'd only eaten at the inn and, as far as dining was concerned, that was very much the same as he would have remembered inns of his day.

Ginny found a coin dealer in the telephone book and had a general idea of its location, but first she headed out of old town toward a McDonald's. Robert's eyes widened as they pulled up and parked. When he opened his own car door, having mastered the inside handle, he lifted his head and sniffed. The smile on his face let Ginny know he was pleased with the smell.

Ginny took his hand and led him inside. She pulled Robert up to the counter. It would be useless to ask him what he wanted so she ordered for both of them. "I'll have a chef's salad with Italian dressing and a diet coke. He's having a 'Big Mac attack'." She chuckled to herself. "Large fries and milk, no, make that a milk shake." She turned to Robert. "Do you like vanilla, chocolate, or strawberry."

"Vanilla, chocolate or strawberry what?"

"Anything."

Robert shrugged.

"Give him chocolate, and an apple pie."

"I can't eat a whole apple pie." Robert whispered in her ear.

"Trust me. You can eat this one."

Ginny picked up the tray and headed toward the condiments where she picked up napkins, and straws. Robert just followed curiously.

This was the second time he saw food wrapped in paper, but this was hot food, the other a cold sandwich. They settled at a table and Ginny set the food out. Robert simply stared at everything until Ginny grabbed a French fry and stuck it in his mouth.

He jumped as he closed his lips over it. "It's hot."

"No, really? That's the idea, dear."

"But how did they cook this so quickly?"

"It's what's known as 'fast food.' No wait, no hassle, lots of calories."

"Calories?"

"Never mind. Just eat."

Enjoying his adventurous meal, Robert picked up the cup and, following Ginny's lead, inserted a straw and sipped.

"It's melted ice cream!" he shouted with delight.

All eyes in the room turned to him. Ginny rolled her eyes and quietly offered, "He's been away a long time."

Most of the other customers turned back to their own meals. A few were obviously discussing the happening.

"Why aren't you eating what I am?"

"You need the fat. I don't."

Robert made no comment, but continued eating. He finished the milk shake long before the rest of the meal, so Ginny got up and bought him another.

"This is excellent. Quite unique."

"Well, now to set your mind at ease, we'll get these coins appraised."

More comfortable with the automobile, Robert rushed in front of Ginny to open her door, but the handle did not respond.

"It's locked." Ginny whispered and inserted the key.

~ * ~

It was a short drive to the coin dealer, but Robert's neck snapped from one direction to the other as he tried to take in all the sights, and he jumped at each car passing in the opposite direction.

"These speeds are so dangerous!"

"Robert, we haven't gotten over thirty-five miles an hour."

"Thirty-five? How fast can this machine travel?"

"Well, the maximum speed limit out on 95 is sixty-five miles an hour, I've gotten as high as seventy-five, when passing a truck, but I'm sure my car can go faster. When I was a kid, some of the turnpikes had speed limits of eighty."

"Doesn't it frighten you?" Robert choked, shaking his head.

"Sometimes. Especially in the snow, though it's not my driving that worries me so much as all the other drivers out there who aren't used to snow. The Orientals, Middle-Easterners, the Indians…"

"Indians! Indians drive these machines?"

"Everyone drives these machines, but I'm probably not talking about the same kind of Indians you are. I mean real Indians, from India, not Native Americans."

Robert didn't respond. Ginny imagined he had a picture in his mind of Indians in war-paint and feathers behind the wheels of cars. She smiled secretly, not wanting to embarrass him.

~ * ~

The coin dealer was in a small shopping center, one of the older ones in Fredericksburg, and outside of the historic district.

When the bell over the door rang, a mousy man with thick glasses came to the counter. "May I help you?"

"Yes, we'd like to have an appraisal of some coins." Ginny spread the coins on the glass counter.

"Are these originals?"

"Yes, they've been in the family for years."

"They're in remarkably good condition." He studied them through a jeweler's glass, then a magnifying glass. "Say they've been in the family for years? Where have they been kept?"

Robert started to reply, "In my poc--"

"In a safe. Yes, a family safe," Ginny offered. "His great-great-great grandfather carried them during the Civil War."

"Do you have any proof these belong to you?"

Robert was indignant. "You have my word, sir."

"We didn't dig up his grandfather and ask for a certificate." Ginny's disgust with the little man sounded.

"Give you *two hundred* dollars for the lot.

Robert was aghast. Virginia's jaw set as she inhaled deeply, her eyes narrowing.

"I never said we were interested in selling them. I *said* we wanted an appraisal. Besides, I know they're worth more than two hundred dollars. "Not t' me."

"Listen you little weasel. I asked for an appraisal. Are you qualified to do that, or should we go somewhere else?" She leaned purposefully over the counter and stared nose-to-nose with the clerk.

"All right, all right. I thought you just wanted some quick bucks. Over there on the wall's my certification. But an appraisal will cost ya. My time is valuable."

"How much?" Virginia gritted her teeth.

"Five percent of the value. Take me 'bout fifteen minutes, if I don't get any interruptions."

"Fine! We'll wait! And you'll do your inspections and comparisons and any referencing you need right out here in *plain sight*. Virginia demanded.

"Yes, ma'am." He must have decided Ginny meant business.

"I'll get my books. They're in the back."

"The coins will stay *here* with *us* while you do."

"Yes ma'am."

The little man disappeared behind a curtained doorway.

"Virginia, do you really think you had to be so, so harsh with the little fellow?"

"He's a shyster, Robert. I wouldn't put it past him to take the coins in the back and switch them. No, these coins stay right here, and I intend to watch his hands every moment."

"I shall as well."

The man returned with several books. Ginny took a position to his left, and Robert stationed himself on the right. Together they watched like hawks as the man leafed through first one book, then another, jotting down notes.

"Ya want this in writin'?"

Ginny forced a smile. "Yes, please."

"Costs an extra two dollars."

"Do it," Ginny ordered.

The man put some figures on an appraisal sheet. "Figure them to be worth about six hundred and forty dollars to a collector."

Ginny smiled at Robert's astonishment. "See, I told you." She reached for the paper.

"That'll be thirty-one dollars for the work, and two more for the report. Thirty-three dollars. Then ya get the paper."

Ginny reached into her purse and pulled out a twenty, a ten and three ones. "Here." She thrust them at the man, and collected the coins off the counter as Robert took the appraisal sheet and turned toward the door.

"Wait!" Ginny shouted at the coin dealer. "There's only seven coins here. We gave you eight!"

The man gave her his most surprised look, until he saw rage in Robert's eyes as he turned back.

"Well, now, what could have happened?"

Ginny moved every book off the counter. Nothing. Then she flipped the pages of each, holding them upside-down. Surely enough, one coin went flying out of a book.

"Now how do you suppose that happened?" The dealer feigned innocence.

"We'll be sure and make a recommendation to our friends-- to stay away from you, that is." Robert fired his words proudly.

~ * ~

"How did you know not to trust that man?" Robert inquired as they got back into the car.

"I'm just suspicious of everyone anymore. Guess I can thank especially my second husband for that."

"You were marvelous." He took her hand and kissed it. "You must add the cost of the appraisal to what you've spent.

Then I want to see that you haven't spent so much you can't recover your money."

"Robert--"

"No, you promised."

"All right, but I'm *not* selling these coins."

"You may do with them as you please. I just don't want to feel I have cost you more than you may be able to recover, should you have need."

"Yes, Robert."

"May we stay out a while longer?"

"If you wish. Is there somewhere you want to go?"

"This may sound irrational, I know it is not my time, I understand that it is 1993, but, well, I'd feel better if I could see…" He stumbled. "I need to see some evidence of the passage of time. I suppose that sounds ludicrous. I just need some means of seeing that indeed time did pass from 1862 to 1993, that God didn't just jump from that terrible war to… Can you possibly understand that?"

"I think so. But I can't exactly think what single place we could go…"

"A cemetery, perhaps?" Robert offered.

"I only know the one next to the battlefield. Would you feel up to that?"

"If you never leave my side." He took her hand between his.

"Only trouble is, I don't know if it's just Civil War soldiers buried there."

~ * ~

In the car, Ginny started in the direction of the cemetery near the battlefield's visitor center. They were both silent as she drove. After a couple of turns, Ginny spied a small, old church with a graveyard of its own. "Maybe if we stop here." She pulled over.

Robert got out of the car and cautiously approached the closest grave. "Born 1907, Died 1973," he read quietly. He walked to a faded marker. "Born 1824, Died 1901." Then he darted about the small cemetery reading all the dates aloud. He walked back to the place where Ginny stood, took her hand and held it to his cheek. Then, with a great sigh, he headed for the car.

"Still want to see the battlefield cemetery," he said quietly. "All right?"

Ginny nodded and got back behind the wheel of the car.

~ * ~

Ginny parked close to the steeply terraced cemetery and began the climb. It had levels of graves, each several feet above the one below it. There were steps in the center leading up from one terrace to the next. At first, Robert contented himself reading only those stones on either side of the stairway path. Suddenly, he pulled Ginny along one row, then another. She realized he was seeking any familiar names.

She tugged with great resistance against him. "Robert, I don't think this is such a good idea." She tugged again, but he'd recovered much strength, and would not be dissuaded.

"Sweet Jesus!" He fell to his knees at one grave and traced the name and date with his finger.

"Robert," Ginny whispered. "Robert, who is it?"

He simply shook his head. Then he closed his eyes, threw his head back and tried to stifle the cry that would not be completely suppressed.

"I did this. I caused this."

"Robert, please tell me." Ginny knelt next to him, placing her arm about his shoulder.

"This is, was, my corporal. The one I entrusted with the note to my commandin' officer telling him where I was going. Perry must have had him killed, too. See the date, 'December 9, 1862.' That's why Perry was so sure they wouldn't look for me. He killed Matthew and took my note. Oh, Matthew, *I'm so sorry.*" Robert doubled over in tears.

"If the general never got my note…he must, they must think me a *deserter. God Almighty."* He rose abruptly from the grave and grabbed Ginny's hand propelling them both down the steep hill. "The books, Virginia!"

As Robert dragged her along, Ginny stumbled and came down hard on her hands and knees.

"Oh, Ginny, I'm so sorry." Robert's hurried apology barely gave her time to climb back to her feet as he raced again toward the car and dragged her after him.

"Hurry!" He commanded as she started the car. "Back to the inn. I *must know.*"

"Robert!" Ginny turned off the motor.

"Virginia, we must hurry."

"Robert! Listen to me. Whether we hurry or not will not change anything in those books."

"But…"

"Shut up and listen to me!"

Robert gave her an indignant look, but did not speak.

"Robert, I've looked. I'm sure there's more than what's in those three books. But I'll be perfectly honest with you, what I gleaned from the books was, well, disturbing. Another colonel, I don't remember his name, but that isn't important--he speculated you had perhaps deserted upon finding yourself in opposition to your son's Union division."

"Barrin'ton!"

"Yes, that was it, Barrington."

"He disliked me. Resented the fact I was invited to dine with Lee whenever we were in the same vicinity." Robert's words were calm--much calmer than Ginny expected. "What else?"

"Well, the report went on to say that General Jackson felt it possible you were captured and ordered you listed 'missing' for the time being."

"That must have been before they found poor Matthew. What else?"

"I couldn't find anything else. I only had a little time to look, when you were sleeping. We can get to the bottom of this, Robert. I have all sorts of books at home."

Robert's eyes were blank, his face expressionless. He did not utter another word as they drove back to the inn.

Seventeen

At the front desk Ginny ordered a light supper to be sent to her room. This would be a long evening.

She showed Robert the few pieces of information she unearthed. Then as he remembered dates and places, he found a couple of other familiar references, some were accurate, some were not. They were unable to find any new passages after the last one Ginny related to him.

"How will we find out more, Ginny? I must know if I was labeled a traitor for all time."

"Robert, we'll find out, but, I think the only way for me to know where else to look is for you to tell me everything you remember."

For a moment, Robert sat in silence collecting his thoughts.

"Start where you left off with Captain Perry when we spoke before."

His gaze drifted, his face blank as if he remembered.

~ * ~

Perry was talking as his men tied Robert to a tree.

"I'm going to enjoy inflicting pain on you, Carter. I've been waiting so long. You and that bitch, Elizabeth, deserved each other. I never really wanted her, but I wanted her family

186

connections. I wanted to be governor of Pennsylvania, maybe even President, someday. They could have bought that for me.

"Now my only path is to be a hero in the war, without risking my neck, of course. What use would it be to become a dead hero? So…" He raised the whip and cracked it across Robert's back and drew blood on the first strike.

"How long this takes, Colonel, is completely up to you." Another crack. "You can tell me exactly where Jackson is camped and how many men he has in his command." A third crack. "Just feel free to speak up whenever you are so moved." A fourth.

"I wouldn't tell you anything, even if I knew." It was difficult for Robert to speak already. He wondered how he would hold out, but he knew he had to.

"You're being extremely foolish, 'Robin.' I know you are privileged among Confederate officers." Crack! "I've followed your career with much interest over the years." Crack! "I was afraid when the war actually broke out you might have sense enough to stay in our army." Crack! "Then I wouldn't be able to use your son to get to you." Crack!

Robert was near unconsciousness now, hanging on the tree.

"You see, 'Robin,' you don't have the stamina of your average slave." Crack! "They can stand up under much worse than this." Crack! Perry turned to a comrade. "Throw some water on him."

It was done, and Robert was once again fully conscious of his surroundings.

"Welcome back, Colonel. Are you ready to tell me Jackson's strength and location, now?"

Robert made no reply.

Perry heaved a sigh as if he didn't want to continue the beating, but even in his depleted state, Robert knew he would not stop until he got what he wanted, whether it was the information he sought or Robert's death.

Crack!

Of course, Robert did not give out any information, much to Perry's chagrin.

"Cut him down! Bring him back to camp." Perry stormed off. "I'll break that son-of-a-bitch, if it's the last thing I do."

A young soldier saluted. "Captain, shall I put something on his back?"

"Not unless it's salt! And don't give him back his shirt. Let him get good and cold. Maybe he'll talk then. No food or water, understand?"

The young man saluted smartly, then hung his head as he turned to go.

Robert was laid on a single wool blanket on the cold ground, far from the campfire, his hands and feet bound. He was given no food or water. Even in the cold, his torn back against the harsh wool of a dirty blanket, Robert didn't talk.

"Father," a faint whisper came out of the dark. "Father." A hand slipped a cup of hot coffee next to him, but Robert's hands were tied, and he didn't have the strength to struggle to sit up.

Harry looked around, and seeing no one watching, he lifted his father to a sitting position and poured the coffee into him. "I'm sorry, Father, I didn't know this would happen. He's *insane.* All my life he's told me how he loved my mother, how you let her die... I'm not pretending I feel like we're family, but I wouldn't have wished this on Jeff Davis himself.

"I don't know what to do. If I try to turn you loose, he'll have me shot, without even blinking. If I report him to the colonel--"

"No Harry, he'll manage to get back at you and ruin your career at the very least. I'll be all right. You stay out of this.

Keep as far away from Perry as possible. He'll bring you down to his level."

"But I can't just--"

"Harry, you might not feel like I'm your father, but I outrank you. I outranked you before I left the Union Army. I'm orderin' you to *stay away*. Now get out of here before Perry catches you. Take the cup with you, and watch your back. Get a transfer as soon as you can."

"Father, they got your--"

"What's goin' on over here?" A voice boomed in the darkness, one of Perry's henchmen.

Robert laid back down on the blanket as Harry scurried off.

"S'pose to bring ya to the captain." The rough voice belonged to a huge, rather witless private who did whatever Perry told him to. He yanked Robert up by one arm and pushed him forward.

Robert slumped as he stumbled toward the firelight.

"Well, Colonel, have you thought better of your refusal to give me the information I seek? No? Well, maybe after you spend the entire night out here, you'll change your mind. Throw him back over there, without the blanket!"

The hulk of a private did as he was ordered, but, returned to the major, stood at attention and said, "Sir, what if the colonel--?"

"That had best be the closest you ever come to questioning me, Albertson!" Perry whipped out a knife and held it to the private's throat. There was no need for Perry to say more. Albertson froze, then saluted as Perry relaxed the knife.

~ * ~

Somehow Robert managed to keep from freezing to death during the night, but the bleeding lashes, and the cold left him extremely weak. He would still not tell Perry anything, even false information to throw them off. He would not speak. Perhaps he couldn't speak.

"Well, Carter, since you won't talk, and I'm running out of time, my orders to move closer to Burnside have come through, I'll just find a way to turn you over as a spy. I'll let someone else have the pleasure of shooting you." He gave a military turn and, shouting orders to his men, walked away.

"Put his shirt and tunic back on him. I'll lead him into camp."

"We got a extra horse, sir," one man offered.

"I didn't call for a horse! He will *walk.* Perry forced the words through clenched teeth, his eyes narrowed in rage.

Robert could tell they were nearing a major camp as he heard more sounds. He tried to keep his eyes open to gather information, in case he somehow escaped, but he could hardly stand, much less keep his attentions focused.

"Throw him in that outbuilding until I get everything set up to turn him in." Perry pointed to a small building near Burnside's headquarters.

Robert was thrust inside.

~ * ~

In a few hours Perry returned. "Think I'm going to turn you over directly to Burnside." He entered with Robert's cape thrown over his arm. Then he pulled the CSA button off the brown side and ground it into the dirt floor of the outbuilding. "See this, Carter?" He held up a US button. "It goes right here where it used be." He held it at the neck of the cape, on the blue side. Then he took his own US hat pin off and put it on Robert's beige slouch hat.

"It would be easy to save yourself from being shot. Being a prisoner of war is better than death. Just give me some information to pass on that will get me noticed enough to get a promotion."

Suddenly, a roar overtook the camp. Orders rang out to fall in. They were marching on Fredericksburg.

"I'll deal with you later." Perry turned to the hulk he previously threatened who was standing in the open doorway. "Make sure that door is secure and leave him in there to rot a while." Perry pushed the man out of his way as he left. He turned back and threw the cape through the door. "Don't think you're free of me yet, Carter." And he stormed off.

~ * ~

Robert's gaze moved back to Virginia's face. "I heard guns, cannon, horses, for two or three days, I'm not sure. The sounds faded away from time to time. There was no light in the stone room, except a sliver from the crack in the roof. Then I heard a great deal of activity, and smelled smoke, not the smoke of guns being discharged, but fires, big fires, like burnin' buildin's.

"Then, sometime, as I lay, my mind muddled, sure I was dying, the door burst open. I caught a glimpse of a face." He squinted, his jaw clenched as he tried to recapture the picture in his mind, his hands on either side of his head, he willed his brain to remember. "It looked...it looked like Harry. But I couldn't be sure. He said nothing. Harry would have said something, wouldn't he?"

Robert looked toward Ginny with soulful, expectant eyes and a pleading expression, as if she could answer his question. Not knowing how to answer, Ginny got up from her chair opposite him, knelt in front of him and simply put her arms around him to hold him tightly. With her cheek next to his, Robert drew from her strength.

"Will you help me clear my name?" he whispered.

"Of course. I can't see myself in love with an accused traitor."

"Do you love me, Virginia?"

"More than I ever wanted to let myself love. More than I thought I was capable of loving. I love you enough to help you, even if it means losing you."

Robert took her face between his huge hands and studied every feature intensely.

"What are you doing?"

"You said it once yourself. I don't want to forget anything about you. I want to be able to see your face every time I close my eyes, when…" His voice dropped off.

"When you're gone," she whispered the inevitable end of his thought.

"I don't know how or if I can get back to my time, but even if I do, what proof would I have of my innocence? I have nothing to show I was lured away falsely, and captured. Besides, I'm an officer, I shouldn't have been so easily fooled," he whispered into Virginia's ear as they continued to cling to each other.

"The scars on your back should be enough proof! Oh, my God!" She pulled back. "Robert, I'm so sorry, I must have been causing you a great deal of pain, my arms wrapped around your body like that."

Robert smiled. "I couldn't feel any pain with your arms about me. If I had you waitin' for me, I would have never been fool enough to get myself captured in the first place. I didn't use my head sometimes."

"If you hadn't been captured, I would never have found you. We would have lived in different centuries, never even knowing each other existed."

Robert kissed her tenderly. "I guess I should thank old Perry, if I ever catch up with him."

"That's it! Let's see what we can find out about what became of Perry and what became of your son. Maybe that will help us find a way to prove your innocence."

Robert kissed her again. "May I selfishly ask if that can wait a while? My 'partner' seems to be getting restless. He nor I can seem to get enough of you." He rose from the chair, drawing Virginia to her feet with him, then he picked her up.

"Robert, you'll *break* your *back.*"

"Shhh."

~ * ~

Robert deposited her gently on the bed, then sat next to her and leaned over her to kiss her again. His lips were tender and so warm. Ginny couldn't remember ever enjoying someone's kiss nearly as much. His mouth tasted sweet, his tongue played sensuously upon her lips and just inside her mouth. Merely kissing Robert was every bit as sensuous as the most erotic love-making she ever had--before Robert, that is. With Robert, it was simply an invitation to more ecstasy than she could imagine possible.

She enjoyed him to the fullest and as much as he seemed to enjoy her. Everything about their love-making satisfied. She was able to fathom the magnitude of his delight, and believe he shared it equally. Yet he seemed just as intent on satisfying her as himself, in turn, heightening his own enjoyment. Never had she felt such ultimate passion.

Robert's hands were so gentle, but strong. Sometimes Ginny thought they had minds of their own, for they were so purposeful as they stroked and caressed. His fingers started on her cheeks, then slid down to her throat, her shoulders, then back to her throat to unbutton her shirt. Then his lips followed down her throat to the top of her "harness", while his hand covered each breast through the cotton and lace of her bra.

Ginny was busily unbuttoning Robert's shirt, letting her fingertips ruffle through the curly hair on his chest. As she raised herself up to kiss his chest, he slipped his hands behind her to unfasten her "harness". Slowly, tenderly they explored each other as if it were the first time. Robert seemed to memorize every curve, and Ginny in turn memorized every muscle, as if they could hold off the inevitable.

Just as he did, she knew in her heart, that they were not slated to be together for long and that somehow Robert would return to his time, or at least disappear from Ginny's. Even in the urgency to fulfill him, and him, her, as often as possible, never would she rush, for the sensations of touching, teasing, thrilling him seemed as important to his enjoyment as any climax.

No one ever touched Virginia's heart so completely by touching her body. With his thoughtful, tender, lingering loving, Robert was every woman's dream-come-true. How wonderful, indeed, to find a man so intent on artful loving, yet radiating more masculinity than any two modern men she'd encountered. How refreshing to leave the macho image to the present, and enjoy this beautiful brush with the past.

She'd never find another lover to compare with Robert. That was a sweet sadness, for she didn't see how she could ever want anyone else to touch her again. Robert was the ultimate lover, and Virginia was just the woman to appreciate it after her unhappy past.

Eighteen

After a couple of hours sleep, Virginia lay, in the darkness, and thought about everything Robert told her. She put all the pieces of the puzzle together. The way to help him get back might be to put everything back as nearly as it had been. He didn't have to be dirty and bleeding, but he had to be in his uniform, with all his possessions, and back at the outbuilding. Perhaps then he would be transported.

What could she do; however, to make sure he had some proof of his capture? The key must be in something he could bring back to camp with him. Something that would show where he'd been or why he'd been gone. The Note! The note written to him to draw him away from his own forces. Perhaps she could create such a note, but how would she get Robert to take it back? He was so full of honor, that he could hardly be expected to present a forgery as the real thing.

She'd worry about that when she figured out how to have such a note produced. She settled back on Robert's shoulder and drifted off to sleep. She at least had some plan to help him, though it would break her heart to have him leave her. She tried to remember that old adage about loving someone and setting them free, if they return... Well, anyway, she loved him, and she knew she must set him free, or at least try to. If her plan didn't work, she couldn't be blamed. If it did work, then she would have given him back his life and his pride.

~ * ~

No longer on Robert's shoulder, Virginia awoke. She turned to his pillow in a panic. He wasn't there. Her immediate thought was that he had been snatched back to his own time during the night. She wanted to scream in grief, but she couldn't breathe. Then she heard water running, and noticed the bathroom door was closed. Her breath restored, she ran to the door and threw it open. There Robert stood at the mirror, shaving.

"Good mornin'." He said chipperly. "You know I'm beginnin' to master this strange razor, but how on earth do you sharpen it?"

Virginia laughed. "You don't, you throw it away." She was nearly hysterical with relief at finding him.

"But the metal is valuable. It shouldn't be thrown away. Surely it could be reused. And this other material, whatever it is, must have some value."

"*Great*, now you're an *environmentalist*."

Robert looked at her questioningly.

"Mind if I watch you shave?"

"Not if it pleases you."

"The last time I watched someone shave, it was my father."

"You loved him very much, didn't you?"

"Yes, I guess that's why I didn't do so well picking husbands. No one quite measured up--until now. That's his robe you're wearing. I've saved it all these years. Never let my husband wear it."

"Which husband?"

"The second. My father died after my first divorce."

Robert touched her cheek as a sign of sympathy or understanding. Then he changed the solemnity of the atmosphere.

"I saved m' shower 'til last. Thought you should scrub my back with that special soap again." He winked.

Virginia smiled and snapped a towel at him. "You're a devil or a leprechaun, I don't know which," she said with a brogue.

"I must be a devil for I've never heard of a leprechaun having a 'partner' quite like mine." Robert's brogue wasn't quite as convincing, but it was amusing.

~ * ~

"Robert," Virginia began as they enjoyed breakfast in the dining room, "do you remember what the note the Union messenger brought you said? I mean, exactly?"

"I shall never forget it. It said:

Colonel Robert Carter, Virginia 5th,
Sir,
I regret to inform you that your son, Lt. R. Harrell Carter, is gravely ill in camp hospital. He is not expected to survive the night. Please come. In the company of the bearer of this note, you will be given safe passage by all Federal forces.
Respectfully,
Col. John G. Howard

"Strange, that message is burned into my brain, but others memories are so unclear."

Unknown to Robert, Virginia was writing every word he told her on a piece of paper under the table, all the while angry at herself that she had never done well in shorthand.

~ * ~

"We still haven't gotten you another shirt. We'll have people wondering about you showing up in the same shirt every day. I think I'll run out after breakfast and buy one."

"Virginia," Robert took her hand, "I don't see the point in spendin' money on more clothes until we see if I can find my way back here."

Her eyes cast downward Virginia took a deep breath. "You're right, of course." Then she raised her chin. "Well, I have to get you some kind of a shirt to go with your uniform. And I have to see what I can do to restore your uniform a little. I can't let a colonel return to his command looking like a ragamuffin, can I?" Her voice cracked with emotion and tears waited to fall from her eyes.

Robert smiled. "We can go out, as soon as I finish my coffee."

"No, Robert, let me go alone. Just this once. I need to think about things, get used to the idea of…you leaving. Please. I won't be gone long, I promise." Virginia put down her silverware. "Robert, you need a hat. What did yours look like?"

"Just a typical officer's slouch hat. I had it in the Union army, just changed the hat pin. I was wearin' it when I left the outbuilding. I'm certain." He rubbed his chin trying to remember.

"I didn't have a very clear head, but I can almost remember it being knocked off my head just before I got to the bridge, just before I saw you."

Virginia remembered the direction from which she observed his staggering form. She would do a quick search under the nearby trees. Perhaps it was still there.

"I don't like the idea of you goin' about without me."

"Robert, I can take care of *myself*. I've been doing it for years."

"It isn't that. I'm afraid if we're separated...you might be all that's keeping me here. If something happens...I might return without even a proper 'goodbye.' Virginia, what if you could return with me?"

She snickered. "Don't think that hasn't occurred to me. I've thought about it many times. But I have responsibilities here, and to be honest, I wouldn't be very good without my modern conveniences."

She didn't wish to tell him her main reason for not wanting to return with him. She feared he might not make it safely through the rest of the war. It wasn't even half over when he left. If he got back to 1862 and her with him, what would she do if he were killed later? She would wind up in some asylum. No, it wouldn't work. She had to stay, and he had to go, if they could find a way.

~ * ~

In the room Virginia collected Robert's uniform but left the cape with him. The uniform over her arm, she stood in the doorway.

"You have a job while I'm gone."

"Good, I'll need to be busy."

"You have to look through those books and see if you can find any other references to Joshua Perry, or your son, Harry." She pointed. "In my computer bag, there's another book that's a day-by-day account of the war. Try looking in that index as well."

"Virginia, let me go with you."

"No, now we'll make more progress if we each do our own thing. I'll be back before you know it."

"I know it already."

~ * ~

Virginia had noticed a tailoring sign at the dry cleaners. She would stop there and see how much repairing they could do to

Robert's uniform. They should be able to tell her where to find a shirt. She jumped in her car and headed for the cleaners.

"Hi, remember me?" she said as she entered the shop, because the same girl was at the counter.

"Yes. Is something wrong? I told you we did our best to save the uniform."

"Nothing's wrong. I didn't come here to complain. I came to talk to your tailor. I want to see if there are any repairs that can be made to the uniform."

"Pop! Customer wants to talk to you," the young girl called toward the back of the store.

An old man came from the back room. He had stooped shoulders and a gray beard.

"This is my grandfather. He's the tailor."

"May I help you, young lady?"

Virginia smiled her brightest. "Yes, I'd like to leave this uniform with you for a day and see how many repairs you can make to it. It's very important. We need it tomorrow for a ceremony."

"Well, I will certainly see what I can do for it. My granddaughter showed it to me when it came in a few days ago. It is rather old, isn't it?"

"Yes, it's very old."

He smiled. "Well, I'll try my best."

"Thank you, I'm sure your best will be fine." Virginia turned to leave, then spun about. She had remembered to bring the button that had been in Robert's pocket. "Oh, here's a button you'll find missing, somewhere. I hope it's the only one."

"We do all the costumes for the two costume companies in town. Do you want us to put back any other buttons which might be missing? We would have to charge you for the replicas, of course."

"Yes, please, replace anything you can. Thank you."

"You may pick it up tomorrow afternoon."

Virginia smiled and nodded.

"Oh, can you tell me where the costume companies are located?"

"Certainly," the young girl said, and pulled out a piece of paper on which she wrote directions.

"Thank you again, I'll see you tomorrow."

~ * ~

Next Virginia went to the bridge. She found a place to pull her car off and put her flashers on so no one would hit her. She ran down the bank in the direction she had seen Robert approach the bridge.

"If a branch knocked it off..." She looked in all directions for low tree branches. Then some low-hanging branches caught her eye and she ran to take a look. Scrambling about under the trees for about twenty minutes, she spied something, not far away, up toward the road. It was a hat--a light brown, cavalry-type hat--with no insignia, a single gold rope with end tassels about the base. It had to be Robert's hat. She smiled, pleased with herself as she walked back to her car.

~ * ~

Virginia's next stop was the first of the costume companies.

"Mornin', ma'am, may I be of assistance?" An elderly man came at the ring of the door bell.

"Do you sell pieces of clothing for costumes as well as rent them?"

"Well, yes, sometimes. What would ya be lookin' t' buy?"

"I need a officer's white shirt for a Confederate colonel to wear--well, I mean for a gentleman to wear with his Confederate colonel's costume. I want it to look as authentic as possible."

"What size is this colonel? Not that there's a great deal of difference. Most shirts were sorta 'one size fits all' like, ya see."

"Well he's rather tall, about six feet two inches, he's got broad shoulders. His winter jacket is a forty-two long. He has a little room inside, but the length of the arms is fine. Wears a thirty-four inch waist."

The man looked through a box of shirts.

"Just got these back from the laundry. The celebration, ya know."

Virginia nodded.

"Ah! Here's one. This should fit. It ain't new, 'course."

"That's fine. The uniform isn't new either." She smiled at her understatement.

"Well, I can let ya have this one for, say twelve bucks."

"Fine."

"Would ya be needin' a separate collar?"

Virginia closed her eyes to picture the shreds she took off of Robert and threw away.

"Most of 'em didn't wear collars under their tunics, if that's any help."

"I think you're right. I don't think I need a collar. Thank you very much."

"Sure, no trouble 't'all. Would ya be needin' anythin' else to go with this?"

"Could you show me a complete uniform? Then I'd be able to see if anything else is missing?"

"Sure, little lady, just step right over here." He showed her to a rack with more Confederate and Union uniform variations than she knew existed.

"Confederate colonel, ya' say?" He thumbed through the rack.

She nodded.

"Cavalry, infantry, artillery…"

Virginia wrinkled her nose and bit her lip.

"Don't you just have one that sort of takes care of it all?" She looked back and forth between the uniforms. One looked more like Robert's than any other. She held it up.

"Cavalry officer's uniform," the old man told her.

There was one thing common to all of the uniforms which she had not seen on Robert, a belt and buckle.

"This." She pointed. "He needs a belt and buckle."

"Well, now, them there are just for rentin'. Cheap imitations, don't ya know, but over yonder, there's the ones we sell to the serious re-enactors. Buckles are actual copies. I might suggest this one'd be fit fer a colonel." He held one up with "CSA" on it.

Virginia nodded again. It was easier to let the man make suggestions, than to try to pick one out herself.

"Thirty-four, did ya say?"

"Yes."

"Well, anythin' else?"

Virginia looked back at the uniforms again. "No, I think that will do."

She bought them with plastic again, and left on her third quest, a print shop.

~ * ~

One in the old part of town had a sign up saying they also did calligraphy. She stopped there.

When the counter-person finished with the customers before her, Virginia stepped up impatiently. She didn't want to be away from Robert so long.

"Do you have a type of paper which has the look and texture of something that might have been used during the Civil War?"

"Lady, this is Fredericksburg. What do you think?" he barked.

"I think you're very impertinent."

"Sorry, I didn't mean to be, that last customer kind of set my teeth on edge. She picked the color of the ink for her invitations, then changed her mind, twice! Let's start again. We have several kinds of paper which are similar in color and texture to those used during the war." He pulled out some samples to show her.

"What do you want printed, then I can help steer you in the right direction."

"Um, I don't want anything printed, actually, well, not in volume, that is. I want a single piece which I can hire your calligrapher to put a message on in a manner that would look like a nib and ink of the Civil War era."

"Sorry, we deal in volume here, lady."

"Are you so busy you can't sell me one piece of paper and the time of your calligrapher for a short note?"

The man sighed in acquiescence. "No, guess not. Tell me what the note is supposed to be like and we'll chose a paper."

Virginia explained and, after assuring the man she wasn't trying to dupe anyone into believing she had found some nineteenth century treasure, he introduced her to the calligrapher.

"Supposed to be from a gentleman or a lady?" The calligrapher inquired.

"A man, but I wouldn't say a gentleman."

"Educated?"

"It was supposed to be from a colonel. Like the note says."

"It'll take a few minutes," the calligrapher told her.

"Fine, I'll just dart next door to that antique shop, and be right back."

In moments, Virginia was back, holding a small bag. The note was exactly what she wanted. She paid and was on her way back to the inn, and to Robert, she hoped. She didn't like having to be away from him for almost three hours, but she had found his hat, and accomplished what she had set out to do.

Nineteen

Virginia fumbled for the key and dropped it. She picked it up again, hastily putting it to the lock and threw the door open.

"Robert!" she shouted happily, but the room was empty. The winter coat he'd been wearing was thrown on the bed. "Robert!" Panicking she called as she looked in the empty bathroom. "Robert, don't tease me!" She opened the wardrobe. Empty!

"*He's gone*. He found his way back, or the powers that sent him here found him. Noooooo!" she cried. "*I'm not ready*." She dropped everything she was carrying and sank to the floor folding her arms tightly about herself. "Robert..." she cried, doubling over and rocking back and forth. She didn't hear the door open behind her.

"Virginia!" Robert ran to hold her. "What is it?"

"Robert! Robert, you're still here. You *didn't* leave me."

"*Of course not.*" I found a dollar in the pocket of the coat. I simply went to the dinin' room for a cup a coffee, and found I had locked myself out. I was sittin' in the dinin' room watchin' for you. I paid for the coffee and came as soon as I saw you."

"I was so afraid you'd left before I was ready. " She kept running her hands over his face, his arms, his chest.

"Shhh, please don't cry. If I had my way I would never leave you at all, surely you know that."

"I know--no, I don't know. I don't feel like I know *anything*." She couldn't stop crying. The strain of possibly loosing him, of wanting him to clear his name, of knowing he could disappear at any moment, took its toll.

He held her tightly.

"I fear I shall squeeze the very breath from you."

"I almost wish you would," she said with a sob.

"Please, darlin', don't cry so. I'm still here. For all we know I may always be here. I can't bear to see you so unhappy." He took her hands and held them to his face.

"You're icy-cold." He picked her up and with her on his lap sat down in the chair closest to the gas fire.

"I don't know what's wrong with me. I can't stop crying." She kept touching his face and running her fingers through his hair.

"I'll hold you until you stop cryin'."

"Then I may never stop. I want you to hold me forever. I feel safe in your arms. I haven't felt that way since--since my father died." *Except, perhaps with Jonathan.*

Robert kissed her forehead and folded his arms about her more tightly. "If only I could. I would be happier than I was when Beth agreed to marry me."

"Happier?"

"Yes, I loved her more than I thought I could love anyone, but I loved her much less than I have come to love you in such a short time. Can you imagine how much I would love you if we had a lifetime?"

"About as much as I love you, I expect," she whispered.

Virginia wiped her eyes and began to brighten. "Look, Robert! Look what I found!" She scrambled from his lap and held out the hat.

"*My hat!* You found it. What a wonder you are, Virginia."

"And here's a shirt, and a belt. Robert, did you have a belt?"

"I did until they used it to string me up. This looks almost like it." He took the belt from her hands.

She smiled feebly. Everything was falling into place.

"They're repairing your uniform." She sniffled. "We can pick it up tomorrow afternoon."

"Virginia," he grabbed her purposefully and held her tight. "You must promise you will not leave my sight again. At least, not until, until we *have* to part, if that happens."

"I promise, Robert," she whispered against his ear, then nibbled at his ear lobe.

"I don't see how I'm gonna to be able to leave you. I'm beginnin' to hope all this fails and I remain in your time. That makes me feel like a traitor. But, on the other hand, I have to wonder how I can go back and fight, knowin' what the outcome will be. Knowin' how many more will die. How will I be able to keep the morale of my men up, when I know so much?"

"Maybe when you get back, you won't remember what you've learned here. Maybe you won't remember me," Virginia mused.

"Could I forget my right arm, my heart? Dear God, I don't want to *forget* you. I *have* to remember."

Virginia went to her tote bag and pulled out the satin pouch she used to carry her jewelry in when she traveled. She withdrew something small and brought it to Robert.

"Robert, I'm sure this is too small for even your little finger. My father made it for me when I was about twelve. It still fits my ring finger on my left hand." She demonstrated. "Can you find somewhere to keep it? Then perhaps you'll remember me. I want you to have something of me with you always. Then even if you don't remember, I'll know I'm with you." Tears streamed as she handed him a small, silver braided ring with a heart in the center. She was right. It wouldn't go past the first knuckle of his pinkie.

"I'll find a safe place, Virginia, I promise. It will travel with me, if I go. But I want somethin' else from you." He removed the locket containing the strand of Elizabeth's hair and opened it carefully. A strand of dark hair was coiled in one side of the locket. "This has two sides, Virginia, would it be an insult to ask for a lock of your hair to fill the other?"

Virginia got the tiny scissors out of her sewing kit and handed them to Robert. He cut a small strand from the nape of her neck, and spun it around in a tight curl.

"It won't show where I cut it."

"I wouldn't care if it did. Between the hair and the ring, if you don't remember me, you'll certainly wonder where you had a good time." Virginia needed to lighten the mood. The idea of Robert leaving knotted her stomach, and crowded her chest like an implanted softball.

Robert smiled and forced a little laugh.

"I have nothing to give you, Virginia. Wait, yes I do." He took off his wedding ring and placed it in Virginia's hand.

"No, Robert, you have to keep this. You have to go back as much like you left as possible. I'll be putting the coins back in the pocket of your uniform, too, when we get it back."

"*No*. The coins are yours. We made a deal. They can't possibly be that important."

"We don't have any way of knowing that."

"I don't want to think about it any more tonight," Robert insisted, his hands in the air in surrender.

"I agree. Let's do something totally *decadent*."

Robert looked toward the big bed and reached to unbutton his shirt. "You won't get any argument from us."

"*Not that.* Well, later, maybe. We had no lunch, and it's almost past dinnertime. Let's go out and have a good, stiff drink and some extravagant desert."

"Well, if you're looking for something good and stiff, there's no need to go--"

"Hush, you *lecherous* varmint."

"Lecherous, perhaps, but I object to bein' classified a varmint."

They laughed, something they both needed to do. It chased away the gloom and doom in which they'd been wallowing.

~ * ~

Virginia introduced Robert to a banana split, while she picked at a hot fudge sundae with chocolate ice cream and lots of nuts.

"I'm being positively wicked, you know. I need this like another hole in my head."

"I've never been offered three kinds of ice cream before, and such a variety of toppin's. It boggles the mind! Once at Oatlands, we had two kinds of ice cream from which to choose. That felt 'positively wicked', too."

"Hey, you didn't tell me if you found anything on Harry, or on Joshua Perry."

"Well, I found nothing about Harry, but I found a passage about Joshua Perry in your daily account of the war. Seems he was court-martialed late in 1864 for deliberately torturin' and killin' over one hundred prisoners of war in a prison camp in Ohio. I gathered it was quite a well-publicized trial for it to have been in that book, for it appears to deal only with the most important topics and movements of each day, but I found no resolution.

"Of course, I didn't have time to read the entire eight hundred pages of the book while you were gone, but I saw no further reference in the index. Perhaps he escaped."

Virginia shrugged. "Guess that's possible. I bet I can find out a lot more when I get home…" Virginia's voice drifted off. "I guess you won't be seeing my little house." She shrugged again. "Oh, well, it isn't much anyway."

"I'll see your home if I don't get back right away. You wouldn't leave me here in this purgatory, would you?"

"Don't be silly, of course not, but I've had a strong feeling all along that you'll find your way back. Now, of course, you'll be taking a big chunk of me with you."

"And I shall leave a great deal of myself behind," he said quietly, his look distant. "Are you sure you couldn't live in my time?"

Virginia smiled. "I've thought seriously about it, even before we met, but I know I wouldn't do well 'roughing it.' I wish it were otherwise, and though there are many things in my world I would love to leave behind, my family is not one of them. We're both tied to our own lives. I just thank God He found a way for our paths to cross."

She reached to hold Robert's hand. "I can face the pressures of my life now, I know I can. You've given me that power."

"I had to travel over a hundred years to begin to live again. I think I was wandering through my life before. I was just a soldier, following orders, giving orders, living by regulations, whether in the regular army or the Confederate army. But how will I go on without you?"

"The same way I'll go on without you, I suppose. With some difficulty, with great strength, and with wonderful memories. I pray we'll have our memories." She closed her eyes. "Dear God, please, don't take our memories."

Robert reached across the table and took her hand, his own silent "amen" to her plea.

Virginia only ate half of her sundae. Her mind was preoccupied.

"Aren't you gonna finish that?" Robert asked, his mouth barely empty of the last bite of his banana split.

Virginia shook her head, and pushed her dish toward Robert, who finished it without hesitation.

All the time Robert ate, Virginia sat making plans. Not only plans on how to go about trying to get Robert back to his time, but plans on how to make him remember her, and how and where to plant the note she had made and hoped he would choose to use when he needed it. She was also trying to decide how to best spend every moment they had left, without even having any idea how many moments that might be.

They held hands as they returned to the room. Suddenly, they seemed to have nothing to say, but they couldn't bear to let go of each other.

~ * ~

Robert led Virginia toward the bed. He sat on the edge of it, and drew her to himself holding her tightly and resting his cheek between her breasts.

"Do you have a plain piece of paper?"

"Of course. I'm a writer. Why?"

"I have something I want to leave you. Something of myself. I'll need a pen or pencil."

"Well, I'm not fond of pencils, but I saw one in the desk." She reached in and handed it to Robert. "Here's some paper, and here's a pen. Not the kind you're used to, I know, but I think you'll like it." She looked at him questioningly and handed him a roller ball-tipped pen.

"You sit here." He stood up and patted the bed where he had been sitting. Then he went over to the desk and sat down. He scribbled on the paper with the pencil, then picked up the pen. After a couple of strokes, he smiled at it. He obviously appreciated the smoothness of the line.

"What are you up to?"

He frowned. "*Don't move.*"

"Robert?"

"Shhh!"

Virginia sat impatiently, dying to know what Robert was doing.

After about ten minutes, which, to Virginia, were torturous, he handed her a piece of the paper. He had drawn her face, and signed it. "Virginia, my love forever, Robert."

Virginia stared at drawing. It looked like her, but, to her, the face staring back at her seemed much prettier. With tears in her eyes, she held the picture toward Robert. "Is this how you see me?"

"That's what you look like. Don't you think I did you justice?"

"Justice? I wish I thought I was this beautiful."

Robert took her free hand in his and sat next to her on the bed. "You are much more beautiful than this poor sketch. If I were a better artist I could portray all that you are in a picture."

"Thank you." Her voice was a weak whisper.

"I used to like to draw, wanted to be a great painter. That's why I excelled in engineering."

Virginia got up slowly, took the picture and placed it carefully in a folder in her computer case to protect it.

"It isn't much of a gift, but it's part of who I am."

"It's a wonderful gift, Robert. It's the most wonderful gift I've ever been given, aside from your love." Her voice was still a choked whisper. "So much love in such a few days."

Robert stood and kissed her, softly, but passionately. Virginia returned his passion, and expounded upon it.

"Robert," she whispered. "I want you to know that I've never loved anyone the way I love you. I can't imagine going on without you, but I know I will, and I know I'll be a better person and, strange as it may sound, a happier person, because I'll have this memory of loving and being so well loved."

Robert kissed her forehead, then each cheek. Then his lips covered hers and his tongue played gently inside her parted lips. His hands stroked her arms, her shoulders, her back, her breasts as she slid her arms about his waist and grasped him tightly to her.

"Love me again, Robert, please." Her voice was barely audible, but Robert didn't need to hear her words. He felt her need and would happily satisfy it, and his own.

He laid her down on the bed and lightly kissed her lips. Virginia reached toward the buttons of her shirt.

"No," Robert took her hands in his, and began to unbutton her shirt himself. Virginia followed his lead, and reached for his buttons.

Slowly they worked at removing every piece of clothing from each other, until they lay together without a stitch, touching, feeling, enjoying, on top the covers.

"I want to know every curve of your body, every inch of your skin. I want to take you with me in my mind," Robert whispered as he moved his lips toward her shoulders, then slid down to her breasts, and paused poignantly to kiss each rosy nipple to fullness.

Virginia was lost in the wonder of his thoroughness, and the tenderness she'd never known existed. Why couldn't modern men be this appreciative? Maybe some were, somewhere, but certainly none she had encountered. She'd be so spoiled after these few days of loving Robert, she'd never want another man to touch her, much less let one close enough to make love to her. Somehow that didn't matter, though. In all her lonely years there was little to look back on with joy, until now.

"I guess I had a little advantage over you, didn't I?" she softly quipped.

"What was that?" Robert whispered without taking his lips from her body, but grasping her wrists with his hands and pinning her down.

"I had a chance to inspect you while you were unconscious."

"Please, don't remind me of that grimy shell you rescued."

Virginia could feel his smile against her waist as he continued to descend.

Robert held all the cards just now. She couldn't reach to put her hands on him anywhere to reciprocate his caresses or to satisfy her own urges.

"Robert," she whispered. "Please, Robert, this isn't fair. I want to play, too."

"When I am ready, madam." He gave her a wicked grin.

"I want to touch you *now*."

He ignored her pleas.

"Robert!" she restlessly wiggled against him. "Oh, Robert, *please!*"

He still ignored her. She tried to wiggle away from him, to make him heed her petition, but he held her wrists with his hands and his lips continued their quest. He rubbed his cheek against the fleece between her thighs. "So soft," he whispered.

"Oh, oh *my!*"

Twenty

Exhaustion and satisfaction brought sweet slumber that lasted the entire night without interruption. Virginia and Robert drifted off to sleep with the gas fire blazing, and only a sheet partially draped over their bodies.

Robert awoke first and smiled as he could see and feel Virginia's head exactly where he remembered. She lay nearly crosswise in the bed, her cheek cuddled into his stomach, her face toward his. The sheet was tangled across his abdomen, around under her arm and draped partially across her middle. He would have gladly lain there for hours just looking at her, but it was only seconds before Virginia opened her eyes.

"I felt you were awake," she whispered, then turned her head to kiss Robert's mid-section.

"Good mornin', my love." Robert spoke softly as he brushed the hair from Virginia's sleepy eyes. "You looked so peaceful there. I was enjoyin' just watchin' you. I don't think you've had much peace in your life. You deserve some." He ran his fingers along her jaw as he spoke.

"No, I haven't had much, but you're making up for it." She inhaled deeply, then with a sigh, stretched.

"We could just stay here all day and make more memories to keep us warm later," Robert offered with a sly chuckle.

"We could, but I want to go out, to feel what it's like just to be with you, just for this one day. We can't make any more plans to get you back until we get your uniform this afternoon. Give me this one day?"

"I would give you the rest of my days, if they were but mine to give." He pulled her tightly to him.

"Hmmm," she rubbed her cheek across his chest. "I love the way you smell. I love the way your skin feels. Your totally naked body against mine sends electrical current surging through me."

Robert just smiled. He had gathered much about electricity's power in his stay, but couldn't exactly figure out how it was made, much less, how it was delivered.

"Am I terribly selfish, Robert, for wishing you wouldn't leave?"

"If you're selfish for wishing, then I am two-fold as selfish."

"Am I shameless for loving you so quickly?"

"Shameless!" He laughed. "Would that all beautiful women could be so shameless."

She pouted. "Now you're making fun of me."

"Hardly, my dear. If women of my time, the wifely ones, that is, were but a fraction as honest with themselves about their own feelin's, a fragment as givin' of themselves as you, a particle as open to enjoyin' love--there would have been no errant husbands patronizing brothels."

"Robert." She looked at him with serious eyes.

"Yes, my love."

"If we weren't from such distant worlds, if I were from your time, or you from mine, do you think I would make you happy? I mean *really* happy? Happy enough that you wouldn't mourn Beth any more? Happy enough that you'd find your son and mend the rift between you? Happy enough to want only me?"

"Virginia, perhaps I should feel ashamed, but I stopped mournin' Beth with our first kiss. I think Harry and I may find each other, if we both survive the war. I don't think he hated me when we parted. Not that he liked me either.

"As for you, I don't know what to say or do to prove my feelings. You doubt yourself so much. If I had a lifetime to devote to you, I would find a way to prove my love. How can I prove it in a few days?"

"By the look I see in your eyes right now." She kissed him softly, rested her chin upon his chest and gazed up into his deep-blue eyes. "I believe you, Robert, I don't know why exactly, but I believe every kind word you say, and I'm storing them in my memory bank to draw from when I need them. I stopped trusting men's words a long time ago, but you're not like the men I meet. I trust you completely."

They gazed at each other for a moment. Then Virginia's eyes showed her desire to say more. She took a deep breath.

"Robert..."

He nodded.

"Will you promise me something?"

"Anything within my power."

"Promise me you'll take extra care through the rest of the war. Don't let me go home and read about you as a casualty in one of my books. Please? For me?"

"I promise I will be a good soldier, and take only the chances I must as such. But I can't promise I will not do everything in my power to save any of my men."

"I wouldn't expect you to do less. But, if you're careful, more careful than those scars of yours would lead me to believe you've been in the past, maybe someday I'll run into one of your descendants, and see your twinkle in his eyes."

"You know, darlin', if I but knew how I got to your time, I would do my duty and go back until the war's end, then return to you." His eyes were distant. His voice reverberated with longing.

"That's a *lovely* thought. Maybe I'll just have to wait for you." Virginia closed her eyes and ran her cheek across his chest.

"*No.* I don't want to think of you wastin' all you have to offer waitin' for a ghost who can never come back. You open your heart, if someone worthy comes along, and allow him to love you." He grabbed her by the shoulders and turned her to face him squarely. "Do you understand me?" He shook her a little.

"Yes. I understand." Her voice had a child-like whimper. "I don't want to think about it. I don't want to think about having to live without you."

"Virginia, you'll never be without me. Not really. I'll live in here." He touched her between her breasts, indicating her heart. "And in here." He tapped her forehead. "I'll always be there. And if there is a heaven, I'll be watchin' every move you make from the moment I leave you, for my time will have been long-since passed when I have left your time."

"But, what about me, Robert. If you go back, I won't even have been born, how can you know I will be in your memory?"

"Because even after what I've seen of the war, after what Perry put me through, I know God is not cruel. He would not give me this taste of you, then take you even from my memory." He raised his shoulders from the bed. "*Now.* I think that is quite enough such talk. We need no further attacks of melancholia here." He took her chin between his thumb and the inside of his first finger and lifted her face to look squarely into her eyes. "I promise you, I will remember you, and you will be my love for the rest of my natural life. I will find some way to let you know that was true. Look for it."

Virginia gave a feeble smile, which slowly grew into an impish one.

"Shower, anyone?" She jumped from the bed and darted for the bathroom.

~ * ~

A towel around her wet hair, and wearing her robe, Virginia approached Robert with a glass of water in one hand, and one of her antibiotic pills in the other. She would make sure he left as healthy as possible. "Here." She held them out to him.

He dutifully took his medicine. He looked like a god standing there in just a towel. Some of the space between his ribs no longer looking so hollow. Virginia's gaze raked over him longingly. "Sit down. Time to put the cream on your back."

"Yes, ma'am." Like a well-mannered little boy, Robert sat on the edge of the bed.

Virginia retrieved a drug store bag from her purse and removed a new tube of antibiotic cream. "This company is making a fortune off your back."

Robert winced at her words. The money still bothered him.

"I didn't really mean 'a fortune.' It isn't expensive. I was just kidding."

His posture eased slightly and Virginia tenderly smoothed the cream over his healing back.

"Your touch is so gentle. I doubt any nurse, much less the doctors who tend our soldiers, could minister so sweetly as you. Too bad I can't take some of that miracle cream back with me. It has certainly been a godsend for these whip marks." He craned his neck to see over his shoulder.

"Well, I wasn't going to tell you until the last minute, but I have a way for you to take some back. I'm not about to chance you getting these things infected." Virginia wiped her hands, walked over to her coat and removed something from the pocket. "I bought this at an antique store." She held up an antique medicine bottle with a cork. "I bought two jumbo tubes of this cream, and I'm going to empty them into this bottle. It's up to you to find a way to get it out and a gentle hand to apply it. The bottle is sturdy and old enough. It should travel well, *even* in time."

Robert just smiled and chuckled. "As I said before, you are a wonder."

"I thought I might get a mortar and pestle and pound some of my pills into powders so you could take that back, too."

"I don't think that will be necessary, but I won't refuse the cream since you've already bought the bottle. Next you'll try to find a way for me to take electricity back with me."

Virginia's fingers moved nimbly to one corner of the towel wrapped around him. Quick as a wink she ripped it from him and snapped it at his naked body.

"Oh, now we are going to play?" Robert chased her about the room and caught her easily. He pinned both her hands behind her with his own. Then spreading one hand, he managed to capture both her hands in one of his. His other hand grasped her by the back of her neck. Then he planted his lips soundly on hers.

For the first time, Virginia did not respond to his kiss. As a matter of fact she froze there in his arms. He leaned his face back from hers without releasing his hold with either hand. Virginia stared, expressionless, right through him. He released her hands and she pushed immediately away from him, catching her breath in small gulps.

"Virginia?" Robert walked toward her, but she retreated to the corner of the room. "Virginia," he whispered, realizing something frightened her. He reached one hand to her and stroked her arm, unthreateningly. "Virginia, are you all right?"

Slowly she responded, swallowing back the tears that wanted to flow, even though consciously she knew Robert posed no threat to her.

"I--" She tried to respond, but her voice was faint. "I'm... I... I don't like to be confined. I don't like small spaces, or having my movement restricted in any way. I'm sorry. I tr...try..." She finally cried.

She had to get it out. It wasn't just her claustrophobia; it was everything about the prospect of losing Robert after falling in love so deeply and so quickly. It was the memory of how she felt last night when she came back and thought he had already left her. How would she be strong? She had to be, for him, but for now, she needed to get all the emotion out, and this was the opportunity.

Her mind raced with flashes of memories--the smokehouse and Jonathan, of being locked in a closet as a child, being pinned down by her first husband because he knew how it frightened her and made him feel important.

Robert waited patiently, shushing, stroking her gently, trying to soothe her senses back to normal without frightening her again. The crying didn't last long, but when it stopped, he was almost afraid to hold her, until she threw herself against him.

"I'm sorry," she whispered.

"No! No. It is my fault, entirely." He kissed and stroked and shushed. "Forgive me."

Virginia inhaled, biting her bottom lip. "There's nothing to forgive. It's my fault. I should have told you before, when I didn't want us both in the bathroom with the door closed."

Robert held her tightly. How he wished he could stay and take care of her. She didn't need taking care of, but she deserved it.

"I've *spoiled* everything ." She pounded her fists into her sides, and her voice reflected her disgust with herself.

"You've spoiled *nothing*. We'll start the day again. Together."

"Okay, I'm all right now." She inhaled and let her breath out slowly. "It's *stupid*. I *hate* being like this." She buried her face in her open hands.

Robert collected her in his arms and held her to his chest.

"Thank you for being so understanding. You reminded me of Jonathan."

"I don't know if I *like* that."

"Why? Jonathan was a nice boy. He was a good friend and he saw me through an episode like this." She looked up at him. "You know sometimes you get an expression on your face that reminds me of Jonathan."

Robert raised one eyebrow.

"What?" She wanted to know what he was thinking.

Robert did not respond.

"What in the world is wrong with you reminding me of someone else I like?"

"*Nothin'. Nothin' at all.*" Robert began pulling on his clothes.

"You *can't* possibly be jealous."

"No, I am not jealous!" Then Robert shook off his mood. "I'm sorry, it's nothing, really. That Jonathan of yours just, well, from a distance he resembled someone I knew. It's impossible, I know. Let's start this day all over again."

Robert reached for Virginia's robe and handily unzipped it, pushing it off her shoulders and letting it drop to the floor. "I'm getting the hang of these zipper things."

"Yes, you certainly are." She slipped her arms about him. "But it's my turn to get dressed now." She ducked away and grabbed her clothes.

He followed her and put his arms around her from behind. "Just one moment like this?" He cupped her breasts in his large hands and she snuggled against him as he leaned his head over her shoulder and kissed her cheek.

Twenty-one

"Robert, I want to know what you'd like to do today."

"T'would be hard to say, when I have no idea what it is customary to do in your world…when you're in love."

Virginia gave a wary smile. "That wasn't quite what I meant. Let's see." She bit her bottom lip and squinted her eyes. "Let's start with what you've missed having to eat most."

"That's easy, cakes, tarts, pies…"

"All right. Now we've got a direction." She grabbed his hand and dragged him out the front door of the inn.

"*Wait*. You mean you're not gonna force some huge breakfast down my throat?"

"Oh, we'll have breakfast all right." With Robert in tow she burst into a playful run toward the car. She knew exactly where she wanted to take him, a bakery, but not just any bakery--the one her friends showed her once before, which was quite expensive, but everything tasted homemade. They didn't skimp or make substitutions with ingredients. They had a few little tables and served coffee and other drinks.

~ * ~

Virginia parked the car and jumped out, racing around to drag Robert from the passenger seat. Inside the door of the bakery, Robert spun around sniffing the air with his eyes closed and looking at all the good things stocking the cases. The hot, heavy fragrance of baking ovens full of heavenly confections intoxicated them.

"The entire Confederate army hasn't tasted this much sugar in a year."

The clerk snickered.

"Pick out *anything* you want." Virginia opened her arms wide and all the while thinking to herself if Robert thought 1862 was lean on provisions, what would he think about the rest of the war?

"I hardly know where to begin. What do you like?"

"Oh, no, I'll pick after you get started. I don't want to influence you."

Robert's mouth watered so much he kept licking his lips and swallowing.

Seeing his indecision, Virginia tried to help. "What's your favorite kind of cake?"

"Any kind, I'm not particular. Really, I don't know what to pick. I could get drunk from just the smell."

Virginia heaved a sigh, shrugged her shoulders, and decided unless she wanted to spend the entire day in the bakery, she'd best take matters into her own hands.

"Okay then. Give us one coffee and two milks," she instructed the clerk, then turned to Robert. "You take the drinks and sit down, and I'll just pick a few things at random."

Robert took the little tray with the coffee and milk and sat down where he could watch.

Virginia pointed, ordering one cup cake, yellow with chocolate icing, one cherry tart, one bear claw, one sticky bun, one éclair, and a large peanut butter cookie for Robert. She chose two French crullers with chocolate icing for herself.

When she approached the table she proudly set the tray down in front of Robert.

"We'll get *sick*."

"No, *we* won't. These are mine." She pointed to the two crullers. The rest is yours." She waved her hand toward the tray.

"*I'll* get sick."

"Maybe, but I doubt it. I've seen you eat. Besides a few more pounds wouldn't hurt. You'll probably lose them anyway…" Her voiced drifted off. "As soon as you go back."

"What are those things you have?"

"French crullers. Here, try a bite." She stuffed one toward his mouth.

Robert made an appreciative sound. "Hmmm." He licked his lips. "It's good, but it's hollow. Should there be something inside?"

"No, I like to fool myself into thinking they have fewer calories because there isn't much to them. It's a lie, but it makes me feel less guilty." She chuckled at herself.

No more words were heard from Robert for quite a while as he sampled first one item then another with great gusto.

He finished the coffee and one of the milks before he half-finished the treats. Virginia gave him the rest of her milk and bought him another.

At last Robert pushed himself back from the table and stifled a belch. "Pardon me, please. I shouldn't have eaten so much so fast. But *oh*, how delicious. Like…"

"Oatlands." Virginia finished for him.

Robert just smiled at her and nodded.

The fact they could so often finish each other's sentences hadn't appeared to escape Robert either. It felt so natural that she never mentioned it. She simply accepted the tendency as she accepted their intense feelings for each other.

The clerk came out from behind the counter to wipe the other tables. Virginia had noticed her watching as Robert put away all the sweets. She paused at their table, facing Virginia. "Ain't it disgustin' how men can pack it in and burn it off?"

Virginia just smiled.

"Can I get ya anything else?" the girl asked.

Robert rolled his eyes thoughtfully.

"How 'bout some more coffee?" she offered.

"I could drink a little more coffee."

Virginia reached for her purse. "Keep it, honey," the clerk said waving her hand. "With a mouth like his to feed, this one's on the house."

Virginia chortled. "Thank you." She turned back to Robert who looked like he would burst any moment. "That was enough sugar to have you bouncing off the walls for a week."

"Excuse me?"

"It just means that much sugar gives you a lot of energy."

"Oh, yes, well, my partner and I know the best use to make of it." He winked.

"Robert!"

"No one's listenin' or watchin' your pretty face blush, but me."

"Let's relax a moment and figure out what we want to do next."

"Can I do anything I want?" he asked.

"That's a loaded question."

"Well, you asked me what I wanted to do, and not knowing much about your time, I know but one thing I would like to try."

Virginia looked at him suspiciously.

"I'd like to try driving your machine."

"My car?"

"Yes. Could I try, please?"

Virginia slid down in her chair and looked squarely at him. She tried to think of where there might be a deserted lot. She couldn't think of any, so she asked the clerk.

"There's a place a couple of miles from town. An abandoned car dealer with a huge lot."

"Thank you," Virginia replied and they headed for the door.

It was against Virginia's better judgment, but she wanted to let Robert have some fun, before he returned, if he returned to his time.

~ * ~

All the way to the lot, Virginia explained the principles of driving the car as Robert watched her intently. In the back of her mind was the concern that removing him from the confines of Fredericksburg might make him disappear.

Virginia breathed a heavy sigh. "Robert, I don't know if this is such a good idea."

"Virginia, I am an experienced engineer. I assure you, with proper instruction, I can handle this machine. I once ran a locomotive."

"Okay, but I want to go on record as saying this is against my better judgment. Get out and come around here."

She opened her door and got out, then, running her hand across the hood in a gesture of fond farewell, she walked in front of the car. She couldn't help wondering if her car would be in one piece by the time this driving lesson ended. Just what would she tell her insurance company? *Oh, a man visiting from 1862 wrecked it.*

Robert tried to slip in behind the steering wheel, but his knees banged against the column, as his head hit the roof of the car. "Ouch!"

Virginia pursed her lips to keep from laughing. Robert was nearly a foot taller than she. "I'm sorry," she sputtered. "I didn't think about moving the seat. Nobody drives my car but me."

"It was custom made to your size?" he asked. "No matter, I will manage." His knees crowded the steering column.

Virginia burst out laughing. "Robert, it's not 'custom made'." She ran back around the car and pushed a button on the open door. She moved the electric seat back and down. *"There.* Is that better?"

"That's positively *astounding.* I'd seen the windows move so, but an entire seat? *Electricity. What a marvel.*" He shook his head.

"Okay, here we go. Boy, am I glad this isn't a standard."

"I should hope such luxury as this isn't standard, it must be very dear."

"What?" Virginia sorted out her words, and his response. "Oh, no, I meant a 'standard transmission,' instead of 'automatic'."

Robert gave her a puzzled look.

Virginia shrugged. "Never mind. This is the gear shift." She explained carefully the principles, then told him to put his foot on the gas peddle, then the brake, then to move it several times between the two to get used to the feel.

"That's just about the most important thing you'll have to do. The other important thing is the steering wheel, of course." She explained all the indicators on the dash, including the speedometer.

"I still find the possibility of such speeds a marvel. I don't think I can truly fathom it."

"I guess I've told you everything I can tell you. You'll just have to try it. Please, please, start slowly! Now, turn the key to start the car."

Robert could see the apprehension in her face. "Virginia, please don't worry. I shall be very careful."

Page 236

Virginia tried to force a smile, but it was impossible. Robert turned the key and the car started easily.

"Put your foot on the brake... Release the emergency brake." She pointed. "Put the gear shift in 'D' for drive... Now let off the brake and..." She took a deep breath. "Put your foot on the gas--*Gently*!"

Robert seemed amazed at the power the motor expended with just a gentle touch of his foot. Needless to say his starting and stopping were less than smooth. All in all, however, even she had to admit that he did quite well. He appeared to have no trouble with the steering and seemed to embrace all the principles of handling the "machine."

"Well, I've mastered driving this around this vacant lot. Let's go out on the macadam."

"Robert, we can't!" Virginia hadn't meant to raise her voice. "I mean. It's illegal." She calmed. "You have to have a driver's license. We don't need to get you arrested. How would we explain who you are or where you came from?"

Robert gave a disgruntled sigh and kept driving around the lot for another few moments.

"I suppose if I'm unable to drive on the macadam, I've satisfied my curiosity." He stopped the car, shifted to "park," put on the emergency brake, and folded his arms in front of himself smugly.

"All right, I confess you did very well." She released her seat belt and leaned over to give him a kiss on the cheek. Then she put her hands on either side of his face and stretched to kiss him on the lips.

"Ooo, tell me what I did to deserve that and I'll do it again."

Virginia made no reply. How could she tell him she was beginning to miss him already and he wasn't even gone? She just smiled and turned toward the passenger door to get out of the car. Trying to bring her philosophical attitude back to the surface, she ambled around the front of the car. When she got to the driver's door, Robert climbed out. He reached to help her back behind the wheel, but as their hands touched, he couldn't resist the temptation to pull her into his arms and hold her.

"I know, darlin'." He sensed her mood. "I know it's impossible to pretend we'll be together forever. But we've been havin' such a wonderful time, we have to enjoy every moment we're given. We have to store up as many memories as we can."

His eyes watered with tears at the thought of leaving her. He must be strong, for Virginia. "Besides, maybe I won't find my way back." Robert tried to sound hopeful. He stroked her hair as she buried her face in his neck.

"No, you have to. I won't let them label you a deserter. We'll find a way. I have some ideas, but I don't want to talk about them now. I don't even want to think about them now." She got in the car, moved the seat back to its normal position, and re-adjusted the mirrors as Robert rounded the car to return to the passenger seat.

"Ready for some more adventure?" Virginia asked, swallowing back her sorrow at the prospect of his return as well. If Robert could put up a brave front, she certainly would. After all, he faced returning to a war he now knew was lost.

"I'm ready for anythin', with you."

"*Good.* I'm taking you shopping."

"Shopping? But there's nothin' I need, and I won't have you spendin' more money on me."

"Okay, you can watch me shop. I need a few things. But mostly, I just want to show you a modern shopping center, and a grocery store. You'll love that."

"I saw a shopping center, when we went to the coin dealer."

"That was just a little group of stores. That kind of shopping center went out thirty years ago. What if I told you there are places with a hundred stores, and more, under a single roof?"

"I'd say you take me for a fool, madam. You've shown me many wonders, but that is impossible. I'll stake my reputation as an engineer on it."

"Well, Robert, say goodbye to your reputation." There was a mall called Spotsylvania Mall, but she didn't know exactly where it was, so she stopped for directions.

~ * ~

On the way to the mall, Virginia spied a large chain grocery store. Robert would be fascinated, so she pulled into the parking lot. All his days in the modern world, Robert hadn't seen the total number of cars as parked in front of this one store.

Virginia led him through the automatic door.

Robert looked for a doorman, but seeing none, his engineer training demanded to know how the door opened. He loosened his hand from hers, returned to the door and inspected every aspect of it. He could not determine by what mechanism it opened, but as he got closer, the reverse door opened. He walked through it, then turned to walk back in the other door. Virginia followed him when he went through again and grabbed his arm dragging him away from the doors.

"Robert," she spoke through clenched teeth, "at this rate we won't get anywhere."

"Sorry," Robert followed her penitently until they reached the first section of food--fruits and vegetables. "*Impossible.*" How can a green-grocer stock all these fresh foods. How could they get here in the dead of winter? Where are there enough people to consume them before they spoil? No one has an icehouse large enough…"

Virginia put her finger to his lips. "Maybe this wasn't such a good idea. There's just too much to see and explain. I've changed my mind. I don't want to spend our time together trying to explain modern shopping conveniences."

"I don't either. I admit I'm fascinated, but I want only to be with you. Perhaps just a quick tour of this one intriguing establishment. I won't ask you to explain things, and I'll just look. Would that do?"

"I suppose. Oh, Robert, it's not that I don't want to show all this to you. There just isn't enough time. I know in my heart if you don't get back soon, well, it just won't work, that's all. I'd like nothing else than to keep you with me forever, but I won't be the cause of you losing your life. All right, one quick tour of this store."

From the fresh fruits and vegetables, they went to the dairy section. Robert did as he promised and refrained from questions, though any number appeared in his eyes. Then to the canned foods. Robert could identify slightly with those. The packaged foods, like cereals were a wonder.

The fresh meats, well, they reminded him he was getting hungry. When they got to the frozen food, Virginia explained a little. She couldn't stand the look of complete confusion in Robert's eyes.

"I won't try to explain microwave ovens." Virginia chuckled as they stood in front of an entire frozen food section that said, "Microwavables." They left the store without buying a thing, because neither of them could decide what Robert should try.

"Is it time for dinner, yet?" Robert inquired.

"Dinner? Oh, lunch." Virginia looked at her watch. "As a matter of fact, it's past time."

"Could we go to one of those 'quick food' places again?"

"Fast food. Do you like fried chicken?"

"That's a silly question to ask a Southerner. I'm glad to know it's still available, I thought maybe they had canned or…" He groped for the word. "Frozen all the chickens."

Virginia laughed. It had to be overwhelming. "Well, I've got the place. "They pulled into a Kentucky Fried Chicken establishment.

Twenty-two

Robert seemed to enjoy the chicken very much, but he wasn't fond of the mashed potatoes, though he liked the gravy. Virginia tried to explain that the potatoes were probably instant, but the concept eluded him.

"The corn is passable, but it would be preferable to use sweet corn, instead of young field corn. Of course, any corn this time of year is a mystery." Robert continued to eat with gusto. "The biscuits are marvelous. We haven't had such light biscuits for months."

"Robert, I know you read some about the rest of the war in my book while I was out. Maybe you'd like to know a little more about history after the Civil War."

Robert nodded as he continued to eat.

"Well, there are fifty states now, from east coast to west coast plus Alaska and Hawaii. We had a brief war with Spain in the late eighteen hundreds, 1898, I think. World War I, in Europe in the early nineteen hundreds, ended in 1918 after the U.S finally got involved and whipped Germany.

"Then came the roaring twenties--women cut their hair short, started getting into the work-force, won the vote, alcoholic beverages were prohibited, that was called 'prohibition.' Gangsters made illegal whiskey and lots of money. Then we had a depression, the stock market crashed, people were poor, the president created the Civilian Conservation Corps to put people to work on public improvement projects. You would have gotten involved in that. They built roads, and bridges, and dams.

"Then came World War II. That time we had two fronts to fight on, Europe--Germany again, and the Pacific against Japan. That ended in 1945. Then the Korean War, that's about when I was born. Then, oh, never mind. I never meant to relate a hundred and thirty years of history counted down by wars."

"I would have thought there wouldn't have been any wars after this one, I mean…" Robert's voice was hollow. The idea of more wars drained him of all energy.

"I know. You'd think people would learn to get along, wouldn't you? But it just hasn't happened. Robert, your time was so much simpler."

~ * ~

When they finished lunch, Robert and Virginia walked slowly to the car and he noticed a roaring overhead. He looked up to see something flying through the air. Instantly, he threw Virginia to the ground and fell on top of her. Nothing else could be booming through the air, but shells of some kind. He must protect her.

"Robert!" Virginia screamed as her face hit the black top, her shoulder crushed beneath him.

Still holding Virginia to the ground, Robert looked cautiously overhead.

"Robert, let me up."

"When it's safe."

"It *is* safe!" She tried to get up, but he was too strong.

"Robert! *Get off me.*" They must be drawing a crowd.

Robert rose and helped Virginia up. There were a few curious on-lookers, but when she asked for no assistance, nor offered any more resistance to her apparent assailant, they dispersed chattering to each other.

Virginia dusted herself off while Robert looked skyward.

"I was just trying to protect you, but I guess the shell didn't explode."

"Shell? What shell?" she barked, painful tears stinging her eyes.

"It must have been some new Federal projectile."

"The only thing in the air was a plane, an airplane. It's like a passenger train that flies."

"I have listened to everything you've said. I have seen amazing things, but *that* is impossible."

Virginia closed her eyes and sighed. Then she looked to the clouds for another plane. She didn't see one right away.

When Virginia looked upward, Robert noticed blood on her cheek. "Oh, God. You're *bleeding*. I've hurt you."

"I am?" She wiped at her face then pointed up. "Look! There's a plane. Don't throw me down again,"

"It looks very high."

"It is. Robert, that size plane holds over a hundred people. There are planes that fly coast to coast, or over the Atlantic or Pacific that hold several hundred people."

Robert was too floored to respond.

"You can fly from New York to San Francisco in a few hours."

Robert just shook his head.

Virginia put her hand to her throbbing mouth, and when she withdrew it, her fingers were covered with blood. "I bit my tongue when you threw me down."

"Oh, Lord. What have I done? I haven't even a handkerchief to offer."

He kissed the blood from her lips. "I feel utterly foolish. Can you forgive me? What can I do to help?"

"You can get in the car and *shut up*." Virginia didn't mean to sound as cross as she did, but her cheek, her mouth, and her shoulder were hurting immensely.

Robert got in the car and said not a single word as Virginia drove back toward town. She stopped in front of an establishment where she said she had left his uniform for repairs. She checked her face in the rear view mirror and wiped the traces of blood with a tissue. Robert started to get out of the car, but she stopped him.

"Just wait here, please. I won't be long."

Her order gave further proof to Robert of her anger.

Virginia left Robert in the car so he wouldn't worry about whatever she had to pay the tailor for the repairs.

"I put on one more missing button, replaced some of the gold braid, mended many places, re-lined the pockets." The tailor held up the uniform.

"It looks like new. I'm very pleased. Tell me how much I owe you." It was difficult for Virginia to talk. She had quite a hole in the tip of her tongue and it was beginning to swell.

"Are you all right, Miss?" The tailor asked, obviously seeing her injuries.

"Oh, yes, thank you. I slipped on a little ice. I'm on my way back to my hotel to take care of it. I'm fine, really," she reassured him.

"I did a great deal of work to the uniform, probably about a hundred dollars, but give me sixty, and we'll call it even."

"Are you sure?"

"Yes, sixty is fine."

~ * ~

Virginia hung the uniform on a handy peg behind Robert.

"You can try it on when we get back to the room," she said quietly as she got back in the car. "I need to get my lenses out. My eyes are burning."

"I've wanted to ask you about your eyes. Sometimes you seem to see very well, and other times you seem to see very little, and sometimes you wear spectacles. I don't understand."

"Robert, I'll show you when we get back. Right now, I'm not feeling very well." She started the car. It was just a few blocks to the inn.

~ * ~

Virginia entered her room. She shook her head and blinked. "Wow, I really need to get these lenses out. Maybe one of them slid off when I hit the ground. You look a little fuzzy."

She went straight into the bath to remove and clean her contact lenses. "Robert, come here, and you'll see what I wear when I don't have my 'spectacles' on." She popped one lens and showed it to him.

"That was in your eye."

"Yes, it helps me see instead of my glasses." She cleaned it and placed it in the case. Then she removed the other and did likewise. "They're a marvelous invention. I see much better with them than I do with glasses." Virginia looked toward the mirror over the sink and pushed her hair away from her face. She had a red knot on her forehead with traces of blue and purple appearing.

"Robert, I think I need some ice." She got a washcloth down and opened it ready to receive the ice, but as Robert brought the ice bucket she reached for it, weaving, then crumbled toward the floor.

Robert threw down the ice bucket, grabbed for Virginia and caught her just short of the floor. He carried her to the bed and saw the knot on her forehead. She probably had a concussion. He gathered some ice from the floor, put it in the washcloth, and held it to her forehead.

"Virginia," he whispered in a panic. "Virginia, please answer. I'm such an oaf. What have I done? I'll get a doctor."

He started for the door, but Virginia roused and stopped him, calling out.

"Robert, it's all right. I'll be all right, really. I feel better already."

"No, I must get a doctor."

"Please, Robert. You didn't let me get a doctor. I'll be all right. I just think I won't stand up for a little while."

"But I caused this with my stupidity. You did not cause my injuries. This is your time. There is no good reason not to call a doctor. You can prove who you are."

"Robert, I don't want to take a chance on them putting me in the hospital for observation. I'll be fine, really. Trust me, please."

Robert defiantly shook his head.

"Please, just come over here and this time you can take care of me. Get some water and the peroxide and clean my cheek. I'll just lie here. I'll be fine."

Robert reluctantly agreed. "I'll put some of the miracle cream on your cheek."

"That's right." Her voice quivered, but, clearing her throat, she tried to hide it. She felt as though she'd been drugged.

"I'll take care of you, Virginia. I'll take good care of you."

"Then that's all I need. Now go get some more ice, and I'll be right here. Take the key!"

~ * ~

Robert left for a moment. When he returned, he went about cleaning Virginia's face and putting cream on the scrape, all the while making sure she kept ice on her forehead.

"Robert, I'd like to get a little more comfortable. Can you help me out of these clothes?"

"With pleasure." He unbuttoned her shirt and removed it gently. Then he sat her up to remove her *harness*. Virginia winced as he did so, and he saw a mass of bruising forming about her shoulder.

"Oh, Virginia," he cried, "what have I done? I'm an idiot, a buffoon, a brute…"

"Enough, already. Robert, you didn't hurt me on purpose. You hurt me out of love, out of a desire to protect me. That's a new one for me. But it's my own fault for not telling you about airplanes. Please stop feeling so guilty and just help me." Her speech was slowing, her words becoming slurred.

Robert didn't say another word. He helped Virginia out of her street clothes and into her nightshirt without so much as an overt glance.

Virginia couldn't stand seeing the pain in his eyes. She feared he'd try to go back on his own, and she wasn't ready to let go. She probably never would be, but she'd have to.

"Robert, will you take care of me tonight?" She reached a hand toward him as he hovered there in a chair next to the bed.

"You needn't ask," he whispered.

"Then, you'll have to go out and get us a sandwich or something later for dinner. Right now, will you just hold me?"

"You should rest. I don't want to do anything else to hurt you."

"Then come over here and hold me. I rest so well in your embrace," she insisted.

Robert came to the bed and stiffly sat down.

"You won't be very comfortable like that. I know, go on out to the desk and order us just something light for dinner. Tell them to bring it about six. Then come back and hold me."

Robert did as she asked, returning with the same pitiful look on his face.

"Now, come hold me. You can use some rest, too. You're still not a hundred percent, you know. I need you to hold me, Robert."

He stretched out on top of the covers, fully clothed. Virginia scooted over and put her head on his chest, then unbuttoned his flannel shirt. He took it off. Then she unsnapped his jeans and unzipped the fly. He slipped them off.

"Now, isn't that better?" Virginia was tired. She waited for Robert to get under the covers, then settled in peacefully. She could feel Robert was tense as he held the ice to her forehead, while trying not to touch her right shoulder. Eventually his shoulders relaxed and he laid the ice aside. He too looked drowsy.

They slept.

~ * ~

A knock at the door awakened Robert several hours later, but not Virginia. He lowered her from his chest to the bed, got up, put on the robe and answered the door. It was the desk clerk with the dinner tray. Suddenly faced with the tray, Virginia asleep, and no money, he was at a loss. He fumbled in the pockets of the robe, then fumbled for something to say.

"I don't have any money on me. Can I come to the desk later?"

"No problem, all you have to do is sign here." The clerk pointed to the ticket and handed Robert a pen.

Robert scribbled his name and thanked the clerk. He'd never been embarrassed like that before, never been dependent on anyone else like he was on Virginia. Robert hadn't done as she had told him and ordered sandwiches. Instead, he ordered the same hot meal they first had in the dining room, turkey, mashed potatoes with gravy, and green beans.

Robert tiptoed over to the bed, stroked Virginia's cheek and hoped that would be enough to awaken her. She did not stir. He leaned close to her ear. "Virginia," he whispered. "Virginia, darlin', supper's here." Still she did not stir. In a panic, Robert threw back the covers and lifted her into his arms to see if she was still breathing. She was.

"Virginia, *please* wake up." He pleaded, more loudly and shook her a little. "Oh, God, Virginia!" He shook her again.

Virginia moaned a slight recognition.

"Oh, Virginia, please wake up. You must have a concussion. I don't know what to do. Please."

Virginia opened her sleepy eyes and sighed.

"Robert, what is it?" Her whisper was barely audible.

"Virginia? Virginia? Can you see me?" Robert's words were frantic.

"Not too well."

"Oh, dear Lord. I don't know what to do."

"Hand me my glasses. Then I'll be able to see you. What on earth is wrong?"

He dropped her back to the bed and reached for her glasses, which he then thrust at her.

When she put them on she could see Robert's distress.

"I couldn't wake you. You weren't just sleepin'. You were unconscious! I didn't know what to do. What should I do?"

"First you should shut up. You're giving me a worse headache."

"A headache. Can I get you somethin' for it? Oh, hell, I don't know what to get you. I don't know anything about your medicines."

"Robert, shhh," she hissed holding up her hands in surrender. "I wasn't unconscious, at least I don't think so. I just had my good ear against the pillow--well, I had it against you, but you moved. I don't have much hearing in my right ear, an injury."

She refrained from saying it was a blow from her first husband which damaged her ear.

"I just couldn't hear you."

"But you always heard me before."

"Not necessarily. I felt the vibrations laying against you, if you spoke when I was sleeping, that woke me."

"Are you certain. I mean. I hurt you when I pushed you to the ground like a complete fool. I...I..."

"Robert..." Virginia held out both arms. "Come here."

Twenty-three

Virginia sat on the side of the bed. When Robert approached, she put her arms around his waist and snuggled her head against his stomach. He relaxed. She must not be hurt as badly as he feared.

"Supper is here," he whispered as he stroked her hair.

"Hmmm, I can smell it. Doesn't smell like a couple of sandwiches, though."

"No, I took the liberty of orderin' hot meals. I thought we could both use the nourishment."

"I certainly don't look malnourished. But I appreciate the thought. What have we got?"

"I wasn't sure what you like, so I ordered the same thing we had the other night in the dinin' room. Turkey, stuffing, potatoes and gravy, green beans…"

"I wish I could have cooked for you."

"I'm sure you're as wonderful a cook as you are a nurse. Does your head hurt much? Or your cheek? What about--?"

"I'm fine, Robert, really. Just a little headache. I can't even feel the scrape on my cheek. Now stop worrying, please. We probably don't have much time left. Let's not waste any of it."

Robert nodded and took her hand and led her toward the table.

Virginia knees wobbled slightly and she sat quickly.

"Would you get my purse, please. I think I'd like to take a couple of aspirin."

Robert raced across the room to retrieve the purse. He wanted so to make amends for her injuries.

"Robert, if you don't relax--" She sighed. "Please sit down."

Robert sat.

"I've been giving this a great deal of thought, how you can get back to your time, I mean. I kind of figure we have to put everything back as nearly as we can to how things were when you left. Your uniform, the place, the time. We need to find the building you were locked in. Do you think you could find it again tomorrow?"

"I don't know. I was rather disoriented."

"Well, I know what direction you came from as you approached the bridge. That's a start. Maybe if we go that way, things will look familiar. It was last Saturday morning when you got there. Do you have any idea how long you'd been walking?"

"The sun was just comin' up when I left the little stone building. I remember that much. The door was broken in a day or two before that. I'm not sure. But I had no strength to get up and get out until that morning. I kept losin' consciousness, I think. It was a struggle to walk this far. I remember that, but the cold air seemed to give me strength." He gazed across the little table at her. "Or maybe I just knew you were waitin' here for me."

Virginia chose to ignore his comment. This was difficult enough without getting swept away every other moment.

"Tomorrow is Saturday, the most important thing we have to do is find the spot you left from. If we find it, we'll know where to take you early Sunday morning. It seems like that's the best plan, anyway. At that time, there are less likely people to be around. I'm guessing here. This is as new to me as it is to you."

"What happens if we don't find the spot?"

"Oh, I don't know. Guess I might just be stuck with you for the rest of my life." Virginia laughed, but she winced at the pain in her head and shoulder.

"Maybe I just won't look very hard," Robert said quietly as he uncovered their dinners.

"Robert…" Virginia reached across the table and took his hand. "I would be the happiest woman in the world if you didn't have to go back, but we both know you couldn't just forget the war and your men, and the fact that you might be labeled a deserter. As it is, we only know that Jackson wanted you listed as 'missing' for the time being. That won't last forever, especially with that other colonel who didn't like you. And once Jackson is…" She hesitated. "Once Jackson is dead, there may be no one to come to your defense except yourself."

"You're right, of course, but that won't make the goin' any easier. I never wanted to stay with anyone so much. But I know you can't go backward to my world. Why would anyone give all these luxuries up?"

"I admit I'm spoiled, but if I thought there was a chance, I'd go with you. Just as I know you can't stay in my time, I know I couldn't stay in yours, even if we managed to get me back there. Now, let's eat the lovely dinner you've ordered, and enjoy our evening together."

"I can't see how you'll enjoy the evening when I've put you in such a miserable state."

Virginia knew her eyes must be twinkling with her wicked thoughts. "I'll manage."

~ * ~

The meal continued in near silence. Only a few brief bursts of conversations interrupted. Virginia wasn't as hungry as she thought. She only managed about half her dinner.

"You know, Robert, since you are responsible for my slight incapacitation, you will have to help me with a few things this evening."

He jumped from his chair. "Anythin'!"

"Well, after you get someone to take this tray, I'd really like to get the rest of the asphalt off my skin and out of my hair. I can't do that by myself. Guess you'll just have to come in and help me in the shower. I hate to ask, but it has to be done."

He smirked. "I'll just have to force myself. What else?"

"Ummm, the winter weather has my skin so dry and itchy, and with this shoulder, well, I can't put any lotion on. Guess you'll just have to smooth it all over me when I get out of the shower."

"That seems like a reasonable request. I'll manage somehow."

"I'll probably need some particularly tender care to be able to get to sleep tonight."

"That shall be my pleasure." He bowed to her, then put all the dinner dishes back on the cart.

"I imagine, since I took a rather long nap that I'll need a little entertaining tonight, perhaps something that would use up some energy…"

"I think that can be arranged. If you feel up to it." He leaned over her shoulder and kissed her injured cheek as softly as a will-of-the-wisp.

Virginia wasn't about to let Robert know she was feeling a bit queasy. When she took the aspirin from her purse, she also got a couple of antacids and hoped to settle her stomach.

"Would madam like to take her shower now?" Robert draped a towel over his arm as he asked.

"No, madam would like to just sit and let dinner settle a little. Come. Sit back down. Let's talk more about plans."

"I'll sit, but I don't want to talk any more tonight about plans that will take me away from you."

"All right. Then let's just talk. Tell me more about your life."

"It's hard to know what to say. When I think back on it, it all seems so empty. Nothing before seems to matter much since I met you. How can I feel so much so fast?"

"I'm certainly not the one to answer that. Maybe it's just because we both have to deal with the idea that we could be separated any moment, and will surely be separated soon no matter what we do."

"I suppose. But I feel like I've spent the last twenty years of my life waitin' for you." Robert took her hand and brought it to his lips. "And it was worth the wait."

"I feel the same. But, you know what? No matter how much I miss you, I wouldn't have had anything or anyone to miss, if we hadn't found each other. So I, for one, will always be grateful."

"I suppose you're right, but I wonder if I shall spend the rest of my life searchin' for a way back to you."

"I guess we're what they call star-crossed lovers. We're just not destined to be together, but I'm glad we found each other for a little while." She grabbed his hand, held it to her face and kissed his palm.

Virginia began to feel better. "Think I'm ready for that shower now. Is it a terrible imposition, Colonel Carter, for you to help me?" She smiled. "You might get wet. Perhaps you should think about shedding the balance of your clothing--just to keep it dry, of course."

He extended his hand to Virginia. "Of course."

~ * ~

The shower was warm and soothing. Robert's always-gentle hands were even more so. He took over completely. He washed Virginia's hair, applied the crème rinse, and let it soak in while he gently ran soapy hands all over her body. From his groans, it was impossible for her to decide just who enjoyed that the most. He rinsed her hair and assisted her from the tub. She wrapped her hair in a towel and took a second to dry her body.

"I'll do that," Robert insisted.

"No, you go on and enjoy your own shower. I'm fine. I'll just be in the other room, waiting for my lotion massage."

"I assure you I shan't be long."

Not wishing to remain in the confines of the small bath, Virginia went into the bedroom to dry herself. She sat down on the bed, with the towels around her. Suddenly she felt a little dizzy so she leaned back on the bed. When Robert emerged, she sat up, not wanting him to suspect she wasn't feeling well.

"I decided to let you dry me after all," she whispered. His face showed his delight.

First he towel-dried her hair, then combed it out, gently. Next he blotted her body, though it was nearly dry from the air. He got the lotion she left sitting on the dresser, put some in one hand, then rubbed his hands together to distribute it before applying it to her body.

"Lie down, face down," he softly ordered.

Virginia complied.

Robert began at her shoulders but bit his lip as he saw bruises appearing on her right shoulder. He said nothing. Using more lotion, he did her arms. Then he made his way to the small of her back, her bottom and hips, her thighs, the backs of her knees, her calves, and finally her feet, with which he took great pains--not only applying lotion, but massaging them.

"That's just about the most relaxing and sensuous thing I've ever felt."

"Now turn over, and I'll do the other side."

"I don't want to move." Virginia sighed and with lazy movements complied.

Again he started with her shoulders, her arms, then he took great care of her hands, doing each finger very deliberately until they felt like limp noodles. Next Robert took more lotion and started on her breasts, gently, kneading them in his hands as he straddled her in only his robe. His skin next to hers was exquisite.

She no longer noticed any nausea. Suddenly she felt all of him next to her, warm, hard, desirous. She wanted him, but he made no move to initiate any real intimacy. He simply kept applying more lotion over the rest of her body. She reached for him, ravenously, but he avoided her hands.

"You're wicked," she chided. "You could drive a woman crazy with all that touching, and not letting her touch in return."

"I told you once I was a very good soldier. A soldier does not let himself become distracted from his duty," he teased.

"Does that mean I have to give you orders?"

"Oh, no, not anymore. You see, I'm off duty now." He ran his hands down her sides, appreciatively. "You could be a model for Raphael, or Rubens, or DaVinci."

"Yup, they appreciated what is laughingly known as us 'full-bodied women'. I've always said I was born in the wrong century."

He shrugged. "Or I was. No matter, we're here now. Let's just enjoy." He leaned down to kiss her lips.

Virginia was already aroused. She needed little encouragement. She slid her hands inside his robe and reveled in the simple feel of his body, the hair on his chest, the muscles in his arms. "Robert," she whispered. He acknowledged with his eyes. "I think your 'partner' and I are on the same wavelength. Please don't make me wait. I want to feel you inside me. I've never felt so complete as I do then."

Those were the most words to pass between them at any time when they were this intimate. Robert didn't need a second invitation. He favored Virginia with his "partner's" entirety immediately and she gasped with pleasure as he filled her. Neither of them moved for several moments and he basked in the sensation of their union. Slowly, automatically, Virginia's hips moved so slightly, it was nearly imperceptible but it was a revelation of pleasure as she enjoyed every centimeter of him.

As Virginia's movement escalated, Robert's arousal grew and he followed her lead until there were no bounds to her pleasure, no rules for her to follow. Time and the universe were the splendor of their joined bodies. There were no yesterdays, there would be no tomorrow's just the complete satisfaction of loving him.

Virginia's absolute arousal and initiation of movement caused her to reach satisfaction first, but it was an incomplete satisfaction for her because she hadn't taken Robert along. She intensified her movement beneath him and he followed quickly.

After a moment of his visibly satiated exhaustion while sprawled on top of her, Robert began to withdraw, but she grasped his buttocks and refused to let him go.

"Stay." Her whisper was barely audible.

"But I'm crushin' you."

"No. *Stay*. I want you to stay."

Robert obliged.

"Do you think I can put my arms around you?"

"Oh, yes."

"I don't want to hurt your back when it's healing so well."

"I couldn't feel anything but ecstasy right now."

Gently, Virginia wound her arms around him. She'd wanted to hold him like this for so long. Now the union was complete.

Every available inch of her skin was against his, and he was deep inside her. She felt whole.

Robert lay motionless upon her and drowsiness drifted over Virginia, but she did not succumb. Then she felt Robert's body tense as he whispered in her ear, "Permission to withdraw from the field, sir."

"You may withdraw, Colonel, but you may not retreat," Virginia whispered. "I have other plans for you."

Robert gently removed himself from his position over her and toppled to the bed next to her.

"Awaiting further orders."

"Just lay there, Colonel. I want to enjoy you." Virginia put her head on Robert's shoulder and ran her hand across his chest and up to the scar on his left shoulder. She traced the scar over and over again. Then she ran her hand down his arm, across his stomach and up the thin trace of hair to his furry chest and back down again, playing in his navel with her index finger. From there she followed the trace of hair to a lower, furry place. She ran her fingers up the length of his partner and back again, several times. She traced his thigh then slid farther down in the bed to touch his knee, his shin, and his foot.

"I'm not objecting, mind you, but may I ask what it is you're about?" Robert made a lazy inquiry.

"Reconnaissance, Colonel. I'm scouting to remember you with my hands. I want to remember how it feels to touch every inch of you. I want to remember it for the rest of my life, the feel, the smell, the taste of you. I won't forget the looks, and I don't want to forget the rest.

"I'll be the only old lady in the nursing home with a lascivious grin as she dozes in her rocking chair."

Twenty-four

Virginia had wanted to take something for the headache and the increasing pain in her shoulder, but she shouldn't because it could disguise symptoms, should the concussion prove more serious than she suspected. She had spent a couple of restless hours trying not to move, as she wished to leave Robert undisturbed. A couple of items in her suitcase were stored in zip-lock plastic bags--her bar of soap, and a facial scrub. About one in the morning, she had managed to slip from the bed apparently undetected as Robert's breathing did not change its rhythm. After emptying the zippered plastic bags, she turned them into efficient ice packs. That had helped immensely. Swelling decreased and the bruises did not continue to grow, nor did the knot on her head.

By now, three o'clock or so, she was experiencing no more nausea. It should be safe to take something for the pain. The aspirin helped and by 4:30 in the morning, she began to rest comfortably. Even if Robert awoke, he would be quiet and allow her to continue sleeping, which she needed, though she hated to miss a single moment with him.

~ * ~

As it turned out, in his still-recuperative condition, Robert didn't wake early. After taking the aspirin, Virginia had rested well and when she opened her eyes, Robert was still there in bed with her, holding her, watching her sleep. She yawned. "Thank you for letting me sleep."

"I haven't been awake very long myself. You didn't go to sleep until this mornin'."

"I...I..." she stuttered, "How did you know?"

"I was concerned. I lay listenin' to your breathin'. I've learned to tell when you're asleep by the sound and feel of you. I'm sorry you couldn't sleep earlier. I know it was the pain." He was ashamed to look her in the eye.

"Robert, if you don't stop blaming yourself, I'm going to scream."

"I'm sorry, I just care so much about you. You're such a part of me, and I feel your pain."

"I know," she whispered. "I felt the same as I tried to take care of you." She struggled up to kiss him. "It really is scary, to love so much, so fast; to know you are the missing piece of my puzzle."

"What is more troublesome, is knowin' we may have to let go soon." He sighed, then forced a smile. "Well, what is our schedule today?"

"We have only one thing we have to do, and that's try to find the place you were being held prisoner. Other than that, I have one stop I want to make. We have a few details to take care of here to be ready for tomorrow morning." She cleared her throat to keep her voice from cracking. "Otherwise, we just have to be together."

"That, you can count on, my love."

Virginia was surprised when she got up, that her head wasn't bothering her much. The worst must be over. The shoulder, she could deal with. "I'm going to take my time getting dressed this morning. Shall we order some toast and coffee? By the time we get out, it will be close to time for lunch, so we don't need much breakfast."

"I'll get dressed and go out to the desk." Robert offered.

"No, you can pick up the phone and order." She pointed to the desk. "Go ahead," she prodded. "Pick up the receiver. You've watched me. Just give the room number, ask for two orders of toast and milk and some coffee for yourself."

Robert didn't move.

"Go on, darling. It's an experience you should have before--" She didn't care to finish her sentence.

Robert walked across the room, rolled back the desktop and, looking toward Virginia for instructions and encouragement, picked up the telephone.

"Put the end of the receiver with the cord coming from it in front of your mouth. Put the free end to your ear."

Robert followed her instructions.

"Now, just dial, well, you don't dial, that's just an expression held over--oh, never mind. Push the 'zero' button and wait for the desk to answer. When they do, say you'd like to order some breakfast."

With obvious trepidation Robert followed her directions. He sighed with relief when he finished his ordered task.

"This is one week of my life about which I will never be able to speak to anyone. They would think me totally mad if I told anyone of my own time about automobiles, telephones, television, airplanes, women voting, holding all the jobs you do, everybody living peacefully. I have seen it and still don't believe it. It's wonderfully impossible."

"I didn't mean to make you believe the world is perfect. It's far from that. After all, how did I start counting down history for you? Mostly by the wars. I didn't touch on women's suffrage, civil rights struggles. I explained about Mr. Lincoln being assassinated. Well, there were others, many others, even another President, and a leading candidate for President who was the dead President's brother, important civil rights leaders. I have lived in a frightening lifetime, but then, so have you."

Virginia put her arms around him. "There are so many things I would like to show you, but it's just too much to absorb. You might be better off to forget it all." She smiled and hugged him "All except me, that is."

A knock at the door gave Virginia the opportunity to escape with misty eyes to the bathroom. "There's breakfast."

"I'll take care of it. I just have to sign the paper." His voice sounded from the area of the door.

~ * ~

Not wanting to leave Robert wondering long, Virginia inspected her injuries quickly. Her cheek was barely noticeable, the lump on her forehead was not very large, and the bruise could be easily covered with make-up. Her shoulder flaunted deep purples, blues, and a little black. It would take time to go away, but it wouldn't be seen, except by Robert. Perhaps she would put a little make-up over it so he wouldn't know the full extent of the damage. She emerged from the bathroom with a smile.

~ * ~

"Now, this is more like my normal breakfast." She sat down at the table. There were two plates, each with four pieces of toast, a dish full of butter and jellies in little sealed packages, which Robert fingered curiously.

Virginia peeled back the paper from a pat of butter, and Robert mimicked. Then she caught the corner of the foil on the top of a jam package and he tried to do likewise, fumbling for the corner.

Virginia took the package from his hands and pulled back the corner far enough for him to catch it.

"My fingers are too clumsy for those tiny things."

"Fortunately, darling, they're not too clumsy for other things." She gave him a wicked grin.

He ate all his toast. Virginia ate only two pieces of her own, then offered the rest to Robert, who had no trouble putting them away.

"I'm sorry, I should have asked you if you wanted more to eat, but I'd like to sit down to a nice lunch and dinner today. Can you hold out a couple of hours until lunch?"

"Of course, I've probably already eaten more in the past few days than I have in three months. Not that our rations are that small," he added quickly. "Not that I want to complain, but it's a habit to minimize the Confederacy's problems. I just never seem to have either the time, or appetite to eat well, especially when we keep movin' about."

"We'll have a big lunch, okay?"

Robert smiled and nodded. "So, where do we start today?"

"By getting dressed, slowly." Virginia snickered as she rose sluggishly from the table.

"I can help, can't I?"

"Maybe, to a point. I'll holler if I need assistance."

Robert rose from the table and stood only inches from Virginia. She looked deeply into his eyes and raised her hand to his cheek. "Robert, no matter what happens, no matter where you go the rest of your life, promise me one thing."

"If I can."

"Promise me you'll remember that I love you and I always will, but I want you to be happier than you were before, when you go back. Try to make a full life for yourself, even if it means…with another woman. Of course, if you don't go back, you can scrub that last part."

She smiled wryly.

Robert put one hand on top of hers on his cheek, reached with his other hand and ran the back of his fingers softly, up and down her cheek. "Whether I am in my own time, or in yours, I'll never love anyone as strongly as I love you. It is impossible."

Virginia turned her face in his hand and kissed his fingertips. Standing in front of her was everything she ever wanted in a man and more, yet she was preparing the way for him to leave her. Was she losing her mind? No, but she was sure she would come close to losing it when, and if he left. She threw herself into Robert's arms. "Hold me," she pleaded urgently.

Robert obliged, kissing the top of her head then resting his cheek against it. "I don't want to leave you, but I know you're right. I have to, for my men, for my son. I have to hope that we'll be able to get together after the war."

He took her hand and led her to the bed. "Come, sit down for a moment, darlin'." He sat and patted the bed next to him.

"We've had a world of happiness in a few days. We've gotten to know each other better than some couples that marry and live together for years." He patted her hand between his. "Virginia, I know some things are botherin' you, besides the possibility that we may never be together again."

Feeling sad, Virginia looked up at him.

"Virginia, I know you're worried that I won't live through the war."

A single tear escaped her eye, which Robert wiped away with a kiss.

"Virginia Berkeley, I can promise you I will survive the war. I will keep this new outlook on life, and if it is possible, I will find my way back to you, or at least find a way to leave word for you somehow. I may have to spend my life wonderin' how your life went, but I will try not to leave you wonderin' as well. Guess I have the advantage here. I can leave a message for the future. You can't leave a message for the past." His eyes twinkled as he smiled.

"I never thought of it that way." She cocked her head and winked. "I promise to stop being so gloomy."

"Neither of us can help how much we care. It's bound to show as our time together grows short."

"You're not only handsome and sexy, you're very wise. I love you very much, Robert. I pray you'll find a way to come back to me." Virginia stood to get dressed.

Robert followed her, put his arms around her from behind and leaned over her shoulder. "And you are beautiful, warm, sensuous, and brilliant. I've never known anyone like you. I've never loved anyone so much."

"Well, here goes." Virginia took Robert's hand as they headed for the door. "We're off to see the wizard."

"Excuse me?"

"Oh, sorry. It would take too long to explain. We're off to find your prison."

~ * ~

Virginia headed for the Chatham bridge. Then, remembering the direction Robert came from as he approached the bridge the previous Sunday morning, she took a left. She went only a short distance, then pulled to the side of the road.

"I found your hat over there under a tree. Can you point us in the right direction from here?"

Robert concentrated, then pointed for her to continue on that same road. Virginia pulled over for him to collect his thoughts a couple of times. Robert seemed to be remembering his route one piece at a time.

Finally he directed Virginia to an extremely familiar road.

"This way?" She pointed to confirm.

Robert nodded.

"That's a strange coincidence. I have friends who live in this direction, and an old house that fascinates me."

"Really?"

Virginia nodded. She slowed down as they came to a main intersection, but Robert directed her to continue straight on across the railroad tracks. They were still going the way she knew well.

"Slow down. I don't think it's much farther. It's difficult to remember, and even harder to judge distance at these speeds."

"Thirty miles an hours is hardly 'these speeds,' dear."

"There! There's the house!" Robert became agitated as he pointed.

"That's not possible--or--"

"That's it. The little stone outbuilding is in the field behind the house."

Virginia passed the house by and pulled into the lot of a garage across the road. She inhaled deeply and put her forehead against the steering wheel for a moment trying to absorb it all.

"Why didn't you stop? Why didn't you turn in? Are you feeling worse?"

"Give me a minute, please." She collected her thoughts and memories of the house and the scene she thought she saw in her rear view mirror, and the smell and fear when Jonathan accidentally forced her inside. Putting it all together like a puzzle in her mind, she began to explain. "This is the house I told you about. I first saw it several months ago when it was for sale. It fascinated me. Jonathan brought me out here on a carriage ride last Friday."

She turned to face him. "Were you locked in the smokehouse?"

"That's odd, I never really thought about it. I was in poor condition after the whippin', and that's when I was put there.

Now that you ask, there was the smell of hickory smoke in the place. Even before I smelled fire outside."

The hair stood up on Virginia's arms and back of her neck as a chill ran down her spine. She swallowed and cleared her throat, then turned to look back toward the house and grounds. "They're renovating the house, but it's Saturday. I guess no one is about. Give me a minute, then we'll walk over, just to be sure this is the place."

Robert anxiously fidgeted while he waited.

At last Virginia signaled when Robert and she could go. Robert jumped out and raced across the road. She wasn't so anxious. Robert made a quick look about but Virginia went no closer than fifteen or twenty feet of the smokehouse.

She saw no reason to relate her trauma there with Jonathan.

"Well, I guess we know where to head tomorrow morning. Please, can we go? I don't want to be here until we have to." Virginia tugged at Robert's arm.

~ * ~

Silence resounded in the car as they headed back to town. Silence that spoke of a lonely future to come, for now they had no excuse to avoid trying Virginia's scheme for Robert's return. She wondered if he hadn't secretly hoped they'd never find the right spot, that he'd have to stay, through no fault of his own.

Now it was inevitable that they must try.

To end the deafening silence, Virginia pushed the cassette in the tape deck. It was Strauss Waltzes. Robert was staring out the window. Wonder where his mind was?

"Stop!" he shouted suddenly.

Virginia pulled over as soon as there was a wide spot in the road.

"Shhh!" Robert put his finger to his lips to indicate she should not speak.

She turned the car motor off to reduce the noise, as Robert fumbled for the button to open the power window. Nothing happened once he found it. It wouldn't work without the motor running, so he opened the door and appeared to be listening for something.

"What?"

"It's gone. You didn't stop soon enough, I guess."

"What's gone?"

"I suppose you couldn't hear it. I forgot about your poor hearing."

"Hear *what*?"

"I distinctly heard a band playing somewhere near, the first familiar music I've heard, except in the camp."

"A band?" Virginia was puzzled. Oh, he heard her car stereo, and of course it was familiar. They were certainly dancing to Strauss in Robert's day. She tapped him on the arm.

"Close the door," she said indulgently. When she turned the motor back on the tape played again. She reached toward the dash and turned the volume up.

"That's it! But, what is it?"

"Car stereo. Remember I told you about radio? Well, this is one step above that." She popped the tape out and handed it to him. "The music you heard is recorded on that tape. It plays in this machine."

Robert held the tape up. "This is made for automobiles?"

"No, I have tape players all over my house and one in my office, and I even have a little one back in our room."

His eyes wide in amazement, Robert could only shake his head. "People still listen to this music, too, besides what I've heard in the stores, and the barber shop?"

"Well, some people do. I do. I used to dream I knew how to waltz like a queen. Wearing a beautiful gown, I would wish to dance to Strauss, with some tall, handsome prince who could waltz me around like we were floating. Of course, a real Confederate officer is closer to a handsome prince than I thought I would ever be." She snickered.

Robert smiled. "I love the waltz. I could teach you."

"Uh, no, thanks anyway." She did not want Robert's last memory of her to be pushing her around a dance floor as she stepped on his feet or tripped over her own.

"I assure you, I'm an excellent dancer."

"I've no doubt." She shook her head. "Thanks anyway. I'm not."

~ * ~

Virginia made a stop at a little jewelry store. "I'll only be a minute. Do you mind waiting for me here in the car?"

"I suppose not. But we promised to stay together."

"Please, Robert. I'll only be a moment."

He shrugged.

"Look," she turned the ignition key to auxiliary, "you can keep listening to Strauss."

Twenty-five

For the nice lunch she promised Robert, Virginia stopped at a restaurant that overlooked the river. They got a table right next to the long row of windows on the riverside, ordered drinks, held hands across the table and in silence, looked out at the river. There was no middle ground; they were either at a loss for words, or clutching each other desperately and trying to hold on to the moment, trying to fit a lifetime of memories into hours.

As he gazed out at the Rappahannock, Robert wondered at the size of the river. It was so much smaller, shallower than he remembered in 1862. He pondered how much easier it would be to cross now, even with the bridge blown. He said nothing as he forced his mind back to the present, to what might possibly be his last hours with Virginia.

Virginia cleared her throat to speak, but the waitress came back with their drinks and asked if they were ready to order. Neither of them had bothered to look at the menu.

"Give us a few minutes, please." Virginia kept her voice low. They were the only customers in the restaurant. Right now, they were the only couple in the world. No rules could cover the kind of parting they were facing--as close to an impending death as anyone could come. Each knew the other would go on living, but so separate and apart there was no room to even dream of being together again.

She took a breath to speak. "Robert, I have something for you. It isn't anything special. It's just, well…" She reached into her purse and pulled out a small box and handed it to him. "You wanted to keep the ring I gave you in a safe place. I just thought…"

Robert opened the little box. He lifted the long, simple silver chain from it with one finger.

"I thought you could put the ring on the chain and wear it around your neck. Then it would have to stay with you when you go. Don't you think?"

Robert smiled. "I think it's an excellent idea, and very kind of you. Now I can wear your ring, even if it is too small for my finger." He took the ring out of his pocket and looked at it. "It's so very small. But then, you said your father made it when you were about twelve?"

"Yes, but it still fits my wedding ring, uh, my left ring finger."

"Really?"

She took the ring from his hand and slipped it on to show him.

"I guess I never noticed how slender and long your fingers are."

"Compared to the rest of me?" she whispered.

"I neither meant, nor thought anything of that nature."

"Sorry, years of conditioning." She took the ring off and handed it back to Robert. She wanted to change the subject. "Let's look at the menu." She opened hers.

Robert put the ring on the chain, put it over his head and tucked it inside his shirt.

~ * ~

Virginia wasn't very hungry, but Robert ate each morsel on his plate, like a bear storing everything away for hibernation.

Holding hands, they left the restaurant. "Let's walk a little," Robert suggested as they walked toward the car.

Virginia nodded. Hand-in-hand, enjoying the afternoon sunshine and crisp, fresh air, they strolled down the street. Conversation was totally absent.

"Isn't this silly? We both have so much we want to say to each other, but it all seems so unimportant now, because we can never get it all said."

"I suppose that is the problem," Robert agreed. "So let's not talk. Let's go back to our room." He sported his crooked grin, which reminded her of Jonathan.

Virginia rolled her eyes at him and, giggling, they began to walk faster. They broke into a run, and laughed wildly as they approached the car--both of them breathless.

It was only a few blocks back to the inn.

When they parked, Robert surreptitiously slipped the tape from the dash into his pocket. Perhaps he could change Virginia's mind about learning to waltz.

~ * ~

As soon as they got inside the room, Robert reached toward Virginia's blouse then fingered the buttons. She put her hand over his and stopped him. "I need to retire to the bath and 'freshen up'," she said dramatically as she slipped from Robert's grasp.

Once in the bathroom, she bit her lip and removed her shirt. It wasn't an easy task, her shoulder felt as though it was wrenched from the socket and not put back in place. She slipped the shirt from her shoulders then her bra and looked at the bruises. They were massive splotches of black and purple with tinges of brown around the edges.

She couldn't cover them completely with make-up and even if she could, Robert would be suspicious. She covered them only enough to make them lighter in color, and smaller in size to minimize their appearance. She downed three aspirin to ease the pain.

She put her shirt back on and returned to Robert, who had disrobed down to his prized modern underwear. He was snapping the waistband with one hand, running the other admiringly over the T-shirt. He had his back to her and she stood admiring him as he enjoyed his underwear.

"I've become spoiled with these new garments. I wish I could take an entire wardrobe back with me at least a wardrobe of undergarments."

Virginia slipped up behind him, put her arms around his waist, rested her head gently against his broad back and made sure she wouldn't hurt any tenderness that still remained there. Robert turned around slowly, reached again for the buttons of Virginia's shirt and slipped his hands inside.

"But, where is your harness?"

"Oh, I took it off in the bathroom, when I 'freshened up'." She hid her eyes from him. He could read her too easily. If they had more time together, they would begin to read each other so well they would become bored. She leaned back and looked into his handsome face. No, she'd never be bored with Robert, even if they had fifty years.

Robert moved Virginia around and seated her at the foot of the bed. He knelt in front of her, snatched her shirt and threw it aside. He untied her walking shoes, took off one sock, then the other, and rubbed each of her feet as he did.

"You're cold."

"Only a little. I assure you I won't be for long." She kissed him warmly, running her tongue slowly along the meeting of his lips.

Robert leaned Virginia back on the bed, and her legs dangled over the end of the high four-poster bed. Tickling her lightly about the waist, he unfastened her jeans and unzipped them. Then he slid them down along with her under pants. He shed his T-shirt and briefs and pulled her toward himself--her legs on either side of him. She wound her legs about him as he stood on the floor and entered her, but left his hands free to explore and caress her.

~ * ~

Sweetly satisfied Robert and Virginia lay in each other's arms. Robert wondered how to make this possibly final evening last them a lifetime.

"We should shower and get dressed for dinner." Virginia whispered lazily. "But I don't want to move."

"You're right, of course. You go ahead. The bathing room is yours. I'll wait."

Virginia's jaw slackened, and her eyebrows drew together quizzically. She looked strangely offended, yet at the same time relieved and Robert chose to ignore it.

Virginia had been so worried about how she would hide the magnitude of her bruises from him when they showered together. He'd always wanted them to. This time, she didn't protest. She would not question providence's solution to her dilemma. She just took her robe and disappeared into the bath.

~ * ~

As soon as Virginia was in the bathroom, and Robert heard the shower water begin, he raced to the telephone. Exhaling rapidly and gathering the courage to use the invention on his own, he picked up the receiver and took care to remember the way Virginia told him to hold it. He pushed the zero.

"Front desk." A pleasant voice answered.

"This is Col--" He stopped himself. "Mr. Carter, in room eleven. I was wondering if your establishment has a private dinin' room."

"Yes, sir, we have a small one which accommodates fifteen to twenty, comfortably."

"Is it engaged for this evenin'?"

"Let me look at the book, sir." The desk clerk thumbed through the pages. "No, sir. It's available. Would you like to use it?"

"What is the cost?"

"There's no cost to guests, if the room isn't booked, sir."

"Can it be set for only two, with the rest of the room vacant for dancing?"

"Yes, sir. That's no problem."

"Then, may I engage it for dinner at eight o'clock?"

"Certainly, sir. That should be sufficient time to set it up."

"This is a surprise. Please do not divulge it to my companion."

"I shall be the soul of discretion, sir. May I do anything else? Would you like to pre-arrange your meal?"

Robert thought a moment. "That would be expeditious. Could we have steak for two, with whatever dishes are appropriate?"

"Certainly, sir."

"Oh, yes, do you have a musical tape-playing machine?"

"We have a small portable system we can place in the room. Would that do?"

"Yes, thank you."

"Is there a preference of music, sir? We have a limited selection."

"If I give you a tape, can you have it installed?"

"Of course, sir. I'll take care of everything." The clerk was gracious. She seemed in tune with their love. At times Robert had thought her nosy. Now he mentally chastised himself for that. She wasn't nosy. She was just curious. Perhaps she just wanted to bask in the light of their love and dream.

Pleased with himself, Robert hung up the telephone. He had mastered it. He strutted toward the partially opened bathroom door and slipped inside.

~ * ~

Virginia stood letting the warm water fall over her shoulder, her back to the showerhead. Robert slipped in between her and the stream of water.

She whirled around, startled. "What?" Her words were cut off by Robert's enveloping kiss. She returned the passion of it and stood quietly, not opening her eyes immediately as Robert withdrew his lips from hers.

His eyes darted instantly to the nasty-looking bruises on her shoulder.

"What in the name of heaven…"

The make-up had been washed away and Virginia hurried to dissuade his concern. "It's not as bad as it looks. Really, I hardly feel it."

Robert's brow and the muscles in his face hardened. "I am desolate. How could I have done this to you?"

"Robert, if you'd done it on purpose, you'd have reason to feel guilty. You thought you were protecting me with your own body. That is the most gallant thing anyone has ever done for me. I love you for it."

Robert's expression did not change.

"In a way, it's my own little battle scar from Fredericksburg. You certainly have yours. But mine will fade in time. Yours will remain."

Robert almost cracked a smile as he pulled her slick, naked body to his. "You're utterly impossible. You have the most peculiar way of turnin' adversity around. I bet you have a hundred reasons why it was advantageous for the South to lose the war."

Indicating she just might, Virginia cocked her head and rolled her eyes.

Robert lowered his head to kiss her shoulder.

"Oh, that makes it much better," Virginia whispered in a deep, breathy voice. Then she planted her cheek on his shoulder.

~ * ~

Her hair damp from the shower, Virginia plugged in her hot rollers. She wanted to look her best for this, their last dinner together.

"I should like to wear my uniform tonight. Will you wear the dress in which I first saw you?"

"If that's what you want." She wouldn't deny Robert anything this evening. The skirt hung in the wardrobe. With the hoops still in it, it filled the closet space. She withdrew it and the lacy blouse.

"Don't you think we'll be a little conspicuous in these?"

"I have arranged for a private dinin' room."

"You have?"

"Yes."

"When did you do that?"

"Before I joined you in the shower."

"But you didn't have time to get dressed and…"

He held up his hand to silence her. "I used the telephone instrument," he proudly related.

Virginia curtsied. "Well, then, by all means, I shall be happy to dress for you, sir."

Robert returned a stately bow.

When he finished dressing, he slipped Virginia's waltz tape from the pocket of his flannel shirt into his uniform pocket.

"While you finish dressin', darlin', I think I'll slip out and make sure everything is arranged." He kissed Virginia's cheek and left the room to give the tape to the desk clerk and make sure there was enough space to teach Virginia to waltz in the private dining room.

~ * ~

When he returned, Virginia stood as radiant as any belle of Robert's day. She wore her hair in long curls, trimmed with ivory silk roses. Ivory fingerless, crocheted gloves covered her hands which held an ivory fan in one, and her small green reticule in the other.

"I have to admit, even I'm pleased with my appearance and I never realized how much difference love, real love, can make in one's looks. This evening we will make a beautiful memory for you to take with you, and for me to treasure always."

"You are a vision," Robert whispered and reached to kiss her hand.

"You, Colonel, are the most handsome man in the whole Confederate army. No, in either army." She curtsied as his lips lingered on her fingers.

"Would you do me the honor, madam?" He held out his arm for hers and escorted her out of the room.

~ * ~

"Excuse me." The clerk rushed out from behind the desk. "Would you mind?" She held up a Polaroid camera. "I took lots of pictures during the celebration, but I didn't see any couple as handsome and happy as you."

Robert looked at Virginia, unsure what it was the clerk held or what she asked of them.

"It's a camera," Virginia whispered in his ear.

"We would be delighted." Robert said, posing stiffly, his hat in hand, Virginia on his arm.

The flash went off and the undeveloped picture shot out. "I'll take one for you, if you like," the clerk offered.

"Oh, yes, please." Virginia smiled realizing she'd taken pictures of the entire celebration, of Jonathan, and the camp, but she'd been so busy she hadn't even thought to take a picture of Robert.

The clerk snapped another and handed it to Virginia.

"Hold this." Virginia thrust the picture at Robert. "Don't go away." Holding her skirt up, she raced back to the room. She returned with her 35mm camera and handed it to the clerk.

"Would you mind taking a couple with my camera?"

"No, but I don't know much about these cameras."

"Oh, don't worry, it's just an inexpensive automatic. You just aim and shoot. Anything more complicated is beyond me."

The clerk obliged, and showed them the way to the private dining room.

~ * ~

As the clerk left them in the doorway, Robert turned to Virginia. "Why did she hand us the paper from her camera?"

"That wasn't just a paper. That was the picture."

"But is has nothin' on it. Not wishin' to embarrass the poor young lady, I put it in my pocket."

"Get it out."

"What for?"

Virginia grinned. "Just get it out. You'll see."

Robert pulled the paper from his pocket and thrust it toward Virginia. She didn't take it from him.

"Look at it," she demanded.

Robert glanced down disgustedly, even though it was a waste of time. To his total disbelief a picture appeared where there had been only a milky blur.

Virginia laughed. "Another modern miracle."

Robert gawked, speechlessly.

Twenty-six

In a few moments a waiter entered the room with an ice bucket and a bottle of wine.

"Compliments of Miss Harriet, the desk clerk," he said as he opened it and poured two glasses.

"How sweet." Virginia was touched, and though she wasn't fond of wine, it was thoughtful.

"To the Union." Robert held his glass up to touch hers. "That's somethin' I haven't been able to say in two years." He noticed the desk clerk looking in the door mouthing the word "now?" He nodded and the music began playing.

"Ah, Tales of the Vienna Woods. May I have this dance, Miss Berkeley?" He held out his hand and bowed to her.

"Robert, I told you, I can't waltz." Disgusted with herself, Virginia spoke through clenched teeth. She wanted so to try, but she didn't want Robert to leave remembering she couldn't follow him or she was as awkward as she feared she would be.

"There is no one here to see, and I told you I am an excellent dancer, and equally as proficient at teachin'. I will not take 'no' for an answer."

Virginia's heart pounded, she was so afraid she would appear clumsy. But Robert bowed and took her hand in his, gently, but firmly, placed his other hand about her waist and held her at a respectable distance to teach her. She put her free hand on his shoulder, and sighed in surrender.

"No, darlin', that's the hand you use to hold your skirt off the floor."

"But I need both hands on you, if I'm to have a prayer of following."

"No, you don't. Trust me."

"Famous last words," she muttered.

Robert began with a simple forward and backward motion to the music, which Virginia followed without problem. Then he added the slow turning that was customary on the dance floor. Virginia was amazed. She wasn't a klutz. She was following him. *She was waltzing.* They floated about the room as if attached to each other. It was every bit as beautiful as she always dreamed.

"Now I'll teach you to reverse."

"Reverse, couldn't we just keep--?" Before Virginia finished her protest, she successfully negotiated the reverse that Robert initiated, then another.

Virginia chortled. "I can't believe it. I'm *waltzing.*"

"I told you it was easy. You are a natural. It would be impossible to think that someone who can sing like you can, could not also waltz."

"It's like floating. I feel like a feather."

"You are, in my arms."

They quickened and slowed with the tempo of the music, reversed time and again, and Virginia never missed a single step, nor did she trample Robert's toes as she feared. Tears of happiness glazed her eyes as she looked into his.

"I wish I could take you back with me, if only for a few days, to show you off."

"I'm flattered, Robert, but you came here without me. I'm afraid you have to return alone as well, but you'll take part of me with you."

"The ring?"

"No, you'll take my heart. I won't need it anymore. You've filled it up. It belongs with you."

~ * ~

"Dinner was delicious, the wine was delicious, the waltz was delicious." Virginia was a little giddy as they returned to their room. "I shouldn't have had any wine. It goes straight to my head." She put her hand to her forehead, and winced. She'd forgotten about her little collision with the pavement.

"I think I'd better get you to bed." Robert directed her through the doorway.

She giggled. "That sounds delicious, too."

Robert began to work at the pearl buttons of her satin blouse. He felt all thumbs trying to maneuver the tiny pearls through the buttonholes. He untied the sash about Virginia's waist, then slipped the skirt from her so he could reach the last couple of buttons of the blouse. He put the skirt and blouse over a chair and returned to help Virginia out of her harness and panty hose.

"Can you climb into bed alone?"

"I suppose I could, but I don't want to."

"Just until I shed this uniform."

"Wait, wait." Virginia reached for her camera again. "Let me take one more of just you, with your hat on this time."

Robert obliged, but wondered if Virginia indeed had him in the camera's view as she listed a bit, unsteady on her feet.

"I have to take my contact lenses out, if you'll excuse me." She stumbled a bit as she tried to curtsy, a rather comical sight with no clothes on. Virginia went into the bathroom for a few moments. When she returned, she waved her arm slowly toward Robert.

"Now Colonel, you have my permission to disrobe."

Robert nodded and tilted his head to excuse himself to the "necessary" for a moment,. He returned to find Virginia sprawled on the bed, sound asleep. He smiled and shook his head as he managed to get her under the covers.

He put his uniform back on the hanger, then climbed in next to her, perfectly content to just hold her as she snuggled to him. He dozed off easily.

~ * ~

After a couple of hours, Virginia got up to use the bathroom. Her head now cleared, this was a good time to sneak the note inside the lining of Robert's hat. It had almost slipped her mind.

By the light of the bathroom, she found Robert's hat and tugged at the band of lining inside. She felt a piece of paper and took it into the bathroom to read it. Without her glasses or lenses she had to hold it quite close to her face. She read the exact words he related to her.

> *Colonel Robert Carter, Virginia 5th,*
>
> *Sir,*
>
> *I regret to inform you that your son, Lt. R. Harrell Carter, is gravely ill in camp hospital. He is not expected to survive the night. Please come. In the company of the bearer of this note, you will be given safe passage by all Federal forces.*
>
> *Respectfully,*
> *Col. John G. Howard*

"*Robert!*" she screamed and ran from the bathroom.

Robert bolted from the bed so startled he searched for his sword or pistol, until he finally realized where he was. Then he feared something happened to Virginia, but, standing in front of the open bathroom door, and holding his hat, she appeared fine.

"Virginia! For God sake, you just scared the life out of me."

She ran to his side. "Robert, *look*. Look what I found in your hat." She waved the note at him.

"Yes, that's where I put it, to keep it safe." He yawned and rubbed the sleep from his eyes then realized she was holding his proof. "How could I have forgotten it was there?" He ruffled his hair, then ran his fingers through to straighten it.

She laughed. "I guess you had about a hundred years in which to forget."

"Virginia, what were you doing with my hat in the first place?"

"I, uh, I was just, I just, uh, I was sprucing it up a little. I was brushing it with the nail brush in the bathroom. I just want everything to be perfect for you. You looked so handsome in your uniform tonight." She sidled up to him enticingly.

"Darlin'." He took her in his arms.

"I'll put the note back, so you won't lose it. Between your scarred back and the note, they'll have to believe you were trapped and captured."

"I suppose. But I don't want to think about that now. How are you feelin'?"

"I'm fine, really."

Robert ran his hands down her naked body. "Fine, I should say you do feel fine." He kissed her softly.

"Let me put your hat down. I don't want to misplace your note." She turned away, and put the note back inside the hat which she placed on the table. Robert followed her, kissed the back of her uninjured shoulder, put his arms around her from behind, covered her breasts with his hands, and spread his fingers to take in their fullness.

Rubbing his chest Virginia leaned her head back against him.

"Your hair's so soft and fragrant. Your skin so smooth, and these marvelous…" He squeezed her breasts gently and moaned his approval.

"Do go on, Colonel."

"I'm still getting used to having you enjoy me as much as I enjoy you."

"I love your body. I love how it looks, how it feels, how it makes me feel. You are the most marvelous lover any woman could dream of, and I will never be the same for having loved you. You've spoiled me for anyone else. I can't imagine ever having another man's hands or lips on me. Needless to say, the idea of any other man, well, any other's partner, is totally obscene."

"I still have some difficulty dealin' with your frankness, my love, because it is not what I am used to. I do, however, appreciate it. It has an effect on me that seems to make my partner 'sit up and take notice'."

They laughed at his pun.

"Robert, love me again," Virginia murmured.

"It shall be my pleasure," he whispered.

~ * ~

There was no sleep for the next couple of hours on this last night together.

"I admit, madam, you are amazing. Every second with you excites me."

"And I am amazed, Colonel, at your ability to perform, over and over again," she whispered.

"We appear to be well matched, my love."

Robert would remember how they lay as they fell into exhausted sleep, both on their sides. Virginia's back curved perfectly against his front--his arms around her and crossed in front of her, and his hands upon her breasts. Virginia's head rested on the inside of Robert's arm. Her arm was flung backward, and her hand spread on Robert's hip. They were as truly one being as they could be. This would be his memory to last a lifetime.

~ * ~

The alarm Virginia set for 5:00 A.M., rudely awakened them, and they clung to each other, wanted the clock to stop, but it would not.

"We have to get dressed," she whispered. "We have to go this morning and try." Her words were chokingly delivered.

Robert said nothing as they both rose slowly from the bed. His face showed all his mixed emotions. He needed to go back, but he didn't want to leave her.

Virginia splashed water on her face, ran a quick washcloth over her body, then dressed warmly as Robert showered alone and shaved. She also took a moment to slip a note of her own, in her own writing, into his hat. He would find it when he retrieved the Union note. She tore up the counterfeit message she had created. She wouldn't have to tell Robert about that.

She didn't feel like bothering with make-up or fixing her hair. She was already despondent and they hadn't yet left the inn. Though she couldn't know if her plan had a chance of working, she must look her best. It might be their last time together.

She did what she could for her outward appearance, including forcing a smile whenever Robert was looking, wanting him to remember her fondly, and at her best.

She could do nothing with the heart that ached inside her tightening chest. "Well, guess we should have a little breakfast," she quipped. "Can't travel on an empty stomach."

"I want nothin' t' eat." His voice clearly reflected his dismal mood.

"I suppose we'd best be on our way then, Colonel. Do you have everything? Let me see, uniform, cape, hat, boots, coins." She placed them in his pocket. "The note is back in your hat."

"Your ring." Robert patted his chest.

"Your locket." Virginia checked his pocket. "The medicine bottle." She handed it to him. "Guess that's it."

Robert nodded. He turned and slowly looked about the room. Then he walked through the door, down the hall, and out the front door of the inn. He didn't look back as they walked to the car.

"Who knows? Maybe we'll be right back here tonight. Maybe this hair-brained scheme of mine won't work at all."

"And perhaps it will." The flatness in his tone made Virginia's throat swell and tears rush to her eyes. She must fight it.

~ * ~

Robert and Virginia rode in silence for the several miles to the house. This morning she pulled into the driveway and around behind the house to try to avoid attention from the road. Pausing every few feet to hug or kiss, they walked slowly back to the smokehouse. Virginia didn't want to go very close to the doorway, but she didn't want to be far from Robert either. She had to fight her fear. As long as she didn't go inside, she would be fine.

They hugged and kissed a farewell and Robert went inside the stone building, but nothing happened.

"It didn't work. Guess you're stuck with me." He was eager to leave. He didn't want it to work.

"No one would be happier than I to have you stay, but you can't be remembered as a deserter. Let's take a little stock here. What is different about you this morning from the moment you left 1862?"

Robert thought. "I'm not bleeding."

"No, that's not it. At least I don't think so. I'm trying to think 'Twilight Zone' here." Virginia sifted through every shred of information Robert had planted in her memory. She took a mental inventory of his clothes, his possessions, such as they were. She thought about her ring and her note, but she needed him to take them.

"Did you have a hat pin on your hat? If you did, you can have mine." She started to remove it from her coat.

"No, I had none."

"Did you have a sword or pistol?"

"No, I was unarmed."

As he turned in disgust, his cape slipped from his shoulders.

"That's it! You said Perry ground the button from your cape into the dirt floor. Maybe we have to look for it. I didn't take your cape to the tailor, so I didn't get a new button for it."

Virginia ran to retrieve her flashlight from the glove box of the car. "Here, I'd like to help you look, but I…"

"I know, darlin', you can't stand small places. That's all right. I'll look." Robert got down on his knees and scrounged and pawed, but found nothing. "I think I shall not be able to return."

He didn't know whether to be glad or sorry.

Virginia crumpled to the grass just outside the doorway. She pulled at the blades impatiently, as Robert continued to search. Suddenly, right in the doorway, she hit something hard and cold with her fingers. She dug around a little trying to find what she struck. She unearthed a tarnished, battered "CSA" button. For an instant, she debated telling Robert, but knew she must.

"Robert," she said weakly. "I think I've found it."

Robert's wheeled, a look of excitement on his face which dissolved into bleak disappointment. "I see," he whispered.

Stepping outside the smokehouse, he took Virginia in his arms and crushed her to himself. Then he kissed her, lingeringly. "I love you, Virginia." He stepped back just inside the doorway of the building and reached his right hand out for hers. He clutched Virginia's left hand, then held out his left hand for the button. The instant he took the button from her, he vanished, leaving only the sensation of still holding her hand.

She clutched her fist to her chest and cried uncontrollably. "R-o-b-e-r-t!" One long scream echoed, wrenching her insides. She shined the flashlight into the darkness of the smokehouse. He was truly gone. No sense standing there crying. She should get back to the inn, pack and go home. Despondently she walked to the car, opened the driver's door and sat down on the seat, leaning down, her fists against her forehead, her feet still on the ground and wept.

She got back out of the car for one more look. She walked again to the back yard and looked toward the smokehouse. It was true. He was not there. Had he really been there, or was it all a dream? No, no dream, she could feel his arms around her, his lips pressed to hers.

She stumbled back to the car, started the motor, and opened her still-clenched fists to put her hands on the steering wheel. Something fell out of her left hand. She scrambled to look. It was the single gold coin. Robert placed it in her hand as he departed.

Her weeping began anew.

~ * ~

An hour passed before Virginia composed herself enough to drive back to the inn. As she pulled away from the huge old house, she kept one eye on the rear view mirror and hoped against hope that she would see him again. She did not.

Convinced he was indeed gone, she must get home as quickly as possible. She had to know if he made it back, if he made it through the war. She would look through her books, and if she found nothing, spend the rest of the day in the library.

~ * ~

The desk clerk on duty this morning was unfamiliar. That was a godsend as Virginia checked out, for she wouldn't have been able to answer any questions about her male companion, particularly from the young woman who shared the previous evening with them.

She haphazardly threw her belongings into her bags. She must hurry. She had to know he was safe. On her way out of the Fredericksburg area, Virginia took one last ride out to the old house, just in case. Her mind raced from a confusion of wishing she'd never found the house and been spared the current pain, to knowing if she hadn't found it, she would not have had the sweetest week of her entire life.

~ * ~

Seeing no sign of Robert when she passed the house again, she headed for route 95. She merged into the highway already ten miles over the speed limit and prayed she would not get stopped as her speed continued to climb.

"Get in an accident, stupid, and you won't be able to find out anything." Then she slowed down and, to keep her impatience in check, set the cruise control. It was the longest hour of her life.

She flipped on the radio to keep her mind occupied. It was tuned to her favorite "oldies" station. The commercial ended and the song that began to play was "Born Too Late." How fitting. Tears streamed down her cheeks.

Twenty-seven

The car had barely stopped in her driveway when Virginia jumped out. She threw open her storm door and fumbled with the key in the door handle, then the dead bolt and impatiently pounded upon her front door to open. She threw her purse down and ran to her little writing room, where the majority of her historical library was kept. The first book she wanted to look at was the book listing all the names of the Confederate soldiers paroled at Appomattox immediately following the surrender.

She pulled books from the shelf and let them tumble to the floor as she searched for the book she wanted. She wasn't finding it. She was frantic. "Think, where did you have it last?" Oh, she had looked at it the night before she left for Fredericksburg. She ran to her bedroom. There it was on the always vacant side of her king-sized bed.

She grabbed the book, roughly leafing through the pages as she knelt on the bed. "Carter, Carter, Carter..." She ran her fingers down the page. "Why the hell are there so many Carters?" Then she saw it! "Carter, Robert William, Brig. Gen. Va. 5th." She screamed, cried, clutched the book to her chest, rocked back and forth on her knees and, glad she bought the book when she visited Appomattox Courthouse with her friend Terry, silently thanked God.

So many tears flowed that her face stung from the saltiness.

Physically, and emotionally drained, still wearing her winter coat, she collapsed on the bed and clutched the book. She was so thankful he returned safely and survived but, at the same time, wishes crowded her that she'd been selfish and tried to make him stay with her. Why had she been so helpful, trying to make everything the same so he could return? Why couldn't she have been selfish, just this once?

~ * ~

Virginia drifted off to exhausted sleep. When she awoke after a couple of hours, she felt mildly renewed. Her eyes were burning, gritty, swollen red masses in her skull. She stumbled to the bathroom to take her lenses out, and was amazed they stubbornly stayed in her eyes in spite of all the tears.

She put soothing drops in her eyes and wet a washcloth with cold water to wipe them. She held the cloth to her face for a few moments, took a deep breath and willed herself to go on and find out as much as she could, not only about Robert, but about his son, and about the infamous Captain Perry.

First, she must bring in her bags. She reached into her coat pocket to retrieve the gold coin. She held it against her cheek. It was all she had left of him. Wonder if Robert found the little note she had written and slipped into his hat with the note from Perry?

The Polaroid picture. She raced for her purse.

At least she had his picture. She pulled it from the front pocket of her purse and turned it over to gaze at him. It was only a picture of herself, looking lovingly at milky, empty space. A wisp of an outline was all that was left where Robert had stood. Gentle tears flowed from her eyes. She wouldn't even have his picture to remember him by, not that she was likely to forget anything about him.

~ * ~

Shoulders drooping, her heart heavy, she dragged in her bags, and her computer. She would unpack later. Right now she wanted to immerse herself in her books and look for every detail she could find about her love. She turned up her thermostat, removed her coat at last, sat on the floor of her writing room and pawed through the books she'd thrown to the floor.

In a who's who-type book of the Confederacy, she found Robert's name. The very brief entry said simply that he escaped from Union forces at Fredericksburg in 1862, and eventually commanded a portion of the Confederate forces that previously served under Stonewall Jackson.

In the counterpart book of Union forces, she found no reference to Harry, but she found a half page about Joshua Perry. He was transferred to Johnson's Island prison near Sandusky, Ohio, chiefly a prison for Confederate officers. There to command a portion of the guard forces after his transfer from Burnside's command.

As Robert found mentioned in Virginia's book recounting the war on a day-by-day basis, Perry was court-martialed and found guilty of activities which directly resulted in the death of approximately one hundred Confederate prisoners of war.

Feeling the mandatory sentence of death would be a possible morale boost to the nearly defeated Confederate forces and conversely, a blow to the morale of Union forces, President Lincoln postponed Perry's sentencing for a more advantageous time.

The death sentence was passed on Monday, April 10, 1865, one day after Lee's surrender. The execution was set quickly for sunrise April 14, 1865, as a sign from Lincoln to the defeated Confederacy that all would be treated fairly, and a sign to Union occupation forces that unnecessary harshness would not be tolerated.

Ironically, Lincoln did not live to see the effects of his decision.

Virginia found much the same account, with more graphic details, in her book about Civil War prisons. Perry confiscated and sold clothing, food and other supplies which the Confederate officers brought with them or received from friends, and even from Northerners who wished to see them treated fairly. He pocketed the money and spent some of it on his unit of guards. It was customary at times to confiscate and sell excess, but the money should have been used for the comfort of the prisoners, and those goods confiscated by Perry were not excess, only the things his wards needed to survive.

Leafing through first one book then another, she sat on the floor. More often than not, she found nothing about the three names, but occasionally she found other names Robert mentioned as friends, foes, or West Point classmates.

The greatest number of references about all three of her interests, ironically, was in the four-volume set of books she once found at the gift shop at the Fredericksburg battlefield. But these were positional, statistical references of what units were where and when.

Going through the listing of forces after each battle account, she found references to Lt. R. Harrell Carter listed among the Pennsylvania units. Then early in 1865, she found a listing for Capt. R. Harrell Carter. She smiled. Robert would have been proud of his son.

Promoted to Brevet Brigadier General early in 1864, Robert then made Brigadier General after exemplary service at Cold Harbor and Cedar Creek. She was so proud of him that she couldn't avoid smiling, even when she wanted to cry for having lost him. One week with Robert had been more wonderful than all the good times of her life to that point rolled into one.

She'd love him forever. She'd miss him forever, but she would not mourn for him. She had done the right thing, and she was well loved for the first time in her life.

Virginia decided to continue to search for information about Robert whenever she saw a book that might offer a tidbit. For now, she was elated to know he made it to the end of the war and was promoted to general before its end.

~ * ~

Finally deciding to leave her books for a while, Virginia had no idea what time it was when she rose from the floor. She looked out the window. It was dark. Her watch read 4:22 AM. She might as well stay up until she could call the office and tell her boss she was taking one more day off.

Slowly, she unpacked her bags and put her clothes away. Each item she pulled out held some memory of Robert. The comb she first used to untangle his long hair, the last disposable razor in the package, and the last pair of socks, as yet unworn. The half-empty can of pet shampoo made her smile. She unscrewed the cap of the sample bottle of aftershave, took a brief whiff, and closing her eyes, remembered how it smelled on Robert. She put the nearly empty bottle on her bathroom shelf.

She came across her camera in her tote bag. She stared at it momentarily, then put it in the drawer of her desk. With the condition of the Polaroid picture, she saw no point in retrieving the film from her own camera.

Tenderly, she picked up the sepia photograph she and Jonathan bought. She stared at his young face. The crooked smile he was trying so hard to suppress reminded her of Robert, and the tears flowed anew.

The last thing in her case was the burgundy robe that had been her father's. She held it close and buried her face in it. It felt and smelled like Robert. She slipped it on over her clothes.

When she finished unpacking, she glanced through her stack of mail, and tossed the bills to one side, the advertisements directly into the trash, and the correspondence into a stack. With little interest, she looked through the letters. A couple from friends in England, a note from Terry, a letter from some law firm in North Carolina.

She looked at the return address, then recognized a familiar name, Blackburn. The firm read Jacobs, McLarin and Blackburn. She wasn't even curious enough to open it. She simply tossed it on the table with the other letters. She would get to it all, eventually.

She called the office and told her boss she needed one more day to tie up a few loose ends, but she would be in tomorrow. She wasn't sure how she'd go in, but she knew she would. Nothing in the present seemed to matter any more, especially getting back to the grind at work. But, Virginia always did whatever was necessary, whatever was expected, no matter where her mind and heart were. She'd do the same again.

She picked up the sepia picture of Jonathan and herself wondering where she wanted to display it, if she wanted to. He looked so gallant in his uniform. Robert's image replaced Jonathan's image. Or seemed to. It was only in her mind. She stared for a moment. Was it her imagination his eyes flaunted the same twinkle lines as Robert's? A long sigh escaped as she placed the picture on her dresser. Robert's face would fill her mind for the rest of her life.

~ * ~

Virginia showered, a long, hot, lonely shower. Her feelings were so mixed up. She was desolate that Robert was gone, and yet grateful to have found him, and proud to have helped him.

It was impossible to question how he was transported from his time to hers and back. God had a reason.

She blow-dried her hair, fastened it back in a clip, dressed, put on make-up and went out. She took the film from her camera with her. She should at least have the other pictures of the festival and of Jonathan to remember her trip.

~ * ~

Her first stop, a huge mall at Tyson's Corner which housed a small jewelry store where she once had a couple of pieces of jewelry made.

"Good morning, Miss. How may I help you today."

Virginia pulled out the gold coin. "I want to have this made into a necklace, but I don't want it drilled or scared in any way. What can you do?"

The jeweler pulled out a couple of coins he had installed rings with loops around and one he had encased in clear acrylic.

"Can you fit this one with one of these rings, a gold one, of course, and encase it in plastic?"

"Certainly! It will take a day or two."

"Oh, no, I can't leave it. It's too precious to me."

"I realize it is a valuable antique, my dear, but we have to have time to work on it. We're fully bonded. You needn't worry, I'll give you a receipt."

"It's not that," she assured him, though the memory of the coin dealer did come to mind. "I'll pay anything you ask, if you'll do it while I wait. I just can't leave without it."

"But even if I do that, it will take at least two hours."

"I'll wait."

"Well, all right. Do you want me to polish it first?"

"Yes, please. I appreciate this. It's a very special gift, and I just can't part with it."

In the immense shopping mall, directly opposite the little jewelry store was a quick photo development studio. She pointed it out to the jeweler. "I'll be right over there."

How would she explain to the man behind the photo counter what might or might not be on her film? They usually didn't make prints of partially developed negatives, but she needed a print of everything, just in case some small fragment or outline of Robert remained.

~ * ~

The mall was unusually empty this morning. Of course Virginia was never in a mall when it had just opened. She hated shopping. She was rarely in a mall at any time.

The young man at the photo counter had time to listen to her, so she tried to explain.

"I'm not sure exactly how to put this…" she began, biting her bottom lip apprehensively. She didn't want him to think she was crazy, but she wanted every possible speck developed on her film, in the off-chance there was some faint image of Robert. She took a deep breath, let it out quickly and tried to keep her composure. "Well, here goes. The majority of this film was taken at a Civil War celebration in Fredericksburg--"

"'Bout a week back?"

Virginia nodded. "But there are a few pictures toward the end, which may appear to have little or nothing on them. I want, no, I need you to make every effort to recover any images you can from those. I can't exactly explain it. Do you have some way of enhancing images or, oh, I don't know."

He winked, but not in a derogatory way. "I've got a computer here that can enhance and clarify just about anything, even a ghost. It costs to get it done, but we can try it on one picture and see if it works. Costs about ten dollars for one picture. When I get it the best I can, then I print it."

Virginia hoped.

"Tell ya what. I'll develop the film and see what we've got, then you can decide if you want me to work on the resolution of one frame."

"Thank you." Dare she hope? Was it possible she might get a picture of Robert after all? He said, "even a ghost."

She took a seat on a bench directly between the jewelry store and the photo lab.

~ * ~

In about an hour, the photo technician motioned for her to come over.

"Look here, what I got! You got some mighty good pictures, the first thirty or so. Then you got these." He held up the negatives. They reflected only her image on a couple of snapshots taken of both of them, and nothing on the ones she took of Robert alone.

"I see." Her lip quivered and disappointment shown in her eyes.

He winked again. "No, ya don't see, *not yet*. But ya will."

There was something familiar about the young man, particularly with his more relaxed speech, but she couldn't think what it was. Racking her brain for some recognition, she sat back down on the bench, but nothing seemed important enough to make her concentrate. His voice was the only familiar thing. He didn't look like anyone she'd met before.

~ * ~

Virginia didn't know how long she had been seated on the bench when the young man came back to the counter. She raced to see what he was waving at her. This time he held a finished picture. It was a little faint, but it was Robert. "You did it!" She screeched, nearly flying across the counter to kiss him.

"Does a cat have whiskers?" he said sheepishly. It was then she recognized his voice, he had said the same thing to her in the Confederate camp.

"Benson?"

"Yes, ma'am."

"That's how you knew when the festival was."

"Yes, ma'am. And there's no charge for experimentin' with this one picture…but if ya want the others done…" On the last words, he dropped his voice to a whisper.

"Oh, yes, please. Do all of them."

"Well, I can do the other one of just the Colonel, but I got t' do some fancy gyrations to get the other two, the ones of ya both. I got to split your image off and bring his image up, then put them back together, but I think I can do it. I'm sort of a freak at this, a kind of computer wizard. Some people think I'm nuts."

"Oh, Benson, you don't know what this means to me."

"I think I do, ma'am. I saw the Colonel. He was a ghost 'r, somethin', wasn't he?"

"Or something, Benson. You don't think I'm crazy, do you?"

"No, ma'am. If you are, I am."

"Thank you. Some time later I'll have sepias made of these so they'll look authentic."

"I can do that, too. Just you leave me these final negatives. I'll fix ya up. Pick 'em up tomorrow, if ya want."

"Oh, yes, Benson, thank you. Make them all 5 x 7's, no, make these two 8 x 10's." She picked out the better one of herself and Robert's outline and hoped it was a good one of him, and the one he already developed of Robert alone. She would frame those to hang in her writing room, on either side of the drawing Robert made of her face. She would frame it as soon as she got home.

~ * ~

By the time the necklace was ready and Virginia selected a chain for it, the pictures were ready. Benson managed to capture the image of Robert in the other picture of him alone, and the two pictures of them both. Virginia would have her memories intact. She told Benson about what happened to the Polaroid picture.

"Bring that Polaroid in some time, let me have a whack at it," he said as he bid her farewell. "You sure do sing pretty, Ms. Berkeley. If ya ever get a hankerin' to visit another camp, look for me. I'm most always there."

"I will Benson. Thank you. And I like you better without the beard," she confided cheerfully.

Twenty-eight

On the way home, Virginia stopped at the grocery store for a few things: bread, milk, fresh vegetables. Even now here at home, remembering her adventure trying to show Robert around a modern super market, brought a secretive smile to her face. She touched the necklace, patted her purse with the pictures. She could face her mail now, and she would be able to face work tomorrow.

She hadn't eaten anything since that last dinner with Robert, over thirty-six hours. Probably the longest she could remember going without food unless she had the flu or something. She sat down with a salad and read her mail.

The note from Terry was just an apology for not being able to accommodate a visit. Virginia smiled. If she had visited Terry she would have missed meeting Robert. Terry asked her to come down soon. She would do that.

She held Terry's letter in her hand. She had just experienced the most important event in her life, and she couldn't tell anyone…not everything at least. Terry might believe her, if the situation were just right at the time of the telling. Terry certainly knew Virginia well enough to know that something monumental had happened. She always noticed such things.

Virginia would never be able to hide her new philosophical attitude toward life. Perhaps, she should just attribute that to Jonathan. Perhaps, Robert wasn't real, was just a ghost, like Benson said. Then she touched the coin necklace. The feel, scent, and taste of Robert permeated her. He was real. For that little while, he was real.

Virginia went on to her letters from England. How she loved the letters from the friends she'd made there. They were always warm and entertaining and there was a note from an aunt to whom she wrote regularly.

At last she opened the letter from the law firm. Yes, it was from Jonathan. He was an attorney. "No wonder his accent and speech patterns slipped from time to time," she said to herself. She would not, however, have pegged Jonathan for a lawyer. The letter was warm and friendly. He explained how he enjoyed being a common soldier at Fredericksburg, and how he wanted to keep in touch with her. He made it sound important to him.

She was flattered, but she wasn't sure she wanted to strike up even a correspondence with Jonathan--not after Robert. She would rather err on the side of caution, than encourage an impossible relationship. She would take her time answering Mr. Blackburn.

~ * ~

Virginia slept well that night, though she reached for Robert many times, only to find the other side of the bed empty, as usual. She was sad and lonely, but she was also fulfilled and happy, it was a strange combination of sensations.

When she dressed for work in the morning, her clothes were a little loose. She got on the scales. She'd lost several pounds while she was gone. "Well, that won't last." She snickered. "Never does."

~ * ~

300

Everyone welcomed Virginia back to work. She smiled graciously as if she were glad to be back, when all the while she would rather have been a hundred and thirty years away.

Her desk was heaped with problems to be solved. Without letting herself get upset or distracted, without letting her blood pressure rise, she tackled them one by one. Her staff members, knowing all the problems they'd been forced to leave for her, seemed amazed at her calmness. When the appointed time for the end of her day came, she left. She didn't feel she needed to work late, or to solve every problem in one day. She would take it all in stride.

~ * ~

The telephone rang.

"Virginia?"

The voice sounded something like Robert and she froze for a moment, without responding, without breathing.

"Virginia? This is Jonathan Blackburn. I just received your refusal to come to Fredericksburg, so I called."

Virginia breathed. The days since then had turned into weeks. She had even lost a few more pounds. Robert had been good for her in so many ways. Jonathan continued to write, and eventually, she answered, in short, formal responses.

"Oh, Jonathan, I'm sorry. I didn't recognize your voice."

"That's not surprising, since we've never spoken over the phone. It's May already. I got your letter today. Virginia, it's very important to me that you come. I have something special to show you."

"I know, you said that in your letter, but..." She was curious, but she wasn't ready to go back to Fredericksburg. Not yet. Maybe not ever. She hadn't even visited her friends who lived there. They were too close to the house.

It's important to my family," he said. "I'd like you to meet my sister and brother. We're having a sort of family reunion.

"I appreciate the offer, Jonathan, but I don't see how I fit into your family plans."

"Virginia, it's very important to me. I thought we became friends in Fredericksburg."

"We did. It's just… I'm really busy Jonathan."

"Please." His voice was pitifully sweet.

"Jonathan--"

"The whole trip's on me. Believe me, I can afford it. Family money. I'm sorry I didn't tell you who I really was in Fredericksburg. Please, forgive me, and humor me, just this once. If for no other reason than that carriage ride."

Virginia smiled, remembering how excited she was to ride in a real carriage, and how sweet Jonathan was that night.

"You'll have a good time, I promise."

"Okay, Okay. I suppose you won't leave me alone until I agree."

"That's right, and I'm a very persuasive attorney."

She agreed to be there, at the inn, early Saturday morning.

"I made you a reservation for the weekend."

"Okay, it'll be nice to see you again, Jonathan." *Maybe it will be nice to see the inn again. Maybe even the house… Well, maybe not.*

~ * ~

That had been Tuesday evening. Since then, Virginia had three more days to "discuss" her decision with herself. She vacillated between wanting to go and not wanting to go, but she said she would and she always tried to keep her word.

She had packed very little to take with her and took her time driving the distance to Fredericksburg. She got off on route 17 and started toward the house, but before she got very far, she turned back toward the town. She was not ready. The inn was the most she wanted to face just yet.

~ * ~

When Virginia got to the inn, Jonathan was waiting. "Virginia!" he called from the doorway of the lobby as if he'd been watching for her.

One look at Jonathan's friendly, boyish face, and Virginia was glad she decided to come. He threw his arms around her and hugged her tightly.

"Hello, Jonny." She kissed his cheek.

"You look absolutely marvelous."

"Thank you," was all that Virginia said. She didn't mention the twenty-plus pounds she'd shed. For the first time in many years, she was actually within a few pounds of where she wanted to be.

"Let me take your bag." He slipped the single bag from her hand and headed for the hallway.

"Ms. Berkeley, welcome back." It was the clerk who was on duty that last night with Robert. "Got room eleven for you again."

Wonder what became of the clerk's Polaroid picture? She didn't want to ask.

The young woman hurried in front of Virginia and Jonathan toward the room.

As they walked down the hall, the desk clerk hesitated. "Ya know that picture I took? Somebody spilled somethin' on it when I left in on the desk. Ruined one side completely."

"I'm sorry." Virginia was glad the clerk had her own explanation.

She unlocked the door and handed Virginia the key. "Here y'are. Home away from home."

"Thank you." Virginia smiled.

~ * ~

Inside there was a stack of boxes on the bed. Virginia turned to catch the clerk to tell her she'd made a mistake, someone was already occupying this room, but Jonathan stopped her.

"It's the right room. Those boxes are for you. It's a special outfit for this evening, with my compliments." Then Jonathan bowed.

"Jonathan--"

He put his finger to her lips. "No argument. It's nothing, really. I told you I can afford it. There was money on my mother's side, but my great, great...grandfather was a big railroad man in the West after the Civil War. He even owned a piece of a gold mine. He made a fortune. We'll never be able to spend it all."

"What was so important you needed me down here?"

"Well, I can't exactly tell you everything right now, but my family and I have something to donate to the historical society here and we wanted you to be present. You'll appreciate it more than most." He took her hand. "Come, have coffee with me. Oops, forgot, you don't drink coffee. Come have a coke." He dragged her in the direction of the dining room.

~ * ~

In the dining room, Jonathan pulled out Virginia's chair. "Were you surprised to find out I was an attorney?"

"Yes, I suppose so. I knew there was something you weren't telling me, but I didn't give it too much thought. I was a little busy after you left."

"Yes, I know."

Virginia gave him a surprised look.

"I mean, I heard. The clerk told me you found a friend."

"Yes, a good friend." She wasn't going to talk about Robert. She wasn't ready to share his memory, nor did she think anyone would believe his coming or going. He was destined to stay in her heart, except for Benson and perhaps Terry.

~ * ~

After two hours of small talk, Jonathan walked Virginia back to her room and kissed her farewell. "I have a few more things to attend to. I'll be back to pick you up at six o'clock. I hope you find everything you need in the boxes. And I hope they fit."

Virginia opened the boxes. Inside were all manner of pieces of clothing, a corset, lady's under drawers, petticoats, hoops, and a beautiful dress. It was black lace over pale peach colored satin. With it were black slippers, a peach and black lace fan, black lace fingerless gloves, a handbag, and a peach and black lace hat. There was also a box with stockings and rolled garters.

I think I'll forego these in favor of panty hose. I'm not sure I even know how to get into all this paraphernalia, but I'll try.

It took almost two hours to master the layers of clothing.

Just what I wanted, layers of clothing to put back every pound I've lost and then some. But after she looked in the mirror, it pleased her that they didn't.

She put her hair in long curls and was as ready as she was going to be. The small tucks she made in the waist of the dress didn't show.

~ * ~

At 5:30 there was a knock on the door. She threw it open. "You're early as usual..." But it was not Jonathan. It was a messenger.

"Miss Virginia Berkeley?"

"Yes."

"Package for you. Will you sign here?" He handed her a small package.

She signed for it, closed the door, and ripped it open. Inside a box was a small leather pouch, which looked very old. Inside the pouch were a note and an antique key. The note was quite old, the paper yellow and brittle. She opened it carefully.

My Dearest Virginia,

If you are reading this note, then someone has found you for me and will give you the box which will only be opened by you and the enclosed key. I have never forgotten you. I know that I am leaving this world soon and have placed this pouch and a strong box in trust for you. You will know everything about my life soon.

Forever, Your Robert
January 4, 1893

Virginia held the note to her breast and took the key out of the pouch. *Did Jonathan have something to do with this? How could he? He never even saw Robert.* The possibilities swimming around in her head were endless.

Jonathan knocked on the door.

Still in a daze, she answered it.

Jonathan gasped. "Oh, Lord, you are beautiful! Good, you got the package."

She held the pouch into his sight. "Then you know about this?"

"Yes, I sent it, but I can't really explain it all right now. I promise you will understand soon. I'll tell you more on the way to the--on the way."

Virginia picked up the handbag and put the note and key inside with her room key and the few items she could stuff into it. She took Jonathan's arm. He was in uniform. A Confederate major's uniform.

"Have you promoted yourself, Sergeant?"

"No, this is what I normally wear when I go to re-enactments, the sergeant's uniform was for your benefit, and so I wouldn't stand out too much while I looked for you."

"Looked for me? What are you babbling about?" She hesitated. "I don't think I want to go anywhere with you until you explain yourself."

Jonathan just grinned at her. "Then you won't know. Will you?

~ * ~

Virginia wanted to know. She had allowed Jonathan to tug her along to the inn's door and open it.

"Are you sure you don't want to go with me?" He swept his arm toward the curb. A beautiful carriage with two gorgeous horses and a driver awaited.

"Well, will you explain in the carriage?"

"Yes, some of it."

Virginia maneuvered the hoops to climb the carriage steps and seated herself.

"Explain!"

"The pouch and much more were passed down to me, uh, to my law firm, to carry out certain provisions of a will made one hundred years ago. Though I was inclined to doubt the instructions and their explanation, I was duty-bound to honor them. We were entrusted with finding one Virginia Berkeley in Fredericksburg, Virginia, in February of 1993 at a Civil War festival. Those instructions were the whole reason I got interested in this re-enacting a number of years ago.

"Being the Civil War enthusiast, I was elected to carry out the provisions of the will. I came here to get the lay of the area in January. Then I returned during the festival and sought you out. My instructions, however, prevented me from divulging myself or my mission to you, as it became apparent you had not yet made the acquaintance of the gentleman who wrote the note and commissioned an attorney, who passed that commission on to another, and so forth, until it reached me.

"It appeared you would not meet him as long as I was around, which kind of made sense. I admit, even the romantic that I am, I found it all impossible to believe, until certain other possessions of the late General Robert William Carter came to us upon my return to North Carolina. Those possessions are what I am taking you to see."

"You mean to tell me you were responsible for what happened to me?"

"Uh, no, no, not responsible. I only knew a little about your chance meeting with a Confederate colonel."

"You knew what was going to happen to me before you left me?" she asked.

"Well, not exactly. I knew the stories passed down, but I can't say I put too much stock in them, not until you led me to the house. Then I knew it was true." He took her hands in his. "Virginia, I'm the one who commissioned the renovation of the house, before I met you. It was part of my instructions. The money was left for it, growing all these years."

She couldn't speak. She was too confused to even form questions.

"The rest, well, it will be easier to just show you. I will tell you, however, that he never married again, though he appears to have lived a very full life." He raised one eyebrow and smiled, then settled back and they rode in silence.

Virginia couldn't help feeling a little pleased that Robert never remarried, but she hoped that didn't mean he never let some other woman close to him. A faint smile crept over her lips as she thought what a waste it would have been if he kept all that masculinity bottled up. Yet somehow she'd hoped there was never another special woman in his life.

Twenty-nine

There it was, the old white house, completely restored. It was beautiful in the early spring evening. There were no more two-by-four's holding up the porches.

"I can't..." Virginia protested softly.

"You have to go in. You're the guest of honor." Jonathan helped Virginia from the carriage and escorted her up the steps.

A lovely woman, wearing a beautiful power blue gown, greeted them.

"Virginia, this is my sister, Elizabeth."

Elizabeth curtsied. Virginia did likewise, then they giggled a little. Elizabeth's hair was indeed bright red, nearly the color of Raggedy Anne.

"Let's go into the front parlor," Elizabeth suggested, then showed the way. "We'll try to explain all this to you, my dear. We weren't allowed to before you saw the house. I'm not sure we believed it anyway. I'm not sure I believed it five minutes ago, but having seen you, I suppose I have no choice."

Jonathan pulled Elizabeth aside and whispered something in her ear. "I don't know where he went, but we can't wait for him," Elizabeth whispered in return, obviously disturbed with someone.

"Virginia," Elizabeth began. "This house will be dedicated tomorrow as the Robert Carter Memorial Museum and Gallery. It's going to be given to the Daughters of the Confederacy to use as a meeting place, and a show place as they see fit. They can rent it out for weddings and such, I imagine."

Virginia was ecstatic. "That's lovely."

"There's a great deal more to the proposition, Virginia." Jonathan took up the story. "You see, Robert Carter not only made a fortune in the railroad, and a gold mine, but he was an artist, though he neither sold, nor gave any of his paintings away. There was a reason."

Virginia remembered the sketch he lovingly drew of her and her heart fluttered, then sank. She longed to feel his arms around her once again.

"The entire collection was passed down in his family after his death, with the explicit instructions that they must be kept together. They are all here, on display," Jonathan continued.

Virginia nodded. "Oh, that's why it's a 'museum and gallery.'"

"Yes," Elizabeth said. "We thought you should see the paintings before the public is allowed to view them, hence this little gathering of family and friends."

"Virginia," Jonathan said. "I have to warn you. Robert Carter managed to place your likeness in every single painting he did, and there are thirty of them. One for each year of his life after he met you. They all depict a place he went or a significant event in his life. He wanted you to know about it all."

Jonathan took her hand. "He also left you this strong box, the key to which was delivered to you tonight."

Virginia's face went pale, her breathing shallow. She didn't know what to make of all this.

"Virginia, are you all right?" Jonathan patted her hand. "Get her some water, Bethy."

Virginia recognized the pet name, but she couldn't speak. She glared at Jonathan. It was too much to take all this in.

"M--may I see the paintings?" Her voice was a tiny squeak.

"Are you sure you're up to it, my dear?" Elizabeth asked.

Virginia nodded, putting the strong box down.

~ * ~

Virginia followed Elizabeth across the hall and Jonathan opened two large, sliding pocket doors to a great hall. At the end of the hall was a flattering portrait of Virginia, in the dress she was now wearing. Her hand flew up to her mouth as she gasped.

"I had the dress made from the picture," Jonathan offered, then escorted her about the room. There were all manner of scenes. A hospital scene in which her likeness was a nurse. A depiction of the driving of the golden spike of the first trans-continental railroad in which she was a small figure in the background, an immigrant's wife.

A picture in which she had dark hair and eyes, and skin the color of a fawn showed her as an Indian princess. Another in an old California setting, in front of an adobe hacienda, she was a Spanish señorita. She was a dance-hall girl in a Barbary Coast saloon. On and on, different costumes, different scenery, different coloring, but always her face. Robert never forgot her face. In confusion she ran from the room into the center hall and out the doors at the rear.

~ * ~

Jonathan started to follow, but Elizabeth grabbed his arm to stop him as they entered the center hall and watched Virginia disappear out the rear doors.

"Give her a few minutes. This must have been quite a shock. I don't think I'd want to walk into a room full of pictures of me and know they were all painted a hundred years before I was even born."

~ * ~

Gazing at the smokehouse in the twilight, Virginia stood in the soft spring grass. She couldn't forget the first time she saw the big old white house, or the first time she saw the smokehouse with Jonathan. Then she found out it was there that Robert was imprisoned, and there he found his way back to his own time.

Squeezing her eyes tightly closed, pressing her chin to her chest, she flung her arms about herself. She longed to have him back, if only for a moment to hold him, to have him hold her. She wished with every ounce of her strength he hadn't returned to his time.

"Virginia?" A male voice came from behind her just as she let out a deep breath. She did not inhale. She froze, unable to turn around, unable to breathe. It was Robert's voice--no, it must be her imagination.

"Virginia?" the voice inquired again.

This time she was sure. It *was* Robert's voice. She whirled quickly and, seeing a Confederate colonel's uniform, her gaze focused in on the face.

"Robert! Robert Carter!" For a split second, she wondered if she was going to faint, but, that wasn't like her. If she were a true Southern belle, if the corset she wore was really pulled as tight... But she was just an imitation.

She gasped a quick breath and threw herself at him. Her arms wound about him as she kissed him soundly, purposefully. He'd found his way back and that was what this entire charade was about. She was ecstatic. His lips were warm and pleasing, but not entirely familiar. She released him and, trying to get her bearings, stood back slightly aghast.

"I've never had such a warm welcome. I don't know what I did to deserve it, but I'd gladly do it again." A lop-sided grin came across the face--Robert's grin--Jonathan's grin.

It was all so confusing. *It's Robert's face looking back at me, Robert's smile. It's Robert's voice I hear, but he no longer has his Petersburg drawl.*

It was not her Robert. That hit her like a sudden punch steeling breath from her body. He looked younger, almost no gray in his hair, where Robert had quite a bit. His uniform was in much better condition and he filled it out more completely.

She stared, her mouth gaping as her gaze took in the entire person before her. What had happened? *Has Robert made his way back to my time, but forgotten me? Has he come back from an earlier time than he left in 1862? Perhaps at the very beginning of the war? No, how would he know my name then?*

She swallowed the lump in her throat, but she couldn't speak, tears of confusion filling her eyes, goose bumps on her skin and a deep chill running down her spine.

"There you are." Jonathan's familiar voice rang out, but she didn't look in his direction. "You found her. Good," Jonathan continued as he approached them.

"Yes, Harry, I found her, but I have a bone to pick with you. Why the hell did you have to go and tell her that Carter is my middle name?"

"Harry?" Virginia whispered to herself. She shook her head nervously. Now she was more confused. Her breath would only come in short, shallow pants. She quivered, putting her hands on either side of her head to stop it from spinning off her shoulders.

"I...I don't understand," she gasped.

"Virginia Berkeley, may I present my brother, Robert, whom I sent to find you," Jonathan offered.

Robert held out his right hand for hers, but she made no attempt to accept it. She recoiled a little as he reached further toward her.

Robert chuckled. "I think we already introduced ourselves, Harry."

Virginia's body would not stop quaking. She had yet to utter an audible word. Her gaze darted from Jonathan to Robert and back again.

"Do you believe me, now, Robert?"

"I seem to have no choice, little brother. She is the same one."

"Virginia…" Jonathan moved closer to her. "I didn't mean to spring Robert on you like this. The resemblance is striking, isn't it?"

"Striking," she whimpered.

"Will you take my arm, Ms. Berkeley?" Robert offered his own, but Virginia didn't move. "I told you this uniform was too much, Harry."

"I…I don't understand." Her voice didn't sound like her own.

"Virginia, this is not *your* Colonel Robert Carter. This is my brother, Robert Carter Blackburn. He's not a colonel. He's sort of a confederate Confederate. If you'll forgive the pun. He's an architect."

"And engineer?" Virginia whispered her question to which Robert nodded.

"And this is my little brother…" Robert spread an arm toward Jonathan. "Jonathan Harrell Blackburn. He's an attorney, but mostly he's a dreamer. And I believe I have something that belongs to you, Ms. Virginia Berkeley."

Robert reached inside the neck of his uniform and withdrew a chain, and pulling it over his head, he handed it to Virginia.

"Your ring. With a slight addition by great, great--" He shrugged, "whatever, Grandfather."

It was the ring she gave Robert.

"Look inside," Robert prodded.

Jonathan gave a disgusted shrug. "Rob, it's too dark to read out here."

Robert took a small flashlight from his pocket and shined it toward the ring.

Virginia strained to see that there was engraved writing inside.

"Don't strain your eyes," Robert offered. "It says, 'V., With All Love, R.'"

Her chin quivering, her tears flowing uncontrollably, Virginia wrapped her fingers around it tightly.

"I've carried that all my life, as did my father, my grandfather, and so forth. Our instructions from the original recipient will were to carry it until 1993, and give it back to Virginia Berkeley in Fredericksburg, VA."

"Yeah, but Robert never believed the stories, not until we were sent the crate, and the strong boxes, one for you and one for us. Ours was to be opened January first, nineteen ninety-three. It was crammed full of instructions. Including this house and bringing you back when it was finished."

"Jonathan, go back inside." Robert spun his brother around by the shoulders and pushed him toward the old house. "We'll be in shortly."

"I...I'll go with you." Virginia tried to leave with Jonathan.

"No, we have to talk," this Robert said. "I realize you don't know me, but I need to tell you something."

Tears still streaming silently down her face, she stood where she was.

Robert ran his thumb across her face and wiped the tears from one cheek. Then he took her right hand in his.

"Virginia, it was never that I didn't believe. I've just always been the rational one. Jonathan was the dreamer. I couldn't let him think I believed in the tales we were told as boys. I'd lose the upper hand as the 'big brother'. Do you understand?" He waited for her nod. "I admit I was skeptical, until I saw you and Jonathan together."

"You saw Jonathan and--"

"The day you came here."

"But, I don't understand. Jonathan..."

"Jonathan had already bought this place in January, as we were instructed in the box. He was paying for the renovation and *I* was doing it. I'm the architect, kind of hands-on-type. I managed the project. Picture me in a hard hat and sun glasses."

He took her hand between his and raised it to his lips. "That ring. It was like Cinderella's glass slipper. I've always felt like I was waiting for the hand with the finger it fit. Now I have it in mine. It was a delicious intrigue for an all-too-practical man.

"There, I said what I wanted to say without my little brother hovering over. He's quite infatuated with you, you know. But I intend to 'give him no quarter' as Grandfather might have said. Now we can go inside, if you're ready. We have a great deal to show you, and to give you. Grandfather set everything up over a hundred years ago."

"But, I have so many questions," she whispered in a tiny voice.

"In good time. We'll answer any questions you have, after."

"After what?"

"After you open your strong box. I have a feeling Grandfather explained everything quite well. If he didn't, I'll be glad to fill in the gaps."

~ * ~

The strong box was full of letters from Robert to Virginia. On top lay an envelope with a large "ONE."

She opened it and read: *"My darling and only love,*

If my instructions have been carried out, you are sitting in the parlor of our special house with my mementos in your lap and my pictures of you all around. You worried that I would someday forget you, but, I believe you now see I did not. Though I have been lonely for you, rest assured, I was not alone, but no one ever captured my heart for I left it in your safe keeping.

I sneaked a look at your driving license and remembered your birth date, so I have written you a letter on your birthday every year of my life and then on Christmas as well. The letter you hold will doubtless be my last as I am weary and old on this June 15, 1893.

Read my letters at your leisure; keep all my memories here in the box. You'll find my wedding ring you refused, the empty medicine bottle, some solid-gold nuggets, and the tag from my under drawers. I shall not part with the 1993 penny, the locket, or the note you left in my hat, and I shall send your ring to my grandson. Yes, my son, Harry and I have been in touch these many years. He has one son and two daughters.

I tire now, my love, but I will visit you in your dreams.

Forever, your loving Robert"

~ * ~

It took some time to digest the treasures she held. Robert had excused himself while she did. When he returned, he asked her to walk back into the gallery with him. She could look at the paintings now.

"He flattered me too much," Virginia quietly observed.

"Oh, I don't know." Robert looked at her. "I think they look like you. Especially that one." He turned her around to look at the painting on the wall next to the door. It was a painting of Robert in his uniform, dancing the waltz with her in her green skirt and ivory blouse.

She turned back to face this new Robert. He had a little scar on his forehead. It was nearly identical in placement and size to the wound she tended on her Robert made by Perry's sword tip. She reached out and lightly touched her fingers to it.

"Oh," Robert snickered. "Like Harry's handiwork? He got carried away with his sword when we were playing war as kids. Well, Harry was still a kid. I was home from college and just humoring him. He was Sir Galahad. I was the black knight."

Virginia didn't say anything about the similar wound, nor the fact that she'd called Jonathan, "Sir Galahad." She just kept staring in amazement at this genetic duplicate, her jaw hanging loosely, her mouth slightly open. If she didn't know better, she'd swear some mad scientist had already perfected cloning.

Robert walked over to a table and pushed a button on a stereo. "Tales of the Vienna Woods" began to play. He bowed to Virginia and took her hand, leading her to the middle of the floor. "May I have this waltz, Ms. Berkeley?"

Epilogue

Robert Carter Blackburn did not give his younger brother any "quarter." Though Jonathan vowed to stay in touch, Robert followed Virginia back to her home in Fairfax. He felt as though he'd waited for her all his life. She felt as though she had a new chance at love.

Robert Blackburn was like Robert Carter in many respects, besides the striking resemblance, but he was modern and forward-thinking, and took her independence in stride. To Virginia, it was as though the first Robert had been an introduction to the second.

She shared bits and pieces of his grandfather's letters. But often the letters seemed distant and dutiful. She supposed it was just the manner of writing then. Robert Carter poured out thirty years of his life to her, but only rarely spoke of his love.

I'm glad Robert was not so distant in person. I'll always love him for the brief time we had together, though it seems a beautiful dream.

Never was there a temptation to compare the two Roberts aloud, for fear of hurting Robert Blackburn. She could not fathom how two men, so many years apart could be so alike.

~ * ~

"Sometimes," she told her friend, Terry, who at least pretended to believe her tall tale, "Robert even starts to talk like his great, great grandfather! When he uses that stilted English, I make fun of him. But I don't know if he's trying to impress me, or thinks perhaps I will love him more that way."

Terry just gave her an indulgent smile.

"Do you think I'm reading too much into this thing. I mean, do you think I'm making myself believe I love Robert, because he's the closest I can get to his grandfather?"

"No," Terry told her, "I see the light in your eyes, and I see the love in his. It's love, okay. A big one!" Terry laughed.

"I've been so afraid to really let myself feel it."

"Feel it, believe it. He's yours and you deserve the happiness."

~ * ~

Much to Virginia's surprise, Robert was an immediate hit with both of her daughters. She and her daughters never agreed on anything, except the fact that their mother was too old to be thinking about men--until Robert.

"I said you will not stay out past midnight, young ladies." Robert jokingly told them over dinner one evening, when the girls were about to go on a double-date. "You are maiden ladies and it is unseemly."

"Maiden ladies", where did that come from? Virginia held her breath, waiting for them to explode. Instead both of them giggled like teenagers.

"Yes, Robert," said one with a contrite expression, followed by a snicker.

"I guess you're right, Robert," the other daughter chimed in.

Robert turned toward Virginia with a smugly satisfied smile pasted on his face. "Your mouth is open, madam."

~ * ~

In October of 1993 they were married, in the house, turned museum in Fredericksburg. Robert wore a Confederate general's uniform, and Virginia wore a beautiful pale green satin dress with hoops that went out for yards. Her daughters were her bridesmaids, Terry her matron of honor. Jonathan, of course, was the best man. Terry's husband gave Virginia away. They all dressed in period, as did the few guests.

As his brother's lawyer, Jonathan would file adoption papers the Monday following the wedding. With their permission, Robert was officially adopting Virginia's twins, no matter they were already of age.

In the middle of the wedding reception, Robert insisted Virginia join him in the gardens of the old house.

"Robert, we have guests," she argued.

"They won't miss us for a few moments. I have to see you alone." He pulled her in the direction of the smokehouse.

"Robert, what is this?"

"Virginia, I have to show you some things and make a confession."

"Robert, I don't like this. What is it all about?"

Robert reached inside his uniform blouse and brought out a yellowed piece of parchment which he unfolded carefully. "Do you recognize these?" He displayed a locket, a note, and a 1993 penny.

Virginia reached out and touched them, fingering each gently. "But...but Robert said he wouldn't part with them." With angry eyes she looked at Robert Blackburn's face.

He touched his fingertips to her cheek. "And so I did not, my darling."

"You...what? Who?"

He placed his fingertips over her lips, then followed with his own lips. This time the kiss was unmistakably her Robert's kiss. He swept her into his arms and carried her to a stone bench that had been placed in the gardens.

"It is I, Virginia. I have returned to you. I am Robert Carter, and Robert Blackburn is now in my place, or should I say was in my place nearly one hundred and thirty years ago. It's quite an involved ruse you see. He wasn't happy in his own time, and I, well, without you, I could not be happy.

"After the war, I came back to Fredericksburg, with the assistance of the penny, the locket with your hair, and your note, I came here to the smokehouse. When I entered, I was transported back to the very day I left you here in February of 1993. But you were gone, and I was not equipped to find you. I slept here that night, and in the morning, Robert Blackburn found me.

"It was quite a revelation. Like staring into a mirror, but when first we touched, I was shot back to my own time. It's quite draining.

"When again I had regained my strength, I returned. Robert was still here working on the house and grounds. He was certain he had seen a ghost, and I suppose, in truth, he had. We spent most of the next few months together. We found as long as we did not touch, we could exist at the same time. But we could not travel together, so the smokehouse became our connection. He could hand me nothing, nor I, him. We had to take great care not to disturb the delicate balance that let us find each other. He left me books to study, I left him writing recounting my past, particularly the war years. He told me about his life to that point. A couple of times, I even took his place briefly at family gatherings to see if I could pass with Jonathan and Elizabeth.

"Never did I send him back to my time, for fear he may be lost forever. I had already been lost in time, but he had no such experience. I had to be sure. He was my grandson, after all.

'Twas my duty to protect him. Truth be told, I believed he might not want to take my place after all the luxury of his time, if he saw what the war had wrought in mine. But it would appear he was content."

"But, no, this isn't possible. What about the letters, the paintings, the fortune?"

"All Robert Blackburn, my love with few exceptions. He wanted my *life*, and I wanted *his* time. We simply traded. Well, not exactly simply. We each studied very hard. I read history and architectural texts, and he picked my brain for details of my time and life. He knew exactly where to go and what to do to amass a great fortune, all in my name, and all I had to do was wait for Jonathan to put it all into play. I wrote the letter delivered to you at the inn and the last letter, which I had to slip into the strong box before it was delivered to you. Robert, my grandson died on June 22, 1893."

"That would explain their loving tone."

Robert nodded.

"Two of the paintings are mine, the balance are his. The one of our last evening, and our waltz, I did from memory during a brief respite before the war's end. The other of mine is the one in the ball gown which Jonathan had made for you.

"If an art expert looked closely at the paintings, he would doubtless see some differences in the brush strokes, though Robert did a good job of imitating my style. If anything happened and I didn't get back to you, and he got back to my time, I still wanted you to know you were never forgotten.

"The letters and other paintings were his promise to me. I would know how he fared, what he did with *my* life. And should my stay in your world be temporary, you must know how much I loved you and would forever. I was sure I was getting the better part of the bargain, even though Robert insisted he was fed up with the pace and clamor of his world. I was coming back to you, to all the wonders of your world. He was going back as a defeated Confederate officer."

"Does Jonathan know?" she gasped.

"I don't believe he does. If he does, he hasn't spoken of it. Nor has Bethy. She looks much like her great, great grandmother. I was, I mean Robert was never as close to them as they are to each other."

"I…I don't believe you!" Virginia jumped up and started for the house.

"Stop!" Robert shouted.

She halted in her tracks, but did not turn around.

Robert came behind her and turned her around to face him.

"That night, the night you met Robert Blackburn. Do you remember when you first saw him in the light?"

"Yes. It was not you, I mean it was not my Robert, not Robert Carter."

"No, it was not. Did he have this?" He pointed to the scar on his forehead.

"No, I mean, I don't know. Yes…Yes, of course he did…you did."

"No, he did not. Close your eyes, Virginia. Think!"

She closed her eyes tightly and pictured his face, the first time she saw Robert Blackburn in the light. She saw no scar.

"He had none," Robert whispered.

She refused to respond.

"After all we shared, Virginia, how can you doubt me now?"

"I just didn't notice at first. That's all."

"No, there was no scar to notice. He left you while you opened the box, didn't he?"

"Yes, I think so." Virginia gasped for breath.

"He left and I returned. I would not let you see me until I knew you still loved me. I found that out when you threw yourself into Robert's arms. We traded places for good that night. I gave him my cape with my CSA button on it. He went back to my place just after the war, and I took his here with you. When we danced, you noticed my scar, and I was sure you had found me out."

She touched her fingers to his face. They were cold, but his face warmed them. Then she ran her fingers through his hair, but said nothing.

"Wondering about the gray? Dye, my darling, just dye, it will return. Have you never wondered why I have never taken off my shirt, even when we have, well, on the recent occasions when we've been intimate?"

"You said you were cold, that you were a little anemic from time to time, but that it was nothing to worry about. No, I won't believe this. You...he...you're different, not the same as my...as the first Robert. Not the same at all."

"Bah! I couldn't let you see the scars, however faint they are, thanks to your miracle cream."

"But--" She glanced toward his crotch. "No, I have proof you are not Robert Carter."

Robert smiled. "You only think you have proof."

"That isn't something you can, well."

Robert laughed out loud. "No, you cannot be uncircumcised once it has been done. And yes, I know you are aware I had not been so."

"Do you have any idea how strange it was to stand before each other totally naked and compare notes with one's very own great, great, grandson? Unnerving, to say the least. He is a full inch taller than I. We had to find a specialist, a urologist, or some such, who was willing to perform the painful deed. And I had to have time to heal properly, else I should have been on you immediately, my darling.

"That alone should tell you how much I love you. 'Twas painful, indeed. And you had been without me for but a few months, whilst I on the other hand had been without you for over three years."

"Robert!" She threw herself into his arms and planted a hundred kisses on his face. "Oh, Robert, it is you, I was too afraid to hope. I just thought it all a happy coincidence. I just thought you were such an experienced lover you knew how to please any woman, not just me."

He shook his head and laughed.

"But…"

"No more tonight, my darling. We have years for explanations."

~ * ~

They honeymooned on a paddlewheel cruise up the Mississippi, stopping at historic places which Virginia devoured and where Robert felt very much at home.

Robert made some minor repairs to Virginia's home and her two daughters moved into it as their own. He moved most of his construction business to Virginia and Jonathan and Elizabeth were frequent visitors to the huge house Robert bought for Virginia until he could build her one of his own design.

~ * ~

"Why do you continue to go into that office of yours? You know you hate it." Robert questioned her after they were settled.

"I like my independence. I need it, to know I can still take care of myself."

"But, my love, I can take care of you. The nuggets Robert left you would give you a handsome nest egg, should you need it."

"Robert, how can I make you understand? I'm not confident yet that this...that you will not be snatched from me again. I can't start all over a third time."

"But--"

"No, we made a bargain. I took a leave of absence to start your--his--your biography, and now that I have a good start, I'm going back to work, just for a while, just until it is finished and you're through moving your business, uh, your grandson's business."

"What will you call my, his biography?"

"'General Robert William Carter, CSA'. After all, who knew him better than I?" She stifled a smile.

With Robert to tell her of the rest of the war and his forty-odd years before Fredericksburg, and nearly thirty years of his grandson's letters to tell her everything about his life after, Virginia had a complete history of the man. Well, to everyone else it would be one man, only Virginia and Robert knew it was one life of two men whom she wove together seamlessly, into one Robert Carter, Civil War general, artist, philanthropist.

She filled in all the gaps, with the help of her husband, and brother- and sister-in-laws. It was her best work, and sanctioned by the subject's family, and two people knew it was sanctioned by the subject, himself. The only part she felt compelled to leave out was the time he spent with her. Who would have believed that in a factual biography?

She made up the manner in which he escaped from Union hands by giving his son, Harry, credit for helping him. She also became a fictitious Fredericksburg woman who nursed him back to health. She allowed for a hint of romance there, but made excuses why they parted.

She gave Robert a few interludes of romance in his later years, to make sure he sounded human, and as masculine as she knew he would have been since he was a chip off the old block.

He hadn't said much about romantic liaisons in his letters, but she had no doubt there were some steamy ones...

The first publisher who read it snapped it up and rushed it to print. It was fast on its way to becoming a bestseller within a month of publication. It was hailed as a "warm, witty, and factual account of a 'should-have-been-famous' man."

Virginia would be able to sell her other writing now. She was no longer an unknown.

"I can finally quit my job."

"My dear, you could have quit long ago, but you refused."

"Robert, I've explained all that."

"Yes, my love, I know. You always say, 'once burned, twice shy, twice burned never trust any man."

"Well, that doesn't apply to you, darling." She drew close and kissed his cheek as he sat at his desk. "I've always worried you weren't real, that someday I would wake up and find this was all a beautiful dream."

"Madam, I believe I have made myself more than real in the bedroom."

"It wasn't just that, Robert. I had to be sure you wouldn't be spirited off again."

He pulled her down on his lap.

"And you're sure now?"

"Oh, yes." She kissed him. "Besides if you are, your grandson has provided for us handsomely." She giggled and jumped from his lap.

"You are a wicked wench, Virginia Carter--uh--Blackburn." He jumped up to chase her.

~ * ~

Robert made sure he fashioned a large library and writing room for her in the house he built. Within eighteen months, Virginia tied up all the loose ends, and left her stressful government job just about the time their house was finished.

Her mother was right when she'd said, "third time's the charm," referring to Virginia's two failed marriages. Robert was all Virginia could have ever wanted. He was the missing part of herself, and he had come such a long way to be with her.

Meet Diana Lee Johnson

Diana Lee Johnson lives in Northern Virginia. She began writing poetry at the age of 6. Her first novel, *Too Late for Tomorrow* was published in 1999. She says, "Writing keeps my sanity after 34 years in public purchasing. Entertaining others gives me great joy."

Her family roots go back to early 17th century America, but the author's fascination with history predated that discovery. The idea of traveling in time has fascinated her since she saw the movie "Time Machine" as a child. Diana loves to include history as she weaves stories that combine romance, humor, and mystery.